**Praise for #1 *New York Times* bestselling author
Linda Lael Miller**

"Linda Lael Miller creates vibrant characters and stories I defy you to forget."

—Debbie Macomber,
#1 *New York Times* bestselling author

"Miller's romance won't disappoint."

—*Publishers Weekly*

"Miller is one of the finest American writers in the genre."

—*RT Book Reviews*

**Praise for *New York Times* bestselling author
Brenda Jackson**

"Jackson's trademark ability to weave multiple characters and side stories together makes shocking truths all the more exciting."

—*Publishers Weekly*

"Brenda Jackson is the queen of newly discovered love… If there's one thing Jackson knows how to do, it's how to pluck those heartstrings and stir up some seriously saucy drama."

—*BookPage*

The daughter of a town marshal, **Linda Lael Miller** is a *New York Times* bestselling author of more than one hundred historical and contemporary novels. Linda's books have hit #1 on the *New York Times* bestseller list seven times. Raised in Northport, Washington, she now lives in Spokane, Washington.

Brenda Jackson is a *New York Times* bestselling author of more than one hundred romance titles. Brenda lives in Jacksonville, Florida, and divides her time between family, writing and traveling. Email Brenda at authorbrendajackson@gmail.com or visit her on her website at brendajackson.net.

#1 *New York Times* Bestselling Author

LINDA LAEL MILLER

ONLY FOREVER

**HARLEQUIN
BESTSELLING
AUTHOR
COLLECTION**

**HARLEQUIN®
BESTSELLING
AUTHOR
COLLECTION**

Recycling programs
for this product may
not exist in your area.

ISBN-13: 978-1-335-40628-6

Only Forever
First published in 1989. This edition published in 2022.
Copyright © 1989 by Linda Lael Miller

Solid Soul
First published in 2006. This edition published in 2022.
Copyright © 2006 by Brenda Streater Jackson

This edition published by arrangement with Harlequin Books S.A.

For questions and comments about the quality of this book, please contact us at CustomerService@Harlequin.com.

Harlequin Enterprises ULC
22 Adelaide St. West, 41st Floor
Toronto, Ontario M5H 4E3, Canada
www.Harlequin.com

Printed in Lithuania

MIX
Paper from
responsible sources
FSC® C021394

CONTENTS

ONLY FOREVER

Linda Lael Miller

For Debbie Korrell, beloved friend.

Remember that serenity is never more than
twelve steps away.

Chapter 1

This particular strain of flu, Nick DeAngelo decided, had been brought to Earth by hostile aliens determined to wipe out the entire planet—starting, evidently, with an ex-jock who owned one of the best Italian restaurants in Seattle.

Sprawled on the couch in the living room of his apartment, he plucked a handful of tissues from the box on the floor beside him and crammed them against his face just in time to absorb an explosive sneeze. He was covered in mentholated rub from his nose to his belly button, and while his forehead was hot to the touch, the rest of him was racked with chills.

He wondered when Mike Wallace would burst through the door, wanting the story. It was time to alert the masses to impending doom.

Did you actually see these aliens, Mr. DeAngelo?

Call me Nick. Of course I didn't see them. They must have gotten me when I was sleeping.

The imaginary interview was interrupted by the jangling of the telephone, which, like the box of tissues, was within reach. Hoping for sympathy, he dug the receiver out from between the cushions and rasped out a hoarse hello.

"Still under the weather, huh?" The voice belonged to his younger sister, Gina, and it showed a marked lack of commiseration. "Listen, if I wasn't afraid of catching whatever it is you've got and missing my exams next week, I'd definitely come over and take care of you."

Nick sagged against the back of the sofa, one hand to his fevered forehead. "Your concern is touching, Gina," he coughed out.

"I could call Aunt Carlotta," Gina was quick to suggest. She was a bright kid, a psychology major at the University of Washington, and she knew which buttons to push. "I'm sure she'd love to move into your apartment and spend the next two weeks dragging you back from the threshold of death."

Nick thought of his aunt with affectionate dread. It was in her honor that he'd slathered himself with mentholated goo. "This is not your ordinary, run-of-the-mill flu, you know," he said.

Gina laughed. "I'll alert the science department at school—I'm sure they'll want to send a research team directly to your place."

Privately Nick considered that to be a viable idea, but he refrained from saying so, knowing it would only invite more callous mockery. "You have no heart," he accused.

There was a brief pause, followed by, "Is there anything I can get you, like groceries or books or something? I could leave the stuff in the hallway outside your door—"

"Or you could just drop it from a hovering helicopter," Nick ventured, insulted.

Gina gave a long-suffering sigh. "Why don't you call one of your girlfriends? You could have a whole harem over there, fluffing your pillows and giving you aspirin and heating up canned chicken soup."

"My 'girlfriends,' as you put it, are all either working or letting their answering machines do the talking. And chicken soup is only therapeutic if it's homemade." Nick paused to emit another volcanic sneeze. When he'd recovered, he said magnanimously, "Don't worry about me, Gina, just because I'm putting you through college and paying for your car, your clothes, your apartment and every bite of food that goes into your mouth. I'll be fine without... any help at all."

"Oh, God," wailed Gina. "The guilt!"

Nick laughed. "Gotcha," he said, groping for the remote control that would turn on the TV. Maybe there was an old Stallone movie on—something bloody and macho.

Gina said a few soothing words and then hung up. It occurred to Nick that she was really going to stay away, really going to leave her own brother to face The Great Galactic Plague alone and unassisted.

There was, Nick decided, no human kindness left in the world. He flipped through the various movie channels, seeing nothing that caught his fancy, and was just about to shut the set off and try to focus his eyes on a book when he saw her for the first time.

She was a redhead with golden eyes, and the sight of her practically stopped his heartbeat. She was holding an urn that was suitable enough to be someone's final resting place, and there was a toll-free number superimposed over her chest.

With quick, prodding motions of his thumb, Nick used the control button on the remote to turn up the volume. "My name is Vanessa Lawrence," the vision told her viewing audience in a voice more soothing than all the chicken soup and mentholated rub in the world, "and you're watching the Midas Network." She went on to extol the virtues of the hideous vase she was peddling, but Nick didn't hear a word.

He was too busy dredging up everything he knew about the Midas Network, a nationwide shopping channel based in Seattle. One of his friends—an executive with the company—had urged him to invest when the economy had gone south, claiming that the new home-shopping network would be a hit with newly spendthrift consumers.

Nick shoved one hand through his hair, causing it to stand on end in ridges that reeked of eucalyptus. Undoubtedly, he thought, he was experiencing some kind of dementia related to the virus that had been visited upon him.

Without taking his eyes away from the screen, he groped for the telephone and punched out the office number. His executive assistant, a middle-aged woman named Harriet, answered with a crisp, "DeAngelo's. May I help you?"

"I hope so," wheezed Nick, who had just finished another bout of coughing.

"You don't need me, you need the paramedics," remarked the assistant.

"At last," Nick said. "Someone who understands and sympathizes. Harriet, find Paul Harmon's number for me, will you please? I'm in no condition to hunt through the contacts on my phone."

It was easy to picture Harriet, plump and efficient, searching expertly for the number. "His office number is 555-9876," she said.

Nick found a pencil in the paraphernalia that had collected on the end table beside the couch and wrote the digits on the corner of the tissue box, along with the home number Harriet gave him next.

The woman on the screen was now offering a set of bird figurines.

"Oh, lady," Nick said aloud as he waited for Paul Harmon to come on the line, "I want your body, I want your soul, I want you to have my baby."

The goddess smiled. "All this can be yours for only nineteen-ninety-five," she said.

"Sold," replied Nick.

Vanessa Lawrence inserted her cash card into the automatic teller machine in Quickee Food Mart and tapped one foot while she waited for the money to appear. A glance at her watch told her she was due at her lawyer's office in just ten minutes, and the drive downtown would take fifteen.

Her foot moved faster.

The machine made an alarming grinding noise, but no currency came out of the little slot, and Vanessa's card was still somewhere in the bowels of the gizmo. From the sound of things, it was being systematically digested.

Somewhat wildly, she began pushing buttons. The words *Your transaction is now completed*, were frozen on the small screen. She glanced back over one shoulder, hoping for help from the clerk, but everyone in the neighborhood seemed to be in the convenience store that afternoon, buying bread and milk.

"Damn!" she breathed, slamming her fist against the face of the machine.

A woman wearing pink foam rollers in her hair appeared at Vanessa's side. "You're on TV, aren't you?" she asked. "On that new shopping channel, the something-or-other station."

Vanessa smiled, even though it was the last thing she felt like doing. "The Midas Network," she said, before giving the machine another despairing look. "Just give me back my card," she told the apparatus, "and I won't make any trouble, I promise."

"I watch you every day," the woman announced proudly. "I bought that three-slice toaster you had on yesterday—there's just Bernie and Ray and me, now that Clyde's gone away to the army—and my sister-in-law has four of the ceiling fans."

In her head, Vanessa heard the production manager, Paul Harmon, giving his standard public-relations lecture. *As the viewing audience expands, you'll be recognized. No matter what, I want you all to be polite at all times.*

"Good," she said with a faltering smile.

She took another look at her watch, then lost her cool and rammed the cash machine with the palms of her hands. Miraculously two twenty-dollar bills popped out of the appropriate slot, but Vanessa's cash card was disgorged in three pieces.

She dropped both the card and the money into the pocket of her blazer and dashed for the car, hoping the traffic wouldn't be bad.

It was.

Worse, when Vanessa reached her attorney's modest office, Parker was there with his lawyer and his current girlfriend.

Vanessa prayed she didn't look as frazzled as she felt and resisted an urge to smooth her chin-length auburn hair.

Parker smiled his dazzling smile and tried to kiss her cheek, but Vanessa stepped back, her golden eyes clearly telling him to keep his distance.

Her ex-husband, now the most sought-after pitcher in

the American League, looked hurt. "Hello, Van," he said in a low and intimate voice.

Vanessa didn't speak. Although they had been divorced for a full year, Parker's presence still made her soul ache. It wasn't that she wanted him back; no, she grieved for the time and love she'd wasted on him. Vanessa's attorney, Walter, was no ball of fire, but he was astute enough to know how vulnerable she felt. He drew back a chair for her near his desk, and gratefully she sank into the seat.

Parker's lawyer immediately took up the conversational ball. "I think we can settle this reasonably," he said. Vanessa felt her spine stiffen.

The bottom line was that Parker had been offered a phenomenal amount of money to write a book about his career in professional baseball and, with the help of a ghostwriter, he'd produced a manuscript—one that included every intimate detail of his marriage to Vanessa.

She was prepared to sue if the book went to press. "Wait," Parker interceded suavely, holding his famous hands up in the air, "I think it would be better if Van and I worked this thing out ourselves…in private."

His girlfriend shifted uncomfortably on the leather sofa beside him, but said nothing.

"There is nothing to work out," Vanessa said in a shaky voice she hated. Why couldn't she sound detached and professional, like she did when she was selling ceiling fans on the Midas Network? "If you don't take me out of that book, Parker, I'm going to drive a dump truck into your bank account and come out with a load of your money."

Parker went pale beneath his golden tan. He ran a hand through his sun-streaked hair, and his azure blue eyes skittered away from Vanessa's gaze. But after a moment, he regained his legendary poise. "Van, you're being unreasonable."

"Am I? That book makes me sound like some kind of sex-crazed neurotic. I'm not going to let you ruin me, Parker, just so you can have a few more annuities and condominiums!"

Parker flinched as though she'd struck him. He rose from his chair and came to crouch before hers, speaking softly and holding both her hands in his. "You feel threatened," he crooned.

It was all Vanessa could do not to kick him. She jerked her hands free, shot to her feet and stormed out of the office.

Parker caught up to her at the elevator, which, as luck would have it, was just arriving. "Baby, wait," he pleaded.

Vanessa was shamed by the tears that were flowing down her face, but she couldn't stop them. She dodged into the elevator, trying to escape him.

Parker squeezed into the cubicle with her, oblivious, apparently, of the fact that there were two men in suits, a cleaning woman and a maintenance worker looking on. He tried again, "Sweetheart, what do you want? A mink? A Corvette? Tell me what you want and I'll give it to you. But you've got to be reasonable!"

Vanessa drew her hand back and slapped the Living Legend. "How dare you assume you can buy me, you pompous jackass!" she cried. "And stop calling me sweetheart and baby!"

The elevator reached the ground floor, and Vanessa hurried out, hoping Parker wouldn't give chase. As it happened, however, he was right on her heels.

He looked exasperated now as he lengthened his strides to keep pace with her on the busy downtown sidewalk. He straightened the lapels of his tailored suit jacket and rasped out, "Damn it, Vanessa, do you know how much money is at stake here?"

"No, and I don't care," Vanessa answered. She was almost to the parking lot where she'd left her car; in a few minutes she could get behind the steering wheel and drive away.

With sudden harshness, Parker stopped her again, grasping her shoulders with his hands and pressing her backward against a department store display window. "You're not going to ruin this deal for me, Vanessa!" he shouted.

Vanessa stared at him, appalled and breathless. God knew Parker had hurt her often enough, but he'd never been physically rough.

Parker's effort to control his temper was visible. "I'm sorry," he ground out, and because he seldom apologized for anything, Vanessa believed him. "I didn't mean to manhandle you like that. Vanessa, please. Sit down with me somewhere private and listen to what I have to say. That's all I'm asking."

"There's no point, Parker," Vanessa replied. "I know what you want to tell me, and my answer won't be any different. The way you portrayed me in that book is libelous—I wouldn't be able to hold my head up in public."

"And I thought you'd be proud when I sent you a copy of that manuscript." He paused to shake his head, as if still amazed at her negative reaction. "Van, people will know I made most of that stuff up," Parker went on presently with a weak smile. "They're not going to take it seriously."

Vanessa arched one eyebrow. "Oh, really? Well, I'd rather not take the chance, if you don't mind. I have dreams of my own, you know."

Passersby were beginning to make whispers that indicated they recognized Parker. He took Vanessa's arm and squired her into a nearby coffee shop. "Two minutes," he said. "That's all I want."

She smiled acidly. "That's you, Parker—the two-minute man."

He favored her with a scorching look and dropped into the booth's seat across from her. "I'd forgotten what a little witch you can be, Van." He paused to square his shoulders. "Darla hasn't complained."

Darla, of course, was the girlfriend. "People with IQs under twenty rarely do," Vanessa answered sweetly. Then she added, "Your two minutes are ticking away." A waitress came, and Parker ordered two cups of coffee without even consulting Vanessa. It was so typical that she nearly laughed out loud.

"The advance on this book," Parker began in a low and reluctant voice, "is seven figures. I can't play baseball forever, Van. I need some security."

Vanessa rolled her eyes. Most oil sheiks didn't live as well as Parker; he certainly wasn't facing penury. "I'll drop you off at the food bank if you'd like," she offered. A muscle bunched in his jaw. Vanessa could have lived for years on the money that Parker's face brought in for commercials alone.

"You know," he said, "I really didn't expect you to be so bitter and frustrated."

The coffee arrived, and the waitress walked away again.

"Watch it," Vanessa warned. "You're trying to get on my good side, remember?"

Parker spread his hands in a gesture of baffled annoyance. "Van, I know the divorce was hard on you, but you have a job now and a life of your own. There's no reason to torture me like this."

He sounded so damnably rational that Vanessa wanted

to throw her coffee in his face. "Is that what you think I'm doing? I want nothing from you, Parker—no money, no minks, no sports cars—and no lies written up in a book and presented as the truth."

"So I was a little creative. What's wrong with that?"

"Nothing, if you're writing a novel." Vanessa could see that the conversation was progressing exactly as she'd expected. "I don't know why I even came down here," she said, glancing at her watch and sliding out of the booth.

"Hot date?" Parker asked, giving the words an unsavory inflection.

"Very hot," Vanessa lied, looking down at Parker. She was meeting her cousin Rodney for dinner and a movie, but what Parker didn't know wouldn't hurt him. She made a *sssssssss* sound, meant to indicate a sizzle, and walked away.

Much to her relief, Parker didn't follow.

Rodney was waiting in the agreed place when she reached the mall, his hands wedged into his jacket pockets, his white teeth showing in a grin.

"Hi, Van," he said. "Bad day?"

Vanessa kissed his cheek and linked her arm through his. "I just came from a meeting with Parker," she replied. "Does that answer your question?"

Rodney frowned. "Yeah," he said. "I'm afraid it does."

Vanessa smiled up at the handsome young man with the thick, longish chestnut brown hair and warm eyes. Her first cousin—and at twenty-one, five years her junior— Rodney was the only family she had in Seattle, and she loved him. She changed the subject. "Aren't you going to ask me about the apartment?"

Rodney laughed as they walked into the mall together and approached their favorite fast-food restaurant, a place that sold Chinese cuisine to go. The apartment over Vanessa's garage was empty since her last tenant had moved out, and Rodney wanted the rooms in the worst way.

"You know I do, Van," he scolded her good-naturedly. "Living over a funeral home has its drawbacks. For one thing, it gives new meaning to the phrase, 'things that go bump in the night.'"

Van laughed and shook her head. "Okay, okay—you can move in in a few weeks. I want to have the place painted first."

Rodney's face lighted up. He was a good kid working his way through chiropractic school by means of a very demanding and unconventional job, and Vanessa genuinely enjoyed his company. In fact, they'd always been close. "I'll do the painting," he said.

It was late when Vanessa arrived at the large colonial house on Queen Anne Hill and let herself in the front door. She crossed the sparsely furnished living room, kicking off her high heels and rifling through the day's mail as she moved.

In the kitchen, she flipped on the light and put a cup of water in the microwave to heat for tea. When the brew was steaming on the table, she steeled herself and pressed the button on her answering machine.

The first message was from her boss, Paul Harmon. "Janet and I want you to have dinner with us a week from Friday at DeAngelo's. Don't bring a date."

Vanessa frowned. The Harmons were friends of hers and they were forever trying to fix her up with one of their multitude of unattached male acquaintances. The fact that Paul had specified she shouldn't bring a date was unsettling.

She missed the next two messages, both of which were from Parker, because the name of the restaurant had rung a distant bell. What was it about DeAngelo's that made her uncomfortable?

She stirred sweetener into her tea, frowning. Then it came to her—the proprietor of the place was Nick DeAngelo, a former pro football player with a reputation for womanizing exceeded only by Parker's. Vanessa shuddered. The man was Paul's best friend. What if he turned out to be the mysterious fourth at dinner?

Vanessa shut off the answering machine and dialed the Harmons' home number. Janet answered the phone.

"About dinner at DeAngelo's," Vanessa said, after saying hi. "Am I being set up to meet Mr. Macho, or what?"

Janet laughed. "I take it you're referring to Nick?"

"And you're hedging," Vanessa accused.

"Okay, yes—we want you to meet Nick. He's a darling, Vanessa. You'll love him."

"That's what you said about that guy who wanted to be 'friends with benefits,'" Vanessa reminded her friend. "I really don't think this is a good idea."

"He's nothing like Parker," Janet said gently. She could be very perceptive. "It isn't fair to write Nick off as a loser without even meeting him."

The encounter with Parker had inclined her toward saying no to everything, and Vanessa knew it. She sighed. She had to be flexible, willing to meet new people and try new things, or she'd become stagnant. "All right, but if he turns out to be weird, Janet Harmon, you and Paul are off my Christmas-card list for good." That damned sixth sense of Janet's was still evident.

"The appointment with Parker and his attorney went badly, huh?"

Vanessa took a steadying sip of her tea. "He's going to publish that damned book, Janet," she whispered, feeling real despair. "There isn't anything I can do to stop him, and I'm sure he knows it, even though he seems to feel some kind of crazy need to win me over to his way of thinking."

"The bastard," Janet commiserated.

"I can say goodbye to any hopes I had of ever landing a job as a newscaster. I'll never be taken seriously."

"It's late, and you're tired," Janet said firmly. "Take a warm bath, have a glass of wine and get some sleep. Things will look better in the morning."

Exhausted, Vanessa promised to take her friend's advice and went off to bed, stopping only to wash her face and brush her teeth. She collapsed onto the mattress and immediately fell into a troubled sleep, dreaming that Parker was chewing her cash card and spitting the plastic pieces out on the pitcher's mound.

She awakened the next morning in a terrible mood, and when she reached the studio complex where the Midas Network was housed, her cohost, Mel Potter, looked at her with concern in his eyes.

A middle-aged, ordinary-looking man, Potter was known as Markdown Mel in the business, and he was a pro's pro. He had ex-wives all over the country and a gift for selling that was unequaled in the field. Vanessa had seen him move two thousand mini food-processors in fifteen minutes without even working up a sweat, and her respect for his skill as a salesman was considerable. He was, in fact, the one man in the world, besides her grandfather, who could address her as honey without making her hackles rise.

"What's the matter, honey?" he demanded as Vanessa flopped into a chair in the makeup room. "You look like hell."

Vanessa smiled. "Thanks a lot, Mel," she answered. "You're a sight for sore eyes yourself."

He laughed as Margie, the makeup girl, slathered Vanessa's face with cleansing cream. "I see by the papers that that ex-husband of yours is in town to accept an award at his old high school. Think you could get him to stop by the studio before he leaves? We could dump a lot of those baseball cake plates if Parker Lawrence endorsed them."

Now it was Vanessa who laughed, albeit a little hysterically. "Forget it, Mel. Parker and I aren't on friendly terms, and I wouldn't ask him for the proverbial time of day."

Mel shrugged, but Vanessa had a feeling she hadn't heard the last of the subject of Parker Lawrence selling baseball cake plates.

Twenty minutes later Vanessa and Mel were on camera, demonstrating a set of golf clubs. Vanessa loved her job. Somehow, when she was working, she became another person—one who had no problems, no insecurities and no bruises on her soul.

The network had a policy of letting viewers chat with the hosts over the air, and the first caller was Parker.

"Hello, babe," he said, after carefully introducing himself to the nation so that there could be no doubt as to who he was. "You look terrific."

Vanessa's smile froze on her face. She tried to speak, but she couldn't.

Mel picked up the ball with admirable aplomb. "Thanks, Parker," he answered. "You look pretty good yourself."

Even the cameraman laughed at that.

"Giving up baseball for golf?" Vanessa was emboldened to say.

"Never," Parker answered confidently. "But I'd take ten of anything you're selling, baby."

Vanessa was seething inside, but she hadn't forgotten that several million people would be watching this. She wasn't about to let Parker throw her in front of a national audience, and she knew the network wouldn't pass on airing a segment with *the* Parker Lawrence in it, even if she begged. "Good," she said, beaming. "We'll put you down for ten sets of golf clubs."

Parker laughed, thinking she was joking. Vanessa wished she could see his face when the UPS man delivered his purchases in seven to ten working days.

Chapter 2

The man was impossibly handsome, Vanessa thought ruefully as she watched Nick DeAngelo approach the table where she and the Harmons had been seated. He was tall, with the kind of shoulders one might expect of a former star football player. His hair was dark and attractively rumpled as though he'd just run his fingers through it. But it was the expression in his eyes that took hold of something deep inside Vanessa and refused to let go.

Suddenly Vanessa's emotional scars, courtesy of Parker Lawrence, got the best of her. She could have sworn they were as visible as stitch marks across her face and she was positive that Nick DeAngelo could count them. Her first instinct was to run and hide.

Grinning, Paul stood to greet his friend. "You survived the flu," he remarked. "From the way you sounded, I didn't think you were going to make it."

A half smile curved Nick's lips, probably in acknowledgment of what Paul had said, but his gaze was fixed on Vanessa. He seemed to be unwrapping her soul, layer by layer, and she didn't want that. She needed the insulation to feel safe.

She dropped her eyes, color rising to her cheeks, and clasped her hands together in her lap. In a matter of moments, a decade of living, loving and hurting had dropped away. She was as vulnerable as a shy sixteen-year-old.

"Vanessa," Paul said gently, prodding her with his voice. "This is my friend, Nick DeAngelo."

She looked up again because she had to, and Nick was smiling at her. A strange sensation washed over her, made up of fear and delight, consolation and challenge. "Hello," she said, swallowing.

His smile was steady and as warm as winter fire. Vanessa was in over her head, and she knew it. "Hi," he replied, his voice low and deep.

The sound of it caressed the bruises on Vanessa's soul like a healing balm. She was frightened by his ability to touch her so intimately and wondered if anyone would believe her if she said she'd developed a headache and needed to go home to put her feet up. She started to speak, but Janet Harmon cut her off.

"I hear you're opening another restaurant in Portland next month," she said to Nick, her foot bumping against Vanessa's under the table. "Won't that take you out of town a lot?"

The phenomenal shoulders moved in an easy shrug. Nick DeAngelo was obviously as much at home in a tailored suit as he would be in a football jersey and blue jeans. His brown eyes roamed over Vanessa, revealing an amused approval of the emerald-green silk dress she was wearing.

"I'm used to traveling," he said finally in response to Janet's question.

Vanessa devoutly wished that she'd stayed home. She wasn't ready for an emotional involvement, but it seemed to be happening anyway, without her say-so. She was as helpless as a swimmer going down for the third time. In desperation, she clasped on to the similarities between Parker and Nick.

They were both attractive, although Vanessa had to admit that Parker's looks had never affected her in quite the same way that Nick's were doing now. They were both jocks, and, if the press could be believed, Nick, like Parker, was a veritable legend among the bimbos of the world.

Vanessa felt better and, conversely, worse. She lifted her chin and said, "I don't think a jock—I mean, professional athlete—ever gets the road completely out of his blood."

Nick sat back in his chair. His look said he could read her as clearly as a floodlighted billboard. "Maybe it's like selling electric foot massagers on television," he speculated smoothly. "I don't see how a person could ever put a thrill like that behind them."

Vanessa squirmed. How typically male; he knew she was responding to him, and now he meant to make fun of her. "I'm not ashamed of what I do for a living, Mr. DeAngelo," she said.

Nick bent toward her and, in that moment, it was as though the two of them were alone at the table—indeed, alone in the restaurant. "Neither am I, Ms. Lawrence," he replied.

A crackling silence followed, which was finally broken by Paul's diplomatic throat clearing and he said, "Vanessa hopes to anchor one of the local news shows at some point."

Vanessa winced, sure that Nick would be amused at such a lofty ambition. Instead he merely nodded.

Dinner that night was delicious, although Vanessa was never able to recall exactly what it was, for she spent every minute longing to run for cover. After the meal, the foursome drifted from the dining room to the crowded cocktail lounge, where a quartet was playing soft music. Vanessa found herself held alarmingly close to Nick as they danced.

He lifted her chin with a curved finger and spoke in a velvety rasp. "Your eyes are the size of satellite dishes. Do I scare you that much?"

Vanessa stiffened. The man certainly had an ego. "You don't scare me at all," she lied. "It's only that I'm—I'm tired."

He smiled, and the warmth threatened to melt her like a wax statue. "You were married to Parker Lawrence, weren't you?"

Suddenly it was too hot in the place; Vanessa felt as though she'd suffocate if she couldn't get some fresh air. "Yes," she answered, flustered, searching for an avenue of escape.

True to form, Nick read her thoughts precisely. "This way," he said, and, taking Vanessa by the hand, he led her off the dance floor, down a hallway and into a large, tastefully furnished office. She was about to protest when she realized there was a terrace beyond the French doors on the far side of the room.

The autumn night was chilly, but Vanessa didn't mind. The crisp air cleared her head, and she felt better immediately.

The sky was like a great black tent, pierced through in a million places by tiny specks of silver light, and the view of downtown Seattle and the harbor was spectacular. Vanessa rested her folded arms against the stone railing and drew a deep, delicious breath.

"It's beautiful," she said, smiling.

Nick was beside her, gazing at the city lights and moonlit water spread out below them. "I never get tired of it," he said quietly. "The only drawback is that you can't see the Space Needle from here."

Vanessa shivered as an icy breeze swept off the water, and Nick immediately draped his jacket over her shoulders. She thanked him shyly with a look, and asked, "Have you lived in Seattle all your life?"

He nodded. "I was born here."

Vanessa marveled that she could be so comfortable with Nick on the terrace when she'd felt threatened inside the restaurant. She sighed. "I grew up in Spokane, but I guess I'm starting to feel at home."

"Just starting?" He arched a dark eyebrow.

Vanessa shrugged. "Seattle is Parker's hometown, not mine." Too late she realized she'd made a mistake, reopening a part of her life she preferred to keep private.

Nick leaned against the terrace and gazed at the circus of lights below. "I've been married before, too," he confided quietly. "Her name was Jenna."

Vanessa was practically holding her breath. It was incomprehensible that his answer should mean so much, but it did. "What happened?"

"She left me," Nick replied without looking at Vanessa.

"I'm sorry," Vanessa said, and she was sincere because she knew how much it hurt when a marriage died, whether a person was left or did the leaving. "A lot of women can't handle living with a professional athlete," she added, and although she'd meant the words as a consolation, she immediately wished she could take them back.

"Jenna bailed out before I got into the pros," Nick said in tones as cool as the wind rising off the water. "When I started making big bucks, she wanted to try again."

Before Vanessa could make any kind of response to that, Nick put an arm around her waist and ushered her back inside. She lifted the jacket from her shoulders while he closed the French doors that led out onto the terrace.

"Did you love Jenna?" she asked, and the words were the most involuntary ones she'd ever spoken.

Nick's expression was unreadable. "Did you love Parker?" he countered.

Vanessa bit her lower lip. "I honestly don't know," she answered after a few moments of thought. "I was in college when I met him, and he was already breaking records in baseball. I'd never met anyone like him before. He was— overwhelming."

Nick grinned somewhat sadly and leaned back against the edge of his desk, his arms folded. "I'd like to know you better," he said.

Vanessa was aware that such straightforwardness was rare in a man, and she was impressed. She was also terrified by the powerful things this man was making her feel. She placed his jacket carefully over the back of a chair, searching her mind for a refusal that would not be rude or hurtful.

She was unprepared for Nick's sudden appearance at her side, and for the way he gently lifted her chin in his hand and said, "It's time to let go of the pain and move on, Vanessa."

The low, rumbling words, spoken so close to her mouth, made her lips tingle with a strange sense of anticipation.

When Nick kissed her, she swayed slightly, stricken by a sweet malaise that robbed her of all balance.

Nick was holding her upright, though whether by means of the kiss or his gentle grasp on her waist, Vanessa couldn't be sure. She knew only that she was responding to him with her whole being, that she'd let him take her then and there if he pressed her. Being so vulnerable when she'd been so badly hurt before was almost more than she could bear.

When Nick finally released her, having kissed her more thoroughly than Parker ever had in even the most intimate of moments, she was so dazed that she could only stare up at him in abject amazement. She made up her mind that she absolutely would not see him again, no matter what.

He was too dangerous.

"Are you working tomorrow?" he asked in a sleepy voice, toying with a tendril of titian hair that had slipped from her hair clasp.

Vanessa struggled to remember, her throat thick, her mind a razzle-dazzle of popping lights. Finally she shook her head.

Nick grinned. "Good. Will you spend the day with me."

No, no, no, cried Vanessa's wounded spirit. "Yes," she choked out.

Nick smiled at her, tracing the curve of her cheek with one index finger, then reached for his jacket and shrugged into it. "We'd better get back out there before Paul and Janet decide we're doing something in keeping with my image."

They went back to the dance floor, and Nick held her. It was an innocent intimacy but it stirred Vanessa's senses, which had been largely dormant for the better part of a year, to an alarming pitch of need.

Every time she dared to meet Nick's eyes, it was as

though he had taken away an item of her clothing, and yet she could not resist looking at him. The dilemma was at once delicious and maddening, and Vanessa was relieved when Nick didn't offer to drive her home at the end of the evening.

Paul lingered on the sidewalk for a few minutes, talking with Nick, while Vanessa and Janet settled themselves in the car.

"Well," Janet demanded the moment she'd snapped her seat belt into place, "what did you think of him?"

Vanessa drew in a deep breath and let it out in an agitated rush. "I think I should have stayed home with my needlepoint," she said.

Janet turned in the car seat to look back at her. "You've got to be kidding. The man is hot!"

Only now, when her nostrils weren't filled with the subtle scent of his cologne and her body wasn't pressed to his could Vanessa be rational and objective where Nick DeAngelo was concerned. "He's also a jock," she said miserably. "Do you have any idea how egotistical those men can be? Not to mention callous and self-serving?"

Janet sighed. "Not every man is like Parker," she insisted.

The conversation was cut off at that point because Paul came back to the car, whistling cheerfully as he slid behind the wheel. Vanessa shrank into the corner of the seat, wishing, all in the same moment, that the night would end, that she could go back in time and say no to Nick's suggestion that they spend the next day together and that tomorrow would hurry up and arrive so she could see him again.

"Thanks," she said ruefully when Paul saw her to her door a few minutes later.

He smiled as she turned the key in the lock and pushed the door open. "Sounds as if you have mixed feelings about Nick," he commented.

Vanessa kicked off her high heels the moment she'd crossed the threshold. "I have *no* feelings about Nick," she argued, facing Paul but keeping her eyes averted. "Absolutely none."

Her boss chuckled. "Good night, Van," he said, and then he was gone, striding back down the front walk to his car.

Vanessa locked the door, slipped out of her velvet coat and bent to pick up her discarded shoes. Her calico cat, Sari, curled around her ankles, meowing.

Sari had already had her supper, and even though she had a weight problem, Vanessa couldn't turn a deaf ear to her plaintive cries. She set her purse, coat and shoes down on the deacon's bench in the hallway and allowed herself to be herded into the kitchen.

Even before she flipped on the lights, she saw the blinking red indicator on the answering machine. Vanessa was in no mood to deal with relationships of any kind that night; she wanted to feed the cat and go to bed. Her own innate sense of responsibility—some calamity could have befallen Rodney or her aging grandparents—made her cross the room and push the play button.

She was opening a can of cat food and scraping it into Sari's dish when Parker's voice filled the kitchen. The first message was relatively polite, but, as the messages progressed, Parker grew more and more irate. Finally he flared, "Why did you change your cell number? And don't you ever stay home? Damn it, call me!"

Vanessa had washed her hands and was about to turn off the machine when Nick's voice rolled over her like a warm, rumbling wave. "You're a terrific lady," he said. "I'm looking forward to seeing you again tomorrow."

Vanessa moaned faintly and sank into a chair, propping her chin in both hands. With a few idle words, the man had melted the muscles in her knees.

"Good night," he said, his voice deep and gentle, and then the machine was silent.

After a few moments of sheer bewilderment, Vanessa got up and checked the locks on both the front and back doors. Then, taking her coat and shoes with her, Sari padding along beside her, she went upstairs.

She hung her coat carefully in the closet and put the shoes back into their plastic box. Soon she was in bed, but sleep eluded her.

She kept imagining what it would be like to lie beside Nick DeAngelo, in this bed or any other, and have him touch her, kiss her, make love to her. Just the thought made her ache.

Sometime toward morning, Vanessa slept. The telephone awakened her to a full complement of sunshine, and she grappled for the receiver, losing it several times before she managed to maneuver it into place.

"Hello," she accused, shoving one hand through her rumpled hair and scowling.

After knowing him such a short time, it seemed impossible, but she recognized Nick's laughter. "Don't tell me, let me guess. You're not a morning person."

Vanessa narrowed her eyes to peer at the clock and saw that it was nearly nine o'clock. She was glad Nick had called, she decided, because that gave her a chance to cancel their date. "Listen, I've been thinking—"

He cut her off immediately. "Well, stop. You're obviously in no condition for that kind of exertion. I'll be over in ten minutes to ply you with coffee."

"Nick!" Vanessa cried, afraid of being plied. But it was too late, he'd already hung up and she had no idea what his number was.

Grumbling, she got out of bed, stumbled into the bathroom and took a shower. By the time Nick arrived, she was clad in jeans and a blue knit sweater and was fully conscious.

She greeted him at the front door, holding a cup of therapeutically strong coffee in one hand. "You didn't give me a chance to tell you on the phone, but..."

Nick grinned in that disarming way he had and assessed her trim figure with blatant appreciation. "Good, you're dressed," he said, walking past her into the house.

"You expected me to be naked?" Vanessa wanted to know.

He laughed. "I'm allowed my share of fantasies, aren't I?"

Vanessa shook her head. Nick was impossible to shun.

He was wearing jeans and a hooded sweatshirt, and he had the look of a man who knew where he was going to spend that chilly, sun-washed Saturday. "Come in, come in," she chimed wryly as he preceded her down the hallway to the kitchen. "Don't be shy."

He grinned at her over one shoulder. "I've never been accused of that," he assured her.

Vanessa had no doubt he was telling the truth. She gave up. "Where are we going?"

"Running," he said. "Then I thought we'd take in a movie..."

Vanessa was holding up both hands in a demand for silence. "Wait a minute, handsome—rewind to the part about running."

Nick dragged his languorous brown eyes from the toes of her sneakers to the crown of her head. "Bad idea? You certainly look like someone who cares about fitness."

She sighed and poured her coffee into the sink. "Thank you—I think."

"I guess we could skip running—just for today," he said, stepping closer to her.

Vanessa's senses went on red alert, and she leaped backward as though he'd burned her. "On second thought, running sounds like a great idea," she said, in a squeaky voice, embarrassed. "You seem to have a lot of—of extra energy."

He favored her with slow, sensuous grin. "Oh, believe me," he said with quiet assurance, "I do."

Vanessa swallowed. It was beyond her how accepting a single blind date could get a person into so much trouble. She swore to herself that the next time Janet and Paul wanted to introduce her to someone, she was going to hide in the cellar until the danger passed.

"Relax," Nick said, approaching and taking her shoulders into his big, gentle hands. "You are one tense individual, Value Van."

Vanessa blinked. "What did you call me?"

"I've gotten kind of caught up in this home-shopping thing," he replied, his dark eyes twinkling. "I thought you should have a professional nickname, like your friend Markdown Mel. The possibilities are endless, you know—there's Bargain Barbara, for instance, and Half-price Hannah…"

Vanessa began to laugh. "I never know whether to take you seriously or not."

He bent his head and kissed her, innocently and briefly. "Oh, you should take me seriously, Van. It's the rest of your life that needs mellowing out."

She gave him a shove. "Let's go running," she said. They drove to the nearest park in Nick's Corvette. He led the way to the jogging path and immediately started doing warm-up exercises.

Vanessa eyed him ruefully, then began, in her own awkward fashion, to follow suit. "One thing about dating a jock," she ventured to say, breathing a little hard as she tried to keep up, "a girl stays skinny, no matter what." Nick started off down the path after rolling his eyes once, and Vanessa was forced to follow at a wary trot.

"Are you saying that I'm not a fun guy?" he asked over one shoulder.

"What could be more fun than this?" Vanessa countered, already gasping for breath. She'd dropped her exercise program during the divorce, and the effects of her negligence were painfully obvious.

When they reached a straight stretch, Nick turned and ran backward, no trace of exertion visible in his manner or voice. "So, how long have you been a member of the loyal order of couch potatoes?" he asked companionably.

"I hate you," huffed Vanessa.

"That really hurts, Value Van," Nick replied. "See if I ever buy another pair of Elvis Presley bookends from you."

There was grass alongside the pathway, and Vanessa flung herself onto it, dragging air into her lungs and groaning. She couldn't believe she was there in the park, torturing herself this way when she could have slept in until noon and sent out for Chinese food.

Nick did not keep running, as she'd expected. Instead he flopped down on the cold grass beside her and said, "I appreciate the offer, but we haven't known each other long enough."

Vanessa gave him a look and clambered to her feet. "Tired so soon?" she choked out, jogging off down the pathway.

At the end of the route, which Vanessa privately thought of as The Gauntlet, the ice-blue Corvette sat shining in the autumn sunlight. She staggered toward it and collapsed into the passenger seat while Nick was still cooling down.

When he slid behind the wheel, she barely looked at him. "What did I do to Janet to make her hate me like this?" she asked.

Nick chuckled and started the car. "I'll answer that when I've had a shower."

Vanessa's eyes flew open wide. Showering was an element she hadn't thought about, even though it seemed perfectly obvious now.

Nick's expression was suddenly serious. "Relax, Van," he said. "It's a private shower, and you're not invited."

To her everlasting chagrin, Vanessa blushed like a Victorian schoolgirl. She was a reserved person, but not shy. She wondered again what it was about this man that circumvented all the normal rules of her personality and made her act like someone she didn't even know.

"It never crossed my mind that you might expect me to share a shower with you," Vanessa lied, her chin at a prim angle, her arms folded.

"Liar," Nick replied with amused affection.

He lived in a condominium on the top floor of one of the most historic buildings in Seattle, and the place had a quiet charm that surprised Vanessa. She had expected a playboy's den with lots of leather, glass accents and stark colors, but the spacious rooms were decorated in earth tones instead. There was an old-fashioned fireplace in the living room and a beautiful Navaho rug graced the wall above the cushy sofa.

"Make yourself at home," Nick said casually, ducking through a doorway and leaving Vanessa to stand there alone, feeling sweaty and rumpled and totally out of place.

She went to the window and looked out on busy Elliot Bay. A passenger ferry was chugging into port, large and riverboatlike, and Vanessa smiled. In the distance, she heard the sound of running water and an off-key rendition of a current popular song.

The view kept her occupied for what seemed like a long time, but when Nick didn't return after ten minutes, Vanessa began to grow uneasy. She approached the big-screen television in one corner of the room and pushed the power button on the nearby remote.

Immediately the Midas Network leaped out at her in living color, life-size. She turned the set off again and began to pace, tempted to sneak out before this nonrelationship with Nick DeAngelo grew into something she couldn't handle.

She was just reaching for the doorknob when his voice stopped her.

"Don't go," he said quietly. "I'm not going to hurt you in any way, Vanessa. I swear it."

She couldn't move, couldn't drop her hand to her side or turn the knob and make her escape.

"Something really important is happening here," he went on. "Can't you feel it?"

Vanessa let her forehead rest against the cool panel of the door. "Yes," she confessed in a strangled voice, "and that's what scares me."

He stepped closer to her and laid his hands very gently on her shoulders. She was filled with the scent of his clean hair, his freshly washed skin. "I won't let anything happen that you're not ready for," he promised, and when he turned her around to face him, Vanessa was powerless to resist.

She looked up at him with eyes full of trust and fear, and he let his hands drop to her waist. He was careful not to hold her too close, and yet she was achingly aware of his total, unreserved masculinity.

"I'm going to kiss you," he said matter-of-factly. "That is, if you're ready."

She slid her arms around his neck and stood on tiptoe, exhilarated and, at the same time, terrified. "I'm ready," she answered, her mouth only a whisper away from his.

Chapter 3

"Want a shower now?"

Vanessa, her energy drained by the kiss, had sagged back against the door when it was overz Her eyes opened wide, however, when Nick's words registered. "I beg your pardon?"

He turned and walked off toward the open kitchen, looking too good for comfort in his jeans and T-shirt. His biceps bulged when he lifted his arm to open a cupboard door, and Vanessa felt vaguely dizzy.

At that moment there was only one thing in the world she wanted more than a shower. She followed him, careful to keep the breakfast bar between them. "I don't have any clean clothes to put on," she ventured to say.

Nick shrugged. "Some of Gina's things are still here. You're about her size, I think."

The name made Vanessa round the breakfast bar. "Gina?" she asked, looking up at him.

He kissed her forehead. "My sister," he assured her.

The relief Vanessa felt was embarrassing in its scope. "I've never had to shower on a date before," she confessed.

Nick chuckled at that. "Never?"

Vanessa looked up into his dancing eyes and felt a painful tug somewhere in the region of her heart. She wanted to appear glamorous and sophisticated, but the truth was far different. She'd never been with any man besides Parker, and, when and if she went to bed with Nick, it was going to be almost like reliving the first time. At last she shook her head and answered, "Never."

He started to put his arms around her and then stopped. "Do you like Chinese food?" he asked.

Vanessa nodded.

"Good. You'll find the clothes and the shower down the hall—first room on the right. I'll go get our lunch while you're changing—okay?"

"Okay," Vanessa answered, not knowing quite what to make of this man. She knew Nick was attracted to her, and yet when he had an advantage, he didn't press it.

The room Nick had directed her to was large, though it obviously wasn't the place where he slept. There was a private bathroom, however, and Vanessa locked herself in before stripping off the clothes she'd worn to run in the park.

When she finished showering, she found the promised clothes in closets and bureaus and finally helped herself to yoga pants and a hoodie. She zipped it to her eyeballs and was just entering the living room when Nick returned with cartons of fragrant sweet-and-sour chicken, chow mein and fried rice.

He smiled and shook his head when he saw the outfit. "Feel better?" he asked.

Vanessa felt a number of things, and she wasn't ready

to talk about any of them. She went to the cupboards and opened doors until she found plates for their food. They ate at the breakfast bar, perched on stools, and Nick insisted on using chopsticks.

"Show off," Vanessa said, spearing a succulent morsel of chicken with her fork.

He surprised her by laying down his chopsticks, reaching out and pulling down the zipper on the hoodie to her breastbone. "The weather's getting nasty outside," he commented, "but it's warm enough in here."

Vanessa blushed, embarrassed. She knew Nick thought she was a hidebound prude, but she didn't have the nerve to prove she wasn't. Not yet.

He leaned over and gave her a nibbling kiss on the lips. "Everything is okay, Van," he promised her quietly. "Just relax."

A light rain spattered the windows, and Nick left his stool to light a fire on the hearth. The crackling sound was cozy, and the colorful blaze gave that corner of the room a cheery glow.

Something Vanessa could not name or define made her leave her place at the breakfast bar and approach Nick. She knelt beside him, facing the fireplace, and said, "I'm not like you p-probably think I am. It's just that you scare me so much."

He turned to her, smiling softly, and slid four fingers into her hair, caressing her cheek with his thumb. "I won't tell you any lies, Vanessa," he replied. "I want you—I have since I turned on the Midas Network and saw you standing there with a toll-free number printed across your chest— but I'm willing to wait."

"Wait?" Vanessa asked. Nothing in her relationship with Parker had ever prepared her for this kind of patience from a man. He had to want something. "You're admitting, then, that there is a plan of seduction?"

He laughed. "Absolutely. I intend to make you want me, Vanessa Lawrence."

Vanessa figured he had the battle half won already, but she wasn't about to say that to him. In fact, she didn't say anything, because Nick DeAngelo had rendered her speechless.

He got up, leaving her kneeling there by the fire, and returned after a few minutes with two glasses of wine. After handing one to Vanessa and setting his own down on the brick hearth, he glanced pensively toward the rain-sheeted windows. "Do you want to go out to a movie, or shall we stay here?"

Even though Vanessa was still wishing that she'd stayed home, indeed that she'd never met Nick at all, she had no desire to leave the comfort and warmth of his fire. She was, in fact, having some pretty primitive and elemental feelings where he and his comfortable home were concerned. It was almost as though she'd been wandering, cold and hungry and alone, and he'd rescued her and brought her to a secret, special place that no one else knew about.

Vanessa shook her head. She hadn't even had a sip of her wine yet, and it was already getting to her.

"Van?" Nick prompted, peering into her face, and she realized that she hadn't answered his question.

"Oh. Yes. I mean, I'd like to sit by the fire and watch the storm." Even as she spoke, blue-gold lightning streaked across the angry sky and a fresh spate of rain pelted the glass.

Nick came back and sat down beside her on the rug. "Tell me about your life, Van," he said, his voice low.

She immediately tensed, but before she could frame a reply, Nick reached out and squeezed her hand.

"I'm not asking about Parker—I know a little about him because we traveled in some of the same circles. You're the one I'm curious about."

Vanessa took a sip of her wine and then told Nick the central facts about her childhood; that her father had died when she was seven, that her very young mother had been overwhelmed by responsibilities and grief and had left her daughter with her parents so that she could marry a rodeo cowboy. There had been cards, letters and the occasional Christmas and birthday gifts, but Van had rarely seen her mother after that.

The expression in Nick's eyes was a soft one as he listened, but there was no pity in evidence, and Vanessa appreciated that. Her childhood had been difficult, but there were lots of people who would have gladly traded places with her, and she had made a good life for herself— generally speaking.

"You've always wanted to be on television?" Nick asked, plundering the white paper bag he'd brought home from the Chinese restaurant until he found two fortune cookies at the bottom.

Vanessa sighed and shook her head. "Not really. I wanted to be Annie Oakley until I was six—then I made the shattering discovery that there was very little call for trick riding and fancy shooting except in the circus." Nick grinned at that. "My childhood dream pales by comparison. I wanted to run my Uncle Guido's fish market."

Vanessa laughed. "And you had to settle for a career in professional football. My God, DeAngelo, that's sad—I don't know how you bore up under the disappointment!"

He had drawn very close. "I'm remarkable," he answered with a shrug.

"I can imagine," Vanessa confessed, and as he touched the sensitive, quivering flesh of her neck with his warm and tentative lips, she gave a little moan. "Is this the part where you start making me want you?" she dared to ask.

Nick nipped at her earlobe and chuckled when she trembled. "Yes. But that's all, so don't get nervous."

"What about what you want?" Vanessa asked.

"I can wait," he replied, and she knew she should push him away, but she couldn't. The attention he was giving her neck felt entirely too good.

Presently his hands came back to the zipper of the hoodie. Vanessa closed her fingers over his, realizing with a sleepy sort of despair that she wasn't wearing either bra or panties beneath the soft blue cotton, but Nick would not be stopped. He was a gentle conqueror, though, and she had no more thoughts of fear or of escape.

She was lying on her back before the popping fire when he bared her breasts and watched the shimmer of the blaze and the flash of lightning play over them. Vanessa had never felt so feminine, so desirable.

With a low, grumbling groan, Nick lowered himself to chart the circumference of her breast with a whisperlight passing of his lips. Vanessa watched in delicious dread as he moved toward the peak he meant to conquer, in an upward spiraling pattern of kisses. A whimper of longdenied pleasure escaped her as he touched her budding nipple with his tongue, causing it to blossom like some lovely, exotic flower.

Beyond the windows, lightning raged against the sky as though seeking to thrust its golden fingers through the glass and snatch the lovers up in fire and heat. Vanessa shuddered involuntarily as Nick's hand made a slow, comforting circle on her belly, his lips and tongue continuing to master her nipple.

He'd said his goal was to make her want him, and he'd succeeded without question. Vanessa longed to give him the kind of intolerable pleasure he was giving her, to be joined with him in a fevered battle that would have no losers. But he was setting the pace, and Vanessa had no power to turn the tables.

Her breasts were moist and pleasantly swollen by the time he brought his mouth back to hers and consumed her in a kiss as elemental as the lightning tearing at the afternoon sky.

"Do you want me to make love to you, Van?" Nick whispered against her throat when the kiss had at last ended.

Vanessa could barely lie still, her body was so hungry for his. "Yes," she admitted breathlessly, her fingers frantic in his hair. "Oh, yes."

He gave a heavy sigh and circled a pulsing nipple with the tip of his tongue before saying the unbelievable words. "You're not ready for that, darlin'."

Although he'd spoken without a trace of malice, Vanessa still felt as though she'd been slapped. "You can't just—just leave me like this..."

"Don't worry," he said, still toying with her nipple. "I don't intend to."

Moments later, he drew her pants down over her hips and legs and tossed them away. He kissed Vanessa thoroughly before trailing his mouth down over her collarbone, her breasts, her belly.

When he reached his destination, the lightning would wait no longer. It reached into the room, scooping Vanessa up with crackling fingers and bouncing her mercilessly in its palm. Only when she cried out in primitive satisfaction did it set her back on the rug in front of Nick's fireplace and leave her in relative peace.

She was crying, and she couldn't bring herself to look at the man who had unchained the lightning.

He covered her gently with an afghan as though she were a casualty of some sort and kissed her on the forehead. "I'll be back in a few minutes," he said.

By the time Nick returned, Vanessa had rallied enough to get back into her clothing. She was standing at the window, looking out on the gloomy spectacle of a city dressed in twilight gray, hugging herself. Nick stood behind her, putting his arms around her, and she felt the chilly dampness of his bare chest against her back and guessed that he'd taken a cold shower.

"Why?" she asked, not looking at him because she couldn't. "I would have given myself to you. Didn't you want me?"

"Oh, I wanted you, all right."

"Then why? Why didn't you take me?"

"Because this is your time, Vanessa. Because I think you're hiding somewhere deep inside yourself and you need to be coaxed into the world again. That's what I want to show you—that it's safe out here."

She turned in his arms, sliding hers around his waist. He wore nothing but a pair of jeans and an impudent half grin. She rested her forehead against his cool, muscular chest.

"It was as though the storm came inside," she confessed. "I've never felt anything like it."

Nick simply held her and listened.

"I'm not some kind of neurotic, you know," she went on. "And I'm not a prude, either."

He chuckled, and his lips moved softly at her temple. "No prude would have responded the way you did."

Vanessa looked up at him. "You were right earlier, Nick DeAngelo—you are a remarkable man."

He favored her with a cocky grin. "You have no idea how remarkable," he teased.

"I think I'd like to go home before I decide to find out," Vanessa replied.

Nick didn't argue, get insulted or try to convince her to stay. He simply put on a shirt and shoes, got her a paper bag for her jeans and sweater and drove her home. "Will you come to dinner on Friday night?" Vanessa asked him, when they were standing in her kitchen and he'd just given her a goodbye kiss that brought faint flickers of lightning to her mind.

"Do I have to wait that long to see you again?" he countered, albeit good-naturedly.

Vanessa nodded. "I'm afraid so. If you're around, I won't get any rest at all, and when that happens, I don't do well on television."

Nick touched the tip of her nose with an index finger. "Okay." He sighed. "I'll content myself with watching you sell cordless screwdrivers and stainless steel cutlery for a week, but be forewarned, when Friday night comes around, you're in for another lesson on why I'm the only man for you."

Vanessa felt a pleasant little thrill at the prospect and hoped he didn't notice. "Eight o'clock," she said.

He kissed her again. "Seven, and I'll bring the wine."

"Seven-thirty," Vanessa negotiated, "and you can also build the fire."

Nick laughed. "Deal," he said, shaking her hand. And

then he was gone, and Vanessa's big, empty house seemed bigger and emptier than ever.

She fed Sari, who had been telling a long and woeful tale in colloquial meows from the moment Vanessa and Nick had entered the house. She had just tossed her jeans, sweater and underwear into the utility room when someone began pounding at the front door.

Thinking Nick had come back, she hurried through the house, worked the lock and pulled the door open wide.

Parker was standing on the step, looking apoplectic. "Do you realize how many messages I've left for you since last night?" he demanded furiously.

Not wanting the neighbors to witness a domestic drama of the sort they'd learned to expect and relish during the last days of the marriage, Vanessa grasped Parker by the arm and pulled him inside the house.

"I've been busy," she hissed, annoyed. She started off toward the kitchen again, leaving Parker to follow. "What did you want, anyway?" she demanded, reaching into a cupboard for two mugs and marching over to the sink.

"I'm going to be on a talk show day after tomorrow," her ex-husband answered in grudging tones, hurling himself into a chair at the table. He named a very famous host. "She wants you to appear, too, since you're in the book."

So that was it. Vanessa's feelings of being cherished was displaced by a sensation of weariness. She wondered who, besides Parker, would have had the gall to suggest such a thing.

"No way, slugger," she breathed, setting the mugs full of water in the microwave and getting out a jar of instant coffee.

"It will mean more sales, Van," Parker whined, "and more sales means more money!"

Vanessa was standing by the counter, her arms folded, waiting for the water to heat. "You live in a fantasy world, don't you, Parker? A place where nobody ever says no to anything you want. Well, listen to this—I'm not going to help you promote that book, I'm going to sue you for writing it!"

The bell on the microwave chimed, and Vanessa took the mugs out and made coffee by rote. She set one in front of Parker with a thump and sat down on the opposite side of the table from him.

He was staring at the hoodie in baffled distaste. "Good grief, Vanessa," he said, "don't you make enough money to dress decently? Whatever that thing is, it's a size too big."

Vanessa sighed. Some things never changed. "I knew you were coming over and I dressed for the occasion," she said sweetly, taking a sip from her mug. Sari made a furry pass around her ankles, as if to lend reassurance. Parker was a master of the quicksilver technique, and he sat back in his chair and smiled warmly at Vanessa.

"I hope I didn't make you feel inadequate," he said.

He'd made a specialty of it in the past, but Vanessa had no desire to hash over the bad old days. She thought of the hours she'd spent in Nick DeAngelo's company and smiled back. "That's about the last thing I'm feeling right now," she answered.

Parker looked disappointed. "Oh."

Vanessa laughed at his frank bewilderment. "Listen," she said after recovering herself, "our marriage has been over for a long time. We don't have to do battle anymore."

He sat up straight. "The things I'm asking for are very simple, Vanessa," he said, sounding almost prim. "And they're also impossible. I'm not going on any talk show to promote a book I'd like to see fade into obscurity."

His expression turned smug. "Suing me will only make sales soar," he said.

"I know," Vanessa confessed with a sigh. "Just tell me one thing, Parker—why did you describe me that way? Was that the kind of wife you wish I'd been?"

Parker averted his eyes, then pulled back the sleeve of his expensive Irish woolen sweater to glance at his Rolex. "What would I have to do to get you back?" he asked without even looking at her.

Vanessa was thunderstruck. Not once in her wildest imaginings had it ever occurred to her that Parker had been harassing her in a sort of schoolboy attempt to get her attention. She put her hands to her cheeks, unable for the moment to speak.

At last Parker met her gaze. "I thought things would be so much better without you," he told her gruffly. "Instead my whole life is going to hell."

Vanessa resisted an urge to take out the brandy she'd used to make fruitcake the year before and pour a generous dose into her coffee. "I'm flattered," she said in a moderate voice, "but I don't think getting back together would be good for either of us."

"You're in love with somebody else," Parker accused. It was too soon to say that what Vanessa felt for Nick was love, but his appearance in her life had made some profound changes.

"That's got nothing to do with anything," she answered. "There is no future for you and me—there shouldn't even have been a past." She got out of her chair and went to the back door, opening it to the chilly autumn wind and standing there looking at Parker.

To his credit, he took the hint and slid back his chair.

"If you'd just let me stay, I could prove to you that getting divorced was a mistake for us."

Vanessa shook her head, marveling. "Good night," she said, and she closed and locked the door the moment Parker stepped over the threshold.

The telephone rang just as she was taking their cups from the table to the sink.

"Was that The Living Legend I just saw leaving your place?" her cousin Rodney demanded.

Vanessa smiled, looking out the kitchen window at the lighted apartment over the garage. "Yes. All moved in, are you?"

"Absolutely," Rodney replied. "I've been painting all day, and the fact is, I think if I close my eyes tonight I'm going to wake up asphyxiated."

"If you're asphyxiated, you don't usually wake up," Vanessa pointed out.

"I'd forgotten how nitpicky you get when you're tired," Rodney teased. "Are you going to invite me to sleep on your couch tonight or what?"

Vanessa laughed. "I haven't got a couch, remember? Parker took it. But you're welcome to spread out a sleeping bag and breathe free."

"I'll be right down," came the immediate response. Rodney arrived within seconds, carrying a rolled-up sleeping bag and a paper sack with the name of a favorite delicatessen emblazoned on the side. "Have you had dinner?" he asked.

Vanessa realized that she hadn't had anything to eat since the Chinese lunch at Nick's, and she was hungry. "Actually, no," she answered.

Rodney pulled out the cutting board and slid the biggest hero sandwich Vanessa had seen in recent memory out of the bag. Her cousin reached for a knife and cut the huge combination of bread and lettuce, cheese and turkey into two equal pieces. "Share and share alike," he said.

Grinning, Vanessa took plates from the cupboard and brought them over to the counter. "I'm overwhelmed by your generosity."

"It's the least I can do for the woman who saved me from spending another night above Jergenson's Funeral Parlor," he replied.

Vanessa put half the sandwich onto her plate and went back to the table. "Someday, when you're a successful chiropractor, you'll look back on living there as a growth experience."

Rodney dropped into the chair directly across from hers. "You're trying to evade the real issue here, which is what did Parker want?"

"I don't think he knows," Vanessa confided, dropping her eyes to her sandwich.

"Damn," Rodney marveled, "he's trying to get you back, isn't he? I wonder how he found out you were seeing Nick DeAngelo. Bet it's eating him up—"

Vanessa gazed directly at her cousin. "How do you know about Nick?" she broke in.

"I saw him," Rodney answered with a shrug. "I go out with his sister Gina sometimes."

Vanessa blushed, remembering that she was wearing Gina's clothes and wondering if Rodney recognized it. "Then you know him?" she speculated.

Rodney shrugged again. "You could say that, I guess. I've been on a few family picnics—when that tribe heads for the island, it's like some kind of Italian exodus."

Vanessa swallowed a weary giggle. "The island?" she asked, trying to sound casual.

The mischievous look in Rodney's eyes said she'd failed roundly. "Nick owns a big Victorian house in the San Juans," he answered. "Don't you ever read the tabloids? He's famous for the parties he gives."

A picture came into Vanessa's mind, the image of herself walking into Parker's condominium on Maui, planning to surprise him by arriving for their vacation a day ahead of time. She'd surprised him, all right—along with the Polynesian beauty sharing his bed.

Her thoughts turned to the storm of that afternoon, and the searing, crackling lightning. Vanessa felt betrayed.

The fiery gentleness of Nick's lovemaking had eased many of her doubts about him, but now she realized that the patience and caring he'd shown had probably been nothing more than pretense. If he liked to party and play the field, a relationship with her wasn't likely to change him any more than it had changed Parker.

Every self-help book on the market was screaming the message that men are an as-is proposition, once a rogue, always a rogue.

Vanessa put her hands over her face, her appetite gone.

"Van?" Rodney sounded worried. "What's the matter? Are you okay?"

Vanessa got out of her chair, carried her sandwich to the counter, wrapped it carefully and tucked it into the refrigerator. Although she didn't say a word, she was shaking her head the whole time.

Rodney's chair scraped against the floor as he pushed it back. "I said something wrong, didn't I?"

"No," Vanessa said, unable to meet her cousin's eyes, "you brought me to my senses, that's all. I'd forgotten that a jock is a jock is a jock." She paused at the base of the back stairway, her hand resting on the banister. "Good night," she said.

Words, Vanessa discovered, did not make it so. The night was not a good one, and the morning showed every sign of being worse.

Chapter 4

The porcelain statuette of a Grecian goddess toppled precariously when Vanessa bumped into it, and it would have shattered on the studio floor if Mel hadn't been so quick to grab it.

Paul Harmon signaled from off-camera, and Vanessa was grateful for the respite.

"Are you all right?" her friend and employer asked, when she left Mel to sell the goddess unaided.

Vanessa drew a deep breath and let it out slowly. She'd been a klutz all morning, crashing into props and sales items, saying nonsensical things, getting prices and details wrong. She splayed her fingers and shoved them through her hair, thus spoiling the coiffure Margie in Makeup had spent twenty minutes styling. "Let's just say I'll be glad when this day is over." She sighed loudly.

Paul grinned. "Nick?" he asked.

Vanessa squared her shoulders. *What egotists men are,*

she thought. *One of them comes along and screws up your life, and all his friends think "what a guy."*

"Nick who?" she countered coolly, turning around and marching back on camera.

An elderly lady from Tucson, calling in to order the statuette for her daughter, was on the air. "I've got all my credit cards up to their limits, but I can't help myself," she enthused. "I just had to get Venus for Allison. She'll love this for her bathroom."

Distracted, Vanessa forgot the cardinal telemarketing rule and said worriedly, "Maybe you shouldn't buy anything for a while. After all, there will be other statues, and you've worked hard to build up your credit…"

Mel looked at Van as though her nose had just grown an inch and elbowed her aside. "Vanessa's kidding, of course," he boomed in his best it's-me-and-you-against-those-guys-who-charge-high-prices voice. "This is a unique piece of art that would grace anybody's bathroom."

Paul was signaling again, but this time he didn't look quite so friendly. When Vanessa reached him, he took her arm and squired her into the makeup room, where fast-talking Oliver Richards was being prepared to go on.

He glanced up at the monitor to let Vanessa know he'd witnessed her gaffe and wriggled his eyebrows. Since the day he'd made a pass at her and she'd set him straight, Oliver had taken pleasure in every setback she suffered, be it major or minor.

"Good work, Van," he said. "Keep this up, and we'll all be in the unemployment line."

Paul gave the former sportscaster a dark look. "Go out and take over for Mel. He's got a dental appointment and has to leave early." Oliver immediately left.

Vanessa lowered her head, braced for a lecture. "My

mind hasn't been on my work this morning," she said. "I'm sorry."

Paul sighed. "This kind of thing happens to everybody at one point or another," he reasoned. "One thing is a given—the board isn't going to be pleased about that little speech you just made. Van, what possessed you to do that?"

"I told you, I wasn't thinking." Vanessa looked up at her friend, feeling defensive. "Besides, what I said was true, even if it wasn't a good sales technique. There are a lot of people out there running themselves into serious debt so they can put statues of Venus in their bathrooms."

"And I should pity the wretched masses and shut down the cameras?" Paul shot back, annoyed. "Is everybody supposed to do without the convenience of home shopping because a few people can't control themselves?"

"I didn't say that!" Vanessa cried.

Just then Nick walked in, looking reprehensibly handsome in gray slacks, a navy blue sweater and a charcoal sports jacket.

"What are you doing here?" Vanessa demanded.

"I'm going out to lunch with a friend," he answered calmly, his eyes dancing with amusement.

"We agreed not to see each other again until Friday," she reminded him.

"You're not the friend," Nick replied in reasonable tones. He looked over her head at Paul. "Ready to go, old buddy?"

Vanessa's face was flushed, and she turned away to hide it. "I'm due on camera," she muttered, striding purposefully toward the door.

"Try not to put us out of business before your segment's over," Paul called after her.

Although Vanessa was seething inside, she smiled at the camera and at Oliver Richards when she stepped back onto the set. A rowing machine had been brought on as the next item to be featured, and Oliver beamed as an idea came to mind.

"The lovely Vanessa Lawrence rejoins us, folks," he announced. "Just in time to demonstrate the rowing machine."

Determined not to lose her composure, Van kicked off her high heels and sat down on the machine's seat, trying to be graceful as she tugged the straight skirt of her cashmere dress modestly over her thighs.

Despite the blinding glare of the studio lights, Vanessa was painfully aware of Nick's presence as she rowed and chatted with customers from all over the country. He'd lingered to watch her make a fool of herself in front of Middle-America.

By the time her replacement arrived, she had developed a megaheadache, but Nick was nowhere in sight when she left the studio complex to drive home.

Upon reaching the house, she felt better, and, seeing Rodney's car in the driveway, she decided to drop in to see if he was settled into the apartment over her garage. Music was blaring through the open door when Vanessa reached the top of the stairs, and she was smiling when she knocked.

"Come in!" cried a feminine voice.

With a slight lift of one eyebrow, Vanessa went inside. A lovely dark-eyed girl, dressed in blue jeans and a T-shirt, with chocolate-colored hair tumbling to her waist, was sitting in the middle of the living-room floor. She was breaking a thread with her teeth, a tangle of fabric and sequins resting in her lap.

Rodney arrived from the kitchen, carrying two cans of diet pop, just as Vanessa was about to introduce herself. He took over the task with admirable grace. "Van," he said proudly, "this is Gina DeAngelo. Gina, my cousin and land-lady, Vanessa Lawrence."

"Hi," Gina said, holding out a hand.

Vanessa was charmed. After returning the greeting, she sank into a chair. "What is that?" she asked, referring to the fabric Gina had been working with.

"It's Rodney's costume," the girl answered, holding up the blue stretchy fabric. "He's got a new act. Why don't you show her, Rod?"

Rodney blushed. Despite the fact that he earned his living, as well as his tuition, by working as an exotic dancer, he was shy. "No way," he answered.

Gina let the subject drop, smiling at Vanessa. "You're dating my brother," she said, her brown eyes twinkling.

Vanessa sighed. "I wouldn't exactly say—"

"It bothers her that he used to be a pro athlete, like her first husband," Rodney put in, speaking as though Vanessa weren't there.

Gina shrugged prettily. "To each her own," she said.

Vanessa felt called upon to say something positive about Nick. "Your brother is the most self-assured person I've ever met," she remarked.

Gina shrugged again. "He'd face down the general membership of Hell's Angels without batting an eye," she said, "but let him get sick or hurt himself and he goes to pieces. Last month he cut his finger chopping vegetables for a salad, and you'd have thought there'd been a chainsaw massacre."

Vanessa laughed. It was good to know the idol was human with feet of clay, she thought to herself. But then she remembered his reputation and the parties he was allegedly so famous for and decided he was probably *too* human. Her expression sobered.

"You look so sad," Gina said, exhibiting her brother's propensity for perception. That she could read minds was evident when she went on. "Nick is a really nice man, Vanessa. And he's mellowed out a lot since the old days."

Vanessa was not comforted, nor could she help drawing certain correlations between Nick and Parker. They were both attractive, sought-after men. While finding Parker in bed with another woman had been devastating, she knew that if history repeated itself with Nick, she would be shattered.

Somewhat awkwardly she told Gina that it had been nice to meet her, made an excuse and fled.

As usual, the light on her answering machine was blinking when she let herself into the house. Dreading more of Parker's nonsense, she nonetheless played back the messages.

The first call was from her grandmother, who wanted to know if she and Rodney would be coming to Spokane for Thanksgiving and Christmas that year. The second was from a local television station, where Vanessa had put in an application just before Paul had hired her to be on the Midas Network.

Her heart practically stopped beating, she was so excited. In the middle of Parker's diatribe on how the divorce had been a mistake, she stopped the playback and listened again. She hadn't imagined it; Station WTBE was interviewing potential hosts for a new talk show and they wanted her to come in to see them.

Vanessa had to take three deep breaths before she was steady enough to return the call. When the producer's assistant answered, her voice elevated itself to a squeak.

The assistant was patient. "What did you say your name was again, please?" she asked.

Van closed her eyes, rehearsing her answer. The way things had been going that day, there was every possibility she'd get it wrong. "Vanessa Lawrence," she managed to reply at some length.

"Would a week from Friday be convenient for you?"

Any day would have been convenient, but Van knew better than to make herself sound desperate by saying so. "That would be just fine," she said coolly.

"Two-thirty?" the woman suggested.

"Two-thirty," Vanessa confirmed, frantically scribbling the date and time on the back of a phone bill even though the information was emblazoned in her mind for all time.

The moment she'd hung up the receiver, she dashed breathlessly up the rear stairs and into her sparsely furnished bedroom. There, she slid open the closet door and flipped on the light, looking for the perfect outfit, the clothes to convince the producers of *Seattle This Morning* that their search for a host was over.

Soon the bed was piled high with dresses, suits, skirts and blouses—none of which quite met Vanessa's specifications. She had just decided to head for the mall when the telephone rang.

Her cheerful hello brought a burst of blustering frustration from Parker.

"Didn't you get my message?"

"Yes…" Vanessa sighed. "Parker, I don't have time to tango right now, okay? Something really important has come up, and I'm going out."

"You've got a date with DeAngelo, I suppose," Parker immediately retorted. "I could tell you a few things about that son of a—"

The pit of Vanessa's stomach twisted. She wasn't ready to hear the things Parker would say about Nick, not yet.

"I've got to run," she interrupted, almost singing the words, "'Bye!"

The telephone started to ring again almost immediately after she'd hung up, and it was still jangling away when she dashed out of the house without turning the answering machine on.

Five hours later she returned with a fitted suit in a shade of ice blue. There was a Corvette to match sitting behind Rodney's battered sports car in her driveway.

Memories of the way she'd behaved in Nick's apartment combined with a not-so-instant replay of the words they'd exchanged at the studio to make her cheeks hot. The man didn't know the meaning of the word Friday, she fretted. Well, maybe it was just as well that he was there. Now would be as good a time as any to tell him that they shouldn't see each other anymore.

She unlocked the back door, let herself in and waited. Nick was obviously up in Rodney's apartment, passing the time of day. In a matter of minutes he would realize that she was home and appear on some flimsy pretext. Twenty minutes passed with no sign of Nick. Vanessa had put away her new outfit, changed into jeans and a flannel shirt and even brewed herself a cup of tea when she finally heard an engine roar to life in the driveway.

He was leaving without even saying hello!

Incredulous, Vanessa raced through the house to peer out one of the front windows. Sure enough, Nick was backing the Corvette out into the road, Gina beside him and, as far as Vanessa could tell, he didn't even glance in her direction.

"I'm becoming obsessive," she told the cat, who had come to steer her back toward the kitchen.

Sari made her usual noncommittal comment, and Vanessa gave the animal supper before setting aside her pride and going outside to climb the stairs to Rodney's apartment.

"Hi," he said, looking surprised to see her.

Vanessa took in the very abbreviated cowboy costume he was wearing, raising an eyebrow.

"I was just practicing a new number," he told her, sounding defensive.

His cousin smiled. "Speaking of numbers, I wonder if you'd mind giving me Nick's?"

Rodney eyed her curiously, then shrugged. "Sure, I've got it here somewhere. Are you going to ask him out or what?"

"That's kind of a personal question, isn't it?" Vanessa countered.

"Touchy lady," drawled Rodney as he searched through the contact list on his phone. "Here it is," he said, scrawling the number onto a piece of scrap paper and holding it out to Vanessa.

She took it, thanked him and left with as much dignity as she could manage.

She gave Nick plenty of time to get home, systematically building up her courage as she waited, and then dialed his number. It was an irony of sorts that she got his answering machine.

The message she left was simple and to the point. "Nick, this is Vanessa. I don't think we should see each other anymore, and that includes dinner on Friday. Goodbye."

It was a long evening for Vanessa, spent with the nervous expectation that Nick would either call or drop by, demanding an explanation for her decision. As it happened, neither the telephone nor the doorbell rang once.

The rest of the week and following weekend was peaceful, too.

On Monday morning, Margie complained about the shadows under Vanessa's eyes as she applied her makeup. "Keep losing sleep like this, kid," the cosmetologist warned, "and you're going to look like a raccoon."

Despite everything, Vanessa laughed. "The beginning of another lovely day," she said.

Just then, Oliver Richards dashed in and switched the channel on the monitor from the Midas Network to a popular national talk show. Vanessa stiffened in her chair as she saw the handsome face of her ex-husband fill the screen. She'd forgotten all about Parker's guest spot.

The program had obviously been in progress for a few minutes, and Parker was smiling boyishly at the applause of the predominantly female audience. "I'm happy to say that Van and I are getting back together," he said. "This time I'm going to be the best husband any woman ever had."

The paper cup in Vanessa's hand dropped to the floor, coffee and all.

"Tell us a little about your ex-wife," the program's famous host prompted, watching Parker with a certain speculation in her eyes.

"It's all in the book," Parker answered proudly, and, to Vanessa's abject horror, he held up a copy for the whole world to see.

Vanessa hadn't expected the book to be published for weeks, so her first shock was compounded by a second. "Oh, no!" she cried.

Oliver, standing beside her chair, was wiping Van's coffee from his pants legs with a wad of tissue.

Parker looked directly into the camera, a besotted expression on his face. "I will say this—I love you, Vanessa. And I forgive you for all the times you've…hurt me."

Vanessa could bear no more. She lunged for the monitor's off button and then covered her face with both hands and groaned in helpless despair.

"Congratulations on the reconciliation, Van," Oliver boomed. "Does this mean we'll be forced to get along without you here at the old network?"

Vanessa glared at him, pointedly ignoring his remark, and stormed out.

That stint on camera was the most difficult of Vanessa's brief career, and when it was over she had to sit through a long meeting with the buyers. The products that would be featured for the next few days were demonstrated in detail, and price lists were passed out.

When she got home, the cleaning lady was there, and the living room was filled to the rafters with flowers. If Rodney had been around, Vanessa reflected ruefully, he'd have thought he was back at the funeral parlor.

As she'd expected, the carnations, roses and daisies were all from Parker, who thought surely he'd won her heart by forgiving her on national television. A headache pulsed under Vanessa's left temple, and she snapped at the cleaning lady when the doorbell rang.

"Shut that vacuum cleaner off!"

Looking wounded, Marita kicked the switch and stomped off into the kitchen. Vanessa opened the door, expecting another shipment of flowers, and found Nick standing there instead of a delivery man.

His jawline looked like granite. "When did you make the decision not to see me anymore, Vanessa?" he demanded, pushing past her when she didn't invite him inside. "Before or after you came to my apartment and let me make love to you? Before or after you decided to go back to Lawrence?"

Vanessa shoved her hands into her hair. "You didn't make love to me," she said lamely. It was a moot point, but she was desperate. "And I don't have any intention of reconciling with Parker. He made the whole thing up to sell books."

Nick was visibly relieved, but only for a moment. "Just how firm is this decision that we shouldn't see each other again?" he asked quietly, facing her now, standing so close that she could feel the heat and power of his body.

She remembered what Gina had said about the way Nick acted when he was sick or hurt, and a wave of tenderness swept over her. She couldn't help smiling a little. "Why do you ask?" she countered, because she didn't know what to say.

He laid his hands on her shoulders. "Because I'm crazy about you, Value Van."

Vanessa stepped back, lifting one eyebrow. "So crazy that you didn't even return my call when I left that message on your machine. Or was it just that you didn't go home that night?"

Nick sighed. "I went to Portland, Van—I'm opening a new restaurant there."

Marita peered tentatively around the door jamb. "Can I come back now?" she queried, poised to run.

"Yes," Vanessa said, closing her eyes.

Nick took her elbow gently into his hand. "What do you say we go somewhere and talk?"

Vanessa could only nod, and they'd reached the sensible solace of Nick's apartment before she spoke. "Do you have any aspirin?"

After favoring her with a grin and a kiss on the forehead, Nick disappeared down the hallway, returning momentarily with two white tablets and a glass of water. Vanessa swallowed the aspirin gratefully and then staggered across the room and threw herself down on his cushy sofa.

"The day was really that bad, huh?" Nick said, sitting down on the sofa and placing her feet in his lap. He slipped her shoes off and tossed them away, then began massaging her aching arches and insteps.

"It was terrible!" Vanessa wailed, her arms folded across her face.

Nick went right on rubbing her feet, saying nothing, and she felt compelled to hurl something into the conversational void.

"Why did you leave football?"

Nick chuckled. "I'd made all the money I needed and I wanted to get out before I ruined my back or one of my knees."

The massage felt sinfully good—in fact, it was beginning to arouse Vanessa, though she would never have admitted that. "Sensible," she said with a sigh. "That's you, Nick DeAngelo."

"Um-hmm," he answered, gently working the taut muscles of Vanessa's left calf.

She gave an involuntary whimper. "Stop," she said with such a lack of sincerity that Nick didn't even hesitate.

"Let's go out to the island tonight," he suggested in a reasonable tone.

Vanessa raised her head to look at him. "I have to work tomorrow," she said.

"So do I. There's ferry service—we can be back in plenty of time."

"But we would spend the night?" Nick didn't look at her. "Yes."

She pulled her leg free and sat up. "I thought we had an understanding about that," she said tautly.

Nick reached out and hauled her easily onto his lap. "I

didn't say we'd sleep together," he said in a deep, sleepy voice.

"Then what's the point of going?"

He laughed. "Get your mind out of the gutter, Lawrence. We could walk on the beach, listen to music by the fire and talk. We could play cribbage, drink wine and bake brownies…"

Vanessa rolled her eyes. "You are weird."

"Saturday I was remarkable. What happened?"

Van was feeling harried, and the idea of spending a peaceful night in an island hideaway was not without appeal. But there were those correlations. "I got to thinking that you're probably a whole lot like Parker," she confessed, looking away.

He took her chin in his hand and made her look at him. "I hate it when you do that," he said in a low, angry voice. "Don't compare me to him, Vanessa."

She shrugged. "He's a jock, you're a jock. He's a party animal, you're a party animal—"

"Tell me one thing, Vanessa," Nick interrupted, his dark eyes hot with quiet anger. "Did he let you decide when the two of you would make love for the first time?"

Vanessa looked away. "I don't see what that has to do with anything."

"Did he?" Nick insisted.

"No," she was forced to admit after a long time. Tears welled in her lashes. "No! I had too much wine on our second date and the next morning I woke up in his bed! Are you happy now?"

Nick closed his eyes. "I'm sorry," he said hoarsely.

Vanessa sniffled and started to get off his lap, but his arms tightened around her and the thought of rebelling didn't even cross her mind.

"Are you still in love with him?" he asked.

"No," Vanessa answered without hesitation.

"Then come to the island with me."

"I have a cat to think about, you know," Vanessa pointed out, as Nick began kissing her neck in much the way he had on Saturday.

"Rodney will feed it," he said.

Vanessa trembled. She wasn't ready for a physical relationship, and yet she wondered how she would endure spending a whole night on an island with Nick without offering herself to him. "Our deal still holds? That I get to choose the time, I mean?"

Nick opened the top button of her blouse. "Yes, but it's only fair to tell you that I'm going to make it hard to wait."

"Oh," Vanessa answered inanely as another button gave way. He slid his hand inside her blouse to caress her breast, and she thought she was going to go insane with wanting him.

As it happened, though, the doorbell rang. Vanessa scrambled to her feet and began righting her blouse while Nick strode, grumbling, across the living room to open the door.

The wonders of the jet age, Vanessa reflected, staring at the visitor in amazement.

Parker glared at Nick as he stepped back to admit him. "It's good to see that you haven't changed, DeAngelo," Parker said furiously.

Nick sighed and ran a hand through his hair. "Is that what you came here to say?" he asked.

Parker had already turned his attention to Vanessa, and he looked for all the world like a betrayed husband, stricken at the discovery of his wife's faithlessness. "How could you, Van?" he rasped. "After the flowers and—"

Vanessa was incensed. "And your generous offer over national television to 'forgive' me?"

"I love you!" Parker bellowed.

"You don't know what love is," Vanessa cried, her chin high and her shoulders square. She took comfort from Nick's presence, but it was even better realizing that she could handle the situation on her own. "Once and for all, Parker, it's over. Now go away and leave me alone."

Parker glowered at Nick, obviously seeing him as the villain of the piece, and then left in a rage, slamming the door behind him.

Vanessa glanced at her watch. "If we're going to the island," she said, "we'd better get started. I need to pick up some of my clothes and feed the cat before we leave." Nick grinned. "Whatever you say, lady," he teased.

"I wouldn't dare cross you."

Chapter 5

Nick's island house was gray with white trim and lattice-work, and it was enormous. Standing hardly more than a stone's throw from the beach, the place had a friendly look about it, and Vanessa's first impression was favorable.

Still, what she knew of Nick's reputation haunted her subconscious, but she refused to entertain the thought. She was tired, even frazzled, and she needed the peace Nick and his grand old house were offering.

The inside was furnished in the same comfortable way as his condominium in Seattle; the sofas and chairs were soft and welcoming, the carpets deep. The paintings were watercolors in muted shades.

Nick led the way through the living room and up the stairway to the second floor. He passed several closed doors, then opened one on the right. "You can sleep in here," he said.

Vanessa bit her lip and slipped past him into a room

decorated for a woman. The curtains and the comforter on the bed were a pastel floral print, and there were two white wicker chairs in front of the window, their seats upholstered to match.

"It's Gina's," Nick said, laying an index finger to Vanessa's lips just as she was about to open her mouth to ask.

He set her overnight case and garment bag on the bed and gestured toward the hall. "Come on, I'll show you where my room is—just in case."

Vanessa laughed. "Just in case what?"

Nick gave her a look. "Did I forget to tell you? The place is haunted. If you hear anything spooky, all you'll have to do is climb in bed with me and you'll be safe."

"I've heard some lines in my time, buddy," Vanessa replied, preceding him out into the hall, "but that one beats them all."

His room was really more of a suite with a fireplace and six floor-to-ceiling windows that overlooked the sea. Vanessa glanced at the bed and quickly shifted her eyes away.

Nick shook his head and pushed up the sleeves of his sky-blue sweater. A look at the half-open door of the closet explained why he hadn't brought spare clothes.

"What we need is some exercise," he said resolutely. "Let's go out for a run before it gets dark."

The way he'd phrased the suggestion made Vanessa feel like an Irish setter, and she did not share Nick's passion for running, but she wanted to be a good sport. She'd brought along an old set of sweats and some sneakers, and she went to put them on.

When she descended, Nick was already downstairs, warming up.

They followed the beach until Vanessa was near collapse, then started back. She knew Nick was adjusting his pace to hers, and she tried not to slow him down too much.

Returning to the house was a vast relief. Vanessa threw herself onto the porch steps, gasping for breath, only to be hauled back to her feet again by Nick. She did seemingly endless cooling-down exercises before he was satisfied that he'd tortured her enough.

"I'm not sure I have the stamina for a relationship with you," she said when they were in the kitchen a few minutes later.

"Why do you think I'm trying to build up your endurance?" Nick got a bag of cookies down from a cupboard and took a carton of milk out of the refrigerator. Sniffing the milk, he made a face and poured it down the sink.

Vanessa grinned, shaking her head. "Your self-confidence overwhelms me."

Nick took two cookies from the bag and stuffed them into his mouth, one right after the other. "I was hoping it would be my charm and good looks," he said. He was standing right in front of Vanessa before she realized that he'd been approaching her.

She brushed a few chocolate crumbs from his lips. "That, too," she conceded.

Her back was to the counter—that was another fact that had sneaked up on her—and Nick had only to lean against her gently to imprison her. He did that without any apparent attack of conscience, and Vanessa ached in response to the hard grace of his body. He bent his head and kissed her, and his mouth tasted deliciously of chocolate cookies and controlled passion.

Vanessa was dazed when he finally broke away, propelled her toward the back stairway and swatted her playfully on the bottom.

"To the showers, team," he said in a hoarse voice, and when Vanessa looked back over her shoulder, she saw him shove a hand through his hair in frustration.

Since Gina's room didn't come with its own bath like its counterpart in the condominium, Vanessa took her shower in the main bathroom. She put on gray pants and a kelly-green shirt, along with a light touch of makeup. Nick was dropping an armload of wood onto the hearth in his bedroom when Vanessa finally gathered the nerve to creep to the doorway and look inside.

He was wearing jeans and a plaid shirt that he hadn't bothered to button over his T-shirt.

Vanessa cleared her throat to let him know she was there, and he gave her a sidelong grin that said he'd been aware of her presence from the first.

"There's a storm coming in from the north," he said, laying a fire in the grate.

Vanessa's eyes widened, the lightning that had changed her forever still fresh in her mind. Her gaze skittered nervously to the big bed and back again.

Nick saw her trepidation and smiled. "Come in and sit down, Van. You ought to know by now that I'm not going to hurl you down and have my way with you."

There were comfortably upholstered chairs in front of the fireplace, and Vanessa went to sit in one of them, watching the motions of Nick's back as he finished building the fire, and thinking.

Ever since she'd met Nick, she'd been pondering the powerful effect he had on her senses and emotions, and she understood at least one thing, Nick DeAngelo was the kind of man most women dreamed of meeting—strong, handsome, successful and far too good to be true.

There had to be a glaring fault that would come leaping out at her when she let down her guard and trusted him—and that was the moment Vanessa feared most. She drew her bare feet up onto the chair and wrapped her arms around her legs.

"Tell me about Jenna," she said, tilting her head to one side.

Nick sighed and reluctantly turned from the fire. "Okay. What do you want to know?"

"Why she left you, for one thing."

"She had a big problem with trust," Nick recalled, looking not at Vanessa but beyond her, it seemed, into the distant past. "I couldn't go anywhere without having her call or drive by to see if I was really where I said I'd be. We started to fight, the marriage fell apart and we went our separate ways."

Vanessa swallowed, remembering her own experience with Parker. "Did you give Jenna reason not to trust you?"

Nick looked insulted that she would even ask the question. "No," he replied with biting directness.

A few moments passed before Vanessa had the courage to speak again. "There was more to it than that, I think," she mused aloud.

"We disagreed about a lot of fundamental things," Nick admitted. "Kids, for instance."

Vanessa sat up straighter. This was a subject that mattered to her. She wanted children of her own more than anything else in the world, including the job on *Seattle This Morning* or a place on a television news team. "She wanted them and you didn't," she blurted out, braced for the worst, expecting Nick to feel as Parker had.

She got another angry, heated look for her trouble. "Wrong," he replied, turning away to throw an unnecessary chunk of wood onto an already thriving fire. "Jenna wanted to be the only child in my life. She was afraid a baby would steal the show."

Vanessa bit her lower lip and looked down at her lap, wishing she'd allowed Nick to tell her what he felt without holding him up against Parker first and then taking her clues from the comparison.

The silence stretched, and Nick finally got to his feet and pushed the screen up close to the fireplace. "What about you?" he asked, keeping his back to her. "Do you want children, Vanessa?"

She swallowed. Here was her chance to distance herself from Nick DeAngelo once and for all, to eliminate him and all the danger he represented from her life. Here was her opportunity to go back to being safe and ordinary.

She couldn't lie to him.

"A houseful," she answered, dropping her eyes when she saw him start to turn toward her.

"What about your career?" he asked. "What about selling foot massagers and wicker birdcages and porch lights?"

He was crouching in front of Vanessa's chair, grasping both its arms in his hands, and there was no way she could escape. "I don't intend to spend the rest of my life selling birdcages and porch lights," she said. "I—I have an interview for another job on Friday, as a matter of fact."

"You're hedging," Nick accused, and the timbre of his voice and the scent of his freshly showered skin combined to make Vanessa slightly dizzy.

"I want to work, Nick," she said quietly, purposefully. "And I want babies, too. When—and if—I remarry, my husband will have to do more than help make children. He'll have to help raise them, too."

"Fair enough," he replied, his voice a husky rumble low

in his chest. He drew Vanessa out of her chair, and she ended up kneeling astride his lap.

"Don't we need to go to the store and buy milk or something?" Vanessa queried, her voice an octave higher than usual.

The sound of Nick's laughter seemed to brush against the hollow beneath Vanessa's right ear. "Milk?" he echoed.

"T-to go with the cookies." Vanessa knew she sounded desperate.

He chuckled and began kissing the delicate flesh of her neck. "Cravings already?" he teased.

Vanessa wondered how in the name of heaven she was going to resist this man until she'd reached that mysterious point of readiness that so eluded her. "Nick," she pleaded.

"Hmm?" He pulled out her tucked-in shirt and then proceeded to unbutton it. The tingling pattern his lips painted on her neck continued without interruption.

"This isn't fair," she whispered breathlessly. Her head fell backward as he pushed the front of her blouse aside. He unfastened the front catch on her lace-trimmed, silky pink bra, freeing her. "Life is never fair," he reminded her.

Against her better judgment, Vanessa leaned back even farther when his hands rose to cup her breasts. "Ooooooh," she said.

Nick was kissing his way down over her collarbone. "My sentiments exactly," he replied just before he closed his mouth over one straining nipple.

Vanessa clasped both hands behind her head, increasing both her vulnerability and her pleasure. Her lips were parted, and her eyes closed as she reveled in nurturing Nick; she could feel and hear his desire, and it heightened her own.

He was moaning as he enjoyed her like a man wild with

fever, and when she would have lowered her hands, he held them in place. The fingers of his left hand rubbed Vanessa's bare back, at once positioning her for his own unrestricted access and stroking her reassuringly.

The moment he released her wrists, Vanessa was peeling off his shirt and tossing it away, tearing at the T-shirt beneath. She would have undressed him completely if his position hadn't made that impossible. His chest was muscular and, as Vanessa had, he leaned back slightly, in effect surrendering at least a part of his body to her explorations. He gave a powerful shudder and moaned low in his throat as she kissed, caressed and nibbled at him.

After a long time he rose gracefully to his feet, drawing Vanessa with him, clasping her close even as he stripped her of her shirt and dangling bra and began unfastening her pants.

"If you want to stop this, Vanessa," he warned, "turn around and walk out of the room right now. Whatever self-control I might have had is gone, and all bets are off."

Looking up into his smoldering brown eyes, Vanessa remained where she was and opened the top button of his jeans. "All bets are off," she repeated, to let him know that she understood what was about to happen, that she welcomed it.

He kissed her then with all the passion he'd been holding back, and Vanessa could only guess at the strength it had taken to restrain such a torrent. She was hardly aware of being carried to the bed or undressed, and even though the sky outside was clear and quiet, the room crackled with lightning.

Nick was poised above her, his mouth covering hers in another mind-splintering kiss, the mattress giving slightly beneath her. Vanessa ran gentle hands up and down his broad, sinewy back, telling him without words that she wanted him.

He took her in a long, slow thrust that set her to twisting her head from side to side on the pillow, delirious in her need.

"Easy," he rasped out, and she could feel the struggle between Nick's mind and his body as he lay perfectly still inside her. "Take it easy, sweetheart. We have all the time in the world..."

Vanessa tried to force him to provide the friction, the motion, that she needed so desperately, but he was too big and too powerful and she could not move him. "Oh God, Nick. Why do you do this to me—why do you love making me wait?"

He chuckled and gave her a single, searing stroke metered to drive her insane, but his expression was serious when he spoke. "I want you to remember this always—it has to be special."

Vanessa arched her neck, felt his lips descend to the fevered skin there. "It is—I swear it. I'll remember..."

His laugh vibrated through his vocal cords and captured her heart like a warm summer wind. "So this is the secret to making you agree to my terms, is it?" he teased.

But he began to move upon her after that, quickening his pace heartbeat by heartbeat, stroke by stroke until Vanessa was covered from head to foot in a fine sheen of perspiration, until she was moaning and flinging her head from side to side.

"Let go," Nick whispered raggedly near her ear. "Stop fighting it and let go." His words broke down the last flimsy wall enclosing Vanessa's soul.

With a series of straining cries, she surrendered all that she was to Nick, all that she'd ever been or ever would be.

The relief was exquisite; for a time, her soul escaped its bonds and flew free.

There was no restraint in Nick's release. He trembled, lunged deep inside her and cried out in satisfaction as pleasure induced its unique seizure.

For a long time afterward there were no sounds in the room except for their breathing and the popping of the fire. Then inexplicably, uncontrollably, Vanessa began to weep.

Nick groaned and rolled over to look down into her face. "Don't do this to me, Van," he pleaded, wiping away a tear with one thumb. "Please, don't be sorry for what we did."

She shook her head. "I'm not," she managed to say. "It's just that—"

He kissed her briefly on the mouth. "It's just that we don't know each other well enough, right?"

She nodded. "Right."

He leered at her and wriggled his eyebrows. "Okay, I'm a modern guy, I can relate. What's your sign, baby?" Vanessa gave a shout of laughter through her tears.

"Stop," she pleaded. "This is a sensitive moment."

Nick squinted at the clock on the bedside stand. "It's also dinnertime, and I'm hungry as hell. Let's make spaghetti."

Vanessa was too relaxed to contemplate getting up and doing any kind of work. "Make spaghetti? I *am* spaghetti."

"I have a hot tub," Nick wheedled, sliding downward and beginning to kiss her neck again.

Vanessa knew where that would lead. She twisted free and sat up. "You have a hot tub," she mused, looking at Nick with shining eyes. "What the devil does that have to do with cooking spaghetti?"

Nick declined to answer that and said instead, "On second thought, let's go out to dinner. I don't want you to get the idea that I'm a cheap date."

They took a shower, this time sharing the same stall, and dressed in the clothes that had been strewn from one side of the bedroom to the other. Vanessa reapplied her makeup and styled her hair.

"I hope this place is casual," she said, giving Nick's jeans and shirt a look.

The restaurant was a few miles away on the edge of the only town the small island boasted, and the spaghetti there was good.

"The owner must be Italian," Vanessa guessed, stabbing a meatball with her fork and lifting it to her mouth.

"Paddy O'Shaughnessy?" Nick teased. "Definitely. He probably grew up in Naples, or maybe Verona."

It was a night full of nonsense, restorative and precious, and Vanessa didn't want it to end. She knew, of course, that it would, and that the morning would bring painful regrets. She concentrated on enjoying Nick, the spaghetti and, later, the hot tub.

There were plants in the glass-walled room where the hot tub bubbled and churned, and Vanessa wrapped herself in the night sky with its glittering mantle of stars. "This must be what it's like when you're on safari," she said after swallowing a sip of wine. "I can just imagine that we're camped alongside a steaming river with crocodiles slipping by, unseen, unheard..."

"Now that's a romantic thought," Nick observed. Vanessa hiccuped and looked accusingly at her wine.

"I've had too much *vino*," she told Nick seriously. "I'd better sleep in Gina's bed tonight."

If Nick was disappointed, he didn't show it. "Whatever you say, princess," he said quietly, taking the glass from her hand and setting it on the tiled edge of the large square tub. "I don't want you to have any regrets when you look back on today."

"I won't," Vanessa said, even though she knew she would. The wounds Parker had left were only partially healed, and she wouldn't be able to disregard the similarities between him and Nick forever.

When she yawned, Nick lifted her out of the tub. "Time for bed," he said. "We have to get up early."

Vanessa scrambled for a towel, not because she was naked, but because she was chilled, and she watched unabashedly while Nick got out of the tub and switched off the jets. He was so incredibly secure in his masculinity that he didn't reveal the slightest qualm about being nude.

When he pulled on a blue terrycloth robe, it was an unhurried action, meant for comfort and not modesty. In fact, when Vanessa came to him he opened the garment long enough to enfold her inside, against his ribs.

They walked upstairs that way, talking idly of spaghetti and hot tubs, and parted after a brief kiss in the doorway of Gina's room.

The sheets were cold. The moon and stars must have all gathered on the other side of the house, for there was no light for Vanessa to dream by. She missed Nick, even though they had parted only a few minutes before and he was just one room away.

Snuggling down determinedly, she closed her eyes and commanded herself to sleep. Despite her utter weariness, oblivion eluded her. She tossed, turned and tossed again.

Finally she got out of bed, put a robe on over her striped silk pajamas and padded across the hall.

"Nick?" she questioned softly from the doorway of his room.

He sounded sleepy. "What?"

"I think I heard something."

A motion in the moon-shadowed bed and a throaty groan of contentment told her he was stretching like some cocky panther. "Like what?" he asked innocently. Vanessa shrugged. "You said there were ghosts…"

"Yup," Nick agreed, "I did." He threw back the covers to make a place for her beside him. "There's only one thing to do, lady. Circle up the wagons and share a bunk."

Vanessa was across the room and between Nick's sheets in a wink. She snuggled up against him, reveling in his warmth and his strength. "I'm going to hate myself when I wake up in the morning," she confessed with a contented sigh.

Nick kissed her forehead. "I know," he answered sadly. "And me, too, probably."

Vanessa rested her head on his shoulder. "Probably," she said, and then she dropped off to sleep.

When she awakened at dawn, Nick was gone. She knew he was probably out running, and she was grateful for the time to sort out where she was and what she'd done the night before.

She'd had her shower and dressed for work by the time Nick returned. Clad in running shorts, a tank top and a jacket, despite the fact that November was fast approaching, he looked at Van warily as he crossed the kitchen. He opened the refrigerator and took out the milk he and Vanessa had stopped for on the way home from O'Shaughnessy's the night before.

"Let's hear it," he started. "You hate me, you had too much wine last night and waking up the morning in my bed was an instant replay of the first time with Parker. Right?"

Vanessa was eating a slice of whole wheat toast slathered with honey. "Do I look traumatized?" she asked, chewing.

He cocked his head to one side, frowning. "No," he said, sounding surprised. "Are you saying you don't regret letting me make love to you?"

"Excuse me," Vanessa said, pouring herself a cup of the coffee that had been waiting when she came downstairs, "but you didn't do everything, you know. I was half of that little encounter." She paused and drew a deep breath, then let it out. "To answer your question, yes and no."

Nick gave her a wry look. "Yes and no. I like a decisive woman."

"It was too soon," she said. "I probably wasn't ready." He set the milk back in the refrigerator and put his hands on his hips. "You seemed ready to me," he replied.

Vanessa blushed at the good-natured jibe and sipped her coffee to avoid having to say something.

"That takes care of the yes. What about the no? What don't you regret, Vanessa?"

Vanessa dropped her eyes. "The passion," she answered after a long time. "You brought me back into the world, Nick, and I'm grateful."

"Gratitude isn't exactly what I had in mind, but it'll do for now," he answered, and then he disappeared up the stairs. When he came back, he was wearing tan cords, gleaming leather shoes and a green sweater.

Vanessa assessed him appreciatively. "How much time have we got before the ferry leaves?"

Nick took in her blue dress and sighed heavily. "Not enough," he lamented. He took her in his arms and kissed her with knee-weakening thoroughness before whispering hoarsely, "I wish we could stay here forever." Vanessa laid her head against his chest. "Me, too," she said, but she knew the magic was already slipping away.

It seemed sadly fitting that, when they drove aboard

the ferry to return to Seattle, dark clouds were gathering in the northern sky.

The storm Nick had predicted was almost upon them.

Chapter 6

When Vanessa finished her segment that morning, Parker was waiting at the door of the women's dressing room. His arms were folded across his chest, and his features were set in a sour scowl.

"Where were you last night?" he demanded in a furious whisper.

Vanessa sighed. "We're divorced, Parker, and that's all I'm going to say about last night or anything else." She started to walk around him, but he reached out and took her arm in a painful grasp.

His nose was an inch from Vanessa's as he rasped, "You slept with him, didn't you?"

Vanessa wrenched free of his hold, her face hot with color. A receptionist was approaching with a folded piece of paper in her hand, looking scared.

"Sh-should I call security, Ms. Lawrence?" Vanessa saw nothing to fear and everything to pity in Parker's eyes at that moment, and she shook her head as he made a visible effort to control himself. "Everything is fine, Karen," she lied.

Karen darted an uneasy glance at Parker and held out the paper to Vanessa. "Mr. DeAngelo called while you were on the air," she explained.

Vanessa scanned the note and suppressed a sigh. There was some kind of problem at the new restaurant in Portland, and Nick would be away until Friday. She bit her lower lip and crumpled the message into a ball. "Thank you," she said to the receptionist, who promptly hurried away.

"Have lunch with me," Parker said.

Vanessa stared at him. "You must be insane."

He treated her to his most endearing smile. "Look at it this way—if you don't, I'll just follow you home and you'll have to feed me anyway."

"I'd be more likely to call the police," Vanessa said.

Parker shrugged. "Whereas a restaurant would be a safe, neutral place—very public."

Vanessa sighed. She was in a glum mood and Parker was the last person she wanted to spend time with, especially when she knew he was going to tell her something she didn't want to know, but she finally nodded. She couldn't hide forever.

While her ex-husband waited, she toned down her makeup, gathered up the list of times she would be selling the next day and braced herself for the worst.

A soft rain was falling as Parker and Vanessa hurried across the employee parking lot to her car. Parker had arrived in a cab, which said a lot about his confidence in his powers of persuasion.

Unable to stand it any longer, Vanessa looked at him out of the corner of her eye as she snapped her seat belt into place. "You're going to tell me something about Nick, aren't you? Something awful."

Parker's expression was one of regretful gallantry. "This thing between you and him is getting serious, and I can't let it go any further."

"What?" Vanessa cried, frustrated beyond all bearing. "What's so terrible about Nick?"

Parker sighed. "All I'm going to say for right now is that he's not husband material. DeAngelo is ten times the bastard I ever was."

Vanessa offered no comment on that, and as she drove out of the studio compound, she gnawed nervously at her lower lip. Normally she wouldn't have given Parker's words any credence—he was, after all, a lying, manipulative cheat. But she had a spooky, gut-level feeling that this time he had something valid to say.

"Where do you want to go for lunch?" she asked even though every trace of her appetite was gone.

He named a nearby bar and grill, and Vanessa drove toward it.

They were settled in a booth with cushioned leather seats and roast beef sandwiches and glasses of beer in front of them, when Parker grinned at her and said, "Just like old times, huh, Van?"

Vanessa rolled her eyes. "Stop it, Parker. Too much has happened for us to be sitting here pretending to have fond memories."

Parker looked hurt. "You don't have any happy memories of us? Not even one?"

Vanessa thought of the early part of their marriage when she'd adored Parker, when everything he said had made her either laugh or cry. She'd lived on an emotional seesaw in those days, believing herself to be happy. In retrospect, she knew she had suffered. "Don't push, okay?" she said, averting her eyes. She hadn't been able to touch her sandwich, but she reached for the glass of beer with a trembling hand.

"You're really nervous, aren't you?" Parker's features darkened, indicating an approaching storm. "Are you that crazy about DeAngelo?"

Vanessa saw no point in lying. "Yes," she said straight out. "I am."

"Why?" Parker demanded, and some of the shaved beef slid out of his sandwich because he was squeezing it so hard.

Vanessa shrugged, trying to look nonchalant even though her stomach was roiling and her throat was closed tight. It wasn't fair of her to try to convict the man she loved on whatever it was Parker was going to say, especially when Nick wasn't there to defend himself. "This is a mistake," she blurted, sliding across the bench to stand and shrug into her coat. "I shouldn't have come here—"

"Vanessa, sit down," Parker said, and something in his tone made her meet his gaze.

Her courage failed at what she saw there, and she dropped back into the seat, covering her face with both hands for a moment and sighing. "Tell me, Parker. Stop playing games and say it."

"He's using you to repay me for something that happened a couple of years ago."

The statement sounded so preposterous that Vanessa almost laughed out loud. Almost. "Like what?"

Parker sighed heavily and, for just a second or so, he looked honestly reluctant. "Did he mention Jenna—his ex-wife?"

Vanessa nodded. "Yes."

The expression in Parker's blue eyes was distant and vaguely arrogant. "What did he tell you about the divorce?"

Powerful forces battled within Vanessa, one faction wanting to stay and hear Parker out, the other clamoring for escape. "He said she had a problem with trusting him, and that she didn't want to have children."

Parker shook his head, as though marveling at some tacky wonder. Then, without further ado, he dropped the bomb. "She and I had an affair, Vanessa. Nick caught us together and he's been out to get me ever since."

For a moment the words just loomed between Vanessa and Parker, quivering with portent. Then they exploded in Vanessa's spirit, and tears of pain filled her eyes. She put a hand to her throat and rose shakily to her feet.

"Tell me it's a lie, Parker."

He shrugged and, incredibly, reached for his sandwich. "I'd like to, babe, but I can't. The truth will out, and all that."

Vanessa turned and stumbled toward the door. The storm had come and rain was pounding on the sidewalk as she stood in the cold wind, heedless and broken. She walked slowly to the car, her hands trembling so that it took several attempts to get the key into the lock and open the door.

When she was inside, she let her forehead rest against the steering wheel and drew deep breaths until the desire to scream had abated a little. She was just fitting the key into the ignition when the door on the passenger side opened, and Parker flopped into the seat, sopping wet. "You shouldn't be alone right now," he said somehow managing to look as though he really gave a damn.

"Get out," Vanessa said. She was soaked to the skin, her hair was dripping rainwater and she knew her mascara was running down her face in dark streaks. She didn't care about any of those things. She wanted to be alone; she needed it.

Parker actually had the gall to reach out and grip her hand. "It's okay, Van—I'm going to take care of you. You'll forget about DeAngelo in no time."

Vanessa was cold and her teeth were beginning to chatter. "Get out," she said again, and after a second's hesitation Parker left the car, slamming the door behind him.

She drove home by rote, tears streaming down her face, and she hadn't had time to pull herself together before Rodney appeared. He let himself in through the kitchen door, took Vanessa by the shoulders and pressed her into a chair.

"Good God," he breathed, "you look awful! What happened? Did somebody die?"

Vanessa nodded. "Me," she answered. "I died, Rodney— fifteen minutes ago in Toddy's Bar and Grill." Rodney put a hand to her forehead and then went to the cupboard for a mug. He promptly filled it with water and shoved it into the microwave. While it was heating, he plundered the cabinets until he found Vanessa's fruitcake brandy.

When he'd made a cup of instant coffee liberally laced with brandy, he set it on the table in front of Vanessa and sat down in the chair beside hers. "Talk to me," he said quietly.

Vanessa reached for the mug, holding it in both hands, letting it warm her fingers. "I can't," she said. "Not yet."

The door opened, and Gina slipped in. "Is everything okay?" she asked.

Vanessa averted her eyes, humiliated. She didn't want Gina to go to her brother and report that he'd broken her. His plan of revenge had succeeded beyond his wildest expectations.

"It's got to be about Nick," Rodney mused. A strangled sob escaped Vanessa.

Gina spoke softly to Rodney. "I'd better go. I'll call you later."

"Sure," Rodney replied with affection, and he kissed Gina's forehead before she left the house.

Vanessa took a steadying sip of the brandied coffee. "So," Rodney said, dropping back into his chair at the table, "tell me about the murder of Vanessa Lawrence back there at Toddy's Bar and Grill." Vanessa shook her head. "Not now."

"Okay," her cousin said, "if you won't talk, at least go upstairs and get out of those wet clothes before you catch pneumonia."

Thinking of the important interview scheduled for Friday, Vanessa nodded woodenly. "Okay." She got up and walked up the stairs, stiff and slow of movement, carrying her coffee with her. She took a brief hot shower, then put on flannel pajamas and collapsed on her bed. "You love Nick that much, huh?" Rodney asked from the doorway. He'd brought another cup of coffee, probably doctored, and he proceeded toward Vanessa's bedside.

She took the cup. "That's ridiculous. I've only known him a few days." And in that short length of time he had recreated her world.

Rodney sat down on the foot of the bed since Parker hadn't left any of the chairs when he moved out. "Why do I get the feeling that your ex-husband had something to do with this?"

Vanessa set her coffee on the bedside table and wriggled under the covers. "Nick's been using me," she said, ignoring her cousin's question. "God, Rodney, what an actor he is—you should have seen him!"

"What did Parker tell you?" Rodney persisted.

"That he had an affair with Jenna DeAngelo and Nick

caught them together," she said, and a new wave of pain washed over her as she said the words out loud.

"And you bought that?" Rodney bit off each word, clearly annoyed. "Van, you know Parker would rather climb the tallest tree and lie than stand flat-footed on the ground and tell the truth!"

Their grandfather had said those very words right after Van had introduced Parker to him. She wished she could be in Spokane now and be held in the old man's strong, gentle arms. "What Parker said was true," she said sadly. "I can't explain how I know, but I do."

Rodney rolled his eyes. "Great. You're not even going to give Nick a chance to tell his side of the story, are you?"

The mention of his name went through her like a lance. As soon as Rodney left, she would roll herself into a fetal ball and die. "He used me to get back at Parker," she said miserably. "Now go away and leave me alone. I'm terminal."

Rodney gave the telephone beside her bed a pointed glance. "I'll be in my apartment if you need me," he told her, and then he was gone.

Vanessa drank the rest of her coffee with brandy and slipped under the covers to wait for the hurting to stop. It followed her relentlessly, even into her sleep.

She awakened hours later, when the room was glowing with moonlight, to find Nick sitting on the side of the bed, looking down at her. She started to pull the covers over her head, but he caught her wrists in an inescapable grasp and held them on either side of the pillow.

"What are you doing in my house?" she spat, struggling, to no real avail, against the hands that imprisoned her with such gentle effectiveness. "Get out, and don't ever come back!"

Even in the half darkness she saw the pain in Nick's eyes. God, how calm and collected he was. He should have been the one to work in the broadcasting business, not her.

He spoke in a steady, though hoarse, voice. "I'm here because Gina called me and told me you were in pieces. Rodney filled me in on the rest."

"It's true, isn't it?" Vanessa ventured to ask, looking at him with wide eyes.

Nick sighed and released her hands. He shoved splayed fingers through his rain-dampened hair. "Part of it. I did come home one night and found Jenna and Parker together."

Vanessa felt herself breaking apart inside. "And you swore revenge?"

"Hardly. I beat the hell out of him and left. He didn't tell you that part of the story, though, did he?"

"You lied to me," Vanessa accused. "You used me to get back at him!"

"I didn't care enough about Jenna to do that, Vanessa," Nick replied, still avoiding her eyes. "In one sense, I was actually relieved that it was finally over between us."

"You're glossing over the fact that you wanted revenge."

"I told you," Nick said with cold patience, "I had all the vengeance I wanted that night. Can you say you don't remember a night when your devoted husband came home with a few cuts and bruises?"

Vanessa shuddered. She remembered all right. Parker had claimed he'd been mugged, but refused to report the incident to the police. He and Vanessa had been married a little over six months at the time. "My God," she whispered.

Nick reached out to touch her face, and she slapped his hand away.

With a sigh, he got up and walked over to one of the windows that overlooked the street. "I think we'd better stop seeing each other for a while," he said after a long time.

Vanessa was stunned and infuriated. If anybody was going to break off this relationship, it was going to be her. She was the one who had been wronged!

She threw back the covers and struggled out of bed. "Wait just a minute, Nick DeAngelo!" she shouted, waving her finger at him.

Instantly he was facing her, and his face was taut with fury. "Listen to me," he ground out. "I won't play these games, Vanessa. I'll be damned if I'll involve myself with another woman who refuses to trust me!"

Vanessa's mouth dropped open.

"Goodbye," Nick said bluntly, and then he walked out, leaving her standing there, in the middle of her bedroom, feeling even worse than she had before.

Throughout the rest of the week, Vanessa functioned like an automaton. She got up in the mornings, fed the cat, got dressed and went to work. When that was done, she went home, fed the cat again and crawled into bed, usually without supper.

By Friday, the day of her interview, she looked less than her best. Wearing some compound Margie had given her to cover the shadows under her eyes, she presented herself at WTBE-TV in her new suit.

The front she put on must have been effective because the interview went very well. Although the program wouldn't actually go into production until after the first of the year, she was informed, the final decision would be made before Thanksgiving. Would she be able to leave the Midas Network by the middle of December? Vanessa answered yes, thanked the woman who had interviewed her and left. Some fundamental instinct told her she was going to get the job. She still wanted it very much, but the excitement was gone.

Since Nick had walked out of her bedroom three days before, so many things had stopped mattering.

She glanced at her watch and saw that it was three-fifteen. She'd promised to meet Janet Harmon for a drink, so she set out for the Olympic Four Seasons at a very reluctant pace.

Janet would probably grill her about the breakup with Nick, and Vanessa didn't want to burst into tears in the bar of a swanky hotel.

Sure enough, her friend looked grimly determined when Vanessa met her in the elegant lobby.

"Paul and I stayed here on our wedding night," she said to make conversation, but it was plain that Janet's mind wasn't on her own relationship. "How did the job interview go?"

"I think they're going to hire me," Vanessa answered dispiritedly as they entered the cocktail lounge and seated themselves.

"Paul will be beside himself," Janet answered, "and not with joy, either."

Vanessa sighed and averted her eyes for a moment. "Stop pretending you didn't ask me here to find out what happened between Nick and me," she said.

Janet, a pretty woman with shoulder-length dark hair and blue eyes, folded her arms on the table top and leaned forward slightly. "I don't have to ask, Vanessa—I already know. Paul is Nick's best friend, remember?"

A waitress came, took their orders and left again. "I'd be very interested to hear Nick's side of the story," Vanessa said stiffly.

"Then why don't you go over to DeAngelo's after you

leave here and ask him to tell it to you?" Janet replied in clipped tones.

"Oh, great," Vanessa complained. "You're mad at me, too!"

"I'm furious. Nick DeAngelo is the best thing that's ever happened to you, and you're not even going to fight for him."

The waitress returned, setting a glass of white chablis in front of Vanessa. Janet was having a martini, and she made a small ceremony of eating the olive.

At any other time Vanessa would have been amused. As it was, she just wanted to go home, feed the cat and slink back into bed. To get it over with, she said, "I admit it. I was going to break off with Nick, and he beat me to the punch."

"He's a wreck," Janet informed her. "Paul says he's never seen Nick so low."

Vanessa took a certain satisfaction in knowing she wasn't the only one suffering. She lifted her wineglass to her mouth and sipped the chablis before answering, "He'll get over it, and so will I."

"I don't understand this," Janet pressed. "You fell in love with Nick the first night you met him—I know because I was there and I saw it happen. And now you're just going to walk away without looking back?"

"I'm not going to crawl to him," Vanessa said firmly. "I still think he used me to get back at Parker and I despise him for it."

"You don't know Nick very well." Janet sighed, sounding resigned at last. "He'd never do a thing like that. He's too open, and he hates games and little intrigues."

"He also hates me," Vanessa said, remembering the look in his eyes when he'd told her goodbye. "Let's drop the subject, please, because if we don't, I'm going to fall apart right here."

Janet must have believed her because she didn't mention Nick's name again. The two women finished their drinks and parted, vowing to meet for lunch before the holidays got into full swing and there was no time. It was four-thirty when Vanessa got home—too early to go to bed and hide from her depression. She changed into jeans and a Seahawks T-shirt, fed Sari and proceeded to the living room, which was still choked with Parker's flowers.

She dropped one fading bouquet after another into a large plastic garbage bag and carried it out to the curb, where Rodney had already set the trash for morning pickup. She was stuffing the bag into one of the plastic cans when an ice-blue Corvette slipped sleekly into her driveway and Nick got out.

He looked as bad as she felt.

"Hi," he said, rounding the car to stand beside Vanessa and effectively block any retreat to the house. Even though she'd rehearsed this moment through a thousand varying versions, she wasn't prepared to face Nick. She averted her eyes and said nothing at all.

Nick sighed, and out of the corner of her eye she saw him wedge his hands into the hip pockets of his jeans. "Damn it, Van, will you at least listen to me? I'm willing to admit I was wrong—I should have told you about Parker and Jenna."

"Why didn't you?" Vanessa asked, raising wary, pain-filled eyes to his face.

His formidable shoulders moved in a shrug. "It was water under the bridge to me. I didn't think it mattered." Vanessa bit her lower lip. "You don't want to be involved with a woman who doesn't trust you—remember?"

Nick swore under his breath. "And you still don't, right?"

Vanessa sighed. "When you've been married to a man like Parker, it doesn't come easy."

"Speak of the devil," Nick marveled as a cab swept up to the curb and Parker got out.

He probably wouldn't have been so brave if he hadn't had another man with him. "That's the idea, Van," her ex-husband said, smiling as he approached, "Toss DeAngelo out with the trash and get on with your life."

Parker's friend, a yuppie-type wearing a three-piece suit, looked at him as though he'd gone mad.

Nick favored Parker with a slow, leisurely grin. "Keep talking," he said. "Right now I'd like nothing better than stuffing you into one of these cans and stomping you down like a milk carton."

Parker paled a little beneath his health-club tan, but he recovered his aplomb quickly enough. "Vanessa," he said, evidently choosing to pretend that Nick wasn't there, "this is Harold Barker. You're getting a second chance, baby."

Vanessa folded her arms, unconsciously protecting herself. "At what?" she asked in suspicious tones.

Parker looked enormously pleased with himself as he explained that Harold was the executive producer of yet another nationally syndicated talk show. "They want you to go on with me next week and help pitch the book."

The idea was born in a rebellious area of Vanessa's mind. She cast a sidelong look at Nick before saying expansively to Parker and Harold, "Come in, come in. This sounds like an interesting proposition."

Nick muttered another swearword, joining them even though Vanessa had made a point of not inviting him.

"Did you want something, Mr. DeAngelo?" she asked

coolly when the four of them were standing in her half-furnished living room.

Nick gave her a look that would have made a vampire cower, planted himself in front of the fireplace and folded his arms across his chest. He was clearly staying for the duration, and that pleased Vanessa, even though she felt a conflicting desire to march over there and kick him in the shins.

Over a drink, solicitously served by a doting hostess, Harold explained his concept of a show including both Parker and Vanessa. He was sure the viewing audience would enjoy hearing her reactions to the things her ex-husband had written about her.

"Of course," he finished, casting a nervous glance toward Nick, "we'll want to discuss your—er—reconciliation with Mr. Lawrence, too."

Vanessa beamed, perching behind Parker on the back of one of the two easy chairs he'd left her and ruffling his hair. "It's a romantic story," she said, well aware that Nick was seething even though she didn't dare look at him.

Parker was obviously baffled, but his tremendous ego served him well in his hour of need. He swelled up like a peacock and then shrugged in that aw-shucks-folks way that had made him such a hit with the fans. "I guess we were just swept away by passion," he said.

At last Vanessa risked a glance in Nick's direction. It was obvious from his grin that he was on to her game, even if Parker and Harold weren't.

Vanessa was still looking at Nick when she responded to Parker's remark. "It was incredible," she said.

Chapter 7

"It's Friday night," Nick said stubbornly, standing in Vanessa's kitchen with his arms folded. "We had a date, remember?"

Vanessa sighed. It was dark outside, even though it was still early, and there was a wintry chill in the air. She took her old sweater from the peg inside the pantry door and put it on. "We can't just go on as though nothing happened, Nick," she reasoned, wishing they could do exactly that.

"Because you still don't trust me," he ventured to guess.

She gently bit her lower lip for a moment. "I want to, but you're so much like Parker..."

His eyes darkened. "I didn't come over here to be insulted," he informed her. "Furthermore, damn it, I'm nothing like that bastard!"

Vanessa took a can of vegetable-beef soup from the cupboard. Since the argument with Nick, she'd been virtually living on the stuff. "You are," she insisted.

When he started to speak, she held up a hand, palm outward, to silence him. "Besides the pro-athletics aspect, there's your reputation. Do you deny that you're known far and wide as a rounder and a ladies' man?"

Nick jerked the soup can out of her hand, stuck it up against the can opener and pushed down on the handle so that an angry whir filled the kitchen. "Who the hell told you that?" he demanded. "Parker?"

Vanessa shook her head, reclaiming the soup, dumping it into a saucepan and adding water. "I'm not sure where I heard it. I just know, that's all." She studied him pensively as she put the mixture on the stove to heat. "You know, I think it's very interesting that Jenna didn't trust you when she was the one who was fooling around. Was yours an open marriage, Nick?"

He rolled his eyes, looking more annoyed by the moment. "Not on my end, it wasn't. As for Jenna, her own guilty conscience made her suspect me."

"Want some soup?" Vanessa asked, getting two bowls down from the shelf even as she spoke because she knew he wasn't about to leave.

Nick sighed. "No, but I'll eat it," he answered. While Vanessa was stirring the broth, he called DeAngelo's and instructed someone to send over two orders of clam linguine and a bottle of white wine.

She was grinning when she brought the steaming bowls of soup to the table. "A man of sweeping power and influence," she commented, as much to keep the conversation moving as anything.

Nick was frowning as he sat down. "How did your job interview go?" he asked.

"They're going to hire me, I think," she answered, reaching for a basket of saltine crackers she'd set out earlier and squashing a handful into her soup. "Of course, if they see me on national television with Parker, they may change their minds."

For a few moments, Nick said nothing. He was busy adding crackers to his soup. When he finally spoke, his tone was serious. "You're really going to do that? I thought you were just stringing Parker along to get rid of him."

Vanessa swallowed. "Yes, I'm really going to do that," she confirmed. "And I'm pretty sure he'll stop being a problem from then on."

"What about us, Vanessa?" Nick wanted to know, and there was a vulnerability in his voice that made her love him all the more hopelessly. "Where do we go from here?"

Inside Vanessa ached. She knew there could be no relationship without trust, and as much as she longed for things to be different, she hadn't reached the point where she could let herself rely on any man's integrity. She looked away, unable to answer.

He reached out and took her hand in his. "Okay, lady. So be it. I'll back off for a while."

The prospect made Vanessa's world seem as dark as deep space. "Don't you dare leave me here to eat two orders of linguine all by myself," she warned, on the verge of tears.

He smiled sadly and stayed, but Vanessa was conscious of the vast distance between them—one that might never be bridged.

Presently he found another subject, seemingly a safe one, and asked, "How did you get into home shopping?" It was a relief to think about something besides her own mixed-up emotions, doubts and fears. "I majored in broadcast journalism in college," she said. "Parker insisted that I drop out when we got married. He was traveling all the time, and I didn't have much to do once the house was clean and everything, so I started looking for work." She paused and lowered her head for just a moment, then went on. "Janet Harmon has been my friend for a long time. When the Midas Network came to Seattle and Paul was hired as production manager, he gave me a job."

"Selling gold chains and kitchen gadgets to the masses," Nick remarked, setting his empty soup bowl aside and regarding Vanessa with puzzled eyes, "is a far cry from broadcast journalism."

She was instantly defensive. "Some of us don't just fall into our dream jobs and become instantly successful," she pointed out tartly. "I had to take what I could get."

The doorbell chimed in the distance like the ringing of the gong between rounds of a boxing match. Nick must have deemed it a good time to retreat to his own corner, for he slid back his chair and disappeared toward the front of the house.

Vanessa hastily rinsed out their soup bowls and put them into the dishwasher, wondering what would happen between her and Nick and how it would be if he did indeed back off for a while.

She had a feeling that life would become as dull a chore as cleaning out an oven or stripping years of wax from a linoleum floor.

When Nick returned he was carrying a sizable white bag and a bottle of wine. Plundering the cupboards and drawers, he brought forth plates, silverware and a pair of dusty wineglasses.

Vanessa immediately took the glasses from him and carried them to the sink, where she washed them in hot soapy water while Nick set out the meal he'd had sent over from his restaurant.

"This house reminds me of your life," he observed when

she finally rejoined him at the table and took up her fork to eat linguine. "Lots of empty spaces."

She glared at him as she chewed the most exquisite pasta she'd ever tasted.

He opened the wine bottle and poured chablis into her glass. "Well?" he prompted, arching one dark eyebrow. "Aren't you even going to fight back?"

"No," Vanessa responded after a few moments of tight-jawed deliberation. "If you want to be a jackass, that's your prerogative. I don't have to jump on the proverbial band-wagon and become one, too."

Nick grinned at her, more in amazement than good humor, and shook his head. "At least you're not denying that there are some gaps that need filling. I guess that's progress."

Although Vanessa was furious, she managed to keep her temper under control. "Thank you for your analysis. And to think some people actually pay psychiatrists when all they'd need to do is ask the great Nick DeAngelo to tell them how to run their lives!"

He sighed, and the sound conveyed an infinite sadness. "It isn't going to work, is it?" he asked, setting down his fork and leaning back in his chair.

A massive, hurtful lump formed in Vanessa's throat. She closed her eyes for a moment, then shook her head. "I don't think so," she said.

Nick stood, taking his leather jacket from a peg on the wall and shrugging into it. "I know it sounds crazy," he said hoarsely, keeping his back to her, "but I love you, Vanessa. When and if that ever means anything to you, call me."

With that, he opened the back door and went out.

Vanessa sat still in her chair for a long time, stunned and utterly confused. Then she got up and scraped the remains of their dinner down the garbage disposal, taking grim satisfaction in grinding it up. She just wished that she could throw in her memories of Nick as well to be pulverized and washed down the drain.

Trying to sleep proved to be a useless effort that night. At the first glimmer of dawn, she called Nick.

He answered on the second ring, sounding wide awake and quietly desolate.

"How could you tell me you love me and then just walk out like that?" Vanessa asked.

"Who is this?" he countered, and she could practically see his wonderful, dark eyes dancing with mischief.

Vanessa laughed miserably. "Damn it, Nick, don't make this any more difficult than it already is."

He sighed. "The whole thing is pretty confusing to me, too, if that makes you feel any better."

"It doesn't."

"You made the call, Vanessa," Nick pointed out. "The ball's in your court."

She shoved a hand through sleep-tangled auburn hair, then bit down on her thumb nail. "I'm in love with you," she finally admitted.

"That's progress," he conceded, but he still sounded the way Vanessa felt—sad.

She closed her eyes against an ocean of scalding tears. "What I'm trying to say, I guess, is that I need some time."

"Fine," he retorted. "How does a hundred years strike you?"

"That was mean!"

Nick was silent for a few moments, and when he went on his voice was low and ragged. "I've told you before," he explained with a slow patience that was patently insulting,

"I don't play games. If I can't be totally committed to this relationship, I don't want any part of it."

Vanessa felt as though he'd slapped her. "I see," she said.

"Should you ever feel ready to take the risk, get in touch with me. If I'm not involved with someone else, we'll see what happens."

Outrage replaced shock. "Of all the arrogant—"

"I'm through shadowboxing with you, Vanessa. I want a wife and a family and I'm not going to wait forever."

"How dare you threaten me that way!"

"It isn't a threat," Nick answered, his words grating together like rusty nails in the bottom of a bucket. "It's a fact."

"Goodbye," Vanessa said after a brief interval. He hung up without returning her farewell.

Vanessa was determined not to fall apart again. She was a modern woman, she told herself, independent with a career. She didn't need Nick DeAngelo to be whole.

Oh, but she wanted him. She wanted him.

When a few hours had passed and she'd recovered her composure to some degree, she dialed the Harmons' number. Paul answered.

Vanessa explained that she had some personal business to take care of and asked for a few days off.

"Are your grandparents all right?" her employer asked, his voice full of concern.

At the mere mention of them, Vanessa ached with homesickness. She would have given a lot to be back in Spokane, pouring out her heart to the people who had raised her, but there wasn't going to be time for that. "They're fine," she answered belatedly, feeling strangely tongue-tied. "It's— it's something else."

Paul sighed. "All right," he said in his kind and quiet way. "Take as much time as you need."

"Thanks," Vanessa replied. She asked Paul to give her best to Janet and then hung up.

She had finished packing and was just carrying her suitcase downstairs when Rodney arrived to check up on her.

"I saw Nick's car here last night," he said, standing in the doorway to the kitchen and eying the suitcase. "I guess the two of you are going away together for a few days, huh?"

Again, Vanessa felt a hollowness inside. "Wishful thinking, Rod," she answered in resigned tones. "I'm flying to New York with Parker."

Seeing Rodney's mouth fall open was the only fun Vanessa had had in days. "What?" he croaked.

Vanessa smiled. "He's been pestering me to tell the world what I think of his book, and that's what I plan to do," she said.

Rodney's eyes rounded, and a grin broke over his face as her meaning struck him. "Wow," he breathed. "He'll kill you."

"He'll want to," Vanessa agreed, and just then the doorbell rang.

"I'll get it," Rodney volunteered, loping toward the front door. Even though he was in his second year of chiropractic school, there were times when he was still the gawky boy Vanessa remembered.

She stood up a little straighter when she heard him talking to Parker. Since there was no love lost between the two men, the exchange was terse.

Seeing Vanessa, Parker smiled fondly as though there had been no ugly divorce and then kissed her cheek. "You are as lovely as ever," he said.

Gag me, Vanessa thought. "Thank you, Parker," she said aloud. "So are you."

He gave her a bewildered look and then glanced at his Rolex.

You'd think a man who could afford a watch like that would at least let his ex-wife keep all the furniture, Vanessa reflected.

"Let's go," Parker boomed in sunny, all-hail-the-conquering-hero tones. "We've got a plane to catch. Thought we'd have dinner at the Plaza."

Why not? Vanessa thought. *He's paying.* "Sure," she enthused. A cloud passed overhead as she considered potential problems. "You did book separate rooms, didn't you, Parker?"

He cleared his throat and looked away for a moment. "Thanks to my agent, we have a penthouse suite. Nothing but the best for you, darlin'."

She arched one eyebrow as they started toward the door, but didn't pursue the point. They could agree on sleeping arrangements later. "You'll feed Sari until I get home and bring in the mail?" she asked of Rodney, who lingered in the entryway, watching her and Parker with a worried expression in his eyes.

He nodded. "Sure."

Some impulse made her hurry back and plant a kiss on Rodney's cheek. *Don't worry*, she mouthed before turning back to Parker.

There was a taxi waiting at the curb, and Parker made a great show of squiring Vanessa to it and sweeping open the door. She almost—not quite, but almost—felt guilty for what she was going to do to him.

They were at the airport, about to board their plane, when Nick suddenly appeared, moving gracefully through the crowds of travelers as he approached. Vanessa felt a lump of dread rise in her throat and averted her eyes momentarily.

Parker was cocky, shoving his hands into the pockets of his tailored trousers and rocking back on the heels of his Italian leather shoes. "I thought you had more pride than this, DeAngelo," he dared to say.

Vanessa gave her ex-husband a wild look and elbowed him, but when she turned her amber eyes to Nick, she was smiling.

"What is it?" she asked sweetly.

Nick took her arm in his hand and pulled her around a pillar, his nose an inch from hers. "You're not actually going through with this, are you?" he demanded in a sandpapery whisper.

She widened her eyes, well aware that Parker, while feigning arrogant disinterest, was actually listening. "I have to," she answered. "Thank you for coming to see me off and goodbye!"

"Goodbye, hell," Nick rasped. "I have half a mind to buy a ticket on this plane and go to New York with you. Wouldn't that be romantic—just you, me and your exhusband."

Vanessa drew in a deep breath, then let it out in a hiss. It was a technique she'd learned once in a relaxation seminar. "Go away." She smiled. "Please?"

Nick bent around the pillar to glare at Parker. "Are you going to sleep with that rat?" he demanded.

"Talk about a lack of trust," Vanessa pointed out, lifting her chin.

Nick closed his eyes for a moment. "You're right," he admitted at length. "I shouldn't have asked you that."

They were calling for the first-class passengers to board the plane, and Vanessa had to leave.

She told him the name of the hotel where she would be staying, adding, "I'll call you as soon as I'm settled."

But Nick shook his head. "I'll be in Portland. We'll talk when you get home."

Vanessa stood on tiptoe to kiss him lightly on the mouth, and Parker took her arm and dragged her away toward the boarding gate.

She was feeling a confused sort of hope when she and her ex-husband were settled in their seats, the coach passengers trailing past them into the body of the airplane.

Some of them recognized Parker and clogged the aisles, asking for autographs, but Vanessa paid little attention to them. She was staring out at the terminal, wondering what Nick was thinking.

For the first time, she allowed herself to hope that things might eventually be all right between them, once she'd dealt with Parker and his book. That would close one chapter of her life, and she'd be able to begin another.

Parker spent most of the trip flirting with a particularly attractive flight attendant; it was only when they had landed at JFK that he turned his efforts back to Vanessa.

A long silver limousine had been sent to fetch them, and Vanessa smiled as she settled into the leather-covered seat. She meant to enjoy every possible luxury while she could since she would undoubtedly leave town on a rail, covered in tar and pigeon feathers.

Twilight was falling as they drove toward the hotel, and Vanessa gazed out through the tinted windows, drinking in the spectacle of light and the cacophony that is New York.

Twice she had to pull her hand out of Parker's fingers. She began to regret the act she'd put on a couple of days before.

"This trip is strictly business," she whispered, hoping

the driver wouldn't hear. "So keep your hands to yourself, Parker Lawrence!"

Parker looked wounded. "How are we going to reconcile if I can't touch you?" he inquired.

Vanessa was tired and hungry and she was beginning to have serious doubts about the wisdom of this venture. "We're not going to get back together ever, and you damned well know it," she said irritably.

She glanced in Parker's direction and saw that he was watching her with a disturbing sort of shrewdness in his blue eyes. "Then why did you come with me?" he asked.

Vanessa sighed. Maybe she should just forget her plan and go home—by way of Portland. The deception seemed too big to carry off now. "I wanted to come to New York," she hedged.

Parker didn't speak to her again until they'd reached their hotel, which overlooked Central Park, and checked in.

The suite was spacious with a breathtaking view of the city and it came equipped with its own bar—and even a glistening black grand piano. There were flowers everywhere, compliments of Parker's agent, and a bottle of Dom Perignon was cooling in a bed of ice.

Vanessa made sure there were two bedrooms and that hers had a lock on the door before taking off her coat and unpacking the few clothes she'd brought with her. She changed into a figure-hugging silk dress for dinner and saw a familiar light in Parker's eyes when she returned to the suite's living room. He was standing by the piano and, grinning, he ran one hand over the keyboard, filling the place with a discordant exclamation.

There was a pop as a waiter opened the champagne. After accepting a tip from Parker, the whip-thin young man—an aspiring dancer, no doubt—slipped out of the suite.

Once again, Vanessa had misgivings. In fact, she wished she'd run after Nick at the airport and made him take her to Portland with him. Her yearning for his voice, his smile, his touch, was an ache deep within her. "You look troubled," Parker observed, his eyes discerning. "What is it, Vanessa?"

She wrung her hands together and drew upon all her courage. The idea that had seemed so just and so wise had turned foolish somewhere along the line. Even infantile. "I was going to humiliate you, Parker," she confessed. "I meant to denounce your book on that talk show tomorrow and tell the whole world what a lie it is." To her surprise, Parker threw back his handsome head and laughed. "Your innocence never ceases to amaze me, Vanessa," he crowed when he'd recovered a little.

"Do you think I didn't know that from the first?" Vanessa's mouth dropped open.

Suavely Parker poured champagne into a crystal glass and extended it to his ex-wife. "Friends?" he said, his voice a throaty rumble.

Vanessa accepted the glass, took an unseemly gulp of its contents and retreated a step, her eyes still wide. She was confused about almost everything in that moment, but one thing was clear as the icicles that lined the eaves of her grandparents' house every winter: Parker had no interest in being her friend.

"Why are you staring at me that way?" he pressed, tilting his head to one side and looking ingeniously baffled.

She finished off her champagne and ignored the question. "Let's go to dinner. I'm starved."

Parker consulted his watch. "Our reservations are for an hour from now, but I guess we could have a few drinks while we wait." Even though the restaurant was within walking distance, he went to the telephone and summoned the limousine.

Vanessa didn't question the gesture, reasoning that people didn't go into Central Park on foot at night if they could avoid it, but her mind and heart were far away as one of the hotel's elevators whisked them to the ground floor.

The Plaza's restaurant was an oasis of light in the darkness, and Vanessa felt more at ease when she and Parker were settled inside with cocktails and a table between them.

"You're still seeing DeAngelo," Parker speculated flatly, and Vanessa was amazed to realize that he'd restrained himself from asking that question for most of the day. Patience wasn't his long suit.

"Yes and no," Vanessa said, her throat hurting. She wondered what Nick would say if she caught a plane to the west coast, took a cab to the restaurant in Portland and surprised him.

"What do you mean 'yes and no'?" Parker demanded. "Damn it, I hate it when you do that!"

Vanessa could be charitable, thinking of how Nick would welcome her. They'd probably go somewhere private, right away, and make love for hours. "We're trying to negotiate some kind of workable agreement," she said.

"You make it sound like a summit meeting," Parker grumbled, looking like a disgruntled little boy. "Doesn't it matter that he was using you?"

Vanessa took a sip of her drink, a fruity mixture that barely tasted of liquor. She was so hungry that she was beginning to feel a bit dizzy. "I'm not sure he was," she said. She looked at her ex-husband pensively, champagne and the cocktail mingling ominously in her system. "He swears he's nothing like you, and sometimes I believe him."

Parker looked roundly insulted. "Am I that terrible?" he demanded.

"You're not a man I'd want to have a lasting relationship with," Vanessa answered with a hiccup.

"Good Lord," Parker grumbled, squinting at her. "You're drunk!"

"I am not," Vanessa protested.

Just then a flash went off, blinding her. For one awful moment, she thought a bomb had gone off. Then she realized that some reporter had recognized baseball's very own bad boy.

For once, Parker didn't look pleased at being noticed. "Get out of here," he said to the hapless person-of-the-press, glaring.

The reporter took another picture before two waiters came and discreetly evicted him from the premises.

"We're very sorry for the annoyance, Mr. Lawrence," a man in a tuxedo came to say. "Your table is ready."

Vanessa was wildly grateful at the prospect of eating. Light-headed, she staggered slightly when she rose too quickly from her chair, and Parker had to steady her by putting an arm around her waist.

Dinner must have been delicious, although Vanessa was never able to recall exactly what it was. She knew only that she consumed it with dispatch and then ordered dessert.

When they reached the hotel, there was a party going on in the suite. Vanessa skirted the room full of laughing, smoking, drinking strangers to let herself into her private chamber and lock the door.

She noticed the message icon was blinking on her cell phone, and she smiled as she read the text. Nick had sent it about an hour before and left his cell number. He was in Portland but he wanted to talk to her.

She punched out the digits on the hotel phone with an eager finger, and when Nick said hello, Vanessa replied with a hiccup and a drunken giggle.

Chapter 8

"Put Parker on the line," Nick said, sounding irritated. Vanessa raised three fingertips to her mouth to stifle another hiccup. "You sent me a text because you wanted to talk to Parker?" she asked, bitterly disappointed.

An exasperated silence followed, and then Nick swore. Completely ignoring her question, he posed one of his own. "How much have you had to drink, Vanessa?"

A hiccup escaped. "Too much," Vanessa admitted. The noise outside her room seemed to be getting louder with every passing moment, and she was developing a headache. "There's some kind of party going on in the living room," she observed out loud.

"Get Parker," Nick reiterated in an ominously quiet voice.

With a sigh, Vanessa laid the receiver on her bedside table and ventured into the next room, weaving her way through the happy revelers until she finally came to Parker.

"Nick wants to talk to you on the telephone," she said.

Parker grinned and touched her cheek, as though she'd brought him good news. "Fine," he replied, and started off toward the nearest extension.

Nick was speaking when Vanessa got back to her room and picked up the receiver again.

"If you take advantage of her, Lawrence," he warned, "what happened two years ago will be nothing compared to what I'll do to you this time."

"The lady made her choice," Parker replied smoothly, no doubt drawing courage from the fact that Nick was on the opposite coast. "She came to New York with me, and she's staying in my suite. If you can't pick up on the meaning of that, maybe you'd better go back to hawking cod at the fish market."

Vanessa sucked in a breath, horrified and furious. They were discussing her as though she were a half-wit, unable to look after herself or make her own decisions. "Wait a minute, both of you!" she cried, her headache intensifying as the music and laughter got louder in the living room. "It just so happens that I have a thing or two to say about all this!"

"Whatever, darlin'," Parker said in a bored tone, and then he hung up. His confidence in his own powers of seduction was an affront Vanessa would not soon forgive.

"Nick," she said, "don't you dare hang up."

"I'm here," he answered, a sort of broken resignation in his tone.

"None of this is at all the way it sounds. I have my own room, even if it is in Parker's suite, and there's no way he and I are going to get back together. Understood?"

Nick gave a ragged sigh. She knew intuitively that he was remembering what she'd told him about her first time with Parker—that she'd had too much wine and woke up in his bed.

"I don't have any claim on you, Vanessa," he said at last. "You can do what you want."

While Nick's words were perfectly true, they were not the ones Vanessa had hoped to hear. She wished devoutly that she'd listened to him and stayed in Seattle, where she belonged.

Vanessa sat up a little straighter on the edge of the bed, thinking of all the women who probably chased after Nick whenever the opportunity presented itself. "Are you telling me that you think we should both see other people?"

Nick made a grumbling sound of frustration and weariness. "Is that what you want?" he retorted.

Vanessa closed her eyes. "No," she admitted. "Good," Nick replied. "When are you coming home?"

"Monday," Vanessa vowed. The door of her room opened, and a woman wearing a leather jumpsuit and stilettos peered in. "I'm sorry, this room is private," she told the intruder.

The woman mouthed an oops and slipped out, closing the door behind her.

"What the hell was that all about?" Nick demanded. "You'd never believe it," Vanessa replied, yawning.

"Shall I just go to Seattle, or make it Portland?"

Nick was quiet for a moment. "Portland. But you have the show to do tomorrow, don't you?"

Vanessa held her breath briefly in an effort to put down another attack of the hiccups. "I'm not staying for that," she said. "I realize now that all my protests will do is make more people rush out and buy the book."

He chuckled, and the sound was warm and low and so masculine that Vanessa ached to be close to Nick. "Speaking of the book, there are a few things I'd like to know about the incident in Chapter Three," he said.

Vanessa sighed. "A circus acrobat couldn't do that," she replied.

Nick laughed outright. "I love you," he said. She hiccuped again.

"Strange that he didn't write about your drinking problem," Nick teased.

"Good night, Mr. DeAngelo," Vanessa said with feigned primness. "I'll see you in Portland sometime tomorrow."

"Text me the flight number, and I'll pick you up." Vanessa nodded, her mind fuzzy, and then remembered that Nick couldn't see her. "Okay. And Nick?"

"What?"

"I love you, too."

"Good night, sweetheart," he said, and his voice was a caress.

After hanging up, Vanessa went immediately to her bedroom door and locked it. Then, after laying out the trim royal blue suit she planned to wear on the flight home the next day, she slipped into her private bathroom and took a long, soothing bath.

When she returned to her room, sleepy and comfortable in her favorite pair of flannel pajamas, Parker was sitting on the end of her bed and the party was still going on full blast in the living room.

"What are you doing here?" she demanded in a furious whisper, pulling on her robe and tying the belt tightly. "How did you get in?"

Parker held up a key. "Relax, Vanessa—for all my sins, I've never forced myself on you, have I?"

Vanessa had to admit that he hadn't, though sometimes his methods had been almost that low-down. She shook her head, still keeping her distance.

"You're not going to do the show tomorrow, are you?" Parker asked, sounding resigned.

"No," she answered. "Are you angry?"

Parker sighed. "It might be to your advantage to go on and show the world that you're not a drunk," he announced.

"A what?" Vanessa demanded, her eyes rounding. With Nick the reference had been a joke, but Parker was coming from a different place altogether.

"You remember that reporter at the restaurant tonight, I'm sure—the one with the blinding flash attachment on his camera? He's from the *National Snoop*, and your delightful face will be propped up beside every checkout counter in America within a week to ten days." He drew in a deep breath and let it out again, his eyes narrowed in speculation. "I can see the headlines now: TOSS-AWAY BRIDE DROWNS HER SORROWS, it will say—or something to that effect."

Vanessa felt the color drain from her cheeks. She had a career of her own to think about, and she couldn't afford publicity of that kind. No one would ever take her seriously if she were seen in such an unflattering light. "Go on the show tomorrow, Van," Parker said quietly, coming to her and taking her hand in his to pat it. "Show the world who you really are."

Vanessa wrenched free of his grasp. "You don't give a damn what the public thinks of me," she hissed, "so spare me the performance. All you care about is selling that rotten book of yours!"

Parker shrugged. "The choice is yours, Vanessa. Go or stay."

She thought of Nick waiting for her in Portland and imagined how it would be to be held in his arms again, to lie beside him in the darkness as he quietly set her senses on fire. She closed her eyes for a moment, torn.

"I'll stay," she said, averting her eyes.

"Um-hmm," Parker agreed smugly, and then he tossed Vanessa the key to her room, went out and closed the door.

She promptly locked it, then hurried back to the telephone, planning to call Nick and explain that she'd changed her mind about doing the talk show with Parker.

As it happened, though, Vanessa set the receiver back in its cradle without pushing the sequence of buttons that would connect her with Nick. She couldn't explain the situation to him when she didn't completely understand it herself.

There was no time to call the next morning because a limousine arrived to collect Parker and Vanessa at an ungodly hour. She rode to the studio in a daze, sipping bitter coffee from a Styrofoam cup.

She promised herself that she would call Nick as soon as she had a chance, but it seemed that the talk show people had every moment planned. The instant they arrived, Vanessa was whisked away to have her makeup redone and her hair styled.

As the cosmeticians worked their wonders, a production assistant briefed her on the structure of the show and the line the host's questioning would probably follow.

None of it was anything like Vanessa expected. In fact, when she and Parker were seated before an eager audience and the lights flared on, all her broadcasting experience seemed to slip away into a parallel universe. It was as though she had never appeared before a camera in her life.

To make matters worse, she had slept very badly the night before, and she probably looked like a zombie.

The audience, mostly female, was clearly interested in

Parker. It was amazing, Vanessa reflected, how the man could flirt with so many women at once.

Numbly Vanessa groped her way through the hour. She answered the questions presented by the host and the audience as best she could and was grateful when the program ended.

Vanessa fled the studio immediately afterward, caught a cab outside and sped back to the hotel. There, she picked up her suitcase and went straight to the airport.

She had to wait three hours for a flight to Portland, and that was routed through Denver and San Francisco with a long layover at each stop. She called Nick from Colorado and told him that she would be in at six that evening.

He didn't sound particularly enthusiastic, and Vanessa could only assume that he'd watched the show, seen her sitting there as stiff as a board, letting Parker display her like a sideshow freak.

A glum, drizzling rain was falling when Vanessa reached Portland, but the moment she saw Nick, her spirits lifted. Although he gave her a rueful look and shook his head at some private marvel, he took her in his arms and held her close, and that made up for a great many things.

"I've had a terrible day," she said, letting her cheek rest against the front of his cool, rain-beaded leather jacket.

He kissed her forehead. "I know," he replied gruffly, and then he put an arm around her waist and ushered her toward the baggage claim area.

After reclaiming Vanessa's suitcase, they went outside and Nick hailed a cab. All the way to his restaurant, they made small talk, avoiding the issues of Parker and her appearance on television. There were long, stiff gaps between their sentences.

"You're angry with me," Vanessa said when the cab had

stopped in front of a towering Victorian building with a view of the water and an elegantly scripted sign that read, *DeAngelo's*.

Nick paid the driver and waited until the cab had pulled away before answering, "Does it matter, Vanessa?"

She sank her teeth into her lower lip. "Yes," she said, after they'd mounted the steps and entered the interior of the restaurant. "Of course it matters."

Wonderful aromas greeted Vanessa, reawakening her appetite.

Nick gave her a look. "Whatever you say," he replied, putting his hand to her back and propelling her toward a set of sweeping, carpeted stairs.

Vanessa decided to save the serious issues they needed to talk about for later when she'd had some aspirin and something to eat. "Do you stay right here at the restaurant when you're in Portland?" she asked, trying for a smile.

He nodded, opening a pair of double doors to admit her to an office that was the size of some hotel suites. "Sit down and relax," he ordered, setting down her suitcase and striding toward the telephone on his desk. "I'll have some dinner sent up. What do you want?"

"Spaghetti," Vanessa answered without hesitation, thinking of the night in the San Juan Islands.

Nick nodded again and placed the order in clipped, brusque tones. It was obvious that he was distracted.

"I thought you weren't going to be on the talk show," he said, when the silence had lengthened to its limits.

So he'd seen the debacle. Vanessa lowered her eyes, embarrassed that she'd been so tongue-tied on the program. Everyone who'd watched—and the producers of *Seattle This Morning* might well have been among them—was probably thinking that she had all the personality of a secondhand dishrag.

"I changed my mind," she replied almost in a whisper. Nick sighed. "That was your prerogative," he replied.

"You're here, and that's all that matters."

Vanessa looked at him with wide, weary eyes full of relief. "You were right," she conceded in a small voice. "I shouldn't have gone. I only made things worse."

Nick crossed the room to sit beside her, and the moment he took her into his arms she burst into tears. He kissed her eyelids and her wet, salty cheeks before taking her mouth and taming it with his own. Vanessa's exhausted body was captured in an instant and largely involuntary response, and she gave a strangled moan when he lifted one hand to caress her breast.

"The spaghetti will be here in a few minutes," Nick muttered against the warm flesh of her neck.

Vanessa laughed even as she tilted her head back in pagan enjoyment of his attentions. "You're so romantic, DeAngelo."

He drew away from her very reluctantly and shoved one hand through his hair. "You'd better reserve judgment on that, lady," he warned.

A sweet tingle went through Vanessa, but she was cool and composed as she arched an eyebrow and queried, "Until when?"

"Until I take you to bed, which will be about sixty seconds after you finish your spaghetti."

Vanessa looked around. "You have a bed here? This is an office!"

Nick pointed toward a closed door on the other side of the room, but said nothing.

She felt her temper flare. "How convenient," she said, folding her arms.

Nick sighed, shook his head and grinned at her. "We party animals like to be prepared," he said.

Vanessa honestly tried, but she couldn't sustain her anger. She was too tired and she wanted him too badly. "Don't tease me," she pleaded.

He touched her nipple and, even through her blouse, it came instantly to attention. "No promises," he said just as a knock sounded at the door.

The spaghetti had arrived, but there was no wine. Diet cola was served instead and Vanessa, who was seated at the small table in front of the windows, gave Nick a knowing glance while the waiter poured it for her.

"Are you afraid I'll lose control of myself?" she asked the moment they were alone again.

"Afraid? Hardly," Nick said, folding his arms and watching as Vanessa ate. "I'm looking forward to it, if you must know."

Vanessa blushed. She did tend to shed her inhibitions when Nick made love to her. "I'm serious, Nick," she said.

"So am I," he replied.

Vanessa tried not to gobble down her spaghetti, but there was no hiding the fact that she was eager to be taken to Nick's bed and driven beyond her own restraints. He was grinning at her when she dabbed hastily at her mouth with the napkin and shoved her empty plate away.

"Go ahead and—er—get settled. I'll be in a few minutes."

Vanessa was possessed of such virginly shyness all of a sudden that she couldn't even look at Nick. She picked up her suitcase.

Those few steps toward the door he'd pointed out earlier

seemed to take half an hour to execute, and when she was finally out of his view, she sagged with relief. The room was not as large as his suite on the island, but it was full of Nick's personality and his scent, and Vanessa felt at home there. With a sigh, she sat down on the edge of a large bed covered with an old-fashioned patchwork quilt and kicked off her high-heeled shoes.

It had been a long day.

In the adjoining bathroom, Vanessa took a hot, hasty shower, then put on her pyjama bottoms and a camisole, wishing she'd brought something sexier. She brushed her teeth and misted herself with cologne, and when she returned to the bedroom Nick was there, waiting for her.

"I missed you so much," she confessed, her chin at a proud angle.

"And I missed you," he answered gruffly, making no move to approach her.

Vanessa knew she would have to go to him this time, but now that they were alone and she was ready for him, it didn't matter. She crossed the shadowy room, which was lit only by the stray glimmers of street lamps outside, and slid her arms around his lean waist.

"Love me, Nick," she whispered, looking up at him, knowing her whole soul showed in her eyes and not caring. "I've been fantasizing about you so much that I'm going to go crazy if you don't touch me."

He cupped his strong hands on either side of her head, stroking her satiny cheeks with the edges of his thumbs. After searching her face with his dark, smoldering eyes for several seconds—as though to commit every feature to memory—he bent his head and kissed her.

His seductive kiss was a gentle kind of mastery, and

Vanessa swayed as Nick gave her a foretaste of the fiery conquering she knew he would make her earn.

When he finally broke away, it was only to slide her camisole over her head and toss it into a chair. Her breasts seemed to swell as he admired them.

Vanessa's knees went weak when he reached out to cup her breast in one hand, the pad of his thumb teasing the nipple. She wanted to lie down and abandon herself to Nick, but he wouldn't allow that. He put his free arm around her waist to support her, and she bent backward by instinct, silently offering herself.

With a groan, Nick bent to taste the nipple he'd already taught to obey him. His hand moved away, sliding down over Vanessa's ribcage to the place where her waist dipped inward to tug at the waistband of her pants.

She trembled as she felt the last barrier give way, cried out softly when he caressed her. The excitement was building steadily, and Vanessa didn't want it to be over so soon.

"Stop," she pleaded, her head bent back. But he didn't stop. With his hand he taught her new levels of pleasure. First he beckoned, then he soothed, now he taunted. "Oh, Nick, please—please—I'm going to..." There was a fierce explosion inside Vanessa, and her hips convulsed as Nick extracted every trace of response from her.

She was still gasping for breath, still so bedazzled that she could barely see when he laid her gently on the bed and began taking off his own clothes. When he was naked, Nick joined her.

Although most of the tension had left her body, Vanessa gave herself up gladly to the slow, skillful massage Nick treated her to. She caught the scent of some fragrant oil, felt it seeping into her skin as he applied it with circling motions of his fingertips.

She asked Nick to take her, but he only turned her onto her stomach and repeated the process with the oil. Vanessa was in an odd state of mingled excitement and sweet satiety, and the thrumming need inside her increased until she couldn't wait any longer. She twisted onto her back again and gasped a fevered plea.

Her hands moved over Nick's chest, his back, his buttocks in a wild, soft urging, and finally, blessedly, his resistance snapped. He took her in a hot, sweeping stroke that made her cry out in welcome and arch her back to receive him as completely as possible.

Her name was a ragged rasp torn from his throat, and though his mouth dipped to hers in an attempt at a kiss, he was too frantic to linger. With a desolate groan, he began quickening his pace by degrees until Vanessa's hips were rising to meet his.

His magnificent head was tilted back in triumph and surrender as he strained, visibly, to prolong the sweet anguish that consumed them both. Finally with a growl of lust he joined Vanessa in the core of a flaming nova. Even when their bodies parted much later, their souls remained fused together.

Vanessa was the first to recover, and she gave Nick a teasing kiss on the belly before sitting up and moving to slide off the bed.

"Don't go," he said, taking her wrist in a painless grasp and holding on.

She allowed him to pull her back down beside him, to kiss and caress her until the treacherous heat was building inside her again. In this second joining, there was no control on either of their parts, no withholding from the other and no teasing. It was fast and it was primitive, and when it was over Vanessa didn't even try to leave the bed because she couldn't move.

She awakened in the depths of the night to find herself alone, and an incomprehensible, unfounded dread forced her heart into her throat. "Nick?" she called, getting up and groping for her robe.

She found him in the adjoining office, half dressed and sound asleep in his desk chair.

Full of love and relief, Vanessa went to him and laid her hands on his shoulders. "Nick?" she said again.

He woke with a start and pulled her deftly onto his lap. "Hi," he greeted her with a rummy yawn.

Vanessa kissed his forehead. "Come back to bed," she said.

He gave another yawn. "This reminds me of page 72," he said.

"Page 72?" Vanessa echoed, completely puzzled.

Nick pulled a copy of Parker's book from underneath a stack of papers and held it two inches from her nose. Vanessa snatched the volume from his hand and flipped through it until she'd found the page in question. Hot color pooled in her cheeks as she read, and her eyes grew wider with every passing word. She'd forgotten this passage.

"I never did any such thing!" she cried, slamming the book closed and flinging it away.

Nick smiled wickedly. "Are you against trying it?" he teased.

Vanessa laughed, her anger fading. "Wretch," she said, giving him a quick kiss on the mouth and a push to the chest, both at the same time.

He rose out of the chair, forcing Vanessa to stand, too, and gave her a little shove toward the bedroom.

There, Vanessa undressed Nick after shedding her robe,

but there was no more lovemaking that night. They slept, legs and arms entangled, heads touching.

The moment she opened her eyes in the morning, however, all Vanessa's doubts and fears were back, lined up at the foot of the bed like an invisible army. This time she sent them packing, determined to enjoy her time with Nick. Things were still far from settled between them, and she didn't want to waste a moment.

He was singing in the shower and she joined him under the spray, although she was nowhere near as brave in the daylight as she had been in darkness.

Nick greeted her with a resounding kiss, then proceeded to lather every inch of her body. The water ran cold long before they came out.

Chapter 9

Until that day, Vanessa's impression had been that Nick dabbled at running his restaurants since he obviously didn't need to earn a living. By noon she knew he worked the same way he made love—with a quiet, thorough steadiness neither hell nor high water could deflect him from.

Watching him fascinated Vanessa, but it also made her restless. She had her own fish to fry, and her thoughts began turning in the direction of Seattle, the Midas Network and the decision being made at WTBE-TV. Leaving Nick in the middle of a loud argument with the chef, she went upstairs where there was privacy and silence and accessed her voicemail to listen to the messages she'd accumulated.

Her eyes widened as she listened. Representatives of six different stations, in that many different cities, had called with requests to "discuss" her career plans. Parker had left word that he'd realized he loved Darla after all and was off to Mexico to be married, and the cleaning lady had imparted that she was going to quit if Vanessa didn't buy a new vacuum cleaner.

When Nick entered the room a few minutes after the messages had ended, Vanessa was still sitting on the corner of his desk with the receiver in one hand, staring off into space.

He frowned as he hung up the telephone and peered into her eyes. "Is everything all right?" he asked.

Dazed, Vanessa nodded. "Parker is getting married and my housekeeper is going to quit," she said.

Nick put a hand under her chin. "You can always get another housekeeper," he said, looking worried.

Vanessa realized that he thought she was shattered by the news of her ex-husband's remarriage, and she laughed. She wanted to reassure him. "I'm glad Parker is tying the knot, Nick," she said truthfully. "Now maybe he'll leave me alone."

"Your eyes are glazed," Nick insisted. "If it isn't unrequited love, what's making you look like that?"

She told him about the messages from the six television stations. "I have to go home, Nick," she finished, resting her hands lightly on his shoulders.

He sighed, and while he didn't seem threatened by her news, he wasn't pleased, either. "You can call them from here, can't you?"

She shook her head.

Nick looked toward the window for a few moments, but Vanessa knew he wasn't seeing the glum weather or the modern skyline. "None of those stations are in Seattle?"

Again, Vanessa shook her head.

He kissed her lightly on the lips. "I've got to stay here until I can replace this chef," he said reluctantly.

Vanessa felt bereft inside, as though some great chasm

had opened between them, and maybe it had. She called the airport and made a reservation on a flight leaving in an hour, then hastily packed her clothes.

Nick offered to see her off, but she declined, needing time and space to think about the future and the unexpected changes it might bring.

Sari greeted her with an annoyed *reoooww* when she arrived home, but was appeased by an early supper. Vanessa returned the calls on her answering machine in a methodical and professional fashion.

Her appearance on national television, far from ruining her in the broadcasting business as she had feared, had sparked considerable interest among the powers-that-be. By the time she'd placed the last call, she had agreed to six interviews, five of which would take place in Seattle for her convenience.

The sixth, in San Francisco, was scheduled for her day off.

Still in something of a daze, Vanessa took a TV dinner from the freezer and shoved it into the microwave. She was eating it when the telephone rang.

"Job offers?" Nick asked, without extending a greeting or even identifying himself.

Vanessa sighed. "Interviews," she corrected. "Did you find a new chef?"

"No," he snapped, and his tone stung like a hard flick from a rubber band. "Did you find a new cleaning lady? Damn it, Vanessa, for once let's not evade the issue here. I'm in love with you, and you're about to be offered a job that takes you to another part of the country. It's halftime, and I'd like to know whether my team is winning or losing."

Vanessa's front teeth scraped her lower lip. "One of us

could commute," she said, knowing the idea wasn't going to please him.

She could see Nick shove his hand through his hair so clearly that she might as well have been standing in the same room with him. "No way," he ground out.

Vanessa stood up very straight, bracing herself. Nick had been so gentle with her, so understanding, but now he was showing his true colors. Now he was going to be the demanding male, trying to dictate her lifestyle and the course her career would take.

He really was as arrogant and egotistical as Parker, he was just more subtle about it.

"I guess we don't have anything more to talk about," Vanessa said, and it took all her strength not to fall apart right then and there.

"We have everything to talk about," Nick argued. He sounded calmer, but there was a note of despair in his voice that told Vanessa they weren't going to be able to work out a compromise this time.

"Goodbye," she said brokenly, and then she hung up and covered her face with both hands.

For two weeks, Vanessa didn't see or talk to Nick. She met with the people sent to recruit her for their local newscasts and talk shows and spent the rest of her time selling merchandise over the Midas Network and telling herself that some people just weren't meant to have it all.

Of the offers she received, the one in San Francisco was the most promising. Her salary would be twice what she was earning at the Midas Network, and she had always had a special affection for the city by the bay.

Vanessa had chosen not to make any hard and fast decisions until she'd gotten her emotions on a more even keel, and she felt like a tightrope walker with no balance pole.

The day before Thanksgiving, Vanessa's grandmother called. "Are you absolutely positive you can't come over for dinner?" she asked plaintively. "It's been so long since your grampa and I have seen you, and you've been looking a little peaky lately. Either that or you shouldn't wear peach."

Vanessa smiled, despite the feeling of quiet despondency that had possessed her since the day she left Portland. "You've been watching the shopping channel again," she said, evading the question her grandmother had asked her about Thanksgiving.

Alice Bradshaw chuckled, but the sound was a little hollow. "I watch every day, sweetie. Last week, I even ordered a cordless screwdriver for your grandfather. Now, are you going to change your mind and come home or not?"

"I have to work," Vanessa apologized, pushing her hair back from her forehead and letting out a long breath. Actually that statement was slightly wide of the truth because she had had the day off but offered to fill in so that another host could spend the holiday with family. Even so, she wasn't in the mood to celebrate anything since Nick was out of her life.

Her grandmother was clearly disappointed. "Can we look for you to visit at Christmas, then?" she pressed.

Vanessa swallowed. Christmas seemed far away, though she knew it wasn't. Maybe by then she'd have a grip on herself. "Okay," she agreed, looking distractedly at the wall calendar on the pantry door. "It's a date."

Alice was clearly pleased and excited. "You could bring that young man of yours along—the one Rodney's been telling us about."

Vanessa closed her eyes, feeling as though she'd just

been struck a blow to the midsection. *When I get through with you, Rodney Bradshaw,* she thought venomously, *it will take every chiropractic instructor in that school to put you back together.* "Nick and I aren't seeing each other anymore," she said with cheery bleakness. "How's Grampa?"

"What do you mean you aren't seeing Nick anymore?" Alice demanded, not to be put off by questions about the hearty health of her husband. "Rodney said this was *it!*"

"Rodney doesn't know what he's talking about," Vanessa said tightly.

Alice sighed. "I knew something was wrong by the way you looked. That man went and did you dirty, didn't he?"

Saying yes would have satisfied Alice, but Vanessa couldn't bring herself to lie. Nick had been stubborn and unbending, but he hadn't made a deliberate effort to break her heart. "Nothing so dramatic," she confessed. "There were a few fundamental things we couldn't agree on, that's all."

The conversation ended a few minutes after that and, just as Vanessa was hanging up, Rodney rapped at the back door and let himself in.

He was obviously ready to make the long drive to Spokane. "Sure you don't want to go along?" he asked slyly.

Vanessa glared at him, her hands on her hips. "I wouldn't go anywhere with you, you big mouth," she said. "What did you mean by telling Gramma and Grampa about Nick?"

Rodney sighed. "Every time I called them they asked how you were getting along and whether or not you had a man in your life. I suppose I should have lied?"

"Of course not," Vanessa said, sagging a little. "Call Nick," Rodney told her. "You're never going to be happy until you do."

Vanessa shook her head. Being a man, Rodney probably wouldn't understand if she explained, so she didn't make the effort.

One of Rodney's shoulders moved in a shrug. "It's your choice, of course. I'll see you on Monday, Van."

She accepted his brotherly kiss on the forehead. "Be careful," she couldn't stop herself from saying. "It's snowing on Snoqualmie Pass."

Rodney grinned. "I'll be okay," he promised, and then, after giving Vanessa a quick hug, he left.

It was time to leave for the studio, so she wrapped herself up in her warmest coat, pulled a fuzzy green stocking cap onto her head and left the house.

When she arrived at work, a message awaited her.

Paul wanted to see her in his office immediately.

Vanessa pulled off her stocking cap and coat as she walked down the hallway and knocked at her boss's door. While she hadn't actually given notice, it was common knowledge at the network that she wouldn't be renewing her contract.

Paul was standing when she stepped through his doorway. "Before we get down to business," he said when Vanessa was seated in a chair facing his desk, "I'm under strict orders to invite you to our house for dinner tomorrow night. We're having turkey and pumpkin pie—the whole bit. Say you'll be there and Janet will be off my back."

Vanessa smiled sadly and shook her head. "I'm in no mood to 'accidentally' run into your best friend," she said.

Paul sighed and spread his hands. "I tried. Janet had some idea that if your eyes met Nick's over the stuffing and candied yams, lightning would strike."

"Nick is going to be there, then?" Vanessa asked, unable to stop herself.

Paul shrugged. "I was going to ask him after you went

to do your segment. Which brings me to the real reason I called you in here. The network is prepared to offer you a sizeable raise to stay on."

Vanessa lowered her eyes and shook her head, but after a few moments she met Paul's gaze steadily. "I hope you don't think I'm ungrateful," she said. "You gave me my first real job, and I'll never forget that."

There was a short silence, then Paul asked, "Have you made any decisions about where you'll go next?"

She sighed, thinking of her ordeal on that talk show with Parker and of the lurid stories that had come out in the tabloids a week afterward. BASEBALL GREAT RESCUES DRUNKEN EX, one of the headlines had read. It still amazed her that the publicity had helped her career instead of ending it once and for all. "No," she answered at last, "but I am leaning toward the job in San Francisco." It was the first time she'd admitted that, even to herself. She wanted to be a long way from the memories of Nick.

"You never heard from *Seattle This Morning*?" Vanessa tried to smile as she shook her head. "Ironic, isn't it? They were probably the only ones who were put off by the article in the *National Snoop*."

"Nobody takes that rag seriously," Paul said, dismissing the subject. "We'll all be very sorry to see you go, Vanessa," he finished.

Vanessa couldn't answer since she had a lump in her throat the size of a football helmet. She paused in the doorway, though, and when she was able to speak again, she asked, "What was Nick's number? When he was still playing ball, I mean?"

Paul thought for a moment. "Fifty-eight, I think. Why?"

Vanessa shrugged. "I don't know," she answered, and

when she looked back at Paul over one shoulder, there were tears glistening in her eyes.

Her boss got out of his chair, crossed the room and simultaneously closed the door and drew her into his arms. "Van, no job is worth this," he said.

"You wouldn't say that if I were a man," Vanessa wailed, completely miserable.

Paul chuckled. "I wouldn't be holding you if you were a man, either," he pointed out.

Vanessa began to sob as the enormity of losing Nick washed over her once again. It was like parting with a lung.

Paul led her back to the chair she'd just left, seated her and buzzed his assistant to ask her to bring in a glass of cold water.

"Nick is a reasonable man," he insisted once the woman had gone. "I'm sure you could come to some kind of agreement if you'd just talk things over!"

She dabbed her eyes with a tissue plucked from the box on Paul's desk and then wadded it into a ball. She was a wreck; she had to pull herself together and stop moping around all the time. "When I was married to Parker," she said in the thick lisp of the terminally weepy, "I had to hand over all my dreams like a dowry. He didn't want me to go to college, so I quit. He didn't want children, so I gave up on the idea of having babies. Do you really wonder why I don't want to wake up one morning and find myself in the same trap with Nick?" Paul sighed. "Take the rest of the day off, Vanessa—you're in no shape to sell ceiling fans. Mel is on a roll today—I'm sure he won't mind filling in for you."

Vanessa refused. She wouldn't have it said that she couldn't pull her own weight.

Fifteen minutes later she went on camera and started pitching musical jewelry boxes. Despite Margie's skill with makeup, a glance at the monitor assured Vanessa that she looked bad enough to scare Hannibal Lecter.

She was demonstrating the ugliest floor lamp in captivity when Oliver smilingly announced that it was time to take a call from a viewer.

"What's your name?" Vanessa's cohost asked, reaching out to touch the lamp fondly.

"Nick DeAngelo," responded the caller. "What's yours?"

Vanessa stepped on the base of the lamp at that moment, causing it to wave madly from side to side. She flung both arms around the thing just as it would have toppled to the floor.

"We've got to talk," Nick said. "Will you have dinner with me tonight, Vanessa?"

"No," Vanessa answered, and it was a struggle to get the word out.

"You're being stubborn," Nick insisted.

"Do you want a floor lamp or not?" Vanessa yelled, wondering when the director was going to cut them off. It was obvious that this was no ordinary viewer.

Nick laughed. "I've missed you, too, lady," he said, and his voice was a brandy-and-cream rumble that brought pink color pulsing to Vanessa's cheeks.

Instead of being angry, the floor director seemed delighted. He stood beside one of the cameramen, signaling Vanessa to continue. Her chest swelled as she drew a deep, deliberate breath in an effort to keep her composure. She tried to smile, but the effort was hopeless.

"This is really not the time or place for this," she said, speaking as pleasantly as she could. "Some of our other viewers are probably anxious to talk to us about these lamps."

Again the item in question teetered dangerously; again Vanessa caught it just in time.

"Far be it from me to stand in the way of free enterprise," Nick replied. "I'll pick you up at seven-thirty."

Vanessa squared her shoulders and looked directly into the camera. "I've moved," she lied, hoping he would take the hint.

"I'll find you," Nick replied.

It was all she could do not to stomp her feet and scream in frustration. "All right, all right. If I agree to see you, will you hang up?"

"Absolutely," was the generous response.

"Then I'll see you at seven-thirty," Vanessa said moderately, seething inside.

The cameramen cheered and, at the end of her shift the director told Vanessa he was sure the orders would fly in when they aired the segment. Everybody loved a lover, apparently.

Vanessa stepped through her front door at five-fifteen, screamed in a belated release of her temper and hurled her purse across the living room. Her cat gave a terrified meow and fled up the stairs, and Vanessa was instantly contrite.

"I'm sorry," she called out, but it was no use. Sari would not forgive such a transgression unless Vanessa groveled and made an offering of creamed tuna.

Nick arrived promptly at seven-thirty, wearing the tailored suit he'd had on the first time Vanessa met him. He was as handsome as ever, although there was a hollow expression in his eyes.

He took in Vanessa's glimmery blue dress with appreciation as she stepped back to admit him. "I half expected that you would have moved out of state before I got here," he said.

Vanessa averted her eyes. She'd fantasized about seeing Nick again for days but, despite all those mental rehearsals, the reality was nearly overwhelming. She couldn't help hoping that he was ready to give some ground where their relationship was concerned so that they could forge some kind of future together.

"You look very dapper," she commented, ignoring his remark. The suit emphasized the broadness of his shoulders, and it was difficult not to touch him.

"Thank you," he replied with a slight inclination of his head.

Vanessa, who earned her living by thinking on her feet, talking for as long as three hours virtually nonstop, was tongue-tied. All the things she longed to say to Nick were caught in her throat, practically choking her.

He seemed to be looking into her soul and reading her most private emotions. "It's all right," he said, touching her face briefly with one hand. "We'll find our way through all this somehow. I promise."

Vanessa wished she could be so sure. As he laid her evening coat over her shoulders, she fought to hold back tears of confusion and fear.

A lot of people would have said she was crazy, she thought, as she and Nick whisked through the rainy night in his Corvette. Jock or no jock, this was a rare and gentle man, the kind most women would have tackled and hog-tied. And Paul had been right when he'd said that no job was worth the kind of pain the loss of Nick DeAngelo had caused her. As if that weren't enough, Vanessa knew she loved the man to distraction.

She'd been holding him at arm's length since the night they met, comparing him to Parker. Down deep, she'd known all along that Nick was as different from her ex-husband as salt was from sugar.

There could be only one reason for her failure to make a commitment, and that was fear—fear of loving and then losing, trusting and being betrayed.

The end of her relationship with Parker had been bitterly painful, even though she'd wanted the divorce and known that she had no other choice. If that happened with Nick, she knew she wouldn't be able to endure it.

She closed her eyes and let her head rest against the back of the seat.

"Don't be afraid, Vanessa," Nick said softly. "Please." Vanessa looked at him, drew in the scent of his cologne. "That's like asking a burn victim not to be be scared of fire," she replied in a sad voice.

Nick sighed. "I'm not the guy who burned you," he reminded her. "Doesn't that mean anything?"

"You have more power over me than Parker ever dreamed of having," Vanessa admitted, unable to keep the words back. "If you wanted to, you could crush me so badly that I'd never find all the pieces."

He turned his head and glowered at her. "You're stronger than you think you are," he said, clearly annoyed. "Give yourself—and me—a little credit."

An uncomfortable silence settled over the car after that, and neither Nick nor Vanessa spoke until they'd reached DeAngelo's and been seated inside a private dining room.

Vanessa had never seen a more elegant room. There was a single table in front of a view of Elliot Bay. The streets were lighted up like a tangle of Christmas tree lights, the colors smudged by the rain that sheeted the windows. Candles provided the only light, and a violinist serenaded Nick and Vanessa as they sat looking at each other, comfortable with the music.

When the music stopped the first waiter appeared, bringing champagne. He popped the cork and poured the frothy liquid into their glasses, being very careful not to look at either Vanessa or Nick.

Vanessa arched an eyebrow the moment they were alone. "No diet cola?" she joked.

Nick grinned. "I'm trying to get past your defenses here, in case you haven't noticed."

"I've noticed," Vanessa said with a sigh, clinking her glass against Nick's as he lifted it in a toast.

"To page 72," he said.

Vanessa laughed and sipped her wine. For the first time in days she felt whole and human. It would be so easy to give herself to Nick body and soul, and that was exactly why she had to keep herself under control.

"I saw a shadow in your eyes just now," Nick said, reaching across the table to take her hand in his. "What were you thinking about?"

"Guess."

His jawline tightened then relaxed again. "The perils of loving Nick DeAngelo?" he ventured.

Vanessa nodded and looked away toward the harbor. "Did Paul and Janet invite you over for Thanksgiving dinner?" she asked in an attempt to change the subject. God knew, the one at hand was a blind alley.

His hand gripped hers for a moment, then moved away. "Yes," he said. "Vanessa, look at me."

She hated the fact that her first impulse was always to do exactly what Nick told her. Before she could do anything about it, her gaze had shifted to his face. "Don't make this any more difficult than it already is," she pleaded. "Please."

"Will you come home with me tonight?"

Vanessa wanted to be flippant. "You move fast," she said, and immediately felt like a bumbling teenager.

"Vanessa."

"No," she said quickly. "No, I won't sleep with you, Nick."

"Why not?"

The nerve. "Because pilgrims don't sleep around, that's why."

Nick tilted his head to one side and studied her. "What?" he asked, looking honestly puzzled.

She smiled, albeit very sadly. "We're doing a special, live show and tomorrow morning I have to get up, put on a pilgrim costume and sell my little heart out. Does that answer your question?"

"Not by a long shot," Nick grumbled as a second waiter appeared with enormous salads.

Vanessa ate with good appetite, having learned her lesson about too much wine on an empty stomach, and by the time the broiled lobster had been served, she felt almost human.

Dessert made her positively daring. When Nick took her home, she invited him in for a drink.

The living room was dark, but Vanessa didn't bother to turn on a light since there was virtually no furniture to bump into. She was leading the way toward the kitchen when a crash and groan behind her made her leap for the switch.

Nick was sprawled on the floor on his back, looking for all the world like someone who had fallen off a ten-story building.

Vanessa dropped to her knees beside him. "Are you all right?" she cried.

"My back is out," he answered, moaning.

There was no time to be wasted. Vanessa went right to

the heart of the matter and panicked. She scrambled for the afghan her grandmother had knitted and covered him with it as if he were a war casualty. His eyes were closed, and he was pale.

"Nick, say something!" she cried.

"I may sue," he replied.

Chapter 10

Vanessa tapped one foot nervously while she waited for Gina to answer the telephone. Finally she heard a breathless "hello" at the other end of the line.

Huddled in her kitchen, speaking in a whisper, Vanessa explained that Nick was lying in the middle of her living room floor, apparently immobilized. "What should I do?" she asked. "Call the paramedics?"

Gina laughed. "It would serve him right if you did. Nick's faking, Vanessa—he probably wants to spend the night."

Vanessa sighed. Of course Nick was pretending, indulging his hypochondria. After all, this was the man who carried on like a victim of Lizzie Borden's when he cut himself. "Thank you," she said.

"See you tomorrow," Gina responded lightly. "Have fun getting Nick off the floor."

"Tomorrow?"

"At Uncle Guido's dinner, of course," came the answer.

Vanessa's hackles rose. Evidently Nick had committed her to a family gathering without so much as consulting her. She said a polite goodbye to Gina and, after gathering her dignity, walked back into the living room.

There, standing beside Nick's prone body, she folded her arms across her chest and nudged him with one foot. "What's happening at your Uncle Guido's place tomorrow, Nick?"

With great and obvious anguish, Nick raised himself to a sitting position. "I could have been killed," he fretted, avoiding her question.

"That could still happen," Vanessa allowed.

Laboriously the man who had once struck fear into the heart of every linebacker in the National Football League hauled himself to his feet. He gave the vacuum cleaner he'd tripped over a look that should have melted the plastic handle, and then sighed. "I suppose you're mad because I told my family you'd come to dinner tomorrow afternoon," he said.

Vanessa was tapping one foot again. "That kind of high-handed presumption is exactly what keeps me from marrying you, Nick DeAngelo!"

He leaned close to her, and she was filled with the singular scent of him. His dark eyes were snapping with annoyance. "Who asked you to get married, Lawrence?" he countered.

Crimson heat filled Vanessa's face. No one, not even Parker, could make her as furious, so fast, as Nick could. "You wanted to shack up?" she seethed.

Nick sighed again heavily. "Time out," he said, making the signal with his hands. "Let's start over. You're the one who brought up the subject of marriage."

Vanessa looked away, her eyes filling with sudden embarrassing tears. She had no idea what to say.

Nick took her arms into his hands and made her look at him. "It's time we stopped playing games," he said hoarsely. "I love you, Vanessa, and I'd like nothing better than to marry you. Tonight, tomorrow, whenever you say."

Vanessa bit into her lower lip. She wanted to say yes so badly that she could barely hold the word back, but fear stopped her. Mortal fear that gripped her mind and spirit like an iron fist, cold and inescapable. She tried to get past it, like a mountain climber working her way around an obstacle by inching along a narrow ledge.

"Maybe I wasn't so far off a minute ago," she ventured to say, "when I asked if you wanted to live together."

Nick stared at her in wounded amazement. "You said 'shack up,' if I remember correctly," he replied.

Vanessa winced at the dry fury in his tone and rushed headlong into her subject. "It seems to me that it would be a good idea for us to live together for a while, just until we could make sure we really love each other."

Nick's eyes glowed with dark heat. "Sure," he mocked, shrugging. "That way you wouldn't have to make a commitment. If you got a job offer in another city, or decided you wanted a different roommate, you could just bail out!"

"That isn't what I meant at all!" Vanessa cried, horrified at the picture he was painting.

"Isn't it?" he demanded. "Tell me, Vanessa—where were we going to set up this romantic little love nest?"

She swallowed. "I thought San Francisco would be nice," she admitted in a very small voice.

"I'll bet you did," Nick retorted, and, unbelievably, he turned and strode toward the door.

Vanessa hurried after him, not wanting to let him go again so soon. "Nick, wait..."

He stopped and turned to face her, but there was a cold distance in his eyes that made her heart ache. "I want a wife and a family, Vanessa—I've told you that. If you can't make a commitment, then for God's sake let me go."

"You're being a prude," Vanessa accused, as he opened the door to an icy November wind.

"Imagine," Nick marveled, spreading his hands. "Me— the party animal. Go figure it."

"Don't be so stubborn and unreasonable!" Vanessa cried, knowing how lonely her world was without him. "Lots of people are living together these days, and they're making their relationships work!"

"Good for them," Nick replied. "As for me, I'm ready for a wife, not a perennial girlfriend. Sleep tight, Vanessa." With that, he went out, closing the door crisply behind him.

Feeling bereft, Vanessa shot the bolt into place and wandered witlessly back to the kitchen, meaning to console herself with a cup of tea. She noticed the light on her answering machine blinking and, after putting a mug of water into the microwave, she pressed the play button on the machine.

There was only one, but it might have made all the difference in the world if she'd only heard it a few minutes earlier. The producers of *Seattle This Morning* wanted her to host the show, not with a partner, but on her own.

Vanessa would have jumped for joy at any other time, but she couldn't forget that Nick had just walked out the front door. She dreaded facing the rest of her life without him.

Thursday was long and it was lonely. Vanessa did her stint on the shopping channel—dressed as a pilgrim—and turned down numerous invitations to friends' houses opting instead to go home alone and cook a frozen turkey dinner in her microwave.

There were messages on her machine and her cell from everyone in the world except Nick DeAngelo. She returned a happy-holiday call to her grandparents and left the others unanswered. All night she lay staring up at the ceiling, trying to imagine herself living with Nick as his wife, bearing his children, sharing his joys and his problems.

The pleasant pictures were all too fleeting. It was easier to imagine him packing to leave her on some rainy afternoon.

All night Vanessa tossed and turned. Long before morning she knew what she had to do. If she stayed in Seattle, she would keep having destructive encounters with Nick, which would break her heart over and over again.

She had to start over somewhere else.

She called the television station in San Francisco first and told them she was accepting their offer, and then she got in touch with a friend in real estate and arranged to put her house on the market. She hoped the new owners would let Rodney go on living in the garage apartment since he liked it so much.

Nick didn't try to contact her again, and Vanessa's feelings about that were mixed. She marveled at her own capacity for conflicting emotions where that man was concerned.

When the fifteenth of December finally arrived, Vanessa's brief career with the Midas Network was over. That evening Mel and the Harmons shanghaied her, dragging her off to a farewell party at, of all places, DeAngelo's.

"How could you?" Vanessa demanded of Janet Harmon in a whisper when the crowd of people from the network had finished congratulating her and gone back to enjoying wine and hors d'oeuvres. It would have been easier if

Nick had been away looking after the other restaurant or something, but he was very much in evidence.

"How could I?" Janet echoed. "Vanessa, how could *you*? Leaving the Midas Network is one thing, but leaving Nick is another. Are you out of your mind? The man adores you!"

Vanessa's gaze went involuntarily to Nick. He was talking to a couple on the far side of the restaurant, laughing at something the woman said as he drew back her chair. Knowing all the while that her reaction was silly, Vanessa ached with jealousy. "Bringing me here was a rotten trick," she said miserably, forcing her eyes back to her own circle. "Thanks a lot."

"We were trying to bring you to your senses, that's all," argued Mel, leaning forward in his chair. He was accompanied by a woman half his age with bleached hair and whisk-broom eyelashes.

Vanessa sighed. "Even if I wanted to stay, it's too late. I've already given up my job and sold my house."

Paul, now her former boss, sat back in his chair. "The spot on *Seattle This Morning* is still open," he said.

Vanessa felt a little leap of hope in a corner of her heart, but it died quickly. She was as afraid of commitment as she'd ever been, and Nick probably didn't want her anymore, anyway.

She wasn't about to find out. Going to him with heart in her hands and being rejected would be more than she could bear. She looked down at the glass of chablis a waiter had poured for her moments before and left Paul's remark hanging unanswered in the air.

Vanessa was in a sort of daze from then on, eating her dinner, sipping her wine, making the proper responses—she hoped—to the things the other people around the large table said to her. She told herself that she had only to get through dessert and a round of goodbyes and then she could escape.

She was coming back from the rest room when she encountered Nick in the hallway. He blocked her way like Italy's answer to Goliath.

"Hello, Nick," she managed to choke out, her cheeks coloring. "How are you?"

He gave her a look that said her question was too stupid to rate an answer and sighed. "It would be easier to forget you if you weren't so damned beautiful," he said raggedly.

Vanessa didn't know what to say in response to that. Inwardly she cursed Janet for having her going-away party here where she couldn't have escaped seeing Nick. She tried to step around him but he wouldn't let her pass. "It's damn easy for you to walk away, isn't it?" he asked in a low, wondering voice. "Didn't any of what happened between us get past that wall of ice you hide behind and touch you?"

Anguish filled Vanessa, but she refused to let her feelings show. She met Nick's gaze, a feat that nearly brought her to her knees. "It was all a game," she lied coldly.

Nick grasped her shoulders in his powerful hands. "If it was," he bit off the words, "we both lost."

Vanessa was on the verge of tears, but she kept her composure and stepped out of his hold. "Goodbye, Nick," she said in a soft voice. This time, when she went to walk away, he allowed her to pass.

She didn't stop at the table and speak to her friends; that was beyond her. She simply kept walking, crossing the dining room, concentrating on holding herself together.

She paused to collect her coat, but she was practically running when she reached the sidewalk.

Snow was drifting down from the sky in great lacy puffs—an unusual event in Seattle—and the magic eased

Vanessa's tormented spirit just a little. She slowed her pace, allowing the weather to remind her of Spokane, of childhood and innocence.

Pike Place Market, with its noise and bustle, reminded her that she was in Seattle. She went inside, making her way through hordes of happy Christmas shoppers, pausing in front of a fish market, watching and listening as salmon and cod and red snapper were weighed and tossed on the counter to be wrapped. Vanessa stepped closer.

"Help you, lady?" asked a young boy with dark hair and eyes. He was wearing a white apron over jeans and a sweatshirt, and Vanessa wondered if he was a part of Nick's vast family.

Vanessa stepped closer, feeling self-conscious in her glittering blue dress, strappy shoes and evening coat.

She opened her evening bag to make sure that she had money. "I-I'll take a pound of—of red snapper, please."

"Red snapper, a pound!" the boy yelled toward the back of the market, and the weighing and tossing process started all over again.

"What's your name?" Vanessa asked.

The young man gave her an odd look. "Mark," he said. "Mark DeAngelo."

She smiled. Nick had told her about working in his uncle's fish market when he was about Mark's age. For Vanessa, it was like looking into the past, seeing Nick as he must have been. "You're Gina's cousin?"

Mark nodded, taking Vanessa's money and making change, still looking puzzled.

Vanessa felt foolish. She put her change back into her purse and reached out for the red snapper, now snug in its white package.

"You a friend of Gina's?" Mark asked just as Vanessa would have turned and walked away.

"Nick's," she confessed.

His wonderful dark eyes narrowed. "So you're the one," he said, and any friendliness he might have shown earlier had faded away.

Vanessa swallowed, wondering what had brought her to this market in the dark of night, what had made her mention Nick in the first place.

"Uncle Guido," the boy said to a heavyset man who had materialized beside him. "This is her—Nick's lady." Guido DeAngelo gave his nephew a quelling look, then smiled at Vanessa and extended one hand over the counter where crab legs and salmon steaks lay on a bed of ice. "You forgive Mark," he pleaded, beaming. "He got no manners. No good manners at all."

Vanessa shifted her bag and her package of fish so that she could shake Guido's hand. "How do you do?" she murmured, completely at a loss for anything more imaginative to say.

Guido's bright dark eyes took in her evening clothes and her special hairstyle. "You have new fight with Nicky?" he demanded. Despite his stern manner, Vanessa doubted that he had a trace of malice in him. The tears came back. "I'm afraid it's an old fight,"
she answered.

Guido rounded the counter and hugged her. "That Nicky. He's a stubborn one. You tell him his Uncle Guido said to quit it out right now!"

"Quit it out?" Vanessa echoed.

"Cut it out," Mark translated from his position at the cash register.

Vanessa smiled and nodded. "I'll tell him," she promised. *If I ever see him again.*

Outside the market, Vanessa hailed a cab. She half hoped to find Nick's Corvette waiting in her driveway, but the only car in evidence was her own. She paid the driver and hurried around to the back door.

The telephone was ringing when she stepped inside the house, and she heard the answering machine kick in.

"Damn it," Janet Harmon said through the machine, "I know you're there, Vanessa Lawrence. Pick up the phone right now or I swear I'll come over and bring the whole party with me!"

Vanessa literally dove for the receiver. "Don't," she cried, "please! I'm here!"

"Well," Janet retorted, "if it isn't the disappearing guest of honor. You might have told us you were leaving, you know."

Vanessa lowered her head, feeling guilty. Her friends had gone to a great deal of work and expense to say farewell, and she had left them high and dry. "I'm sorry," she said. "It's just that—"

"Don't tell me," Janet interrupted, "I can guess. You ran into Nick, went a few rounds with him for old times' sake and then crawled off to lick your wounds."

Vanessa was incensed. "It wasn't like that at all," she said, even as one part of her insisted that Janet was exactly right. Mostly in self-defense, she began to get angry. "In some ways, Janet, it serves you right. If you'd picked any other restaurant besides DeAngelo's, this wouldn't have happened!"

Janet was quiet for a moment while Vanessa regretted having spoken so sharply.

"I'm sorry," they both said in unison. After that they laughed in chorus, and then cried.

"What are your plans for the holidays?" Janet wanted to know when they'd each gotten a hold on themselves. "I'm going home to visit my grandparents," Vanessa said.

"After that?"

"I'm due in San Francisco on January second."

"Do you have an apartment?"

Vanessa glanced at the clock, stretching the telephone cord so that she could walk to the refrigerator and toss the package of red snapper inside. "No," she answered. "The station is putting me up in a hotel until I can find something. Where are you calling from?"

"Nick's office," Janet replied. "The party's still in full swing—why don't you come back?"

Vanessa relived the encounter she'd had with Nick in the hallway and nearly doubled over from the pain the memory caused her. "I couldn't," she said.

"What did you say to each other?" Janet wanted to know. "You sound like someone in Intensive Care, and I think Nick is out on a ledge even as we speak."

"What do we always say to each other?" Vanessa countered. She knew the question would confuse Janet, and that was exactly what she wanted. "Listen, my friend—Nick DeAngelo is old news, all right? I don't want to talk about him anymore. Not tonight, at least." Janet sighed heavily. "Okay," she conceded. "But let me go on record as one who thinks some of your wires are stripped."

Vanessa smiled sadly, though there was no one there to see her. "Thank you for giving the party—I really appreciate it, even though I didn't behave as if I did."

"I understand," Janet said. And that was why she was

such a good friend—Vanessa knew without a doubt that she really did. "Will we see you again before Christmas?"

Vanessa promised not to leave Seattle without saying goodbye and hung up. She didn't sleep well that night, but that was nothing new.

In the morning she was up early. Dressed in jeans, sneakers and a hoodie, she was busy packing in the living room when Rodney startled her out of her skin by bursting into the room from the kitchen.

He was dragging an enormous Christmas tree behind him.

"You didn't," Vanessa said painfully, looking at the evidence. The lush scent filled the near-empty room.

Rodney beamed. "Yes, Lady Scrooge, I did. You're going to have a tree whether you like it or not!"

"I'm not even going to be here!" Vanessa wailed. "Where's your Christmas spirit?" Rodney demanded, looking hurt.

Vanessa had never been able to take a hard line with Rodney. Loving him was a lifetime habit. She shoved a hand through her hair. "Do you promise to take it down before we go home? The Wilsons want to move in the first week in January."

Rodney was mollified. "You have my word, Van. I'll not only take it down, but I'll vacuum up the pine needles and the stray tinsel."

Vanessa laughed. "Wild promises, those," she said just as the doorbell rang.

A delivery man was standing on the porch holding a massive pink poinsettia in a pot wrapped in gold foil and tied with a wide white ribbon. Vanessa accepted the plant, scrounged up a tip and tore open the card the moment she'd closed the door.

"Let's part friends," it read. "Call me. Nick."

A hard, aching lump formed in Vanessa's throat, and tears smarted in her eyes. Against her better judgment and without a word to Rodney, she stepped into the kitchen and dialed the familiar number of his cell.

"Thanks for the poinsettia," she said when he answered.

"I'm sorry about last night," Nick replied.

Vanessa hugged herself with one arm. Just the sound of his voice tied her in knots; she wondered what she was going to do without him. "Me, too," she said.

"You've sold your house," he said, evidently determined to keep the ball rolling.

"I should have done it a long time ago." Vanessa wondered what kind of talk show host she was going to make when she could hardly carry on an intelligent conversation with the man she loved more than life.

"I guess you'll want a small place when you get to San Francisco," he ventured.

So he knew she'd accepted the job there. Vanessa closed her eyes for a moment. "Probably," she responded.

"I'd like to see you before you leave."

Nick's words shouldn't have surprised Vanessa, but they did. It was a long time before she could speak.

"I wonder if that's such a good idea." Her voice was faint and shaky. "We don't seem to do very well on a one-to-one basis."

Nick gave a hollow chuckle. "There's an obvious response to that remark, but I'll let it pass out of chivalry."

Vanessa had to smile. "Is that what you call it?" she countered.

"I hear you met my uncle last night." She let out her breath. "Yes."

"He gave me a long, loud lecture about mistreating lovely ladies," Nick went on.

Vanessa laughed softly. "I suppose I looked pretty forlorn," she confessed.

"I'm sorry," he responded, his voice a velvety caress.

"Did Uncle Guido tell you to say that?" Vanessa teased.

"Yes," Nick answered. "As a matter of fact, that was part of my penance. Vanessa, will you spend the afternoon with me?"

"I've got to pack and do some Christmas shopping—"

"Please?" he persisted. And when Nick persisted, he was nearly irresistible.

"There's no point—"

"I'm not going to pressure you, Van," Nick broke in gently. "All I'm asking for is this afternoon, not the rest of your life."

It took Vanessa a long time to answer. She wished she had the courage to offer the rest of her life, but she didn't. "Okay," she said.

Nick came to get her at noon, dressed casually in jeans, a sweater and a leather jacket. There was a sad glow in his coffee-colored eyes as he took in Vanessa's gray pants and sweater.

"Hi," he said.

Vanessa resisted an urge to hurl herself into his arms and beg him never to hurt her, never to betray or reject her. "Hi," she answered.

They went to Pike Place Market and walked through it, hand in hand, visiting the different shops and talking about everything but Vanessa's new job and her impending move to California. They had lunch in a fish bar on the waterfront and then drove to a Christmas-tree lot well outside the heart of the city.

Nick inspected tree after tree, consulting Vanessa about each one. She played a dangerous game in her heart, pretending that they would always be together at Christmas, selecting trees, stuffing stockings, putting dolls and tricycles out for little ones to find.

"How are you going to get that home?" Vanessa wanted to know when Nick had at last settled on a seven-foot noble pine with a luscious scent.

Nick looked puzzled by her question. With the help of the attendant, he bound the enormous tree to the top of his Corvette, and Vanessa held her breath the whole time.

She couldn't help comparing Nick's apparent carefree attitude with Parker's paranoia about his car's paint job.

The tree rode with them in the elevator, scratching their faces and shedding its perfume.

"I didn't get any shopping done," Vanessa complained, once they'd dragged the tree inside Nick's condominium and set it up in a waiting stand.

He was dusting his hands together. "I need to get something for Gina," he said. "Let's hit the mall."

Vanessa did a lot more pretending that afternoon, but, like all fantasies, her time with Nick had to end. When he saw her to her door, he didn't even try to kiss her.

"You really didn't pressure me," she marveled as he turned to walk away.

Nick looked back at her over one shoulder, his soul in his eyes. "When I make a promise," he said, "it's good forever."

Vanessa swallowed, thinking of promises that involved loving, honoring and cherishing. "W-will I see you again?" she asked.

He shrugged. "That's up to you," he said. "The next move is yours."

With that Nick walked away without looking back.

Chapter 11

Their grandparents' Christmas tree was a muddle of color in the front window, and Rodney and Vanessa exchanged a look of delight as they pulled into the familiar driveway.

John and Alice Bradshaw had heard the distinctive purr of the sports car's motor and were huddled together on the front porch, waiting. Rodney and Vanessa raced up the walk to greet them with exuberant hugs.

"It's about time you got here," John complained good-naturedly, and then he and Rodney went off to carry in the presents and suitcases that were jammed in the little car.

Vanessa, in the meantime, was led into the kitchen by her spritely redheaded grandmother and divested of her coat and purse. The room was filled with the scents of Christmas—cinnamon, peppermint, a hint of evergreen from the boughs surrounding the striped candle at the center of the table.

"I'm so glad to be home," Vanessa said, and then, re-markably, she burst into tears.

Alice made a clucking sound with her tongue and squired her granddaughter to a seat at the table. "Tell me all about it, sweetheart," she said, patting Vanessa's hand.

Rodney and John had arrived with their arms full by then, and Alice had to go and open the door for them. Vanessa waited with her head down until her cousin and grandfather had passed diplomatically into the living room.

"It's Nick, isn't it?" Alice persisted once they were alone again. She'd brewed a pot of tea, and she poured cupfuls for herself and Vanessa before sitting down.

Vanessa had regained some control of herself. "He's so unbelievably wonderful," she sniffled, plucking a tissue from the little packet that was stuffed into a pocket of her sweater. She was getting to be a regular old maid, carrying on all the time and having to stave off bouts of weeping.

Alice arched one finely shaped eyebrow. At sixty-seven she was still a lovely woman. Her green eyes were as bright and full of humor and love as ever, and her skin was flaw-less. She wore her rich auburn hair in a braided chignon and dressed elegantly. Vanessa adored her.

"That's what you said about Parker," the older woman remarked.

Vanessa sighed. "I know," she said. "That's part of the problem—what happened with Parker, I mean." She paused to pull in a deep, shaky breath and let it out again. "Nick used to be a professional football player." Alice was ap-parently reserving judgment on that, for she took a sip of her tea and shrugged in a way that meant for Vanessa to continue.

"He was a party animal, too," Vanessa elaborated, thinking, for the first time, how thin her argument sounded. "Surrounded by women," she added uncertainly.

Alice didn't look convinced. "Lots of men carry on like that when they're younger," she observed. "Parker probably won't ever stop."

Vanessa sighed as memories flipped through her mind like rapidly turning pages in a scrapbook—Nick running backward in the park so that she could keep up, eating spaghetti at that café on the island, bringing the lightning inside while he loved her, tying a Christmas tree to the roof of his Corvette.

"I'm so scared, Gramma," Vanessa confessed, and her teacup rattled in its saucer as she set it down.

"But you love him?"

"More than my life," Vanessa answered.

"How about your fear? Is your love greater than that?"

Vanessa bit her lip. "No one in the world has more power to hurt me than Nick DeAngelo does," she said. "There are two sides to that coin," Alice reminded her with a certain loving sternness in her voice. "No one else could make you happier, either—did you ever think of that? There are times in this life when we come to a crossroad, Vanessa, and we have to make a choice."

Vanessa looked down at her hands. "I've already made the choice," she said, even though she'd told her grandparents about her decision to move to San Francisco soon after it was made.

"Choices can be unmade. Vanessa, if Nick is a good man—and Rodney certainly seems to think he is—and you love him, then take the risk, for pity's sake!"

"What if he dies?" Vanessa whispered. "What if he decides he doesn't love me anymore and runs off with another woman?"

Alice looked exasperated. "What if you both live to be a hundred-and-four and die loving each other as much as you do today? You're being silly, Vanessa—silly and cowardly.

"Remember how it was when we'd go to the lake in the summertime when you were a little girl? You'd stand on the bank, dipping your toes in the water for an eternity while all your cousins were already swimming. By the time you finally took the plunge, the rest of us were ready to go home and you cried because you'd missed all the fun."

Vanessa smiled ruefully, recalling those incidents and others like them. She'd always been too cautious, except when she'd married Parker and that resounding failure had only made her more careful than ever before. "I am a bit of a coward, aren't I?"

"I don't want you thinking badly of yourself," Alice said firmly. "You're not the most daring person I've ever known, but there's something to be said for thinking things through and taking the slow and steady course, too."

"But I could be more of a risk taker," Vanessa ventured.

"Where this new man is concerned, I think you could," Alice allowed, pouring herself a second cup of tea.

That night, sleeping in her childhood bed in a room where cheerleading pom-poms and pictures of movie stars still graced the walls, Vanessa thought of the last time she'd seen Nick. *The next move is yours*, he'd said. In the morning, Vanessa awakened and went downstairs in her old bathrobe to find her grandfather in the living room, building the fire in the Franklin stove. John's blue eyes twinkled beneath bristly Santa Claus brows as he looked at her.

"Good morning, sunshine," he said. "You're up early." A thick Spokane snowfall was wafting past the windows that overlooked the street. Vanessa went to her grandfather and kissed his cheek. "So are you," she pointed out. "But that's nothing new, is it?"

He closed the door of the stove, put the poker away and smiled at her. "We're going to miss tuning in the shopping channel and seeing you there every day," he said.

Vanessa glanced at the clock and wondered if Nick was still in bed or out running through wet, dark streets. Then she slipped her arm through her grandfather's and teased, "You were probably spending too much money trying to make me look good."

John laughed. "You don't need any help to look good, button—you never did." He paused, watching her with wise, gentle eyes. "And the way you keep looking at the clock makes me think maybe there's somebody you want to call."

Vanessa swallowed. She'd been thinking all night, and she'd decided her grandmother was right. It was time she gritted her teeth and took a chance. "There is," she confessed. "But I don't think I'm ready to do it yet."

The old man shrugged. "No one can decide when the time is right but you," he said, and he and Vanessa went into the kitchen where he poured fresh coffee for them both.

"Did you ever wish you hadn't married Gramma?" Vanessa asked, watching the snow through the window above the sink. It gave her a peaceful, secure feeling.

"A thousand and one times," John answered. "And I'm sure she wished she'd never laid eyes on me now and again, too."

Vanessa was staring at her grandfather in surprise, the lovely and mystical snow forgotten. "But you love each other!"

"That's no guarantee that two people are going to get along all the time, Vanessa," her grandfather pointed out reasonably, leaning against the counter as he sipped his coffee. "Show me a marriage where neither party ever gets mad and yells, and I'll show you a marriage where one or both partners just don't give a damn."

Vanessa made swift calculations. Christmas was just three days away. Perhaps, if she were very lucky, she could get a plane back to Seattle, do what she she needed to do and be home in time for the festivities.

She searched online for a flight, but there wasn't an available seat on any of the planes leaving Spokane until after Christmas.

Discouraged, Vanessa called the train station. The prospects were much more encouraging there, but when she hung up she saw her grandmother standing nearby, looking sad.

"I'll be back before Christmas, I promise," Vanessa said.

Alice was a woman who had made bravery a habit. She squared her shoulders. "Bring the football player back with you," she ordered, tightening the belt on her bathrobe and then smoothing her hair with one hand.

"I'll try," Vanessa promised. She took only her purse and coat, leaving her suitcase and gifts as a pledge that she would return.

The train trip was slow—it took eight hours—but the journey gave Vanessa plenty of time to assemble her thoughts. It was six o'clock in the evening when she reached downtown Seattle, and catching a cab turned to be such a competitive pursuit that it might have become an Olympic event.

Finally, however, she reached DeAngelo's and hurried upstairs to Nick's office, where he'd kissed her the night they met.

Nick's middle-aged assistant looked her over warily.

"Ms. Lawrence?" she echoed after Vanessa introduced herself. "You're Nicky's friend?"

Nicky. Vanessa bit back a smile and nodded. "Yes."

The woman made a harrumph sound, as if to say "some friend," and then announced, "He's not here. Mr. DeAngelo is sick today."

Vanessa was alarmed. "Sick? What's the matter with him?"

A shrug was the only answer forthcoming, so Vanessa hastily excused herself and ran outside again. Cabs were still at a premium with so many last-minute shoppers in the downtown area, and it wasn't far to Nick's building. She hurried there on foot and was breathless when she fell against his doorbell.

"Who is it?" yelled a thick voice from inside. Vanessa smiled. "It's Mrs. Santa Claus. Let me in!"

The door was wrenched open, and Nick stood in the chasm, wrapped in a blue terry-cloth robe. He smelled of mentholated rub, and his hair stood up in ridges as though he'd run greasy fingers through it.

Vanessa wrinkled her nose and stepped past him. "Your assistant tells me you're sick," she said.

Nick sneezed loudly. "I've seen colds like this develop into pneumonia," he said.

Vanessa rolled her eyes, but let the remark pass. After slipping out of her coat and laying it across a chair, she started toward the kitchen. "What you need is some hot lemon juice and honey," she said.

Nick stopped her by grasping her arm in one hand and whirling her around to face him. "What are you doing here?" he asked.

Inside she was trembling. She felt like a person standing on the edge of a cliff, about to pilot a hang glider for the first time. "You said the next move was mine. This is it, handsome."

His mouth dropped open. "You mean—"

"I mean that I love you, Nick."

"Wait a second. You've said that before. What's changed?"

"My mind. I'm not going to San Francisco, Nick, and if you still want to marry me..."

He gave a shout of joy, crushed her against him and whirled her around as though she weighed nothing at all. The scent of mentholated rub was nearly overpowering. "If? Lady, you just say when!"

Vanessa made a face as he set her back on her feet. "You smell awful," she said.

"God, this is romantic," Nick enthused, beaming. He sprinted off down the hall, and Vanessa set about finding lemon juice and honey.

When Nick returned minutes later, he'd showered and pulled on jeans and a T-shirt with the number 58 imprinted on the front. His hair was still damp and tousled, and Vanessa combed it with her fingers, smiling at his miraculous recovery.

He kissed her, and Vanessa knew she would catch his virus—if he had one—but she didn't care. When he lifted her into his arms, she made no protest.

"Just how long do you want me to stick around, woman?" he asked, his lips close to hers.

Vanessa touched his mouth with her own. "Only forever," she replied.

He kissed her again. "You've got it," he promised.

His bed was unmade and rumpled, but Vanessa barely noticed. She gave herself up to sweet anticipation as Nick removed her clothing article by article, making a game of kissing and caressing each part of her as he unveiled it.

Vanessa settled deep into the mattress, giving a sigh of contentment, trusting Nick so fully that she clasped the headboard in her hands and abandoned herself completely to his loving.

He was tender, sensing that she was giving him her whole self this time and not just her body. She whimpered with pleasure as he circled one nipple with the tip of his tongue and held on tight to the headboard lest she drift away.

Nick teased her nipple, rolling it between his tongue and his teeth, then took it hungrily. When he'd had his fill of her breasts, he moved down over her quivering belly, taking tantalizing nips at her satin-smooth skin and deepening her whimper to a soft, steady croon.

And then he lifted her up in both hands, as he might take water from a cool, clean stream, and drank of her. The glory of it stunned her, but soon she was in a delirium of pleasure, tossing her head from side to side and letting go of the headboard to tangle her fingers in his hair. Shameless pleas fell from her lips, which felt dry even though she continuously ran her tongue over them, and her body was in mutiny against her mind, wildly seeking its own solace.

She sobbed his name as he brought her over the brink and introduced her to a new world—a world of unchained lightning and velvet fire. Her face was wet with tears when he finally poised himself above her, asking for her permission with his eyes.

Vanessa nodded, unable to speak, and ran her hands up and down the taut, corded muscles of Nick's back as he eased himself inside her. The pleasure was quiet at first— she'd already been wholly satisfied—but watching Nick's climb toward glory excited her all over again. When he reached the pinnacle, shuddering upon her and giving a fierce lunge of his hips, Vanessa met him there, arching her back to accommodate him, crying out in triumph and submission.

He buried his face in the curve of her neck when it was over, still trembling and breathing raggedly. Vanessa caressed him gently, wanting to soothe him.

Her body was utterly relaxed, but her mind was active. "I did promise my grandparents that I would come home for Christmas," she said. "They want me to bring you."

Nick sighed, his breath warm against her flesh. "Okay, but don't make any plans for next year without consulting me."

"Yes, sir!" Vanessa laughed.

He raised his head and gave her a sound, smacking kiss on the mouth. "Don't give me the old 'yes, sir' routine," he said, trying not to grin. "You're going to be nothing but trouble, woman, and you know it."

Vanessa was nibbling at his neck, giving him back some of his own. "Um-hmm," she agreed, "trouble."

Nick groaned as she slid downward beneath him, tasting first one of his nipples and then the other. "Give me a break," he pleaded. "I'm Italian, not superhuman."

Vanessa giggled beneath Nick and the covers. "Same thing, to hear you tell it," she said. She didn't stop, and Nick was finally forced to submit to her attentions.

He was a very good loser.

The train pulled into Spokane at 11:50 p.m. on December 23, and Nick and Vanessa caught a cab to her grandparents' house.

Golden light spilled onto the snow outside their windows. "They're waiting up," Vanessa said, touched. "That's so sweet."

Nick paid the cabdriver and collected his suitcases, obviously nervous. "What if they don't like me?" he asked.

Vanessa smiled, pulling him toward the front door. "After the buildup Rodney's been giving you, they won't be able to help it," she said.

Her grandmother hurled open the door just as they reached it and hauled them inside. The Christmas tree glittered in front of the window, piled high with gifts, and a cheerful fire danced in the Franklin stove.

"So this is Nick?" Alice demanded, looking him over.

"Number fifty-eight," John said reverently, extending a hand to his future grandson-in-law.

Vanessa rolled her eyes. "What will that make me—Mrs. Fifty-eight?"

Only Rodney laughed at her joke. He'd always been a sport.

Nick and Vanessa were properly welcomed with eggnog and cookies, then sent off to their respective beds. For the first night in weeks, Vanessa slept soundly, and visions of sugarplums danced in her head.

When she awakened, her grandmother informed her with glowing eyes that Nick had gone out shopping with Rodney. "He's a fine man," she added, pouring coffee for Vanessa and herself. "You don't need to worry with that one."

Vanessa nodded, her eyes shining as she sat down at the table with Alice. "I love him so much," she said.

Alice's mind had turned to more practical matters. "What about that job in San Francisco?"

"I called and told them I'd changed my mind," she said.

"You're going to stop working then?" Alice asked, trying to be subtle.

Vanessa shook her head, smiling. "I love working. I got in touch with the people at *Seattle This Morning* while I was in town, and we're going into production right after the first of the year."

Alice sighed. "Does that mean there aren't going to be any babies?"

Vanessa patted her grandmother's hand. "There will definitely be babies," she promised. A quick mental calculation indicated that there might be one sooner than anybody expected. She put all the inherent joys and problems of that prospect out of her mind, determined to enjoy Christmas. "Let's go shopping, Gramma. I need to get something for Nick."

The stores were crowded, but Vanessa still enjoyed the displays and the music and the feeling of bustling good cheer. In one shop there were enormous colored balls hanging from proportionate boughs of greenery, and Vanessa felt like a doll standing under a Christmas tree.

She was full of joy when she and Alice arrived home with their packages to find the house crowded with relatives. All of them were gathered around Nick eating take-out chicken and reliving a certain Rose Bowl game.

There was no private time with Nick at all that day, but when Vanessa crept into the living room to put the gifts she'd bought under the tree he was there.

"If you were hoping to catch Santa," he said, turning from the window where he'd been looking out at the steady snowfall, "you're too late. He's already been here."

Vanessa went to Nick and stood on tiptoe to kiss him. "Mistletoe alert," she said, just before her lips touched his.

He laughed and held her very close. "I love you," he said.

Vanessa pretended to pout. "Oh, yeah? Where's my present?" she demanded.

Nick took a small red velvet Christmas stocking trimmed in white fur from a branch of the tree. "Right here," he said.

Vanessa's hand trembled as she pulled a small box from the stocking and looked inside. Nick's gift to her twinkled even in the relative darkness of the living room, and she drew in her breath.

"It's official now," he told her hoarsely. "I'm asking you to marry me, Vanessa. Will you?"

She looked at the ring and then up at Nick and she nodded, her throat too constricted for speech.

He took the ring from its box and slid it on to the proper finger. Christmas magic seemed to shimmer all around them, and it made a sound, too—like wind chimes in a soft breeze. Vanessa hurled her arms around Nick's neck and held on.

Nick stirred a cup of coffee and leaned on the breakfast bar in the kitchen of the house he and Vanessa had bought soon after they were married. His eyes were trained on the television screen that hung under one of the cabinets along with the coffee maker and the can opener.

As many times as he'd watched Vanessa do *Seattle This Morning*, he was never bored. If anything, he found her more appealing now that she was obviously pregnant and so, apparently, did her viewers. The ratings were sky-high.

The theme music filled the kitchen and there was Vanessa looking like a shoplifter trying to make off with a basketball. Nick smiled and took a sip of his coffee.

"Good morning, Seattle," she said. "This is Vanessa DeAngelo, and today we're going to talk about…"

Nick heard the buzzer on the dryer go off and wandered into the utility room to take his shirts out before they could wrinkle. He put each one on to a hanger and then meandered back into the kitchen. Once Vanessa's show was over, he'd go down to the restaurant, but for now he was a house husband.

He grinned, watching out of the corner of one eye as Vanessa chatted with a group of haggard-looking men. Nick wondered what disaster they'd survived, but he didn't stay to find out. He took the shirts upstairs and hung them in his side of the closet. Then, after peering into the master bath, he shook his head.

As usual, Vanessa had left the place looking like a demilitarized zone. He picked up her towels, hung up her toothbrush and scraped her hairbrush, makeup and other equipment into a drawer.

By the time he got back downstairs, a commercial was on. He was just pouring himself a second cup of coffee when the telephone rang.

"Hello," he said into the receiver, waiting to see what Vanessa's subject for the morning was. She'd told him, but he'd been half asleep and the information had slipped his mind.

"Nick?" The voice belonged to Gina. "I'm calling to remind you about the baby shower. You're supposed to get Vanessa to the restaurant by seven. Can you handle that?"

Nick chuckled, thinking the whole thing sounded like a scene in an espionage novel. "I think so," he said as Vanessa came back on the screen, smiling and telling everybody to stay tuned.

Nick had every intention of doing just that. "Don't worry, Gina," he reassured his sister. "All systems are go."

"Great," Gina said. "What are you doing?" Terrific. The kid felt sociable.

"I'm trying to watch Vanessa's show," he answered pleasantly.

"Oh. Well, goodbye, then."

"See you tonight," Nick responded.

After laying the receiver back in its cradle, he went back to the TV and turned up the volume slightly.

"Don't you think this is a case of plain and simple hypochondria?" Vanessa was asking of one of her guests.

The man looked, as one of Nick's many aunts liked to say, as if he'd been dragged backward through a knothole. "Absolutely not. If my wife gets a cold, I get a cold. If she stubs her toe, mine hurts."

Nick grinned. The world was full of nut cases. "When my wife was pregnant," offered the next guest, "I was the one who suffered morning sickness." Just then, Vanessa was shown in full profile. She was probably going to have twins, Nick thought, and just that morning she'd been a little on the queasy side.

He slapped one hand over his mouth and ran for the bathroom.

* * * * *

Also by Brenda Jackson

HQN

Catalina Cove

Harlequin Desire

Forged of Steele

Visit her Author Profile page at Harlequin.com,
or brendajackson.net, for more titles.

SOLID SOUL

Brenda Jackson

To Gerald Jackson, Sr., my husband and hero.

To my sons, Gerald and Brandon,
who constantly make me proud.

To my agent extraordinaire, Pattie Steele Perkins.

To my editor, Mavis Allen, who asked me to
be a part of the Kimani Romance line.

To my readers who have supported me
through forty books.

Beloved, I wish above all things
that thou mayest prosper and be in good health,
even as thy soul prospereth.
—3 John 1:2

Prologue

"My mom needs to get a life!"

With a sigh of both anger and frustration, fifteen-year-old Tiffany Hagan dropped down into the chair next to her friend, Marcus Steele.

"I thought you said that the reason you and your mom moved here to Charlotte a few months ago *was* for a better life," sixteen-year-old Marcus said after taking a huge bite of his hamburger as they sat in the school's cafeteria.

Tiffany rolled her eyes. "Yeah, that's what I thought, but now it seems that her idea of a better life is making mine miserable. Just because she got pregnant at sixteen doesn't mean I'd go out and do the same thing. Yeah right! I don't even have a boyfriend and if she keeps up her guard-dog mentality, I never will. She needs a life that doesn't revolve around me."

"Good luck in her getting one," Marcus said, taking a sip of his soda. "My dad is the same way, maybe even worse. He's so hell-bent on me making good grades and getting into an Ivy League college that I barely have time to breathe. If it weren't for my three uncles I probably wouldn't be playing football. Dad sees any extracurricular activities as a distraction."

Tiffany shook her head in disgust. "Parents! They're so controlling. Can't they see that they're smothering us?"

"Evidently not."

"I wish there was some way that I can shift my mom's attention off of me," Tiffany said, unwrapping her sandwich. "If only she had another interest, like a boyfriend or something. Then she could get all wrapped up in him and give me some breathing space. I don't remember her ever dating anyone."

After taking another bite of his hamburger, Marcus said, "My dad has dated occasionally since my mom died seven years ago, and although I'm sure some of the women have tried, none of them holds his attention for long."

Tiffany laughed. "Then he better not ever meet my mom. One look at her and he'll be a goner for sure. I hate to brag but my mom is hot," she said proudly.

"Hey, my dad doesn't look too bad, either." Marcus grinned. "Maybe we ought to get them together since it seems that neither of them has a life," he added teasingly.

Tiffany was about to bite into her sandwich when Marcus's suggestion sank in. A huge smile curved her lips. "Marcus, that's it!"

He looked at her, baffled. "What's it?"

"My mom and your dad. Both are single, good-looking and desperately in need of something to occupy their time besides us. Just think of the possibilities."

Marcus began thinking. Moments later, he smiled. "Yeah," he agreed. "It just might work."

"It *would* work. Think about it. If we got them together, they would be so into each other that they wouldn't have time to drive us nuts."

"Yeah, but how can we get them together without them getting suspicious about anything?" he asked.

Tiffany smiled mischievously. "Oh, I bet I could think of something..."

Chapter 1

Less than a week later

Kylie Hagan regarded with keen interest the handsome specimen of a man dressed in a dark business suit, who had just walked into her florist shop. That was *so* unlike her. She couldn't recall the last time a member of the male species had grabbed her attention. Denzel Washington didn't count, since each and every time she saw him on the movie screen it was an automatic drool.

She continued watering her plants, thinking that the woman he was about to buy flowers for was indeed very lucky. The good news was that he had selected her florist shop—she was the newbie in town, and Kylie needed all the business she could get, since she'd only been open for a couple of months. Business was good but she needed to come up with ways to make it even better.

Her heart jumped nervously when, instead of looking

around at her vast selection of green plants and floral arrangements, he headed straight for the counter. Evidently he was a man who knew what he wanted and what he needed to woo his woman.

"May I help you?" she asked, thinking that with a face and physique like his, he probably didn't need much help at all. He stood tall, six-three at least, with a muscular build, a clean-shaven head, chocolate-brown eyes and skin tone of the richest cocoa, altogether a striking combination. The drool she usually reserved only for Denzel was beginning to make her mouth feel wet. As she continued to look at him, waiting for his response, she suddenly noticed that he wasn't smiling. In fact, he appeared downright annoyed.

"I'm here to see Kylie Hagan."

Kylie lifted her eyebrows and the smile on her face began fading at his rough and irritated tone of voice. What business did this man have with her? All her bills were current, which meant he couldn't be there to collect anything. And if he was a salesman, with his less than desirable attitude, she wouldn't be buying whatever it was he was selling.

"I'm Kylie Hagan."

Surprise flickered in his drop-dead gorgeous eyes. "You're Kylie Hagan?"

"That's right and who are you?"

"Chance Steele."

The name didn't ring a bell, but then she had only recently moved to the area. "And what can I do for you, Mr. Steele?"

He stared at her for a moment, and then he said, "The only thing you can do for me, Ms. Hagan, is keep your daughter away from my son."

Kylie froze. The man's words were not what she had expected. For a long moment she stared back at him, wondering if she had misunderstood. But all it took was the deep scowl on his face to let her know she had not.

"Keep my daughter away from your son?" she repeated when she finally found her voice.

"Yes. I found this note yesterday that evidently dropped out of Marcus's backpack. They were planning on cutting school together on Friday," he said as he pulled a piece of paper out of the pocket of his jacket.

"What!" Kylie shrieked, grabbing the paper out of his hand.

"You heard me and you can read it for yourself," he said, crossing his arms over his chest.

Kylie read, then after the first few lines she wished she hadn't. Three emotions enveloped her: hurt, betrayal and anger. Tiffany had always promised that if she ever got serious about a boy that she would tell her. Granted, she and Tiffany hadn't been that close lately, but a promise was a promise.

"Now can you see why I want your daughter kept away from my son?"

Chance Steele's question sliced through Kylie's tormented mind and grated on her last nerve, deepening her anger. She came from behind the counter to stand directly in front of him. "Don't you dare place all the blame on Tiffany, Mr. Steele. If I read this note correctly, she was merely responding to a note your son had sent asking *her* to cut school. The nerve of him doing such a thing!"

"Look, Ms. Hagan, we can stand here all day and we won't agree who's to blame. But I think we will agree on the fact that your daughter and my son shouldn't even be thinking about cutting school. I have big plans for my son's future that include him attending college."

Kylie glared at him. "And you don't think I have those

same plans for my daughter?" she snapped. "Tiffany is a good kid."

"So is Marcus," he snapped back.

Kylie breathed in deeply and closed her eyes in a concerted effort to calm down before a blood vessel burst in her head. They weren't getting anywhere biting each other's heads off.

"Ms. Hagan, are you all right?"

She slowly opened her eyes to focus on the man looming over her. Concern was evident in his gaze. "Yes, I'm fine."

"Look, I'm sorry I came barging in here like this," he said, the tone of his voice calmer, apologetic. "But after reading that note I got upset."

She nodded. "I can understand why. I'm pretty upset myself."

"Did you know our kids were hung up on each other?" he asked. She could tell that he was trying to maintain a composed demeanor.

"Mr. Steele, until you walked into my shop and dropped your son's name, I had no idea he even existed. Tiffany and I moved here a few months ago from New York State, right before the start of the new school year. I knew she had made some new friends but she's never mentioned anyone's name in particular."

"Okay, so as parents, what do you think we should do?" he asked.

His voice was drenched in wariness and Kylie could tell he was deeply bothered by all of this, but then he wasn't the only one. "The one thing we shouldn't do is demand that they not see each other. Telling them to stay away from each other will only make them want to see each other more. Teenagers will always deliberately do the opposite of what their parents want them to do. And once they start rebelling, it will be almost impossible to do anything."

She didn't have to tell him that she knew firsthand how that worked. Her parents had tried to keep her and Sam apart, which only made her want him more. The more she and Sam had sneaked around, the more risks they had taken until she had eventually gotten pregnant at sixteen...the same age Tiffany would be in about ten months.

"We have to do something. In confronting Marcus about that letter, I've thrown a monkey wrench into their plans for Friday. But how can we be sure this won't happen again?"

At the sound of Chance's voice, Kylie dragged her thoughts back to the present. "I'll talk to Tiffany and, like I said, she's a good kid."

"Yes, but it appears that my son and your daughter are at the age where overactive hormones cancel out good sense. We need to do what we can to make sure those hormones stay under control."

"I fully agree."

He reached into his pocket and pulled out a business card. "This is how to reach me if you need me to do anything further on my end. I talked to Marcus but things didn't go well. I did the one thing you indicated I should not have done, which was demand that he stay away from Tiffany. I don't think I've ever seen him that angry or rebellious."

Kylie nodded as she took the card from him. She didn't want to think about her upcoming talk with Tiffany. "I appreciate you dropping by and bringing this to my attention."

"Like I said earlier, I apologize that my approach wasn't more subtle. But Marcus's last words to me this morning were that nobody would stop him from seeing Tiffany. I was furious and still riled up when I decided to come over here."

He sighed deeply and then added, "It's not easy raising a teenager these days."

"Don't I know it," Kylie said softly, feeling terribly drained but knowing she would need all her strength when she confronted Tiffany after school.

"Well, I'd better be going."

"Again, thanks for coming by and letting me know what's going on."

He nodded. "There was no way I could *not* let you know, considering what they'd planned to do. Have a good day, Ms. Hagan."

As Kylie watched him walk out of her shop, she knew that as much as she wished it to be so, there was no way that this would be a good day.

The moment Chance got into his truck and closed the door, he leaned back against the seat and released a long sigh. If the daughter looked anything like the mother, he was in deep trouble. No wonder his usually smart son had begun acting downright stupid.

Kylie Hagan was definitely a beauty. He had noticed that fact the moment he had walked into the flower shop and headed straight toward the counter. When she had come from behind that same counter and he'd seen that she was wearing a pair of shorts and a T-shirt, he'd thought the outfit fit just right on her curvy, petite body and showed off her shapely legs too perfectly. Braided dark brown hair had been stylishly cut to accent her face. Her creamy chocolate skin complemented a pair of beautiful brown eyes, a perky nose and an incredibly feminine pair of lips.

How in the world could she be the mother of a fifteen-year-old when she looked barely older than twenty herself? She looked more like Tiffany's sister than her mother. Perhaps Tiffany had been adopted. There were a lot of questions circulating around in his mind, but the foremost was what the two of them could do about their kids who seemed hell-bent on starting a relationship that neither was ready for.

He understood Marcus's interest in girls—after all he was a Steele—and Chance could distinctly remember when he was younger. He had fallen in love with Cyndi when he'd been just a few years older than Marcus, and had married her before his nineteenth birthday after she had gotten pregnant.

Pregnant.

He would never forget that day when Cyndi had come to him, a mere week before he was to leave for Yale University, to let him know she was having his baby. He had loved her so much he decided not to accept a full college scholarship and leave her alone. Instead, he had married her, gone to work at his father's manufacturing company and attended college at night. It hadn't been easy and it had taken him almost six years to get a degree, but he and Cyndi had made the best of it and he could look back and honestly say that although there were hard years, they had been happy ones.

And then the unthinkable happened. Cyndi had noticed changes in a mole on the side of her neck, a mole that was later determined to be cancerous. Even after surgery and chemo treatments, four years later, on the day Marcus should have been celebrating his ninth birthday, they were in the cemetery putting to rest the one woman who had meant the world to Chance.

He straightened and started up his truck. Although he would never think of marrying Cyndi as a mistake, he couldn't help but remember her plans of attending college;

plans that had gotten thrown by the wayside with her pregnancy. If he had it all to do over, he would have been more responsible that night when they had gotten carried away by the moment.

And then on top of everything else, he couldn't forget the promise he had made to Cyndi on her deathbed; a promise that he would make sure that their son got to do everything they hadn't done, and take advantage of every opportunity offered to him, which included one day attending a university that would give him the best education.

That was the reason he was driven to make sure Marcus did well in school. Of course it was Chance's hope for him to one day join the family business, the Steele Corporation, but if Marcus wanted to do something else after finishing college, then he could do so with Chance's blessings.

As he began backing out of the parking lot, he contemplated the emergence of Tiffany Hagan in Marcus's life. He didn't think his son's interest in the girl was going to fade away anytime soon, regardless of what kind of talk Kylie Hagan had with her daughter. That meant Chance needed to have a "Plan B" ready. Under no circumstances would he let Marcus succumb to teen lust and ruin the life he and Cyndi always wanted for him.

His thoughts shifted to Tiffany's mother again, and he felt lust invading his own body. The difference was he was a man and he could handle it.

At least he hoped he could.

After reading the note, Helena Spears glanced up at the woman who'd been her best friend since high school. "Are you sure Tiffy wrote this, Kylie?"

The two of them had met for lunch and were sitting at a table in the back of the restaurant. Kylie shook her head.

Leave it to Lena to try to wiggle her goddaughter out of any kind of trouble. "Of course I'm sure. I can recognize Tiffany's handwriting when I see it and so can you. Those curls at the end of certain letters give her away and you know it."

Lena shrugged as she handed the note back to Kylie. "Well, the only thing I have to say in defense of my god-child is that if Marcus looks anything like his daddy, then I can see why Tiffy fell for him."

Kylie didn't want to admit that she'd thought the same thing. "You know Chance Steele?"

"Oh, yeah. There are few people living in Charlotte who don't know the Steele brothers. They own a huge manu-facturing company, the Steele Corporation. There are four of them who were born and raised here. They're not trans-plants like rest of us, and they are very successful, as well as handsome. Chance is the CEO and his brothers have key positions in the corporation. There are also three fe-male cousins, one of which works in the PR Department. The other two chose careers outside of the company, but all three are members of the board of directors."

Lena took a sip of her drink before continuing. "Chance is the oldest and the one I see most often with my charity work. He's a big supporter of the American Cancer Society. His wife died of cancer around seven years ago."

Kylie, who had been putting the note back in her purse, suddenly lifted her head. "He's a widower?"

"Yes, and from what I understand, he's doing a good job raising his son."

Kylie frowned. "Not if his son is enticing girls to cut school with him."

Lena laughed. "Oh, come on, Kylie. You were young once."

"I remember. And that's what I'm afraid of," she said, meeting Lena's gaze with a concerned expression. "You recall how I was all into Sam. I thought I was madly in love. It was like my day wasn't complete until I saw his face. I was obsessed."

Lena shook her head. "Yeah, you did have it bad. You thought you were in love, and nobody could tell you differently."

"And you saw what happened to me. One day of acting irresponsibly changed my entire life. I was pregnant on my sixteenth birthday."

And rejected at sixteen as well.

She would never forget the day Sam told her that he wanted no part of her or the baby, and that he would get his parents to give her money for an abortion, but that was about all she would ever get from him. He intended to go to college on a football scholarship and under no circumstances would he let her mess up his future with a baby he didn't want. He agreed with his parents that there was no sense in him throwing away a promising career in pro football because of one foolish mistake. So instead of hanging around and doing the right thing, he had split the first chance he got. Even now she could count on one hand the number of times Tiffany had seen her father. Sam did get the football career in the NFL that he'd wanted, at least for a short while before an injury ended things. Now he was living in California, married with a family, and rarely had time for his daughter.

Emotions tightened her throat as she remembered that time she had gotten pregnant. She had hurt her parents something awful. And disappointed them as well. They had had so many high hopes for her, their only child, including her attending college at their alma mater, Southern University.

She had eventually gotten a college degree but that was only after years of struggling as a single parent and trying to make a life for her and Tiffany. And now to think that her daughter could possibly be traveling down the same path was unacceptable.

"Yes, I did see what happened to you, but look how much you've accomplished since then, Kylie," Lena said. "The only thing you didn't do was allow another man into your life because of Sam's rejection, and I think you were wrong for turning away what I knew were some good men. You never gave yourself the chance for happiness with someone else after Sam. I tried to tell you how arrogant and selfish he was but you wouldn't listen."

Kylie sighed. No, she hadn't wanted to hear anything negative about Sam. She had been too much in love to see his faults and refused to let anyone else talk about them, either. A sickening sensation swelled in her stomach at the thought that history was about to repeat itself with her child. "That's why I can't let Tiffany make the same mistake I did, Lena."

"Don't you think you and Chance might be overreacting just a little? It's not like Tiffy and Marcus planned to cut the entire day of school. They were skipping the last two classes to go somewhere, probably to the mall," Lena pointed out.

"And that's supposed to be okay?" Kylie's nerves were screaming in frustration and anger each and every time she thought about what her daughter had planned on doing. She remembered when she had cut school with Sam. Instead of going to the movies like the two of them planned, he had taken her to his house, where they had spent the entire day in his bedroom doing things they shouldn't have been doing and things neither of them had been prepared for. But all she could think about was that Sam Miller, the star player on the Richardson High School football team, was in love with her. Or so she'd thought. Silly her.

"You need to calm down before you talk to Tiff, Kylie. I understand you're upset, but your anger won't help. You know how headstrong she is. She's just like you when you were her age."

Kylie sighed deeply. Again that was the last thing she wanted to hear. "She broke her promise to me, Lena. We've had a lot of talks. She had promised me that she would let me know when she was interested in boys."

"And had she come and told you about Marcus, then what? Would you have given her your blessings or locked her up for the rest of her life? Girls like boys, Kylie. That's natural. And you've had so many talks with Tiffy that she probably knows your speech by heart. Has it ever occurred to you that maybe you're laying things on a little too thick? Tiffy is a good kid, yet you're judging her by the way you lived your life, by your own past mistakes. It's important to you that she 'be good' because you don't think that you were."

Kylie's eyes began filling with tears. "I only want what's best for her, Lena. I made a foolish and stupid mistake once and I'll do anything within my power to keep her from making the same one."

Lena got up, came around the table and hugged her friend. "I know. Tiffy is going to be fine. I'll be here to help you anyway that I can. You know that. I just don't want you to build this brick wall between you and her. That same kind of wall your mother built with you."

Kylie wiped away a tear from her cheek. Although she

and her mother had a fairly decent relationship now, Kylie would never forget when Olivia Hagan had let down her only daughter by upholding her belief that by getting pregnant out of wedlock, Kylie had committed the worst possible sin.

"I'll never let that happen," Kylie vowed quietly.

Chapter 2

"That's the crisis you called this meeting for?" Sebastian Steele asked, turning away from the window and looking across the office at his brother with both amazement and amusement on his face.

Chance glared first at Sebastian, and then at his other two brothers, Morgan and Donovan. They were sitting in front of his desk and looking at him with the same expressions. "Your nephew is putting a pretty face before his studies and that doesn't add up to a crisis to any of you?"

When all three chimed the word "no" simultaneously, Chance knew talking to them had been a waste of his time.

At the age of thirty-six, Chance was the oldest of the group. Next was Sebastian, fondly called Bas, who was thirty-four. Morgan was thirty-two, and Donovan was thirty. Of the four, Chance was the only one who had ever been married. Bas was presently engaged, but the other two claimed they enjoyed their bachelor status too much to settle down anytime soon.

"Look, Chance," Morgan said as he stood up. "It's normal for boys Marcus's age to like girls. So what's the problem?"

Chance rolled his eyes heavenward. "The problem is that the girl is only fifteen and they were planning to cut school together and—"

"No," Sebastian interrupted. "They planned to cut a couple of classes, not school. There is a difference."

"And he of all people should know," Donovan said, grinning. "Considering the number of times he used to play hooky. I understand they still have a desk in Mr. Potter's math class that says, 'Sebastian Steele never sat here.'"

"I don't find any of this amusing," Chance said.

Morgan wiped the grin off his face. "Then maybe you should, before you alienate your son."

"How about chilling here, Chance," Sebastian interjected. "You act as if Marcus committed some god-awful sin. We know the promise you made to Cyndi, but there is more to life for a teenager than hitting the books. He's a good kid. He makes good grades. Marcus is going to go to college in a couple of years, we all know that. One girl isn't going to stop him."

"You haven't seen this girl."

Morgan raised a brow. "Have you?"

"No, but I've seen her mother, and if the daughter looks anything like the mother then I'm in trouble."

"I still think you're blowing things out of proportion," Morgan countered. "If you make a big deal out of it, Marcus will rebel. You remember what happened last year when you didn't want him to play football."

Yes, Chance did remember, although he wished he could

forget. He rubbed his hand down his face. Regardless of what his brothers said, he needed to talk to Marcus again. He didn't have any problems with his son being interested in girls, he just didn't want Marcus losing his head over one this soon.

Kylie was waiting in the living room the moment Tiffany walked through the door. She took one look at her daughter's expression and realized Tiffany knew the conversation that was about to take place. Kylie tried not to show her anger, as well as a few other emotions, when she said, "We need to talk."

Tiffany met her mother's stare. "Look, Mom, I know what you're going to say and I don't think I did anything wrong."

So much for not showing her anger, Kylie thought. "How can you say that? You planned to cut classes with a boy and you don't consider that wrong?"

Tiffany rolled her eyes. "My last two classes of the day are boring anyway, so we—"

"Boring? I don't care how boring they are, you're supposed to be in them and you *will* be in them anytime that bell sounds. Understood?"

Tiffany glared at her. "Yes, I understand."

Kylie nodded. "Now, about Marcus Steele."

Tiffany straightened her spine and immediately went on the defensive. "What about Marcus?"

"Why didn't you tell me about him?"

"Why? So you could find some reason for me not to like him, Mom? Well, it won't work because I do like him. You're the one who wanted to leave Buffalo and move here. And I'm the one who was forced to go to another school and make new friends. Not all of the kids at school like me. They say I talk funny. Marcus has been nice to me. Extremely nice. He asked me to be his girlfriend and I said yes."

"You're not old enough to have a boyfriend, Tiffany."

"That's your rule, Mom."

"And one you will abide by, young lady."

"Why? Because you think I'll get pregnant like you did? That's not fair."

"It's not about that, Tiffany. It's about such things as keeping your reputation intact and not getting involved in anything you aren't ready for."

"It *is* about what happened to you when you were six-teen, Mom. And how do you know what I am or am not ready for? You want to shelter me and you can't. You've talked to me, but the choice of what I do is ultimately mine."

"No, it's not," Kylie bit out. "As long as you're living under my roof, I make the rules and you will abide by them."

"I can't, Mom. I care too much for Marcus and we have news for you and Mr. Steele. We are madly in love!" she almost shouted. "And nothing either of you say is going to make us not be together, whether it's at school or some-place else."

"What's that supposed to mean?"

"It means," Tiffany said stalking off to her room, "that I don't want to talk anymore."

Chance leaped to his feet. The sound of his chair crash-ing to the floor echoed loudly in the kitchen. "What do you mean you might not go to college but stay in Charlotte to be closer to Tiffany Hagan?" he shouted. His anger had clearly reached the boiling point.

"There's no reason to get upset, Dad. What's the big deal

if I decided to hang around here and go to college? One university is just as good as another."

Chance rubbed his hand down his face, trying to fight for composure, and quickly decided to use another approach. "Marcus," he said calmly, "I'm sure Tiffany Hagan is a nice girl, but you're only sixteen. In another couple of years you'll finish high school and go to college where you will meet plenty of other nice girls. You have such a bright future ahead of you. I'd hate to see you get too serious about any girl now."

A stubborn expression settled on Marcus's face. "She's not just any girl, Dad. Tiffany is the girl I plan to marry one day."

"Marry!" Chance nearly swallowed the word in shock. "How did marriage get into the picture? You're only sixteen! I know you think you really care for this girl and—"

"It's more than that, Dad, and the sooner you and Tiffany's mother realize it, the better. Tiffany and I are madly in love and we want to be together forever. There's nothing either of you can say or do to stop us, so you may as well accept it."

"Like hell I will."

"I'm sorry to hear that," Marcus said as he walked out of the kitchen toward his bedroom.

Total shock kept Chance from going after his son and wringing his neck.

Kylie paced the floor. Her nerves were stretched to the breaking point. Tiffany hadn't come out of her room yet, which was probably the best thing.

Love!

At fifteen her daughter thought she was in love. Madly in love at that! Kylie swallowed a thickness in her throat when she realized how her mother must have felt sixteen years ago, dealing with her when she'd been obsessed with Sam Miller.

She paused when she heard the phone ring and quickly crossed the room to pick it up, thinking it was probably Lena checking to see how things with Tiffany had gone. "Hello."

"We need to talk, Ms. Hagan."

Kylie blinked at the sound of the ultra sexy male voice. It didn't take a rocket scientist to figure out who the caller was, or to know he'd evidently had had another talk with his son. She sighed. Yes, they did need to talk. "You name the place and I'll be there."

"All right." After a quiet pause, he said, "They *think* they're in love. Madly in love."

Kylie shook her head. "So I heard. Louder than I really cared to, in fact."

"Same here. Do you know where the Racetrack Café is?"

"Yes."

"Can you meet me there around noon tomorrow?"

Considering what was going on with Tiffany and his son, she really didn't have a choice. Hopefully, together they could devise a way to stop the young couple before they got into more trouble than they could handle. "Yes, I can meet you there."

"Fine, I'll see you then."

Chance arrived at the restaurant early to make sure they got a table. Jointly owned by several race car drivers on the NASCAR circuit, the Racetrack Café was a popular eatery in town. He hadn't been seated more than five minutes when he glanced over at the entrance to see Kylie Hagan walk in.

He had hoped his mental picture of her from yesterday had been wrong, but it hadn't. Kylie Hagan was an attractive woman. Every man in the place apparently thought so, too, judging by the looks they gave her. Not for the first time he wondered about her age and how someone who looked so young could have a fifteen-year-old daughter.

He watched her glance around before she spotted him. There wasn't even a hint of a smile on her face as she walked toward him. But, he quickly decided, it didn't matter. Smiling or not, she looked gorgeous dressed in a pair of black slacks and a blue pullover sweater. And those same curves that he'd convinced himself had to be a figment of his imagination made her slacks a perfect fit for her body. Even her walk was mesmerizing and sexy.

When she got closer, he saw the wariness around her eyes, which led him to believe that she'd probably gone a round or two with her daughter sometime during that day, as he'd done with Marcus. He wondered if the discussion had been about the "his and hers" tattoos Marcus had indicated he and Tiffany were thinking about getting.

Chance stood when she reached the table. "Ms. Hagan."

"Mr. Steele."

He thought they were overdoing the formality, but felt it was best to keep things that way for now. After all, this was nothing more than a business meeting, and the only item on the agenda was a discussion about their children.

After they had taken their seats, he asked, "Would you like to order anything? They have the best hamburgers and French fries in town."

A small smile touched Kylie's lips. "So I've heard. But no, I'm fine, you go ahead and order something if you'd like. It's just that my most recent conversation with Tiffany has killed my appetite."

Chance heard the quiver in her voice and recalled his own conversation with Marcus that morning before he'd left for school. "I take it Tiffany told you about the tattoo."

He watched her nostrils flare as she drew in a silent breath. "Yes, she told me. Matching lovebirds on their tummies right above their navels, I understand."

"That's my understanding as well." A soft chuckle erupted from his throat. There was a cloud hanging over his head that refused to go away and he had to find amusement anywhere he could to keep his sanity. But he had to believe this was just one part of parenthood that he would get through, and for some reason it was important to him for Kylie Hagan to believe that as well.

"Things are going to be all right, Ms. Hagan," he said soothingly. "That's why we're meeting today, to make sure of it." He flashed her a smile.

She glanced up and met his gaze. "I want to believe that," she said quietly. "Under the circumstances I think we should forgo formality. Please call me Kylie."

"Okay, and I'm Chance." After a pause he said, "Kylie, I want you to believe things will work out. We have to think positively that we'll get through this particular episode in our children's lives. We have good kids—they're just a little headstrong and stubborn. But I believe with some parental guidance they'll be fine."

"I hope so. Otherwise if they continue with the route they're going, they're bound to make a mistake."

Chance raised a brow. "By mistake, you mean…?"

"Taking their relationship to a level they aren't ready for, Chance."

He liked the way his name easily flowed from her lips. "I take it you mean sex."

"Yes, that's precisely what I'm talking about. Over the

years, I've had the mother-daughter talks with Tiffany, but when teenagers are in love, or think they're in love, they believe that sex is just another way to show how much they care."

They paused in their conversation when a waitress came to give Chance his beer, hand them menus and fill their water glasses.

"And you think that's going to be on their minds?" he asked.

"Of course. Raging teenage hormones are the worst kind."

He picked up his glass to take a sip of beer. "Are they?"

"Yes, trust me, I know. I had Tiffany when I was six-teen."

Chance's glass stopped midway to his lips. His mouth opened in surprise. "Sixteen?"

"Yes. So I hope you can understand why I'm upset with all of this. I don't want Tiffany to make the same mistake I made as a teenager."

Chance nodded. That explained the reason Kylie didn't look old enough to have a fifteen-year-old daughter. That meant she was around thirty-one, but still she didn't look a day over twenty-five. "Did you and Tiffany's father get married?"

Her laugh was bitter. "Are you kidding? He had to make a choice between me and a football scholarship to Hampton University. He chose college."

"I didn't."

Kylie glanced up from studying her water glass. "You didn't what?"

"I was faced with the same decision as Tiffany's father. My girlfriend, Marcus's mother, got pregnant when we were seniors in high school. We were both eighteen and had plans for college. We acknowledged our mistake and felt that no matter what, we loved each other and loved the child we had made. Instead of going to college, we got married, remained here in Charlotte and made the best of things. I later went to college at night. My wife died of cancer when Marcus was nine."

Chance finished his beer. A part of him regretted that the man who had gotten Kylie pregnant hadn't done the responsible thing. "It must have been hard for you, pregnant at sixteen," he said.

"It was." He could tell by the way her lips were quivering their conversation was bringing back painful memories for her. "I disappointed my parents tremendously, embarrassed them. When it was determined that the father didn't want me or his child as part of his future, my parents tried talking me into giving up my baby for adoption, but I refused. That caused friction between us the entire nine months. Things got so bad at home that I had to go live with my best friend and her mother the last couple months of my pregnancy."

After taking a sip of water, she said, "The day the nurse brought Tiffany to me for the first time after I'd given birth to her, I gazed down at my beautiful daughter and knew I had made the right decision, no matter how my parents felt."

"Did they eventually come around to your way of thinking?"

"Years later when they realized they were denying themselves the chance to get to know their granddaughter. But at first they wanted me to know what a mistake I'd made in keeping her. They'd intended to teach me a lesson. I couldn't move back home so I continued to live with my friend's family until I was able to get an apartment at seventeen. I finished high school at night while working at a grocery store as a cashier during the day. My best friend, who also became Tiffany's godmother, kept her at night so I could finish school. It was hard but I was determined to make it work. After high school, I went to college and I struggled for years as a single parent before I finally earned a degree. I got a management position and later purchased a modest home for me and Tiffany."

"What made you decide to move here?"

"The company where I worked as a supervisor decided to downsize. My position was no longer needed so they gave me a pretty nice severance package. Instead of seeing losing my job as the end of the world, I decided to turn it into an opportunity to do something I'd always wanted to do."

"Open up a florist shop?"

"Yes. The reason I decided on Charlotte was that Lena had moved here after college and I liked the area the couple of times I'd come to visit her."

"Lena?"

"Helena Spears, my best friend from high school."

Chance smiled. "Helena Spears? I've met her on several occasions. She's a Realtor in town and is very active with the Cancer Society. I think her father died of the disease some years ago."

"He did, when Lena was fourteen. In recent years her mother has taken ill. I admire Lena for taking on the responsibility of her mother's care the way she has."

Kylie leaned back in her chair. "So knowing my history, Chance, I hope you can understand why I don't want Tiffany to make the same mistakes I did. I don't have anything against your son personally. I'm sure he's a fine young man. I just don't think he and Tiffany are ready for any sort of a relationship just yet."

"And I totally agree. So what do you think we should do?"

"I think we should meet with them, tell them our feelings, let them know we understand how they feel, or how they think they feel, since we were young once. But we should try to do whatever we can to slow down things between them. They're moving too fast. One day I didn't even know Marcus existed and now my daughter is claiming to be madly in love with him."

When the waitress came back to take their order, Chance glanced over at Kylie. "You're still not hungry?"

Kylie smiled. "Yes, in fact I think I'm going to try a hamburger and fries."

Chance returned her smile. "I think I will, too."

"I'm glad we had our little talk," Chance said as he walked Kylie to her car an hour or so later.

"So am I," she said honestly, although the whole time she'd sat across from him she'd had to fight back her drool. She was amazed at the thoughts that had crept into her mind. Thoughts of how Chance Steele had to have one of the sexiest mouths she'd ever seen. And the type of physique that drew feminine attention. Watching him eat had been quite an ordeal. She'd had to fight the urge to squirm in her seat each time he bit into his hamburger. Her attraction to him was truly bizarre, considering the real problem was finding a way to keep their kids in line.

But she would be crazy not to acknowledge that she was drawn to him in a way she hadn't been drawn to a man in years. Sexual longings were something she hadn't had to deal with for quite some time. Being in Chance's company she had been reminded of just how long it had been.

"So we've decided that I'm to bring Marcus over to your place for Sunday dinner so the four of us can sit down and talk," he said when they reached her car.

"Yes, that's the plan."

"And I think it's a good one. We need to talk to them, but even more importantly, we need to let them talk to us. And no matter what, we're going to have to keep our cool, even when we'd like nothing better than to ring their little necks. The situation we're dealing with calls for strategy and tact, not anger."

She tilted her head up and looked at him. "Strategy and tact I can handle, but it's going to be hard keeping my anger in check," she said, thinking of the conversation she'd had with Tiffany that morning before the girl had left for school. Her daughter was intent on being stubborn, no matter what.

"We'll not only get through it, we'll succeed," Chance said.

Kylie knew he was trying to alleviate some of her worries and she appreciated it. "Okay, then I'll see you and Marcus on Sunday. I'm looking forward to meeting him."

"And I'm looking forward to meeting Tiffany as well." As he held the car door for her he shook his head and laughed. "Matching lovebird tattoos. Have you ever heard of anything so ridiculous?"

Chance drew Kylie into his amusement. "No, and what's really crazy is that Tiffany is petrified of needles."

"Well, it's been said that love makes you do foolish things."

Later that night Chance swore as he got out of bed. For the first time in eight years, a woman other than his wife had invaded his dreams. Every time he'd closed his eyes, he'd seen Kylie Hagan's face.

It seemed as if he couldn't keep his mind from dredging up memories of her. First there was her appearance yesterday when a T-shirt and a pair of shorts covered her shapely body. And today, at the café, the slacks and sweater she'd been wearing had made him appreciate the fact that he was a male.

And then there were the times she would do something as simple as drink water from her glass. He couldn't help but watch the long, smooth column of her throat as water passed down it. He had wanted to kiss every inch of her neck and had wondered how it would feel for her to grip him the way she was gripping her glass.

Chance dragged a hand down his face thinking it had been a long time for him. Way too long. Sexual cravings were something he'd barely had to deal with, but now he was having several sharp attacks. In addition to the lust he was feeling for her, he also felt a deep sense of admiration.

She had given birth to a child at sixteen, hadn't given in to her parents' demand that she give the child up for adoption, and had struggled the past fifteen years as a single parent who'd gotten a college education and had provided for herself and her daughter. He considered what she'd done a success story. What he really appreciated was the fact that her past experiences enabled her to foresee what could be a potentially dangerous situation for Tiffany and Marcus. It was clear as glass that she didn't want them to make the same mistake she'd made.

As he left the bedroom and headed for the kitchen, he thought about his own situation with Cyndi. They had been blessed in that both sets of parents had been supportive of their decision to keep their child and marry. And when Marcus was born, there was no doubt in Chance's mind that Cyndi's parents, as well as his own, loved their first grandchild unconditionally. His heart went out to both Kylie and Tiffany when he thought about what they had been denied.

His pulse began racing when he thought about dinner

at Kylie's place on Sunday when he would be seeing her again. That was one dinner engagement that he was looking forward to.

Kylie awoke with a start, finding that she was drenched in sweat…or heat, since what had awakened her was an erotic dream.

Chance Steele had kissed her, touched her, made love to her. At first she had moaned in protest but then they'd become moans of pleasure. But at the exact moment he was about to do away with all the mind-blowing foreplay and enter her body to take total possession, she had awakened.

She pulled herself into a sitting position and struggled to calm her ragged breath. Perspiration cloaked her body, a sign of just how long she had been in denial. For a brief moment, everything had seemed real, including the way his skin felt beneath her palms, how thick and solid his muscles were against her body and just how good those same muscles felt melding into hers.

With a deep sigh of disgust, she threw the covers back and got out of bed. Why, after fifteen years, did she finally become attracted to a man who just happened to be the father of the boy who could become her worst nightmare? On the way to the bathroom, she inwardly cursed for finding Chance so damn handsome.

As she turned on the shower and began stripping out of her damp nightclothes, she thought about how her life had been over the past fifteen years. Sam was the first and only man she had slept with. Once Tiffany had been born, her precious little girl had become the most important thing to her, her very reason for existing, and the years that followed had been busy ones as a single parent. Although a number of men had shown interest, a relationship with any of them had taken a backseat. It was either bad timing or a lack of desire on her part to share herself with anyone other than Tiffany. In essence, she had placed her needs aside to take care of the needs of her child.

But now it seemed that those needs were catching up with her. Something sharp, unexpected and mind-blowingly stimulating was taking its toll. For years she had been able to keep those urges under control, but now it seemed a losing battle. It was as if her body was saying, *I won't let you deny me any longer.*

As she stepped into the shower and stood beneath the spray of water, she knew that she was in deep trouble. Not only did she have to deal with the situation going on with Tiffany and Marcus, but she had to deal with her own attraction to Chance. It was sheer foolishness to become this enamored with a man she had only met a couple of days ago, and the very thought that she had gone so far as to dream about him making love to her was totally unacceptable.

No matter how intense the sexual longings invading her body, she had to get a grip. And more than anything, she had to remember that men couldn't be depended on to always do the right thing. Sam had proven that to her in a big way, and so had her father. He had let her down when he'd meekly gone along with her mother's treatment of her when she'd gotten pregnant.

Moments later when she stepped out of the shower, dried off and donned a fresh nightgown, she had to concede that the water hadn't washed any thoughts of Chance from her mind. She had a feeling that even when she went back to bed she wouldn't experience anything close to a peaceful sleep.

Chapter 3

"**Y**ou actually invited Marcus and his father for dinner on Sunday!"

Kylie lifted a brow as she washed her hands in the kitchen sink. Surprised at the excitement she heard in her daughter's voice, she turned to meet her gaze. "I take it that you don't have a problem with it."

The enthusiasm in Tiffany's voice dropped a degree when she shrugged her shoulders and said, "No, why should I? Just as long as you and Mr. Steele aren't going to try and break us up, because it won't happen. Marcus and I are—"

"Madly in love," Kylie rushed in to finish, stifling her anger as she dried her hands. "I know." If she heard her daughter exclaim the depth of her love for Marcus Steele one more time she would scream.

"I thought it would be a good idea for me to finally meet Marcus, considering how you feel about him," Kylie said.

"Why is Mr. Steele coming?"

"Because he's Marcus's father and, like me, he wants what's best for his child."

"Oh, then, he won't have to worry about a thing because I am the best."

Kylie rolled her eyes thinking her daughter was getting conceited lately—another of Sam's traits rearing its ugly head.

"So the two of you have been talking a lot?"

Kylie frowned as she began making the pancakes for breakfast. "The two of who?"

"You and Mr. Steele."

"More than we've wanted to, I'm sure," Kylie said with forced calmness. The last thing her daughter needed to know was just what an impact Chance Steele was having on her. Just as she'd figured last night, she hadn't been able to go back to sleep without visions of him dancing around in her head.

"How does he look?"

Many of the descriptive words that came to mind she couldn't possibly share with her daughter. "He's handsome, so I take it that Marcus is handsome, too."

Tiffany beamed. "Yes, of course." Then seconds later she said, "I heard Mr. Steele is nice."

Kylie expelled a deep breath. "I don't know him well enough to form an opinion but I have no reason to think that he's not." Although she pretended nonchalance, she couldn't stop herself from glancing over at Tiffany and asking, "Who told you he was nice?"

"Marcus. He thinks the world of his father."

Kylie's first reaction at hearing that statement was to ask why, if Marcus thought the world of his dad, he was causing Chance so much grief.

"He doesn't date much."

"Who?"

"Mr. Steele."

With his good looks and fine body, Kylie found that hard to believe. "Don't you think you need to start getting dressed for school?" she prompted, not wanting to discuss Chance any longer.

Tiffany nodded. "I'll be back in time for pancakes," she said as she rushed out of the kitchen.

When she was gone, Kylie leaned against the counter wondering why Chance had dominated their conversation. Was there a possibility that Tiffany was nervous about meeting Marcus's father? She couldn't help but remember the first time Sam had taken her to meet his parents. They hadn't been impressed with her and hadn't wasted any time letting her and Sam know they thought the two of them were too young to be involved.

Too bad she hadn't taken the Millers's opinion seriously. How differently things would have turned out if she had. But then she could never regret having Tiffany in her life, even now when her daughter was determined to make her hair gray early.

So, she thought as she pulled the orange juice out of the refrigerator, Chance didn't date often. Rather interesting…

Chance leaned back in the chair and stared out his office window. Instead of reading the report from the research-and-development department, he was sitting at his desk thinking of a reason to call Kylie Hagan. After that dream last night, he had awoken obsessed with hearing her voice.

Gut-twisting emotions clawed through him. It was bad enough that his son was totally besotted with the daughter, now it seemed he was becoming obsessed with the mother. He hadn't even managed to brush his teeth this morning without Kylie consuming his thoughts. He gritted those same teeth, not liking the position he was in one damn bit.

It wasn't as if he hadn't dated since Cyndi's death. But he quickly admitted that Kylie was different from any woman he'd taken out. She had a strong, independent nature that he admired. She had raised her child alone and when times had gotten tough with the downsizing of her job, she had made what she'd felt were the best decisions for the both of them. Even considering all of that, he still wondered what about her had not only grabbed his attention but was holding it tight. Could it be that now that he was getting older with a son who would be leaving for college in a couple of years, the thought of being alone scared him? Of course, he had his brothers, but they had their own lives.

Sebastian was the corporation's problem solver and troubleshooter. The Steele Corporation was more than just a company to Bas; it was his lifeline. Bas had been the last brother to join the company, and of the four, he had been the one to give their parents the most grief while growing up. Cutting school on a regular basis had been minor considering the other things he'd done. His reputation for getting into mischief was legendary. Trouble had seemed to find Bas, even when he wasn't looking for it. His engagement had mystified his brothers since he was the last Steele anyone would have thought would want to tie the knot.

Then there was Morgan, who headed R & D. Although he dated, everyone teased Morgan about holding out for the perfect woman. So far he hadn't found a woman who qualified for the role, although he was convinced one existed.

Last but not least was Donovan, who women claimed could seduce them with his voice alone. The youngest of the Steele brothers headed product administration, but unlike Bas, who was married to the corporation, Donovan always managed to carve out some play time.

"It doesn't look like you're busy, big brother, so I'll just come in."

Chance turned his head and watched as Bas entered his office. He sat up, a little surprised that anyone, including his brother, had made it past his secretary without being announced. "Where's Joanna?" he asked. It was a rare occurrence for Joanna Cabot to leave her post without advising him.

Bas smiled. "Just where is your mind today, Chance? Have you forgotten that Robert Parker is retiring and today's his last day in sales? We were all at the celebration downstairs and wondering where you were. I made an excuse for you by telling everyone you probably had gotten detained on an important call."

Chance muttered a low curse. He had forgotten about Robert's retirement party. Robert had been part of the Steele Corporation when their father, Lester Steele, had run things. Now their retired parents were living the life in the Keys, doing all the things they'd always dreamed of doing, and had left the family business in the hands of their capable sons and niece.

"Yes, I'd forgotten about it."

Bas leaned against the closed door. "Umm, and you were just talking about it yesterday, which makes me wonder what's weighing so heavily on your mind."

Chance stood and quickly slipped into his suit jacket. "Trust me, you don't want to know."

Bas scowled. "You aren't losing sleep over that Marcus affair, are you? You are chilling like we told you to do, right?"

Chance decided not to tell Bas that the Marcus affair

had conveniently become his own personal affair, thanks to Tiffany Hagan's mother. "Yes, I'm chilling."

Bas laughed. "You wouldn't know how to chill if your life depended on it."

Chance rolled his eyes, grinning. "Look who's talking."

It was a couple of hours later that Chance arrived back in his office. A part of him was still obsessed with hearing Kylie's voice. Deciding not to fight it any longer, he pulled out his wallet to find the business card she had given him the other day at the café. He picked up the phone, then put it back down. Damn, he wanted to do more than talk to her. He wanted to see her.

He reached for the phone and punched in the number to connect with his secretary. "Ms. Cabot, I'm leaving early today. If an emergency comes up you can reach me on my cell phone."

Strategy and tact were the methods he'd mentioned to Kylie for bringing their children around. Little did she know he was about to apply that same technique on her.

Kylie turned at the sound of the shop door opening with a smile of greeting on her lips. The smile quickly faded when she saw it was the one man who had invaded her dreams last night.

She took a calming breath, remembering her reaction the first time she'd seen him when he'd walked through her door two days ago. Nothing had changed. Dressed in another power-house business suit, he looked drop-dead gorgeous.

She tried not to stare at him like a love-struck teenager, but found she was helpless in doing so. Chance Steele wasn't just any man. He was the one man who had started her blood circulating again in some very intimate places.

He was definitely a man who was the very epitome of everything male.

"Hi," she said, deciding to break the silence when they just stood there staring at each other.

"Hi." He then glanced around. "You're not busy."

"No, the lunch crowd has come and gone."

"Oh. Would you like to go out?"

She raised a brow. "Out where?"

"To lunch."

Surprise flickered in the depths of Kylie's dark eyes. "To lunch?"

"Yes," he said, giving her a smile that made her stomach clench. "Would you go to lunch with me?"

"Why? Do we need to talk about the kids again?"

"No."

That single word sent her mind into a spin. He wanted to take her out but not to talk about the kids. Then what on earth would they talk about?

Chance must have seen the question in her eyes because he said, "I discovered something very important yesterday at the café, Kylie."

"What?"

"I enjoyed your company a lot. A whole lot." Then as an afterthought, he added, "I don't date often."

His confession was the same as Tiffany had said that very morning. Although she knew it probably wasn't good manners, Kylie couldn't help asking, "Why?"

He shrugged. "For a number of reasons but I can probably sum it up in one rationale."

"Which is?"

"Lack of interest."

Kylie knew all about lack of interest. She'd been dealing with it for over fifteen years. She hadn't wanted the drama of getting into a hot and heavy relationship with someone, nor had she wanted to expose Tiffany to the drama, either. "Oh, I see."

"Do you?"

Nervously, Kylie stared down at her hands, confused by a lot of questions, the main one being why she was more attracted to Chance than any other man. She lifted her head. "Then maybe I don't see after all."

Her heart began racing when he started crossing the room. When he came to a stop directly in front of her, he placed his finger under her chin, lifting her gaze to meet his. "In that case, for us to go to lunch together is a rather good idea."

She was warmed by his touch. "Why would you think that?"

"Because it would make things easier for us on Sunday if we were honest with ourselves about a few things now."

Kylie's eyes clung to his, knowing he was right. There was no need to play dumb. There was something happening between them that she didn't need or want, but it was happening anyway. And they needed to get it out in the open, talk about it and put a stop to it before it went any further. How could they help their kids battle lust when they'd found themselves in the same boat?

She drew in a deep breath. "All right, if you'll give me a second, I need to close up and put the Out to Lunch sign on the door."

He nodded. "Take your time. I'm not going anywhere."

Chance stood to the side while Kylie went about closing her shop. His eyes roamed over her with more than mild intensity. For some reason, today she looked even younger than she had the other days. She was wearing shorts and a top again, and he thought her legs were just as shapely as he remembered and her body just as curvy.

He couldn't help the desire that quickly escalated to extreme hunger and hit him in the gut. For one intense moment, he felt a burning desire to walk across the room and take her mouth with his. The need to taste her was driving him insane.

"I'm ready."

He blinked, realizing she had spoken. He inhaled a calming breath and fought for composure. He was ready, too, but doubted they were ready for the same thing.

"One of these days I'll take you to a place that serves something other than hamburgers and fries."

Kylie smiled as he led the way to their table. To save time they had decided to grab a quick lunch at Burger King. "I don't mind," she said, as butterflies began floating around in her stomach. Did he realize he'd just insinuated that he would be taking her out again?

"It's not too crowded," he said, pulling the chair out for her.

"No, I guess the lunch crowd has come and gone."

"Which is fine with me. Before I go order, I think I need to do this." He pulled off his tie and stuffed it into the pocket of his jacket. Then he reached for the top of his shirt and worked a couple of buttons through the holes. "I'm a little too overdressed for this place."

Kylie watched as he walked off toward the counter, thinking that an overdressed Chance was the last thing on her mind. Thoughts of an undressed Chance seemed to be cemented into her brain. In a suit he looked handsome, professional and suave. And she would bet that even in a pair of jeans and a shirt he would look rugged and sexy.

She didn't want to think about how he would look without any clothes on at all. But she had, several times, day and night, and that wasn't good.

It didn't take long for him to return and they began digging into their food. It was only when they were halfway through their meal that Chance spoke. He leaned in close, smiled and said, "I was wondering about something."

"What?"

"Since we've assigned ourselves the task of monitoring our kids' behavior, to make sure they stay out of trouble, whom should we assign to do the same thing for us?"

Chapter 4

That was a good question, Kylie thought as she held Chance's gaze from across the table. Who would make sure the two of them stayed out of trouble?

The smile on Chance's lips matched the one in his eyes. Still, she knew that, like her, Chance realized this was a serious discussion. A part of her wished she could forget that he was Marcus's father and that they'd met because of their children. But she couldn't forget, even while her attention focused on nothing but the shape of his mouth. It taunted her to lean in and cop a taste.

She drew in a deep breath, trying to regain control, and got a sniff of his cologne. The manly scent of him was unnerving, totally sexy.

"Don't look at me like that, Kylie."

She blinked and saw more than a bare hint of challenge in his eyes. She didn't have to wonder just how she'd been looking at him. The throb between her legs told the whole story and then some. It was a deep ache and it was all she could do to keep from asking him to relieve her of her pain.

She was astounded with her lack of strength where Chance was concerned and wished she could ignore how he made her feel, dismiss the longings he stirred inside of her. But at the moment she couldn't. At least not while her heart was beating a mile a minute and the heat was taking her body to an intolerable degree.

Regardless, she knew she had to fight temptation and take control. She wasn't a lustful teenager. She was a grown woman of thirty-one. A woman with a teenage daughter she should be concerned about. Tiffany was important. Tiffany was the only thing that mattered.

With all the strength she could muster, she broke eye contact and busied herself with pulling napkins out of the holder. "I don't want this, Chance," she said, knowing he knew full well what she meant.

He nodded. "To be honest with you, I don't want it, either, Kylie. So tell me how we can stop it."

She shrugged. It wasn't as if she had any answers. She was definitely lurking in uncharted territory. The only thing she knew was that around him she had the tendency to feel things she'd never felt before. No man had ever made her breathless, excited and hot. When it came to the opposite sex, she felt just as inexperienced as her daughter. Oh, sure, she'd engaged in sex before, and at the time she'd thought it was pretty good, once she'd gotten beyond the pain. But Sam had been just as young and inexperienced as she had been, and she figured what she'd always thought of as satisfaction was nothing more than an appeasement of her curiosity and the elation of finally reaching womanhood at the hands of someone she thought she loved.

But she wanted more than that for Tiffany. More than

teenage lust eroding what could be a wonderful experience with the man she married. That was the reason she was sitting here, a little past one, with the sexiest man alive. It wasn't about them. It was about their children. They needed to realize that and get back on track.

"I think the first thing we should do is to remember the reason we're here in the first place. You have a business to run and so do I, but our kids take top priority. Nothing else. My wants and needs have always come second to my daughter's and things will continue to be that way, Chance."

She paused briefly before she continued. "It's going to take the two of us working together to keep things from going crazy between Tiffany and Marcus. Shifting our concentration from them to us will not only make us lose focus, but will have us making some of the same mistakes they'd be making."

"So, you're suggesting that we pretend we don't have urges and that we aren't attracted to each other? You think it will be that easy?" he asked.

The frustration in his tone matched her own feelings. "No, it won't be easy, Chance. To be quite honest with you, it will probably be the hardest thing I've had to do in fifteen years."

She thought about the men in her past who had shown interest in her and how she'd sent them away without a moment's hesitation. There had been that new guy at work who tried hitting on her several times; then there was that guy who worked at the post office who had enjoyed flirting with her. Not to mention that handsome man at the grocery store who gave her that "I want to get to know you" smile. But none of them had piqued her interest like Chance had. None of them had offered any temptation. Chance was too incredibly sexy for his own good. Even worse, he was a pretty nice guy.

"We have to keep our heads," she said. "Or the kids will take advantage without us realizing it." Kylie hoped—prayed—that he wouldn't give her any hassles. They needed to be in accord. They needed to be a team with one focus.

He leaned over the table, closer to her. "I know you're right but…"

She lifted an arched brow. "But what?"

"At this very moment, the only thing I want is to kiss you."

His blatant honesty, as well as the heat of his gaze, burned her. She could actually feel the flame. His softly uttered words only intensified the throbbing between her legs, and made fiery sensations rip through her stomach. It wouldn't take much for her to lean in to him and mesh her lips with his, satisfy at least one craving they evidently both had. And without any control, her body began doing just that, leaning closer…

They jumped apart at the sound of a car backfiring. Kylie's eyes widened and her cheeks tinted with embarrassment. They were sitting in the middle of Burger King thinking of sharing a kiss, for heaven's sake!

"Are you ready to go?" Chance asked.

Kylie drew in a deep breath. Yes, she was ready. The sooner she got back to the shop the better. There, she could regain her sensibilities, take back control of her mind. No doubt Chance had more experience dealing with this sort of thing than she did. Regardless, she knew she couldn't depend on him to keep things in perspective. An affair with Chance was the last thing she wanted. No matter what, she had to remember that.

* * *

"Thanks for lunch, Chance," Kylie said to him as he backed out of Burger King's parking lot.

"You're welcome. I enjoyed it."

For the next few minutes they shared pleasant conversation in which he told her about his parents retiring to Florida and about his three brothers and three female cousins. It wasn't hard to tell that the Steele family was close.

"So how is your flower business?"

She appreciated him asking. It was a good idea to stick to general conversation. "So far business is good. Before moving here I did my research, made sure adding another florist wasn't overcrowding the market."

"You have a good location since it's an area ripe for development."

"Yes, and I owe it all to Lena. She put her real estate skills to work and gave me a call one day. It was just what I was looking for, exactly what I needed. I grow a lot of my own plants in the greenhouse out back. Those I don't grow I get from a pretty good supplier."

She paused briefly as he glanced over at her. He hadn't put back on his jacket or tie, which made her wonder if he planned to go back to the office or just chill the rest of the day. She scolded herself when she realized what Chance did was really none of her business.

"If you don't mind, I need to make a stop. It won't take but a couple of minutes. I promise to get you back to your shop before two."

"All right."

She blinked seconds later when he pulled up to a car wash. She thought his SUV looked pretty clean. It was definitely in better condition than her car.

"I have those pesky bugs on my fender," Chance said, as he eased his truck into the bay.

The automatic equipment began moving around the truck, blasting water over it and hiding them from the outside world in a cocoon-like waterfall. The insides of the truck suddenly got dark, intimate, warm.

She didn't want to but she couldn't help but glance over at Chance. Seeing the seductive look in his eyes, she knew this was no coincidence. Coming here had been deliberate on his part.

"This is the first time I've done this. I've never brought a woman with me to get my truck washed," he said in a husky voice. "But I want to kiss you, Kylie."

Kylie swallowed at the passion she heard in his voice. She hated admitting it but she wanted to kiss him as well. But still...

"Chance, I thought we decided that—"

"Please." His tone vibrated with a need that touched her when she knew it shouldn't. "Ten minutes is all I ask."

Kylie blinked. *Ten minutes? A car wash took that long?* As if reading the question in her eyes, he said, "I'm getting a heavy-duty wash."

"Oh." Still, she'd never been kissed for ten minutes.

"Come here, Kylie. Please."

The knot in her throat thickened. She knew he wanted her to slide over to him, and heaven help her but she wanted it, too. Without stopping to question the wisdom of her actions, she unsnapped her seat belt and scooted toward him. When she got close enough he pushed back the seat and pulled her into his lap. His arms automatically closed around her shoulders as he held her in a warm embrace.

"Thank you," he said huskily, before sweeping his tongue across her lips and taking her mouth, hungrily, thoroughly. The first touch of his mouth on hers had her automatically parting her lips. And now with the insertion of his tongue, he brought out a responsive need in her so deep, she began to intimately stroke his tongue with hers.

She had never been kissed this way, had never known that such a way was possible. But it was clear as glass that Chance had a special, skillful technique. His tongue was stroking the top of her mouth, sliding over her teeth, entwining his tongue with hers, sucking relentlessly on it.

Her breasts, pressing against his chest, felt full, sensitive and tight. Instinctively, she wrapped her arms around his neck as they greedily consumed each other. She tasted every inch of his mouth while pressed against him, feeling the way his body had hardened beneath her bottom.

The kiss went on and on as his mouth continued to take hers, skillfully, thoroughly, tantalizing every bone in her body and making her conscious of just what a master he was at igniting sensations.

And they were ignited—by sensations she had never felt before. She was experiencing the emotions of a woman and not a sixteen-year-old girl. In reality, this was her first taste of passion and Chance was delivering it in grand style.

There was a need hammering deep within her that she didn't understand, but evidently Chance did, since he seemed to sense just what she wanted, just what she needed, even if she wasn't certain. The only thing she was sure about was that he had taken their kiss to a level she hadn't known possible.

The sound of a car door slamming made her remember where they were and what they were doing. The honking of a horn indicated that someone was behind them waiting for their vehicle to move. Still, Chance took his time easing his mouth from hers. She could barely think. She could barely breathe. And she could barely break the connection of the dark eyes locked with hers.

"I think the truck is clean enough now, don't you?" he asked throatily against her moist lips with a sound that sent sensuous chills down her body.

Kylie didn't trust herself to speak at the moment. When he released her, she slid out of his lap and back across the seat. She'd read about women being kissed senseless but never in her wildest dreams had she thought such a thing was possible. Boy, had she been wrong.

She snapped her seat belt back in place as she felt the truck move forward. When they were back in the sunlight, a dose of reality struck. They'd been in the midst of making out in his truck like teenagers. She inhaled deeply, wondering how she could have let things get so out of hand.

"It was inevitable, Kylie."

She glanced over at him. Just because what he said was true didn't mean she liked hearing it.

"Please don't have any regrets," he said softly.

How could she have regrets when she had been a willing participant, just as much into the kiss as he had been? However, she did intend to have her say. "We need to have more control, Chance. How can we expect our kids to have control if we don't?"

He pulled the truck to the side and parked it, and then glanced over at her. "They're kids, but we're adults, Kylie. Our wants and needs are more defined than theirs. And a lot more profound."

"Sounds like a double standard to me."

"It's not. That kiss we shared has nothing to do with our kids. That was strictly personal, between me and you."

She stared at him, hoping he understood what she was

about to say. "I don't have any regrets about the kiss but it can't happen again, Chance."

A slow smile played across his lips. "That's easier said than done, Kylie. I tasted your response. You're a very passionate woman, moreso than you even know. You've denied yourself pleasure for a long time and now that your body has savored just a sampling, it's going to want more."

She didn't like what he was insinuating. Okay, so she had been a little greedy back there, but still, she had her morals.

"And your principles have nothing to do with it," he said as if he'd read her mind. "So don't even think it. It's about needs that are old and primitive as mankind. I have them and you have them, too."

She frowned. "And I'm supposed to jump into bed with any man just to appease him?"

"No. Only with me."

He evidently saw the startled look in her face, because he then added, "But I'm willing to wait until you're ready."

Kylie inhaled and decided it would be a waste of her time to tell him that no matter how much she had enjoyed their kiss, when it came to an affair, she would never be ready. Especially not with him.

Another night and Chance couldn't sleep a wink. But at least tonight he wasn't being kept awake wondering how it would be to kiss Kylie since he'd gotten a real down-to-earth experience earlier that day.

And it had been better than he'd imagined.

The moments their lips had connected he had felt a slow sizzle all the way to his toes. The more he'd kissed her, the more she had wiggled closer for a better connection, and while his truck was getting the wash it really hadn't needed, he was inside with her locked in his arms, and getting hotter by the second.

She had felt like she belonged in his arms and the firm breasts that had been pressed against his chest had felt like they were meant to touch him that way. More than once he had been tempted to ease his hand under her blouse and cup her breasts, massage them, lift her blouse and lower his head and actually taste them.

The only reason he had finally lifted his mouth from hers had been to breathe in some air. He had heard the car behind them blowing the horn but he would have stayed right there and ignored the sound if he hadn't needed to breathe. What he'd told her was true. She was one responsive woman but he hadn't meant it as a bad thing. He was beginning to realize that everything about Kylie Hagan was all good.

He glanced over at the clock. It was a few minutes past eleven. He wondered if she was still awake. He reached for the phone, deciding there was only one way to find out.

Trying to get to sleep that night was torture for Kylie. The vivid memory of their kiss in Chance's truck, her sitting in his lap while his tongue stroked her mouth into sweet heaven, kept her wide awake.

She remembered the feel of her breasts, their fullness, their sensitivity, and how at one point she had wanted his lips to bestow the same magic on them that he was giving her mouth. Then there was the feel of his body growing hard beneath her bottom. She would have given anything to feel that same erection cradled into the V of her thighs.

Feeling frustrated in the worst possible way, she was about to get out of bed when her telephone rang. She reached over and picked it up. "Hello."

"I just wanted to hear your voice one more time tonight."

Kylie breathed deeply at the seductiveness of Chance's tone. She had wanted to hear his voice again, too, but hadn't had the nerve to call him. He was definitely bolder than she.

"Kylie?"

She swallowed hard before saying, "I'm here."

"Yes, but I wish you were here."

She shook her head. "That's not a good idea."

"Your opinion and not mine."

"We all have opinions."

"Yes, and we all have the capability of getting a good night's sleep. At least some of us do."

She lifted her eyebrows. Was he having trouble sleeping as well? "Try counting sheep."

"I tried that and it didn't work. Any more suggestions?"

She pulled herself up in bed and relaxed against the huge pillow. "We could talk."

"About what?"

"Anything you want to talk about—except what happened this afternoon."

There was a pause, and then he said, "Okay, fair enough. I'll let you choose the topic."

"All right. Tell me about Marcus. Whenever I ask Tiffany about him the only words she can fix her mouth to say are, 'Oh, he's simply wonderful.'"

Chance chuckled. "Hey, I'm the kid's father. Do you expect me to admit to any of his flaws? If she thinks he's wonderful, then who am I to disagree?"

"Be serious, Chance."

Evidently there was something he sensed in her voice that let him know she needed to know about Marcus before actually meeting him on Sunday.

"On a scale of one to ten with ten being exceptional, I'll

give Marcus a nine. He isn't perfect but for the past six-teen years he has been a son any father would be proud to claim. He's smart, and he's also sensitive, something he inherited from his mother. Cyndi was a warm, loving and sensitive person."

The undisguised love she heard in his voice let her know that he had cared for his wife very much. "How old was Marcus when his mother died?"

"He was nine and he took her death hard. Thankfully, he had my parents, Cyndi's parents and my brothers and cousins. Still, there were times when I worried about him. I made Cyndi a promise the day before she died that I would do everything within my power to make sure that Marcus had all the opportunities that we either didn't have or didn't take advantage of, especially when it came to college."

She nodded. No wonder he was so intense about his son staying focused to get into a good university.

"Marcus knew of his mother's dreams for him and after she died it was as if he was trying to honor her memory by doing everything that she'd wanted. He was always at the top of his class, and I never had to remind him to do homework. He tried so hard to please me because I think in his mind, pleasing me meant pleasing his mom as well."

"And then here comes Miss Tiffany…"

Chance chuckled again and in her mind she could actu-ally see a smile lighting up his eyes. "Ahh, yes, here comes Miss Tiffany. But before Tiffany came football. I hadn't wanted him to play. I had played in school and I knew how grueling practice could be. I wasn't sure Marcus could han-dle it and still keep his grades up. I think that was the first time the two of us butted heads."

After a pause he said, "Luckily he had his uncles on his side. It took my brothers to make me see that I was being unrealistic and that it wasn't all about making good grades. Marcus had a few more years in high school to go, and kids these days need to be well-rounded and I was keeping him from being that."

"So he started playing football?"

"Yes, and the girls started calling...and calling and calling. My phone was a regular hotline. But I think they annoyed him more than captivated his interest. At least until Tiffany."

"Tiffany used to call your house all the time?" Kylie asked, somewhat surprised.

"No, and that's what's so strange. I can't recall her ever calling. That's why I was taken aback when I found that note and was stumped further when Marcus told me, in no uncertain terms, just how he felt about her. It was as if she appeared one day out of the clear blue sky."

Kylie nodded. It was as if Marcus had appeared out of the clear blue sky as well. He'd definitely been one well-kept secret.

"Now it's your turn."

"My turn?" Kylie echoed.

"Yes, to tell me all about Tiffany so I can be prepared."

Kylie's lips tilted into a smile. "I don't think anyone can ever get fully prepared for Tiffany. She's smart, funny and extremely outgoing. An extrovert if you've ever seen one. I think that's why she's having trouble making friends at school since we moved here. I don't think the kids know how to take her. They see her genuinely exuberant nature as being insincere and phony."

Kylie's smile then widened. "There is, however, something that I do think you should know."

"What?"

"I told Tiffany that as Marcus's father you would want what was best for him."

"And?"

"And she feels certain that you're going to like her when the two of you meet because she is definitely the best."

Chance laughed. "Sounds like a person with a lot of confidence."

"A little too much at times. It comes from her dad's side of the family."

"Hey, there's nothing wrong with having an overabundance of confidence."

"Remember you said that when you meet her on Sunday."

There was a hint of amusement in Chance's voice when he said, "I will. And by the way, is there anything you need for me to bring?"

"Yes, a lot of prayer just in case Tiffany and Marcus don't want to go along with our plans for them."

"Hello."

"Marcus, are you awake?"

Marcus clutched the phone as he buried his head back underneath his pillow. "Tiffany, it's Saturday morning. Nobody gets up before eight on Saturdays."

"I do. Some of us have chores to do and the earlier they get done the better. I only called this time of the morning because you said your dad always plays basketball every Saturday morning with his brothers, and you told me to call if I had anything to report."

Marcus removed the pillow. She had gotten his attention. "And you have something to report?"

"Yes. Your dad called here last night. And it was late."

Marcus lifted a curious eyebrow. "How do you know?"

"Your phone number showed up on our caller ID this morning and it showed the time as close to midnight. That means our parents are talking after-hours. That's a good sign."

"But what if he just called to get directions to your house or something?"

"At midnight? Think positive, Marcus."

"Okay. But we should be able to tell if anything is going on when we see them together tomorrow, right?"

"I hope so, Marcus."

"Yeah, I hope so, too, considering how much of a pain in the butt I've been to my dad over the past week."

Chapter 5

By the time Chance and Marcus arrived at Kylie's home on Sunday evening, Chance was chomping at the bit to see her again.

The moment they pulled into her driveway, he saw her standing in the backyard in front of a barbecue grill. Kylie looked up the moment she heard his truck and their gazes connected. His gut clenched when an irrepressible smile lit her face.

"Wow! Tiffany was right. Her mom is a knockout," Marcus said with such profound amazement that Chance sharply turned his head to look at his son.

Marcus's gaze was glued to Kylie, so Chance let himself stare at her, too, letting his eyes roam over her features. Kylie was a beautiful woman, and that was the main reason he—a man known to have good self-control—had been in such a bad way since meeting her. She was wearing a sun-dress and the turquoise color flattered her.

"Isn't she pretty, Dad?"

Chance swallowed. In his book she was more than pretty, or beautiful or even gorgeous. There wasn't a word he had to define just what she was, although the word *perfection* came pretty close. And not for the first time he wondered how she'd succeeded in keeping men at bay all these years.

"Dad?"

He knew his son was waiting on his response but he dared not look at Marcus for fear of him recognizing the lust in his eyes. "Yes, she's pretty."

Moments later, Marcus asked, "Aren't we going to get out?"

Feeling a lot more confident that he had regained a semblance of control, Chance glanced over at Marcus. "You sound rather anxious."

Marcus chuckled. "I am. I want you to meet Tiffany. She's really something else."

Chance nodded as he opened the door to the truck, thinking that, evidently, it ran in the family, because he thought Kylie was something else as well.

As Kylie watched Chance get out of the truck, she could no more stop the flash of desire and excitement that raced through her body than she could have denied her next breath. And to make matters worse, Chance's eyes were glued to her and she knew he was remembering their kiss as much as she was.

She had thought about it a dozen times since it had happened. Her response to him had surprised her, overwhelmed her, until she'd come to grips with the fact that Chance Steele wasn't your typical man.

Today he was wearing a pair of jeans and a crisp white shirt, and it was the first time she'd seen him dressed in

anything other than a suit. He looked the epitome of masculinity, fine and sexy.

She forced her gaze from him to the young man walking by his side. So this was Marcus, the potential root of
her troubles. He favored Chance and was almost as tall.
He had the look of youth, but like his father, Marcus's
features were sharp and well-defined. And she was glad
to see that he eschewed the popular baggy pants and was
dressed neatly in a pair of shorts and a shirt. It wasn't lost
on her that he was checking her out with as much curiosity as she was him.

"I hope we aren't too early," Chance said, breaking into
Kylie's thoughts when they reached her.

They *were* early; a good thirty minutes to be exact, but
she didn't have any complaints. "No, Mr. Steele, you're
right on time," she said, addressing him formally. They had
decided not to let the kids know they had been in constant
communication with each other. They didn't want to run
the risk of Marcus and Tiffany thinking they were gaming
and plotting behind their backs, even if they were.

"Tiffany is inside getting dressed and I was setting up
the grill. I hope hamburgers and hot dogs sound okay."

Chance chuckled. "You aren't trying to pay me back
with the hamburgers, are you?"

"Pay you back for what?" Marcus asked.

Both Chance and Kylie glanced at him. "Nothing,"
Chance said quickly, clearing his throat. She knew he hadn't
meant to let that slip.

"You must be Marcus," she said and then gave him her
full attention and offered him her hand.

His grin was unrepentant as he took it. "Yes, ma'am.
And you've got to be Tiffany's mom. You're pretty just
like her."

Kylie smiled. This kid was a real charmer and before the evening was over she intended to see if his charm was the real thing or not. "Thanks."

"Do you need our help with anything, Ms. Hagan?" Chance asked, glancing around at her big backyard.

Kylie looked up at him and smiled. "I think it would be fitting if you called me Kylie, that is if you don't mind me calling you Chance."

He smiled. "No, I don't mind at all."

"In that case, Chance, there is this one little thing I might need help with. Tiffany thought it would be a good idea to put up the volleyball net in case anyone was interested in playing after dinner. If I can get you and Marcus to set it up, that would be wonderful."

"Consider it done. Just tell us where it is and where you want it to go."

"It's over there and I think that would be a good spot," she said, turning to point to an area of her yard.

"I think so, too. That should be fun. I haven't played volleyball in years."

"Should I be worried about that, Dad? I don't think we have anything for sore, aching muscles at home," Marcus said, grinning.

Chance's mouth curved into a smile as he glanced over at his son. "I might be a lot older than you, Marcus Pharis Steele, but I think I can still manage to hit a ball or two over a net."

That's not all he's capable of doing, Kylie thought, shifting her gaze from Chance to Marcus. No matter what disagreements they might have had since Tiffany had appeared on the scene, it was rather obvious that Chance and his son had a close relationship.

"You're going to have to prove that big-time, Dad."

"Hey, kid, you're on," Chance countered and then turned his attention to Kylie. "What do you think?"

"I think that this I got to see," she told him, laughing.

"You'll more than see it. I want your participation as well. The young against what this pup considers as 'the old'. I think we need to show our children just what we're made of. How about it, Kylie?"

She grinned. "I'm game if you are."

"Mr. Steele?"

Chance cast a quick glance over his shoulder, blinked and did a double take. He turned around and blinked again, shaking his head in disbelief. He looked into the face of what had to be a younger version of Kylie. Her daughter looked so much like her it was uncanny. He watched as her mouth curved into the same type of smile Kylie wore.

He automatically smiled back. "Yes, and you must be Tiffany," he said, taking the hand she offered. "Marcus has told me a lot about you."

"And it was all good, right?"

Chance chuckled, remembering what Kylie had said about her daughter's high confidence level. "Yes, it was all good."

She glanced around. "And where is Marcus?"

"I sent him to the store to pick up some more sodas."

"Oh. Mom told me to tell you that she'll be back outside in a minute. She's finishing up the potato salad and thought I should come out and keep you company."

He smiled. "That would be nice since I'd like to get to know you. So what are your plans for the future?" he asked as he leaned against the stone post holding up the covered patio. Kylie had assigned him the task of cooking the hamburgers and hot dogs, something he had convinced her he was pretty good at.

Tiffany laughed. "You don't have to worry about me and Marcus rushing off doing anything stupid when we become of age, like getting married or something."

Chance grimaced. God, he hoped not. "That's good to hear. What about the two of you making plans to cut school again?"

She grinned. "Okay, I admit that wasn't a smart idea, but like I told Mom, our last two periods of the day are boring."

Chance folded his arms across his chest and regarded her directly. "And I'm sure your mom told you that it doesn't matter how boring the classes are, you and Marcus belong in school."

Tiffany's expressive eyes filled with remorse. "Yes, sir, and Marcus and I talked about it. We didn't intend to get you and my mom upset with us, but Mom thinks I'm too young to start dating and you—"

When it seemed that she had encountered some difficulty in finishing what she was about to say, Chance lifted an eyebrow. "I'm what?"

She leaned in closer and squinted her eyes against the smoke coming from the grill. "Don't take this personally, Mr. Steele, and Marcus says you're a nice dad and everything, but at times you can be too overbearing where his education is concerned."

Chance couldn't help but laugh. He was being told that he was overbearing by a fifteen-year-old girl! She might have inherited her high confidence level from her father but her directness had definitely come from her mother. "Marcus thinks I'm overbearing, does he?"

"Yes, and you don't have to be, you know. Marcus is one of the smartest guys I know. In fact, the way we became such good friends is because the teacher had him help me on a class assignment that I was having problems with. He wants to go to the best college one day, just like you want him to. You're just going to have to trust him to do the right thing. And he will because he wants those things for himself as well as for you."

Chance's smile widened. Tiffany's expressive eyes had gone from being filled with remorse to being filled with sincerity and he liked that. He also liked what she was saying, and had to admit that his curiosity was piqued about something. "And where will all this leave you, Tiffany?"

"Me?"

"Yes, you. Where will that leave you when Marcus goes off to college two years from now?" Assuming your relationship lasts that long, he wanted to add.

Tiffany shrugged. "When he leaves I'll have another year of school to complete and then I'll be leaving for college myself. I doubt it will be to the same college Marcus will be attending since my grades aren't nearly as good as his, but it won't matter. Marcus and I have decided that the best thing for us to do is to make sure we both get a good college education. Then we will return home afterward and be together."

Chance's eyebrows drew together in surprise. The last time he and Marcus had talked, his son had threatened to hang around Charlotte and go to a local college. He released a satisfied sigh. He was certainly glad to hear this recent turn of events and was about to tell her so when they heard his truck pulling into the driveway, which meant Marcus had returned.

"Mr. Steele, Marcus and I can finish cooking if you want to go into the house and keep my mom company. I'm sure she's bored making the potato salad."

Thoughts of being inside the house alone with Kylie had his mind reeling. "You think so?"

"Yes."

He rubbed his chin thoughtfully. "Have you told your mom what you and Marcus have decided about your futures?"

"No, not yet."

"Do you mind if I do?"

"No, I don't mind. It's not like me and Marcus won't be girlfriend and boyfriend until he leaves for college, because we will. But we won't let anything interfere with him going away to a good university, I can assure you of that. We want what's best for our future." Then with a smile on her face she said, "I'll go help Marcus with the sodas."

Chance watched her walk away, thinking he really liked Tiffany Hagan.

"So what do you think?" Tiffany whispered to Marcus while helping him unload the soda from the truck.

Marcus grinned. "I think my dad likes your mom. In fact I have a feeling that they may have seen each other another time in addition to that day he visited her flower shop."

"What makes you think that?"

"Because they're too friendly with each other to have met only that one time. And then there was this private joke they shared."

"What private joke?"

"It had something to do with hamburgers."

"Hamburgers?" Tiffany raised a confused brow. "So you think he likes her?"

"He definitely notices that she's a woman, which is more attention than he's given other ladies, including those at church who are always vying for his and my uncle Morgan's and my uncle Donovan's attention. They know it's a lost cause with Uncle Bas since he's already engaged."

After placing the soda cans in the cooler, Marcus continued. "When we pulled up today and I saw your mom for the first time, I commented on how pretty she was and he agreed with me. And he kept staring at her with this funny look on his face. He's been smiling a lot since he got here. I don't recall ever seeing my dad smile this much."

Marcus then gave Tiffany a questioning glance. "You do think we're doing the right thing, don't you? Making our parents think something is going on between us so we can get them interested in each other?"

Tiffany nodded her head. "Yes, I think we're doing the right thing. I have to admit that at first I was doing it just to get Mom off my back because I thought she needed a life, but today she was actually humming. She was humming because she's in a good mood, and I think the reason she's in a good mood is because of you and your dad's visit. Seeing her that way made me realize just how lonely my mom probably has been. All she's ever had is me. Like I told you, I don't ever recall her dating anyone. In a few years I'll be leaving for college and she'll be all alone if she doesn't meet someone and get serious about him."

Marcus nodded. "Yeah, Dad will be all alone when I leave for college, too, in two years. He has his parents and his brothers and cousins but it won't be the same. He needs to get involved with a nice lady like your mom. I really like her."

When they reached the backyard, Marcus glanced around. "Speaking of our parents, where are they?"

Tiffany's face glowed with excitement when she said, "My mom is inside making the potato salad, and I suggested to your dad that he go inside and keep her company, and that you and I were capable of doing the cooking."

Marcus smiled down at her. "It seems our plan just might be working."

Tiffany tipped her head back and looked up at him, returning his smile. "Yes, it certainly appears that way. Now it's going to be up to us to make sure they get to spend more and more time together."

Chance strode into Kylie's house, rounded the corner that led from the utility room to the kitchen and stopped dead in his tracks. For the first time in his life, he forgot how to breathe.

Kylie was standing on a stool trying to get something out of a top cabinet. Stretching upward, the sundress she was wearing had raised, showing off a pair of luscious hips and those legs of hers that he admired so much.

His conscience gave him a hard kick. He shouldn't be standing in the middle of her kitchen ogling her this way. The truth of the matter was that he couldn't help it. The tantalizing sight of her had captured his attention and wouldn't let go. Pure, unadulterated hunger filled his gaze, keeping him focused primarily on her. She had a gorgeous body and, with the fantasies playing around in his head, he could just imagine his hands all over it, followed by his mouth.

He inhaled deeply when he felt his body getting hotter by the second. The need to escape back outside suddenly overwhelmed him. He had to get out of there, right now, this very instant, before he went up in flames or—even worse—before he did something outside of his control like cross the room, snatch her off that stool and take her into his arms and kiss her senseless.

* * *

Kylie wasn't certain if she'd heard a sound behind her or if her own body had alerted her to the fact that Chance was near. Whichever it was, she turned around so fast that she almost slipped off the step stool and had to fight to regain her balance.

Within an instant she was gathered into strong arms, avoiding a possible fall.

"You okay?"

The soft husky words from Chance's lips that fanned against her temple raised her temperature ten degrees. "Yes, I'm okay. You startled me. I hadn't heard you come in."

Instead of offering her any kind of explanation, he simply nodded as he held her body in his strong arms. For the next couple of seconds her mind questioned the sanity of them standing in her kitchen that way. What if the kids walked in?

She panicked at that possibility. "I'm okay, Chance. You can put me down now," she said, although she knew her voice lacked conviction.

"Are you sure you're okay?" he asked, his tone deep and rich, and his gaze remaining steadily on hers.

No, Kylie thought. She wasn't sure. Desire, the likes of which she'd never encountered before, raced through her, igniting her awareness, her attraction and her fire. Her eyes locked with his and at that instant she felt safe and protected in his arms, even with the feel of his body growing hard beneath her, which reminded her of the kiss they had shared Friday at the car wash.

With her teeth she caught the edge of her bottom lip, thinking she was just where she had dreamed of being last night—in his arms. Would it be so terrible if she stayed there just a little longer?

"Where are the kids?" she asked softly, tilting her head back and not breaking eye contact.

"Outside, cooking the rest of the meat."

"That should take at least five minutes."

"I'm counting on at least ten," he said.

She felt him sliding her down his body, lowering her feet to the floor. But he kept his hand at her waist, not intending for her to go anywhere out of touching distance. When she was standing, her legs automatically parted slightly to gain her balance; ironically it was just enough room for him to pull her close and place his thigh between them. She felt him again, the hardness of his erection that was resting between her legs.

"Why didn't you let me know that you had come inside?" she asked as intense heat shot up her core.

An apologetic smile touched his lips. "I couldn't have spoken even if I had wanted to, Kylie. Seeing you on that stool like that had me barely breathing. Has anyone ever told you that you've got one hell of a nice figure?"

She tried not to be touched by the thought that he liked the way her body looked. "Yes, but it never really mattered."

"Oh."

"Until now."

He bent toward her. "You're sure?"

"Positive."

He intended to be certain of that. Moving his hand to the swell of her hips, he gently pulled her closer as he leaned down and slanted his mouth over hers. She tasted sweeter than he remembered and he was helpless to do anything but deepen the kiss. He knew the exact moment she placed her arms around his neck, bringing their bodies closer into a locked embrace.

What he was sharing with her was a degree of passion

he hadn't shared with any woman in over seven years, and he was desperate for anything and everything she was offering. He suddenly felt it, a primitive need to bind her to him in the most elemental way. But he also knew he wanted more from her than just her body. He wanted her mind and soul as well.

The sound of their kids' laughter came through the closed window and they parted quickly, but he didn't release her. Resting his forehead against hers, he breathed in deeply, seeing the passionate look in her eyes and knowing it mirrored his own.

He motioned his head toward the back door. "You don't think they're outside burning our dinner, do you?" he asked, making an attempt at gaining control.

"I hope not," she replied, trying to breathe again normally.

"I came inside to keep you company. Tiffany suggested it."

"Did she?"

"Yes. Is that a bad thing?"

"Only if it meant doing so would give her more time alone with Marcus."

Chance gave her an incredibly sexy smile. "I didn't think of that. But I guess there's only so much they can do outside in the open."

Kylie smiled. "Thank heavens for that."

"And she happened to mention something to me that she said she hadn't told you about yet."

"What?" she asked, her voice barely above a whisper, hoping whatever it was would not make her fall dead in a faint. She had asked, and Tiffany, although upset with her for asking, had assured her that she was still a virgin.

Evidently Chance heard the panic in her voice and an

easy smile touched his lips. "Relax, Kylie, that isn't it. Far from it."

"Thank goodness for that."

"I personally don't think they've taken their relationship to that level, which is a good thing. In fact I'm a little more confused than before by what she said, although it pleases me."

"Dammit, Chance, don't keep me hanging," Kylie said in a near desperate voice. "What did Tiffany tell you?"

"Our kids have decided that although they intend to remain girlfriend and boyfriend, they also intend to further their education by going off to college, after which they'll return here and then decide their future."

Kylie blinked. "Are you sure that's what she said?"

"I'm positive."

She shook her head. "It doesn't make sense. Earlier this week she was ranting and raving about how madly in love they were and nothing and no one would ever break them apart."

"I heard the same thing from Marcus. I guess they sat down and talked about it and in the end decided to take our advice. They were getting too serious way too fast."

"Whatever made them decide to slow things down, I'm extremely grateful for it. Do you think we still need to lay out the rules we came up with?"

Chance nodded. "They may think this way now but it might be a different story tomorrow. Besides, either way, there's plenty of trouble they can get into before Marcus actually leaves for school in two years."

And it was the kind of trouble Kylie was definitely familiar with. She agreed with Chance. It wouldn't hurt to let the kids know exactly where she and Chance stood and how they planned on handling the situation of them being a couple.

"Ready to go outside?" he asked.

"Just about. I just need to find that lid for the bowl of potato salad. That's what I was looking for when you came in."

"Then let me look for it."

Kylie watched as he crossed the room and, not needing a stool, reached up and opened the cabinet. He pulled out several lids. "Will one of these work?"

"Yes."

He placed them on the counter then crossed the room to her. He reached out and caressed his finger against her cheek. "Thanks for the kiss, Kylie. I needed it more than you will ever know."

He really didn't have to thank her. She'd needed it just as much as he had, although she wished she hadn't. "I think we need to get back outside now."

As much as Chance wanted to stay inside with her, a part of him knew she was right. "All right. Is there anything else you need for me to do before I go?"

A smile touched her lips. "No, but it might be a good idea for you to wipe your mouth. You're wearing the same shade lipstick I'm wearing."

"Now that the both of you are well fed, there's something Chance and I would like to discuss with you."

Both Marcus and Tiffany looked up from eating their ice cream. Marcus's smile faltered somewhat and Tiffany rolled her eyes heavenward. "I knew this day was going too good to last," she said. "What do you want to talk with us about, Mom?"

"Your relationship."

"What about it, Ms. Hagan?" Marcus asked her in a respectful tone.

Kylie glanced over at Chance, who nodded for her to continue. "Chance and I talked about the best way to approach the situation, especially since Tiffany isn't old enough to date yet."

"But I should be old enough, Mom. The other girls at my school began going out with boys when they were thirteen."

Kylie frowned. "I'm not going to discuss what the other girls are doing, Tiffany. You're my concern. And for me it's not a particular age but a maturity level. I personally don't think you're ready to begin dating."

"If you had your way I would never date!"

"That's not true. You're the one who has to prove to me that you're ready. But Chance and I do understand you and Marcus would like to spend some time together, so we came up with what we feel is a workable solution."

"And what solution is that?" Marcus asked when Tiffany refused to do so.

It was Chance who responded. "You and Tiffany can date only if the dates are chaperoned."

Tiffany glanced over at Marcus before looking back at their parents. "You mean that you'll be coming with us to the movies? Bowling? On picnics?"

"Yes," Kylie answered. "So what do you think?" She braced herself for her daughter's tirade.

"I think it's a wonderful idea," Tiffany said, smiling.

Kylie blinked. "You do?"

"Yes. Since Marcus and I will be getting married after college, I think it would be good that all four of us get to know each other." She smiled at Marcus. "Don't you agree, Marcus?"

He smiled back at Tiffany. "Right, and in the process we can prove to our parents just how responsible we are."

Kylie glanced over at Chance knowing he was just as confused as she was. Tiffany and Marcus were beaming. If anything, Kylie and Chance had thought their suggestion would be met with some pretty strong opposition.

"Well, if everyone agrees with our plan then that's great," he said.

"So how soon can we go someplace?" Tiffany asked excitedly.

"Where would you like to go?" Chance asked.

"Umm, I've never been camping and Marcus said you take him all the time."

Kylie rolled her eyes. "Tiffany, we're not talking about a family outing. We're talking about a date."

"I don't have a problem with Tiffany coming along the next time Marcus and I go camping," Chance said. "Of course, that means that you'll have to come, too, Kylie."

"Yes, Mom. You've never been camping before, either."

"Yes, but that doesn't mean we can just invite ourselves on a camping trip, Tiffany."

"But Mr. Steele invited us."

"Yes, but only after you—"

"It's okay, Kylie, honest," Chance cut in to say. "Marcus and I would love for you and Tiffany to go camping with us. My family owns a cabin in the mountains so we're really not talking about roughing it too much. The cabin has two bedrooms, so you and Tiffany can take one and Marcus and I can take the other."

"I'm not sure that's a good idea," Kylie said as her gaze moved from one person to the next. "When Chance and I thought of supervised activities we didn't mean anything that involved staying any place overnight."

"Yes, but it would be fun and different, Mom, and you and I have never done anything fun and different."

Kylie leaned back in her chair. She thought the two of them had done several things that were fun and different. How about that train ride from New York to California a few years ago? And then there was that vacation to Disney World for Tiffany's twelfth birthday. Had it really been three years ago? Okay, so they hadn't actually spent a lot of time doing fun and different things together on a regular basis. But she really hadn't had the time since she'd been busy going to school and trying to move up the corporate ladder to provide for her and Tiffany.

"Please, Mom, just this once. Mr. Steele did say it would be okay."

Kylie glanced over at Chance. "Are you sure you don't mind?"

He smiled. "No, I don't mind. In fact I think it's a wonderful idea."

Chance's statement should have had a calming effect on her but it didn't. She was no longer concerned for Tiffany, but for herself. She didn't want to think about a weekend spent in a mountain cabin with Chance in such close quarters. With all the heat they could generate, the kids might think something was going on between them when it really wasn't.

"Well, Mom?"

The enthusiasm she heard in Tiffany's voice almost made her say yes, but a part of her held back. This was something she needed to really think about.

Instead of answering Tiffany, she looked over at Chance. "Let me think about it some more and I'll give you my answer within a week."

Chapter 6

With a sigh of resignation, Chance walked into his office Monday morning and met his brothers' inquisitive gazes. He knew why they were there. Marcus had mentioned to them that they'd been invited to Kylie's for dinner and no doubt they wanted to know how things went. But he wouldn't make it easy for them. He would pretend that he hadn't a clue why they graced his office with their presence.

"Good morning. Is there any reason the three of you have taken over my office?" he asked, placing his brief-case down on his desk.

After a few moments, when no one replied, he exhaled a long sigh and said, "I don't recall us having a meeting this morning. I know I have a meeting with Bas later today, but what's up with you guys? Is anything wrong?"

Not surprisingly, it was Bas who stepped forward and said, "How about cutting the bull, Chance. You know why we're here. We want to know how things went yesterday."

Chance looked at him. "Was there a particular way they were supposed to go?"

"You tell us," Morgan said, frowning. "You were the one who was all bent out of shape last week when you found that note. Can we assume you blew things out of proportion and Tiffany Hagan isn't the threat to our nephew's future that you assumed she was?"

Chance leaned back in his chair. A part of him wanted to tell his brothers that Tiffany was no longer a threat but her mother definitely was. But there was no way he could do that and have a moment's peace from their inquisition. "No, Tiffany's not a threat and although I'm not going to say I overreacted, I will say that I think Kylie and I have everything under control."

Donovan quirked an eyebrow. "Kylie?"

"Yes, Kylie Hagan. Tiffany's mother."

Donovan smiled. "Oh, yeah, the one who's such a good-looker."

A dark scowl suddenly appeared on Chance's face and he leaned forward. "And how do you know that Kylie is good-looking?"

Donovan was taken back by the bite in his brother's tone. "You told us, don't you remember? In fact your exact words were, 'If the daughter looks anything like the mother then I'm in trouble.'"

"Oh." Too late, Chance recalled having said that. He leaned back in his chair again, ignoring the curious glances his brothers were now giving him.

"You know what, Chance?"

Chance glanced over at Morgan and frowned. "What?"

A smile curved Morgan Steele's lips. "I hate to tell you this, but I have a feeling that you've gotten yourself into some trouble."

* * *

"So there you have it, Chance," Bas was saying after handing him the written report. "I'm glad to say that considering everything, we're doing well. Although some of our competitors have gotten bruised by the severe trading conditions of the past few years, we've been successful because we're a company that sets the pace and doesn't just follow the trend. Still, whether we like it or not, sooner or later we're going to have to give some thought to the possibility of outsourcing in order to stay competitive. I don't like it any more than you, but that's the way things are going now and we need to continue to adapt to change, even change we don't particularly like."

Chance tossed the report on his desk. Bas was right. He didn't like the thought of outsourcing as a means to stay ahead of the game. With the new importance being placed on countries like India and China, for the past year he'd seen huge restructuring taking place in a number of manufacturing and production companies.

As the corporation's problem solver and troubleshooter, Bas kept them in the know. He was an expert at tackling the company's complex problems. So far the Steele Corporation was not unionized because, during the twenty-five years of its existence, the employees had always been pleased with the fair treatment they'd received. Their salaries were more than competitive, and the Steele Corporation had a reputation of never having laid off an employee, even during some of the company's rough times.

However, according to Bas, there was talk in the production area that the Steele Corporation would be outsourcing to a foreign country.

"I'm still not ready to go that route, Bas. Our employees are loyal and we owe them for all the hard work they do.

Our people are the reason this company is successful, not the products we produce and deliver. What we're going to have to do is to continue to focus on developing our employees and executing those manufacturing strategies that integrate people, processes and technologies to assure us tangible results. Until that stops happening, I refuse to entertain the thought of outsourcing to another country."

Bas smiled. "I fully agree with you. So what do we do about those rumors that we're headed that way the first of the year?"

"Before I leave for Dallas next week, how about setting up a meeting between me and the production department heads? I want to make sure they're delivering the same message to our employees. There's evidently a communication breakdown somewhere. And make sure you include Vanessa. She will be back in the office then," Chance said of his cousin Vanessa Steele, who headed the PR Department and was presently vacationing in Europe.

"All right. Consider it done."

Chance studied his brother as Bas placed the items back into his briefcase. Bas was a hard worker—too dedicated at times since he lived, ate and breathed the Steele Corporation. That would make one wonder when he had time for a social life, which he evidently had since he was engaged to be married. "Seems to me that you need to chill more than I do, Bas."

Bas glanced up and his lips curved into a lethal half smile. "I beg to differ, Chance. You're the one who's tackling woman troubles. I'm not."

"It's hard to believe Cassandra is that understanding."

Bas shrugged. "Frankly, she's not but she knows how far to take her complaints."

A frown pulled at Chance's lips. Not for the first time

he wondered what had possessed his brother to become engaged to Cassandra Tisdale, a staunch member of Charlotte's elite social group. Cassandra and Bas were as different as day and night. The woman was so incredibly self-absorbed, it boggled Chance's mind that Bas had even given her the time of day, let alone become engaged to her. She had a tendency to think she was the most important thing that existed in this universe. And while she was shining and polished, it was known that Bas was more than a little rough around the edges and had a few tarnished spots on his reputation from a few years back. But Cassandra was determined to do something nobody had ever been able to do—make Sebastian Steele sparkle.

Chance and his two brothers wondered how in the hell she planned to accomplish such a feat. If nothing else, they would give her an A for trying. They knew, even if she didn't, that it would be a wasted effort. The woman who would eventually capture Bas's heart would be the one who accepted him as he was, and not try to make him into something that he wasn't.

"Dinner is at six tonight, if anyone is interested," Chance decided to say, since his brothers had a tendency to drop by for a meal unannounced.

Bas chuckled. "I'll pass the word on to Morgan and Donovan."

"What about you?"

"I'm invited to dinner at the Tisdales'. My guess is that Cassandra's mother will try to get me to finally commit to a June wedding."

Chance nodded. That was eight months away. "Will you?"

"There's no reason for me not to, I suppose. Being engaged for almost six months is long enough, don't you think? See you later."

When the door closed behind Bas, Chance stood and walked over to the window and looked out. Deciding to rid Bas and his issues from his mind, he turned his thoughts to his own problem.

Kylie Hagan.

He couldn't help wondering whether she'd made a decision about the camping trip yet. Several times that day he'd been tempted to call her but had changed his mind.

He felt excited at the prospect of having her at the cabin for an entire weekend, even with the knowledge that their kids would be around to keep them company. It would be hard to keep his attraction to her at bay, but he would.

He figured the reason she was hesitating was because the thought of them spending the night under the same roof bothered her. She was well aware that the kids would have to go to sleep eventually, and when they did, it would be parents' time.

She was fighting the chemistry between them. He knew that just as he knew it was a fight she wouldn't win. But he would let her try, up to a certain point. He'd give her until the end of the week and if he didn't hear from her by then, he would take some necessary action.

"So, have you decided whether or not you and Tiffy are going camping with Chance Steele and his son?"

Kylie glanced up from the meal she and Lena were sharing during their weekly lunch date at a popular restaurant in town. "Who told you about that?" she asked.

Lena smiled. "Who else? My goddaughter, of course. She's all excited at the thought of going camping."

Kylie rolled her eyes. "I'm beginning to wonder if it's the camping trip that has her excited or the thought of being around Marcus an entire weekend. If it's the latter then she might as well get unexcited because if I do decide to go, I'll have my eyes on her and Marcus the entire time. Any time they spend together will definitely be supervised."

Lena couldn't help the small smile that tugged at her lips. "So you think she has an ulterior motive for wanting to go?"

"Hey, remember I was young and in love once, and when you are their age, you look for every opportunity to be together, whether you're under your parents' watchful eyes or not."

"Yes, that could very well be, but at some point you're going to have to start trusting her, Kylie. You can't continue to judge Tiffy by the way you behaved with Sam. The more you do, the more she's going to resent it."

There was anguish in Kylie's eyes and a wee hint of guilt. "It's so hard being a parent these days, Lena. You want the best for your kids and you go on the premise that experience is the best teacher, but then you're faced with the question of how you can be there to protect them without suffocating them."

Lena nodded, clearly understanding. "I think for you it's more difficult because Tiffy is all you have. Over the years she has become your life. Have you given thought to becoming involved in other things?"

"Other things like what? I have a florist shop to run, Lena. It's not like I don't have anything else to do with my time."

"Yes, but only when Tiffy is at school. Other than that you're a full-time mother who really doesn't have a life other than her child."

Kylie knew where this conversation was leading since they had been down this road several times. It was the one topic she and Lena didn't agree on. Lena felt it was a crying shame that she didn't have a man in her life and hadn't had one since high school.

Her thoughts shifted to Chance Steele and how much she had enjoyed his company on Sunday. It had felt strange sharing her time with anyone other than Tiffany, but she had to admit it had felt good, too. Too good. After they'd eaten they'd played a game of volleyball, the young against what Marcus and Tiffany had considered as "the old."

Kylie had been surprised at how much energy Chance had. The kids had been surprised, too, and she and Chance had won the game, showing Tiffany and Marcus that age was nothing but a number. Afterward, they had eaten ice cream and the cake she had baked.

As much as she had enjoyed Chance's company, she knew it out of the question for something to develop between them. There was no way she would start depending on him or any other man for her happiness. She had done so once and refused to go that route again.

"I don't want a man in my life, Lena, at least not now," she decided to say. "Maybe when Tiffany leaves for college I'll feel differently and I'll get involved with someone, but I'm not interested now." She then turned her attention back to her meal.

"Okay," Lena said, placing her glass of iced tea aside. "Tell me about Chance Steele."

Kylie looked up again, giving her friend an uncomfortable stare. "What do you want me to tell you about Chance that you don't already know?"

"Well, Tiffy couldn't stop singing his praises when I picked her up from school yesterday. He definitely made a positive impression on her. She thought he was cool and fun to be around."

Kylie smiled. "She's right. He was a lot of fun."

She quickly resumed eating her meal, afraid that Lena might see all the lust that filled her eyes. The last thing she wanted was to tell Lena that Chance was the cause of her surging hormones lately. Which was exactly why she didn't think going on a camping trip with him, Marcus and Tiffany was a good idea. The longings he stirred within her could be relentless at times, and it took all the willpower she could muster to hold on to her sanity. Her needy libido and her out-of-control hormones confined in a cabin for the weekend with Chance Steele were way too much to ignore. Especially when she'd have to stay focused on Marcus and Tiffany.

"Chance is not a bad catch you know, Kylie. He's good-looking, wealthy, intelligent and generous to a fault."

Kylie glanced up. "Umm, sounds like someone you should be interested in, then."

A sad smile tugged at Lena's lips. "You know the story of my life. Because of Mom's failing health, the two of us are a package deal and not too many men want that. At least none I've met so far. The moment I mention that I'm my mother's caretaker, they conveniently drop out of the picture. However, I do believe Chance would be different, but he and I never connected that way. I can only see him as a friend and nothing more."

Unfortunately, Kylie could see Chance as a lot more than a friend but she blatantly refused to go there. But right now, at that moment, her main concern was not the issue of her and Chance. It was Lena. She silently searched her mind for something to say that would ease the raw pain she'd heard in her best friend's words.

Propping her chin in her hand, she gave Lena a serious smile. "There's a man out there for you, Lena, who will be more than happy to take you and whatever and whoever comes along with you. I've always known that if I got interested in someone, that person would have to love Tiffany as much as he loved me. For some men it's easy to accept a package deal. For others it's not. And those who can't are the ones that women like us do better leaving alone."

Lena reached across the table and took her hand. "And I believe that there's a man out there for you, too, and believe it or not, he can be depended on. I know Sam and your dad let you down but you can't continue to judge all men by their actions, Kylie. Every young girl needs a good male role model in her life. Because of Dad's death, I missed having that, and you're cheating Tiffy of having that as well. I think as a single mom you've done an admirable job in raising her. But don't you think at some point she needs to see you in a loving relationship with a man?"

Kylie looked Lena squarely in the eye. Conversations like this tended to expose emotions that she would rather keep under wraps because along with the emotions came the memories of the hurt and pain that Sam and her father had caused.

"Even if I did, Lena, that man can't be Chance Steele. For heaven's sake, he's the father of the boy that my daughter thinks she's madly in love with."

Lena placed her elbows on the table and laced her fingers together. "And what does that have to do with anything? More specifically, what does it have to do with you and Chance?"

"I don't want to confuse her, nor do I want to send out a negative picture about anything."

Lena shook her head. "Your daughter and my goddaughter is a lot smarter and mature than you think, Kylie. Kids these days know the score. They aren't as naive as we want to think they are. If something is going on between you and Chance, she'll be able to pick up on it, and personally, I doubt if she'll see anything wrong with it."

"She might not see anything wrong with it but I will. How am I going to lecture her about the difference between love and lust when I'm having problems knowing the difference between the two myself?"

Lena smiled. "So you are attracted to Chance." It was a statement and not a question.

"Yes, more than I want to be," she said, deciding to finally be completely honest with her best friend. "Around him I feel things that I've never felt before, Lena. We've kissed. Twice. And I'm not talking about a little kiss, either. The man takes kissing to a level I've never experienced before. All he has to do is get close enough to breathe on my mouth and my lips automatically open. Isn't that pathetic? Now can you understand why I'm hesitating about going on that camping trip?"

"Yes and no."

At Kylie's confused expression, Lena explained, "Yes, I can see why you're hesitant about going, and no, I don't agree with your assessment of the situation. So what if you have the hots for Chance? You're both adults and should be able to do whatever you want to do. Your attraction to him shouldn't have any bearing on what's going on between Tiffany and Marcus and how you're handling their situation. I know you and no matter what you do, you will always set a good example in front of Tiffany. However, what you and Chance do in private is your business. But then, like I said earlier, I think it's important for Tiffy to see you in a loving relationship with a man, and I can't think of a better person for that man to be than Chance Steele."

"There are bound to be complications, Lena."

"Only those of your own making, Kylie. Take it from

someone who knows. Good men are hard to find, so if you meet one who's interested, you better grab him, hold on tight and not let go."

Later that night Kylie got into bed, wrestling with the knowledge that the main reason she didn't want to go on that camping trip was because of her growing feelings for Chance. She had to finally admit those growing feelings to herself after having lunch with Lena.

Their discussion had made her realize two things. She found Chance attractive and sexy, and thought he had a body that was all that and a bag of chips. But there was more to him than that. He'd already proven that he was dependable, unlike Sam and her father. When Chance and his girlfriend had been faced with a teen pregnancy, instead of leaving her in a fix like Sam had done to her, Chance had done the noble, honorable and responsible thing. He'd made whatever changes the situation called for to make a home for his wife and child. She could tell by his relationship with Marcus that he was a good father and from what she read in the business section of the *Charlotte Observer*, he was also a highly respected businessman. And she wanted to believe if he had shown up at her shop that day to tell her that their kids were involved in an unplanned pregnancy versus a plot to cut school, he would be angry, true enough, but nothing would make him turn his back on his only child, as her father and mother had done to her.

She sighed. One of the problems she was having trouble coming to terms with was the knowledge that their relationship—if they could call it that—had developed because of their kids. She doubted they would have met any other way. There was a strong possibility that if they'd been in the same room together at any given function, he wouldn't have given her a second look. So in her mind their meeting was a twist of fate rather than by their own choosing.

She jerked her head off the pillow at the sound of the phone ringing. The last time she had gotten a call this late it had been Chance. Sensations raced through her at that possibility and she quickly reached over and picked up the phone. "Hello."

"Sorry to call so late," Lena was saying. "But I forgot to mention today that the American Cancer Society is sponsoring their annual ball and I'm on the committee. The price of the tickets is high but it's all for a worthy cause, of course. Would you like one?"

Before Kylie could answer, Lena quickly inserted, "In fact you can get two if you like and bring a date."

"I'll take one ticket, Lena," Kylie said softly, hoping Lena didn't pick up the disappointment in her voice. A part of her had hoped the caller was Chance. She hadn't seen or talked to him since Sunday, which was three days ago.

"Sure you don't want two?"

Kylie rolled her eyes. "No, I only want *one* ticket, Lena. I won't have a date that night. Will that be a problem? I either come alone or not at all."

"No, that won't be a problem but I was hoping there was someone you could ask. Someone like Chance, perhaps?"

Kylie sighed. She knew where this conversation was leading and wasn't in the mood. "No. Only one ticket, Lena. Good night." She then hung up the phone.

A few seconds later, before Kylie could reclaim her comfortable position in bed, the phone rang again. She frowned. There were times when Lena was worse than a dog with a bone. She didn't know when to let up.

Snatching the phone, not giving her best friend a chance

to say anything, Kylie said, "Look, Lena, forget it. There's no way I'm going to ask Chance to go with me."

There was a brief pause and then...

"And just where is it that you won't ask me to go, Kylie?" Chance Steele asked in a deep, husky voice that bespoke more than mild curiosity.

Kylie's eyes widened and hot color rushed into her face. If she'd been standing she would have melted to the floor in embarrassment. Instead she found solace in burying her face under the pillow.

But even that couldn't drown out the sound of Chance's voice when he said, "Okay, Kylie, tell me. What's going on and why won't you ask me to go wherever it is that you're going?"

She closed her eyes and moaned. Her only saving grace was that she'd heard the teasing in his voice and was glad he had such a good sense of humor, even if it was at her expense.

"Kylie?"

She pulled her head from beneath the pillow. "What?"

"Are you going to tell me voluntarily or do I have to come over and tickle it out of you?"

The thought of Chance actually tickling anything out of her had a stimulating effect on her rather than an amusing one. Yet she couldn't help but smile. "I doubt if you can tickle anything out of me, Chance."

"Don't let me come over there and prove you wrong," he warned in an even huskier tone of voice.

Kylie closed her eyes and in her mind she could envision him lying in bed saying what he'd just said. He would be propped back against the pillow with a sexy smile on his lips and a teasing glint in his dark eyes.

She allowed her mind to go a little further by envisioning him lying on top of the bedcovers completely naked. Her overactive imagination spread warmth through her as she envisioned her gaze moving down his muscular chest and firm stomach before coming to rest on his exposed groin. He was hard as steel.

She inhaled deeply and wondered what it would be like to touch him there, caress his body all over, bury her face in the curve of his neck, taste his skin and nibble him in a few places to brand him hers. She would let his musky scent fill her nostrils before pressing her mouth to his, getting the deep, tongue-tangling kiss she knew awaited her. She would let her hand reach down to touch him in his most private area, feeling the heat of him, hot, hard and thick. The mere thought of seducing him that way had blood racing recklessly through her veins.

"Kylie?"

She swallowed, trying to bring her thoughts back in check. "Yes?"

"Tell me."

The sensuous tone of his voice was playing havoc on her sensibilities. She leaned back in bed, letting her body cool from the heated thoughts that had flowed through her mind earlier. Her lids lowered and for a long second she didn't say anything, wondering if she should. But she knew he wouldn't let up until she told him.

"Lena mentioned that the American Cancer Society is having their annual ball and she's on the committee," she started off by saying. "So quite naturally she's trying to get rid of as many tickets as she can. I told her I'd get a ticket to support the cause and then she tried talking me into getting two, knowing full well I wouldn't have a date that night."

"And?" he asked when she paused briefly.

That single, softly uttered word stirred an area of her body that it shouldn't have. "And...Lena suggested that I invite you."

"So that's what you meant when you screamed in my ear."

Color rushed into Kylie's face again. "Yes, that's what I meant."

"I see. Don't I have a say in the matter?"

"No. The only reason we met, Chance, is because of the kids," she said, giving voice to her earlier thoughts. "If we had been at any function together you wouldn't have noticed me. I'm not the type of woman you would have been drawn to enough to show any real interest in."

"You think not?"

"Yes."

"What if I said you're wrong?"

"We'll never know, will we?"

When he had no comeback, she said, "Besides, I don't date. I mentioned that to you before."

"Yes, you did mention it. Is that also the reason you won't go camping, because you see that as a date?"

"No, that in itself is a whole other set of problems, Chance. I just think the two of us spending a weekend at a cabin isn't a good idea, even with the kids there. Especially with the kids there."

"Why?"

"I think you know the reason without me having to go into any great detail. For some reason, we're like magnets—we attract."

"And you see that as a bad thing?"

"Yes. Our focus should be on our kids. What would Marcus think if he thought you were attracted to me?"

Chance chuckled. "He would probably think the same

thing I did when I finally got to meet Tiffany. That he has great taste. She's a nice girl and so is her mother."

Kylie couldn't help but smile, pleased with his compliment, but still... "Can't you see the problems it will cause if our kids think something is going on between us?"

"No."

"Chance," she said, moaning his name in frustration.

"Kylie. We've had this conversation before and my feelings on the matter haven't changed. We're adults and what we do is our business. In fact I think Marcus will find it strange if I'm not attracted to you. He thinks you're beautiful, so quite naturally he'll assume that I'll think you're beautiful, too. And I do. I also think you're someone I'd like to get to know better. He would assume as much as well. But you're right. The camping trip will be about Marcus and Tiffany and not about us. Our time will come later."

She wondered what he meant by that.

"Will it make you feel better if I promise to be on my best behavior when we go camping?"

Kylie shrugged. How could she explain to him that his behavior really had nothing to do with it? It was her own behavior she was concerned about. He didn't have to do anything in particular for her to get turned on. Her dilemma was the fact that just seeing him did that.

"If you don't go, you know what might happen, don't you?"

Chance's question recaptured her attention. "No, what?"

"The kids are going to feel that they can't depend on us to keep our end of the bargain. We did tell them that we would agree for them to take part in supervised activities."

"But we never said anything about overnight activities, Chance."

"Neither did we clarify they had to be only daytime activities. They won't understand what the big deal is since we will be there as chaperones. They will only see it as a cop-out on our part. I don't think it's fair to cancel out a weekend of fun for them just because we can't keep our hormones in check for forty-eight hours. It makes us sound pretty damn selfish, don't you think?"

Kylie sighed deeply. It hadn't before, but since he'd put it that way, yes, it did make them—her in particular—sound selfish. Tiffany had never gotten the chance to go camping. Kylie had been too overprotective to even let her go with the Girl Scouts that time when she was ten. And now all her daughter wanted was to experience her first camping trip and her selfish mother, who couldn't keep her overactive hormones in line, was standing in her way.

"Okay, you've convinced me. I'll go."

"Great! The kids will be happy."

She laughed. "Yes, I'm sure they will be."

"I'll make the arrangements for next weekend. Will that work?"

"Yes, that will work."

"And,. Kylie…?"

"Yes?"

"The kids aren't the only ones who'll be happy. I'm going to be happy as well. Good night."

Before she could say anything, he hung up the phone.

Chapter 7

A few days later Kylie was praying that at some point her life would resume a sense of normalcy. Since she'd told Tiffany of her decision to go camping, her daughter had been nothing but a bundle of mass excitement. So much, in fact, that Kylie had to wonder whether being with Marcus was the primary reason for her daughter's happiness or the camping trip itself.

With teenage exuberance, Tiffany had gone on and on about all the things she planned to do, like swimming in the lake, fishing in that same lake, having a picnic by that lake and taking oodles and oodles of pictures of that lake. And she intended to do a lot of bird watching and had even checked out a library book on the various species. Of course, that meant she would need a pair of binoculars, which her godmother had been quick to buy for her.

Kylie hadn't talked to Chance anymore until he'd called early Saturday morning saying he would drop off a list of items she might want to bring along. The cabin's kitchen was well-stocked with cooking utensils, but he thought it would be good if they cooked outside on the grill or a camp stove. He'd gone on to tell her that although the cabin had electricity, usually he and Marcus enjoyed faking it by using candles and lanterns.

Anticipating his visit, she had been a mass of nerves, and once she opened the door not even the loud wail of a fire truck siren could intrude on her jolting awareness of him. She pulled in a deep breath. And then another. Neither did a thing to stop the pounding of her heart or the barrage of sensations that overwhelmed her.

Standing before her in jogging pants, a T-shirt and a pair of what appeared to have once been expensive tennis shoes, Chance Steele was the epitome of everything hot and spicy. He looked like a man capable of doing anything he pleased, whether it was in the boardroom or in the bedroom. Especially in the bedroom. However, at that very moment she had to concede that there was nothing sophisticated about Chance's appearance. He looked like a man ready for some play time, and his darkly stubbled jaw, which meant he hadn't yet shaved that morning, only added to his sharply male features.

"Here's the camping checklist I told you about," he said, breaking into her heated thoughts.

She took the paper he handed her. "Thanks."

"The only things you'll need to bring for you and Tiffany are the items listed under the first-aid section."

She nodded and quickly scanned the list, okay with everything she saw on it until she noted the snake bite kit. She lifted her gaze back to his. The eyes that met hers were dark, sexy and full of sexual interest he wasn't trying to hide, which made her thankful for two things: that she was a woman and that she was decently dressed. "Snake bite kit?"

A smile touched his eyes. "Yes, just as an added precaution. But I have one if you have trouble finding it. It's a rather popular item this time of the year."

An uninvited shiver ran through her. That wasn't exactly what she wanted to hear. She cleared her throat. "Would you like to come in? Tiffany and I were just sitting down to breakfast. You're welcome to join us."

"No, thanks. I'm on my way to the gym. It's tradition that my brothers and I play basketball every Saturday morning. It helps get rid of any competitive frustrations we might have before the start of a new week."

She lifted a brow. "Competitive frustrations? Does that happen often?"

"I guess with four adult males it can't help but happen occasionally, given the closeness of our ages and our competitive natures. Then of course there's Donovan, who often forgets that I'm the oldest and he's the youngest."

It wasn't the first time she felt that an extreme closeness existed between the Steele brothers. It was there in his tone whenever he spoke of them. "Well, enjoy your game."

"I will. And just so you'll know, I'm catching a flight out first thing Monday morning to Dallas. I'll be there until Thursday. Marcus will be spending time with my brothers until I return."

"All right, thanks for letting me know," she said, missing him already, although she didn't want to feel that way. "Have a safe trip."

By the way he was staring at her, she knew without a doubt that if Tiffany hadn't been home he would have come inside and kissed her goodbye. That knowledge caused an ache in certain parts of her body. Their connected gazes were holding just a little too long. She knew it and was fully aware that he knew it as well.

"I'll call you," he finally whispered huskily.

Kylie nodded. A promise made and one she knew he intended to keep. "All right."

She wrapped her arms around her waist, hugging herself so she wouldn't be tempted to reach out and hug him.

He took a step back and looked deeply into her eyes one last time before turning back to his truck.

During the next four days Kylie spent her free time shopping for the items on the list Chance had given her. After that was done, Tiffany had convinced her that they needed to spruce up their wardrobes, with a collection of new outfits suitable for camping.

Kylie enjoyed this carefree, happy-go-lucky side of her daughter. It had been a long time since she'd seen it and she couldn't help but count her blessings now.

She and Tiffany returned home from one of their shopping trips rather late on Wednesday night and were in her bedroom unwrapping their numerous packages.

"Mom, can I ask you something?"

"Sure, honey, you can ask my anything."

"Why don't you have a boyfriend?"

Kylie's hand went still on the new blouse that she was about to place on the hanger. You can ask me anything but that, she wanted to say but decided it was a good question. If only she could give her daughter what she felt was a good answer. She decided to go for the truth…but only after she found out why Tiffany wanted to know.

"Why do you ask?"

"Because I think you're so pretty and all the other girls at school whose moms are single always talk about their mothers' boyfriends. In fact Trisha Nobles's mom is getting married next month."

Good for Trisha Nobles's mom, Kylie wanted to say. But she knew the only reason Tiffany had asked the question was because the answer was important to her.

"I've been too busy to have a boyfriend," she said honestly. "Running the shop takes up a lot of my time."

"But even before we moved here and you worked for that marketing firm you never went out on a date or anything."

Kylie lifted an eyebrow. "And that bothered you?"

"I really never thought about it until recently."

Kylie sat on the bed next to her daughter. "And why recently?"

"Because now I know how it feels to care for someone and I think it's sad that you never cared for anyone before. It doesn't seem right."

Kylie pulled her daughter into her arms and was mildly surprised when she came willingly. "Oh, honey, but it's okay. Some things aren't just automatic. Another reason I never went out was because I'm a very selective person."

"Nitpicky?"

Kylie laughed. "Yeah, nitpicky. Only a certain type of man appeals to me."

Tiffany pulled back and glanced up at her. "Really? And what kind is that, Mom?"

Kylie immediately thought of Chance and forced him from her mind. "First and foremost he has to be willing to be a good father to you. Then he has to treat us both good, look good, be health-conscious, fun to be around, be someone I can always depend on even during my darkest hour, and someone who loves me unconditionally."

"Unconditionally?"

"Yes. Someone who would love me no matter what and

who would take me as I am—the good, the bad and the ugly."

Tiffany smiled. "You know that's funny."

"What is, honey?"

"Marcus said he recently asked his dad why he never remarried. And it seems that he's nitpicky, too."

"Really?"

"Yes. And he gave almost the same exact answers as you did." Tiffany chuckled. "Boy, adults sure are strange."

"Strange in what way?"

Tiffany gave her mother a beaming smile. "If all of you are looking for the same thing in a person, then why is it so hard to find someone?"

Before Kylie could answer her daughter's question—not that she thought she had an answer anyway—the phone rang. Tiffany quickly picked it up. "Hello?"

Kylie watched her daughter's dark eyebrows lift curiously. "I'm fine, and yes, sir, she's here. Just a moment please."

Her daughter then stared at her with bright, penetrating eyes and whispered, "It's for you and it's Mr. Steele. He's probably calling to make sure that you got everything on that list for the camping trip this weekend."

Kylie took the phone her daughter handed her. "Yes, I'm sure that's why he's calling," she said, trying to keep her voice neutral but feeling she'd failed miserably. She hoped Tiffany hadn't picked up on anything.

"That's really nice of him to call us all the way from Texas, isn't it?"

"Yes, it is."

"Well, it's late and I have school tomorrow so I'm going to bed. Thanks for taking me shopping, Mom. Good night."

"You're welcome and good night, sweetheart."

With quiet gravity Kylie watched Tiffany leave the room, closing the door behind her. It was only then that she turned her attention back to the phone and the man waiting on the line to talk to her.

"Hello?"

"Sorry about that, Kylie. I assumed Tiffany would be in bed by now."

"Usually she is but that's okay. I took her shopping after school and we just got back a little over an hour ago."

Chance chuckled. "Must have been some shopping trip."

Kylie smiled. "Trust me, it was." She didn't want to sound too excited but she was glad to hear his voice. "How are things going?"

"Busy. This is one of those annual meetings where the CEOs of various corporations get together, leave egos at the door and work on something we all need to improve within our companies."

"And what's that?"

"Employee relations. But I didn't call to talk about that. I wanted to see how you and Tiffany were doing."

"We're fine." Actually there was something concerning her. Maybe Chance could shed some light on it. "I know Tiffany talks to Marcus every day, but I'm a little concerned about something."

"What?"

"Although I told him on Sunday that it would be okay if he wanted to visit with Tiffany for a few hours after school on occasion, he hasn't done so."

"Umm, even with football practice I'm surprised he hasn't jumped at the chance at least once. Does Tiffany seem bothered by it?" Chance asked.

"No, and I know for a fact that they aren't mad at each other." Kylie sighed. Maybe things were different with teenagers today. She and Sam had practically tried living out of each other's pockets. It had gotten so bad that he had become a regular fixture around her parents' house although they had wished otherwise.

"Maybe I'm assuming too much here, Chance, but I thought with them being so 'madly in love' that once I gave the go-ahead for supervised visits that Marcus would become a constant visitor."

"That's strange, because I know that I would."

"You would what?"

"Become a constant visitor if you ever gave me the go-ahead."

Chance's voice was hardly more than a whisper but she heard the underlying meaning loud and clear. Kylie's breath hung in her throat for a brief second and then she took a deep, calming inhale, which was followed by a series of flutters in her stomach.

"Kylie?"

"Yes?" She was glad to say anything, even that one single word, to assure her that her vocal cords were still working and they hadn't drowned in all those sensations overtaking her.

"May I ask a favor of you?" Chance asked.

"Sure," she said with a small shrug, certain he wouldn't ask her to do anything indecent or immoral.

"Would you pick me up from the airport tomorrow around lunchtime?"

Surprise flickered in the depths of her dark eyes. "You want me to pick you up?"

"Yes. My car is at the dealership getting serviced while I'm away. I can get one of my brothers to pick me up but I would like for you to…if it won't be any problem."

"No, it won't be a problem. But can I ask you something?"

"Yes."

"Why do you want *me* to do it?"

"You'll find out when I see you."

The sound of his voice held promises she wasn't sure she wanted him to keep. She'd been having a lot of mixed emotions since meeting Chance. A part of her knew that getting involved with him was not a good idea, but then another part of her—the one that lately was constantly reminding her that she was a woman with needs—was egging her on to enjoy what he was offering. At least within reason.

"All right. Would you like to give me your flight information now?" For the next minute or so, she jotted down the information that he gave her.

"Well, I'll let you go now. I'm sure the shopping trip tired you out."

"Yes, it did somewhat. I appreciate you calling."

"I told you I would. I just hope my doing so hasn't raised Tiffany's suspicions. I know how much you don't want the kids to think anything is going on between us."

"No, I don't think your call did. In fact she said she thought it was very considerate of you to call and make sure we were all set for this weekend."

"And are you all set for this weekend, Kylie?"

More than I need to be, she thought, thinking of all the new outfits she had purchased with the hopes that he'd like each and every one of them. "Yes, I found all the items on the list including the snake bite kit."

"Good girl. Now do something tonight when you go to sleep."

"What?"

"Think of me."

* * *

Chance settled back in the bed after placing the phone back in the cradle. He hadn't been able to concentrate on the summit all week, because Kylie was on his mind. Hell, for the last couple of nights, he hadn't been able to sleep a wink.

It had been during Horace Doubletree's speech that day when he'd suddenly came to the realization that it was a waste of time trying to fool himself any longer and that things for him had moved past him trying to get to know Kylie better. The truth of the matter was that he knew all he wanted to know. His heart had decided. He had fallen in love with her.

How such a thing was possible he wasn't sure; especially when the woman had been sending out conflicting signals since the day they met. She was attracted to him, although she was determined to fight that attraction every step of the way. Her independence, while a turn-on, had ironically become a major obstacle to the relationship. That meant he needed to probe deeper and somehow break through her defenses. He also needed to take one day at a time and wipe away the fifteen years of hurt and pain she'd endured and prove that with him there would only be happier days. Even without her realizing she'd been doing so, for the past couple of weeks she had been extracting an unusual type of strength from him.

A strength of will.

He'd been fighting an intense longing, a deep-rooted desire for her since that day he'd walked into her florist shop. He could now admit that the first time their eyes had connected his heart had slammed into fifth gear. No wonder lunch at the Racetrack Café had seemed fitting as a place for their first date. Even then he'd known that something special was within his grasp.

After Cyndi died he'd actually thought that he could never love another woman again. And even with the few affairs he'd indulged in over the years, he'd never allowed his emotions to go any deeper than affection or desire. Yet here he had fallen hard for a woman whom he had never actually taken out on a real date, had never slept with and had never really spent more than a few hours with at a given time. His brothers would say such a thing was utterly insane. They would call in the shrink to have his head examined, or they would take him out somewhere and beat some sense into him. But then they would one day realize that some things in life were not meant to be understood, just accepted. Today he had accepted the fact that he had fallen in love.

And he knew he had his work cut out for him.

There was more than gentle pride in every bone in Kylie's body. He knew just from the time he'd spent with her that she could be stubborn, willful and defiant. That was all well and good if she was dealing with any other man than him. But he refused to wait around for her to bolster her courage to take a chance and fall in love again—this time with a man who wouldn't let her down. He still wouldn't rush her into doing anything, but he definitely planned to show her how good things could be between them. He planned to jar her emotions, jump-start her heart and make her stare the truth in the face.

There were chances in life worth taking and he was one "Chance" she should definitely take. In high school he and his brothers had been pegged as guys who were forged of steel. It was time to prove to Kylie that no matter what, he was a man with the endurance to withstand just about anything.

* * *

The next day at noon Kylie was at the airport waiting for Chance to arrive. As usual, no matter what day of the week it was, Douglas International Airport was busy. People were scurrying to their connecting flights or to their rendezvous with their loved ones.

When Chance's flight number was announced, she turned and glued her eyes on the gate. Evidently he traveled in first class because it didn't take long for him to exit the jetway. He was dressed in an expensive suit, and his stride was long and confident as he passed through the gate. There appeared to be an aura of power and authority surrounding him. Chance Steele was one dynamic, compelling and forceful man.

He looked so dependable, like the kind of man at whose feet a woman could leave her worries knowing he would take care of them and she wouldn't ever have to carry them on her shoulders again. He also looked like the kind of man who could drive a woman crazy with desire. She could definitely attest to that.

Her breath caught the moment their gazes met and she felt that immediate quiver of anticipation in her middle. He was going to kiss her. Somehow she knew, and heaven help her but she wanted that kiss more than anything.

She watched his long, elegant stride eating the distance separating them. And with each step he made, a delicious heat inched its way through her veins, making her blood hot and leaving her wondering, not for the first time, how this particular man could affect her so. He was the type of man that fantasies were built on, and who made realities even more poignant. And with every step he took toward her, he was making anticipation that much sweeter.

When he was within five feet of her, she saw the undisguised longing on his face. She could actually feel his desperation. There was a lot she didn't understand but at that moment the one thing she did accept was that in less than a minute, now more like a few seconds, she was going to be kissed senseless.

All the while he'd been walking toward Kylie, the one thought that kept churning in Chance's mind was that she was the woman he wanted and needed in his life.

She was the woman he loved.

Other than his mother, he had never kissed a woman at an airport, but that thought was pushed to the back of his mind when he pulled Kylie into his arms and captured her lips with his. And as their lips engaged in one hell of a lockdown, he wished she could feel all the emotions flowing through him at that very moment.

Knowing he had to get a grip before the kiss really turned raw and primitive, he reluctantly pulled back, but kept his arms around her waist, refusing to let her go anywhere. "Now that was worth coming back to," he whispered softly.

Kylie struggled for breath and then noted they had become the center of attention. "We've caused a scene."

He smiled. "Yes, but some scenes are worth causing."

She looked up at him. "Is this what you had in mind when you asked me to pick you up last night?"

He reached out and caressed her cheek. "Not entirely, but it's definitely a start. Come on, let's get my luggage so we can get the hell out of here."

Chapter 8

Kylie couldn't remember the last time she had a problem with keeping her eyes on the road while driving. But Chance's presence in her car was interfering with her concentration and wreaking havoc on her senses.

After claiming his luggage, he had taken her hand as they walked out of the terminal to her parked car. Once he had placed his bags in her trunk, his arms had clamped around her waist, pulled her to him and he'd sunk his mouth down on hers in another kiss. The moment their lips connected, heat had exploded through her and the heavy bulge of his erection pressed to her middle had caused her entire body to ache.

"We've got to stop doing this," she'd said the moment he had released her mouth.

"Why?" he had whispered hotly against her moist lips.

"Because it won't lead anywhere. It's a dead end."

His gaze had pinned her with a measured look. "And what if I told you that I see things differently?"

"Then my response is that you need a new pair of eyes."

"I have very good vision, Kylie." He'd then strolled to the passenger side of her car and got inside.

Bringing her thoughts back to the present, she took another quick glance over at him. He was sprawled in the seat next to her. His muscular body fit nicely into her Altima, although his broad shoulders took up a lot of space. His legs were long and his seat was pushed as far back as it could go to accommodate his height. His head lay back against the headrest and his eyes were closed.

Evidently the trip had tired him out, but not enough to stop him from engaging in a little mouth exercise with her a couple of times. She had begun thinking of their kisses as TST—taste, stroke and tangle—because each time they kissed he tried a new technique on her mouth that centered around those three basic elements.

"You're tired," she decided to say when she came to a traffic light. "Are you sure you want me to take you to the dealership to pick up your truck instead of taking you home? It might be a good idea for you to go to bed."

He opened his eyes, titled his head and let his gaze fasten on hers. "If you were to take me home and I got into bed, would you get in there with me and keep me company?" he asked, his voice low and sexy.

She inhaled deeply. Although he had phrased the question in a roundabout way, technically he had just hinted at the possibility of her sleeping with him. "No. I'd take you home and put you to bed, but I wouldn't get in that bed with you."

He smiled. "Spoilsport."

She chuckled and turned her attention back to the road when the traffic light changed. "I might be at that, but it seems I'm the one destined to keep us out of trouble."

"Some trouble I might like," he murmured in a low voice leaden with exhaustion, before closing his eyes again.

"And what if Marcus had that same attitude?"

"When he gets to my age he's welcome to it, but while he's underage, I decide what he likes and doesn't like. And stop comparing us to our kids, Kylie. Like I told you before, we're adults. They aren't."

"Sorry, I keep forgetting," she said sarcastically.

"It will behoove you to remember. The next time you forget it will cost you."

She lifted an eyebrow. "Cost me what?"

"A kiss. Right then and there. Even if it's in front of those two kids of ours."

She frowned and took a quick glance at him and saw that his eyes were opened and he was staring at her. His expression was serious. "You wouldn't dare."

"I wouldn't count on that if I were you."

And Kylie was smart enough to know not to. She pulled her car into the dealership, parked it and turned to him. "And just what would doing something like that prove?"

"It would prove that our kids wouldn't have a problem with anything developing between us."

"But I'd still have a problem with it. I won't let any man use me to slake his sexual cravings."

In a flash Chance snapped the seatbelt off his body and before she could get out her next breath he loomed over her. Blatant anger was carved in his features. "This isn't about me slaking any sexual cravings, Kylie. But you're so out of practice with men that you wouldn't know that, would you? Well, let me tell you something, not about men in general but about this man in particular," he said pointing to himself. "I won't ever use you just to slake any sexual cravings, so don't try making my wanting you as anything sullied or dirty.

"It's the most natural thing in the world for a man to desire a woman and vice versa. I won't apologize for it. When we do make love, Kylie, it will be a mutual thing. You'll want it as much as I do, so don't kid yourself into believing otherwise. And when it comes to me there's something else you need to keep in mind."

"And what's that?" she asked softly.

"When there's something I want, I won't give up until I get it."

"When we do make love, Kylie, it will be a mutual thing. You'll want it as much as I do, so don't kid yourself into believing otherwise..."

The words Chance had spoken earlier that day woke Kylie up more than once that night. This time she knew she had to deal with them before trying to go back to sleep.

Taking the pillow from the other side of the bed, she wrapped her arms around it and hugged it to her chest, wondering how in the world one man could be so utterly self-confident, so damn arrogant. The nerve of him making such a statement as if it was a foregone conclusion they'd go to bed together. Well, she had news for him, she thought bitterly.

After this camping trip was over she would put rules into place where their relationship was concerned. The only thing between them would be Marcus and Tiffany. As parents they would have some connection in order to keep their offspring on the right path, but that would be as far as things went. It wouldn't bother her in the least if she never saw the infuriating man again.

Turning over on her side, Kylie gazed despondently at

the digital clock on the nightstand. It was almost midnight, way too late to be having this sort of conversation with herself. She should be resting peacefully in a sound sleep, but thanks to Chance she was wide awake.

He had upset her so badly that afternoon that it had been a good ten minutes before she'd been able to pull herself together to drive away from that dealership. And twice during dinner Tiffany had asked her if anything was wrong.

And to think she would be spending an entire weekend in Chance's presence. If there were any way she could cancel their plans without disappointing Tiffany she would, but she knew better than anyone how much her daughter looked forward to this trip.

The phone on her nightstand rang and not for the first time she wished that like the phone in the living room this one had caller ID. But somehow she knew it was Chance and reached out and picked it up. "Hello?"

"I need to apologize, Kylie."

It was his deep, rich, husky voice, more than the words he had spoken, that sent a sensuous shiver through her. "Do you?"

"Not for everything—just for getting upset with you. I won't apologize for our kisses. But your words caught me off guard. Never in my wildest dream did I assume you'd think I would want to use you that way."

"Okay, Chance, maybe it was a bad choice of words, but what I was trying to say was that I'm being logical here. I don't see things as you see them, and when it comes to a lot of man-woman stuff, you're right, I'm way out of my league. You aren't. So I have to protect myself."

"You'll never have to protect yourself from me, Kylie. I'd never hurt you, take advantage of you or use you. I give you my word."

"Thank you."

"But I won't give you my word that I'll stop pursuing you, stop trying to make you want me as much as I want you, stop trying to—"

"Get me in your bed?"

"No, I won't stop trying to get you in my bed, Kylie, because I think that's where you belong. And once I get you there I intend to keep you there for a long time. But it will be for all the right reasons."

"When is an affair good for any reason?"

"When the two individuals agree that it is. You and I have a long way to go, Kylie. We haven't even gone on what I consider a real date. I want that but you don't."

She sighed deeply. "It's not that I don't want it, Chance, it's just that I don't think it's wise, considering the kids."

"So you prefer that we do things behind their backs?"

"No, I prefer that we don't do anything at all. Why is that so hard for you to understand?"

"And just what is it that you're afraid of?"

She was taken aback by his question. "I'm not afraid of anything."

"I think you are."

"Then think whatever you want."

"I will, and right now I think it's time that I show you something, Kylie Hagan."

She didn't like the way that sounded. "Show me what?"

"What this man-woman thing is all about. Like I said earlier today, you've been out of the game for so long you don't know what's acceptable between couples and what's not. Maybe it's time that I start teaching you a few things and—"

"Teach me a few things?" she interrupted shortly.

"Yes, then maybe you'll realize that you're not immune to me as you want to believe. Good night, Kylie."

The phone had already clicked in her ear before Kylie could recover her power of speech.

"Mom, isn't this place simply beautiful?" Tiffany asked in a high-pitched voice that was filled with enthusiasm and wonder.

"Yes, it is," Kylie replied, trying to direct her gaze out of the cabin window and not on Chance and Marcus as they brought in the items out of the truck.

Especially on Chance.

Instinctively, she took one hand and checked her pulse at her wrist, not surprised to find the strong beat racing beneath her fingertips. Already Chance was having an effect on her. He had shown up at her place wearing a pair of faded jeans and a T-shirt. The moment she'd seen him those wacky hormones of hers began soaring. She wished there was some type of injection she could take to build an immunity against him.

"Mom, you don't sound excited about being here. Are you okay?"

Kylie turned to meet Tiffany's concerned gaze and suddenly felt guilty. The last thing she wanted was her daughter worrying about her needlessly, which would place a damper on all the fun she'd planned for the weekend. "Yes, sweetheart, I'm fine, and it's going to be a wonderful and fantastic weekend. Now let's put this stuff down and go outside to see if Marcus and Chance need our help."

Once they had stepped back outside, Kylie glanced around. The spacious log cabin that sat on the shore of a huge lake blended well with the surroundings. Trees of all kinds provided plenty of shade, as did a sprawling front porch that had several wooden rocking chairs and a rustic porch swing. Kylie had to agree with Tiffany's earlier assessment. The place was beautiful.

"The air is so crisp and clean here. I can't wait until Marcus teaches me how to fish, and Mr. Steele said he would help. Isn't that nice of him?"

"Yes, that is nice of him."

They walked back toward the truck while Tiffany excitedly rambled on about what fun she planned to have and what a nice man Chance was.

"Need us to help carry anything else inside?" Kylie asked Chance and Marcus when they reached them.

"No, Dad and I can handle things, Ms. Hagan," Marcus said, not giving Chance an opportunity to respond. "But remember we don't use electricity, so you and Tiffany might want to unpack and get familiar with the inside of the cabin. Right, Dad?"

Chance smiled. "Right."

Kylie could feel Chance's eyes on her but she refused to look at him. She was beginning to feel ridiculous and out of sorts because a part of her was still upset about yesterday. He, however, was acting like their conversation never took place. To her chagrin, he was in the best of moods.

"So what's for dinner?" Tiffany would have to be the one to ask.

"I thought it would be nice if we grilled something outside on the open fire," Chance said. "Any ideas?"

Kylie saw the opportunity to make peace and seized it. She glanced over at Chance. "Anything but hamburgers," she said softly, as a tentative smile touched her lips.

Chance met her gaze, immediately recognized their private joke and smiled back. "Okay, no hamburgers."

"What about a hot-dog roast?" was Tiffany's suggestion.

"That's a great idea and we have plenty of hot-dog sticks to use," Marcus chimed in.

"Okay, all that sounds good," Chance said, as an amused grin eased up the corner of his mouth. "But because I need something a little bit more filling, I'll throw a couple of steaks on the grill, too."

He lifted the last box into his strong arms. "Come on, let's go inside and get this show on the road."

Kylie inhaled a deep breath as she stepped out of the bedroom she and Tiffany were sharing. More than a dozen candles were strategically scattered about and a couple of huge lanterns blazed in the corners of the living room.

She couldn't help but smile, thinking of all the fun they'd had so far. Chance had given both her and Tiffany a quick lesson on camping and had shown them how to assemble a tent in case they ever needed to use one. Roasting hot dogs on the stick had been fun but she'd appreciated Chance's idea of grilling the steaks when Marcus and Tiffany over-cooked the weiners.

And then later, before it had gotten dark, Chance had taken her out in a canoe to the other side of the lake. The scenery there had been just as breathtaking with numerous trees, flowering plants and a catfish-filled stream. Kylie smiled and thought that a person could get spoiled by so much of nature's beauty.

"Marcus is out like a light."

Kylie's smile froze when she turned and saw Chance coming out the bedroom that he and Marcus were sharing. She thought he had turned in for the night.

"So is Tiffany." She gave him a curious look and said, "I thought you had gone to bed, too."

"Not without first putting out the candles and lanterns. Fire hazards, you know."

She nodded. "I never realized there was so much to know about camping."

"There is but it's an excellent way to get back to nature. My mom agreed up to a point, which is why my parents purchased this place. She didn't mind getting back to nature but wanted all the comforts of home while doing so."

He grinned as he moved around the room to put out the candles and lanterns. "I hate to say this but we had more fun when we left her at home. Dad was too laid back to worry about us turning over in the canoe or eating berries off the bushes without washing them first. And the only reason we have hot and cold running water is because she refused to let us bathe in the lake. Good old Mom always came with a strict set of rules."

Kylie chuckled. "Haven't you figured out yet that's one of the things we're best known for? Your mother sounds like my kind of woman. I would love meeting her one day."

And I intend for you to do just that, Chance thought as he glanced over at her. Mom would be happy to know that her oldest son has found love again.

All the candles were out but one, and the luminescent glow from that one candle seemed to focus on Kylie, making her skin shine with an ethereal radiance. Her hair had been up in a ponytail earlier but now she'd taken it down, and the mass of braids fell in soft waves around her shoulders.

"Well, I guess I'll call it a night and—"

"Will you sit on the porch with me for a while?" he asked.

Kylie looked at him then shook her head. "I don't think that's a good idea."

The corner of his mouth tipped upward into a smile. "Has anyone ever told you that you think too much?"

"Possibly," she said slowly. "But I won't absolutely admit to anything."

Chance chuckled. "I didn't think you would."

"Now who's thinking too much?"

"Oh, that's real rich," Chance said, laughing. "Come on. I think you'll get a kick out of watching the stars." He reached out and offered her his hand and, only after hesitating briefly, she took it.

Chance was right. She was getting a kick out of watching the stars. Sitting here on the porch and rocking in the chair made Kylie realize all the little things she hadn't taken time to do before.

"Sure you don't want to come over here and share this swing with me?" Chance asked.

She chuckled as she glanced over at him. "I'm positive."

"But you aren't sitting close to me."

"I'm close enough, Chance."

"I beg to differ."

She shook her head grinning. "Tell me something. Are your brothers like you?"

"No, I'm one of a kind."

"Thank God."

"Hey," he said with affront. "What's that supposed to mean?"

"Let's just say I'm glad after you were born that they broke the mold. I can't imagine another one like you."

"I'll take that as a compliment."

"You would." After a brief moment of silence she said, "Tell me some more about your brothers."

"All right. Like I told you that day at the Racetrack Café,

Bas is eighteen months younger than me and he's the troubleshooter for the company."

"He's also the one engaged to be married, right?"

"So we hear."

She stopped rocking and looked over at him, studied his
features from the glow of the moon. "Why do I have a feeling that it's one of those 'I'll believe it when I see it' deals?"

"Because it is. Cassandra Tisdale and Bas are as different as day and night."

Kylie raised a brow. "Tisdale? As in Tisdale who owns
a number of car dealerships around town? As well as those
two restaurants?"

"Yes, the dealerships belong to her father and the restaurants to her uncle. Same family."

"Why do you think Ms. Tisdale and your brother aren't
compatible?"

"Because they aren't."

"He evidently thinks they are."

"Remember you're the one who thinks too much. In this
case, I don't believe Bas is thinking at all. But I have all
the faith in the world that he'll come to his senses before
doing something stupid."

Kylie frowned. "You're serious, aren't you?"

"Quite." After a brief moment he said, "But only because
I know my brothers, and Bas in particular. All through his
life he's been known as the 'not so stainless Steele.'"

"Meaning?"

Chance frowned at the memories. "He was considered
the black sheep of the family because he used to get into
so much trouble. I guess you can say he went through quite
a rebellious stage while growing up. You name it, he probably did it. It was a good thing my father was good friends
with Sheriff Blandford since Bas had a penchant for stray-

ing to the wrong side of the law. Most of the time it wasn't him but the crowd he hung out with. But you know what they say about guilt by association."

Yes, she knew. "So when did his future change for the better?"

"When he was about twenty. He dropped out of college after deciding he wanted to see the world. He was gone for a year without us knowing where he was most of the time. All we know is that when he returned he had a new outlook on life. He went back to college, graduated with honors and then came to work at the Steele Corporation, starting from the bottom. He was determined to learn everything he could. Now he's a vital asset to the company. I depend on him to keep me in the know and to put out small fires."

"What about the other two?"

"Morgan is Morgan. He has this thing about finding the perfect woman and until he does he won't settle for less. Then there's Donovan, who thinks he was born to have fun. He's serious enough while at work but otherwise there's really never a serious moment with him. My mother predicts he'll probably be the one who lives the longest because he enjoys life too much to get stressed about anything."

"Does that also mean he's having too much fun to settle down and get married?"

"So he claims. He just hasn't met the one woman to tame his game."

"Quite an interesting bunch."

"Yes, they didn't refer to us as 'Forged of Steele' for nothing."

Kylie lifted a brow. "'Forged of Steele'?"

"Yes. We were known for our endurance. We thought we could outlast anything."

She decided not to ask their endurance in what. "The

possibility that Marcus might be a chip off the old block now has me worried. Should I be?"

Chance chuckled. "No, he's a good kid."

"Yes, I noticed and I'm appreciative of that. I was prepared not to like him, you know."

"Yeah, I know, and it was likewise with me and Tiffany. But I like her. You did a good job raising her, Kylie."

"So did you with Marcus."

"Thanks."

Kylie stretched and then stood. "Well, I think I'm going to call it a night."

"Already?"

"It's probably close to two in the morning, Chance, and I still have to take a shower. That checker game you played with the kids lasted quite a while."

"Only because your daughter didn't know how to play. I've never heard of such a thing. That's un-American."

"Well, I hate to tell you but her mother doesn't know how to play checkers, either."

"Then I guess I'll add that to my list of all the other things I intend to teach you."

"Don't do me any favors."

"Trust me. It will be for my benefit as well as for yours. The more you know and understand, the better off we'll both be."

Kylie knew they weren't talking about checkers but about the intricacies involving a male and female.

But was she willing to learn?

Chance lay in bed and could only stare up at the ceiling as he heard the shower going, imagining Kylie, naked and standing beneath a full spray of water that flowed down her breasts, flat stomach, thighs…

He tried tuning out the sound and turning his attention to his snoring son, who was sleeping on the opposite bunk. Damn, he sounded just like Donovan. Chance chuckled as he remembered that while growing up no one wanted to share a bedroom with Donovan because he snored.

After a few moments he released a groan and decided listening to Kylie in the shower was a lot better than putting up with Marcus. He smiled, thinking he had really enjoyed their conversation on the porch tonight. She seemed interested in his family, which was just as well, since if he had his way the Steeles would be her family one day.

God, he loved her.

Heat sizzled along his nerve endings at the thought of just how much. A slow, sinful grin touched his lips when he thought about what he'd told her last night. There was a lot she didn't understand about man-woman relationships and he intended to teach her. Things had definitely changed since her last date, especially in the bedroom. If he remembered correctly, that was the year the Hubble Telescope was launched into space, Nelson Mandela was finally freed from prison and George Bush Senior was president.

Hell, she probably wasn't aware that these days men and women who were in a serious relationship openly discussed such things as foreplay and orgasms, or that trying different positions in the bedroom was now the norm and not the exception. And she'd probably be startled to know that oral sex was pretty popular these days.

A slow smile rolled around his lips. Yes, he would enjoy teaching her all the finer things in life with one goal in mind: to make her fall as deeply in love with him as he was with her.

Chapter 9

"Well, Lena, how do I look?"

Lena stood with her hands on her hips and gave Kylie an assessing stare. The two of them had been shopping for gowns to wear to this weekend's ball and it seemed as if Kylie had hit the jackpot.

"Girl, that dress is gorgeous and it looks fabulous on you," Lena said. "But of course you have the figure for it. You have more curves than the Daytona Speedway. You'd be nuts not to buy it."

With her courage bolstered, Kylie looked down at herself. Lena was right. The dress was a sexy black form-fitting georgette mini with a halter crisscross bodice and a low-cut back. She had to admit it did look rather flattering on her, though it showed more skin than she would like.

"You don't think it's too daring?" she asked Lena.

"Heck, no, like I said you have the body for it. Everyone can't say that. I most certainly can't."

Kylie frowned at her friend. "Hey, there's nothing wrong with your figure."

"That losing fifteen more pounds won't hurt?"

"Don't complain. A lot of men like full-figured women. You have a small waist, nice size hips, a gorgeous pair of legs—"

"Strong bones and a good set of teeth," Lena tagged on. They laughed, remembering other times they had gone shopping together when they were much younger and faced with the same dilemma. Kylie always thought she was too thin and Lena had made up in her mind years ago that at size sixteen she was too thick.

"So, are you going to buy it?" Lena asked as she walked around Kylie, admiring how the dress fit.

"Probably not," Kylie said, still looking down at herself. She felt half-naked wearing it. "But it's gorgeous, though."

"And it has your name on it."

Kylie glanced up at Lena. "You think so?"

"I wouldn't have said it if I didn't. Besides, since you've decided to be my date for the ball what I say counts, right?"

"Right."

"So what are you going to do?"

Kylie grinned. "I'm going to take it."

An hour or so later they were back in Lena's car and exiting the mall. "You never told me how things went last weekend with the camping trip," Lena said.

Kylie glanced over at her. "Didn't think I had to. I'm sure Tiffany told you everything you needed to know."

"Yeah, but she didn't mention anything about you and Chance."

"Was she supposed to?"

"I guess not, if the two of you are keeping your affair a secret."

Kylie gave her friend a direct stare, although Lena's eyes were glued to the road and didn't notice it. "Chance and I are not having an affair."

"Oh. The two of you just meet every so often to lock lips, right?"

Kylie rolled her eyes heavenward. "So, we kissed a few times, no big deal."

"I would think after fifteen years of abstinence that for you it *was* a big deal. And you even admitted he was a good kisser."

"Oh, my gosh, he's the best," Kylie breathed and then regretted that she'd admitted it.

Lena laughed. "Bingo. So how did you manage to keep those overzealous hormones under control?"

"It was hard but I managed."

"And the two of you didn't kiss not even once?"

"No, not even once. Marcus and Tiffany kept us much too busy. They wanted to do everything and by the end of the day we were too tired to do anything but sleep."

"Oh, how sad."

Lena and Kylie looked at each other and burst out laughing again. A few moments later, Lena said, "You know he's coming to the ball, don't you?"

Kylie tried to keep her attention on an object outside of the car's window. "What Chance does is his business."

"And he's bringing a date."

Kylie jerked her head around. "What!"

Lena laughed out loud. "Gotcha!"

Kylie frowned. "That's not funny, Lena."

"It is, too. You should have seen the way your head snapped around. It's a wonder you didn't break your neck.

For someone who claims what Chance Steele does is his business, you were definitely interested in that piece of news."

"Well, is it true? Is he bringing someone?"

Lena shrugged. "Don't know. Cassandra Tisdale mentioned at committee meeting yesterday that her cousin was going to be in town that night from D.C. and she was going to ask Chance to be the woman's date."

"Good for her."

"Umm, do I detect a little jealousy in your voice?"

"Not on your life."

Lena smiled. "Okay, if you say so."

Lena was right, Kylie thought as she got ready for bed that night. She was jealous. Of all the nerve!

She had to admit that Chance had been on his best behavior last weekend, probably because she didn't give him the chance to be otherwise. After that first night when he had invited her to sit out on the porch with him, she had gotten smart and made sure the opportunity never presented itself again. She went to bed when Tiffany went to bed and she stayed there.

Still, she thought things had gone rather well that weekend and Marcus and Chance had been perfect hosts. They had seen to all of her and Tiffany's needs, and with Tiffany and Marcus carrying on more like siblings instead of a couple the majority of the time, it was as if the four of them were a family.

Chance had been wonderful with Tiffany when he showed her the proper way to use a rod and reel, after Marcus had thrown up his hands and given up. And then there was the time Chance taught Tiffany how to paddle the canoe, and how he was the only one who actually seemed interested in her obsession with bird-watching. Seeing them together actually made her wonder if perhaps Tiffany had lost out by not having a father figure in her life all these years. At least Tiffany would have the chance to spend time with her grandfather this weekend. Kylie's parents had called a few days ago and asked if Tiffany could go with them to Disney World for the weekend.

Since both Friday and the following Monday were teachers' planning days, things worked out perfectly. Kylie would put her on the plane Friday morning and then pick her up from the airport on Monday evening. That meant she wouldn't have to worry about her daughter while she attended this weekend's ball.

The phone rang and Kylie glanced over at the clock, knowing it was Chance. How could he talk to her every night and not mention he was taking someone to the ball? It didn't matter to her one iota that she hadn't taken Lena's advice and invited him herself. It was the principle of the thing.

She frowned when she picked up the phone. "Hello."

"How did things go at work today?"

This was how they began their conversation each night. He would ask her how things went with her job and she would ask how things went with his. They would hold a pleasant conversation for a good forty-five minutes and then they would say good night. Sometimes she wondered about the real purpose of them talking, other than to hear the other's voice each day.

"Things at the shop went okay. Business has really picked up this week. I got a lot of pre-Thanksgiving orders." Then she said, "I closed early. Lena and I went shopping for gowns for the ball this weekend." She wondered if he would mention if he were going, or more specifically if he had a date.

"Did you find something you liked?"

"Yes."

"What color is it?"

"Black."

"I bet it looks good on you."

"Lena thought so."

"Did she?"

"Yes."

There was a pause and then he said, "Marcus is going away this weekend."

Kylie raised an eyebrow. This was news to her since Tiffany hadn't mentioned it. "He is?"

"Yes. Cyndi's parents are coming through on their way to—"

"Not Disney World?" she asked, immediately jumping to conclusions and hoping they were the wrong ones.

"No, Busch Gardens in Virginia."

Thank goodness. "Oh."

"Why did you think they were going to Disney World?"

"Because that's where Tiffany is headed this weekend."

"Ahh. And you thought that perhaps they had manipulated their grandparents so the two of them could be in the same place and at the same time."

"It's been known to happen."

"I'm sure it has but I doubt they would go that far."

"Hey, you never know," Kylie said.

There was another pause and then Chance said, "We're going to have to start trusting them at some point, Kylie."

Tucking a braid behind her ear, she took a deep, frustrating breath. "I know but for me it's hard, Chance, because I remember all the tricks I used to pull to be with Sam."

"Yes, but is it fair to judge them by what you did?"

"No."

"All right, then."

Kylie tilted her lips in a smile. Even if he were bringing a date to the ball, she still enjoyed her nightly talks with him. Although she had decided that they could never be lovers, it seemed that he had made up his mind that they would be friends. And deep down she didn't have a problem with that.

She'd always had Lena as another female to bounce her ideas and thoughts off of, but there had never been a guy she felt close enough with to do the same. Lately she had asked Chance's opinions about a lot things, including how she should handle situations that had arisen at work. Being the savvy businessman that he was, he had always given her good, sound advice.

"So, how are things going at the Steele Corporation?" she asked.

"There was a development today that I wished could have been avoided."

"Oh? What?"

"We had to let a man go who's been with us for over ten years."

She heard disappointment, as well as regret, in his voice. "Why?"

"We found out he'd been stealing from the company. He was padding figures and having the products delivered elsewhere. Bas had suspected him for a while but we only got the proof we needed today to do anything about it."

They talked for the next thirty minutes or so and that night Kylie slept with an inner peace that she hadn't known in a long time.

* * *

"So you think they will have their first date this weekend?" Marcus asked before biting into his sandwich.

Tiffany smiled. "Yes. They're going to that ball although they aren't going with each other. I can't see how it won't turn into a date with the both of us gone for the weekend. Didn't you see how they were looking at each other last weekend when they thought no one was noticing? I think we did the right thing by contacting our grandparents."

Marcus nodded. "I hope you're right."

Tiffany took another sip of her soda, smiled and said, "Just think, Marcus, if we actually pull this off, you'll be the big brother I've always wanted."

Marcus grinned. "Yeah, and then I can give Rhonda Denton my full attention. I think she likes me."

Chapter 10

He wanted her.

That thought rammed through Chance's mind the moment he saw Kylie enter the ballroom. His heart began hammering in his chest and he actually felt his pulse rate spike drastically. And if that wasn't bad enough, his body got hard as a rock.

At that moment he was grateful he was standing behind a waist-high plant that could shield the physical evidence of just how much he desired her. That, coupled with the knowledge of how much he loved her, was setting his loins on fire.

The minidress she was wearing was definitely a shocker he could sum up in three words—short, sassy and sexy. It fit her body to perfection, showing off all her curves and the luscious length of her long, shapely legs. And if the dress wasn't jaw-droppingly seductive enough, then there was the way she had her hair piled atop her head with a few swirling braids crowning her face.

"Who are they?" Morgan leaned over and whispered, while raising an impressive eyebrow. "I don't know either of them," he said as if it were his God-given right to be acquainted with every beautiful woman in Charlotte.

Chance studied his brother's face for a second and noted his gaze wasn't as glued to Kylie as it was to Lena Spears. That was a good thing since it would have been of waste of Morgan's time to show any interest in Kylie. When it came to her he could get downright territorial. "The one in the black dress is Kylie Hagan, and she's mine," he said, deciding to state his claim here and now. "The woman in the fuchsia dress is her best friend, Lena Spears."

"Spears? Where have I heard that name before?" Morgan asked.

"I have no idea. She's a part of the committee that put on tonight's ball and owns a real estate office in town."

"A real estate office?"

"Yes."

Morgan glanced over at Chance after taking a sip from his wineglass. "You know her, then?"

"Yes."

Morgan's dark eyes sparkled in the glow of the huge chandelier that hung over their heads. "Good. I want an introduction." He then glanced back over at the two women. "So the one in black is Marcus's girlfriend's mother?"

At Chance's nod, he said, "Umm, definitely good-looking. But she doesn't look old enough to have a fifteen-year-old daughter."

"Well, she does," Chance answered, with no intention of going into any details as to how that had happened.

For a brief moment Morgan didn't say anything and then

he spoke. "It seems she's caught Derek Peterson's eye. He didn't waste any time going over there to talk to her. If I were you I'd go claim what's mine."

Chance had noticed the man's flight across the room to get all in Kylie's face. Derek Peterson, twice divorced, had a reputation as a skirt chaser and it seemed that he wasn't wasting any time making Kylie's acquaintance. "I think I will."

"Aren't you going to introduce me to your friend, Lena?" Derek Peterson asked.

"I'll think about it," Lena responded noncommittally.

Kylie raised an eyebrow. Lena was known for her friendly disposition. If she was giving this man the cold shoulder, there must be a good reason.

"Since Lena won't cooperate, I guess I have to introduce myself," the man said, capturing Kylie's hand in his. "I'm Dr. Derek Peterson."

Upon recognizing the name, Kylie understood her friend's less-than-friendly attitude. Derek was a doctor who had at one time shown interest in Lena until he discovered she was her elderly mother's caretaker. He'd told her there was no way the two of them could get serious since she came with "extra baggage."

"And I'm Kylie Hagan," Kylie said, in an attempt to be polite.

He gave her a smile that showed perfect white teeth. "Ms. Hagan, it is a pleasure to meet you. You must be new to town."

Kylie decided she didn't like him any more than Lena did, probably because his gaze was focused more on her chest than her face. "I've been living here for almost four months now."

"What section of town do you live in?"

"Myers Park."

"Myers Park?"

"Yes." She heard his impressed tone. Myers Park, one of the first suburbs of Charlotte, featured large stately homes that were canopied in willow oaks. More than any other neighborhood in the city, Myers Park had preserved its true character over the years. The "front-porch" neighborhoods had the traditional sidewalks, funky shops and restaurants. The house she had purchased had cost a pretty penny but thanks to Lena's negotiating skills, the owners, who'd needed a quick sale, had readily agreed to her offer.

"Then I must definitely get to know you. We're neighbors," Dr. Peterson said, "though I don't ever remember running into you while out and about."

Kylie was just about to tell him that she was both a full-time mother and a working woman who didn't have time to be "out and about," when she felt a sudden quiver in her midsection. She knew without a doubt that Chance was in close range.

She didn't want to seem too obvious when she scanned the crowded ballroom, but knew from the way her heart began hammering that she didn't have to look far. He stood on a raised dais, staring directly at her. The person standing by his side was a man and not a woman, which gave her some relief. It was easy to tell the man was one of his brothers, as the resemblance was striking.

What was also obvious was the intensity in Chance's eyes. She could almost drown in the look she saw there. Male interest. Male appreciation. Male longing. Even a novice like her could recognize the three. He was silently sending her a message, one her body fully understood. Her hormones were on ready, set, go. But she knew there was something else involved here; something she hadn't counted on happening. It was also something she wasn't prepared for.

Emotional feelings of the deepest kind.

Now she understood why she'd been having all those vibrant and uncontrollable urges since meeting Chance. And why her body was so aware of him whether he was with her in person or was talking to her on the phone. The thought that he easily ignited her fire had always bothered her because she hadn't understood the why of it. Whenever he kissed her she got caught up in his special skill of tongue-play, as if his tongue was made for her and hers for him. She hadn't wanted to get in the same fix she'd been in with Sam; something she now thought of as forbidden obsession.

She was old enough now to know better. She was at that age of maturity where she no longer took things at face value. She didn't trust easily and had a tendency to expect the worst. But standing here being absorbed in Chance's heated gaze she knew at that moment that it wasn't about obsession, nor was it about lust. It was about love.

She had fallen head over heels in love with him.

"And what do you do for a living, Kylie?"

She tore her gaze away from Chance upon hearing Dr. Peterson's question. "I own a florist shop."

"Oh? Where?"

"In the newly developed section of town, Hazelwood."

"That's a nice area, but if you ever want to move to another location, a friend of mine owns a couple of buildings that he's leasing downtown and—"

"Good evening, everyone."

That deep, husky voice made the pounding of Kylie's heart increase. She glanced up and met Chance's direct gaze.

"Chance! It's good to see you," Lena said, deliberately showing a lot more enthusiasm upon seeing him than she had Dr. Peterson.

"Thanks, Lena, and it's good seeing you as well."

He then gazed back at Kylie and held out his hand. "Hello, I'm Chance Steele. And you're…?"

Kylie wondered what game Chance was playing, but at the moment deciding to go along with him. "Kylie Hagan."

"Well, Ms. Hagan, it's nice meeting you. And I'd like to introduce my brother, Morgan." He then proceeded to introduce Morgan Steele to both her and Lena. It was only then that she noted that he'd given Derek no more than a cursory glance. Kylie immediately felt the tension that surrounded the three men and was bewildered by it.

"Derek," Chance acknowledged.

"Chance. Morgan. I thought you guys ran in packs. Where're the other two?"

Chance's smile didn't quite reach his eyes. "Bas and Donovan are around here somewhere. Why? Are you looking for them?"

"No." Derek then turned his attention to Kylie. "It was nice meeting you, Ms. Hagan, but I'm being beckoned elsewhere."

"And it was nice meeting you as well, Dr. Peterson." The man quickly left. Once he was no longer in sight, Kylie turned to Chance to inquire what that had been about, but found her hand enveloped in the warmth of his when the orchestra began playing.

She met his gaze and all thoughts of Derek Peterson were forgotten as she was immediately swept away by the intensity in Chance's dark eyes and the warmth of the smile that spread across his features. "Would you dance with me?" he asked quietly.

She wondered if he could sense her inner turmoil. Did he know the emotions she was feeling were real and far exceeded the ones she'd assumed she had felt for Sam all those years ago? What she'd felt then was the passion of a young, naive girl. What she was experiencing now was the passion of an adult woman who had discovered love for the first time and knew there was no place for her to run, and no place for her to hide. There was nothing she could do but accept her fate.

Love was staring her in the face in the form of Chance Marcus Steele.

"Yes, I'll dance with you." His hand on hers tightened gently and she felt the warm strength of his touch as he led her toward the dance floor.

Once there he pulled her into his arms, close to the solidness of his form, the heat of his body. She wondered how long she could continue to stand and not melt at his feet with all the sensations overtaking her. Finding out at thirty-one that you had the ability to love again was definitely a shocker.

"You look beautiful tonight, Kylie," Chance said, claiming her absolute attention. "Without a doubt you are the most gorgeous woman here."

Kylie lowered her gaze to study the Rolex watch on his wrist. "Your date might have a problem with you thinking that."

"I didn't bring a date."

She raised surprised eyes to his. "You didn't?"

"No. What made you think I did? Or even more important, what made you think I would?"

"Your brother's fiancée mentioned to Lena that some

woman in her family was coming to town and that you would be bringing her to the ball."

He shrugged. "Cassandra did call and try convincing me to escort her cousin tonight but I refused."

"Why?" she asked swiftly, then regretted doing so. It was really none of her business.

"Because the only woman I want to be with tonight was going to be here, although she didn't ask me to be her date."

Kylie couldn't help but smile, elated he'd come alone. "Oh, what a pity," she commented teasingly.

"Yes, I thought so as well. But now that she's here, right where I want her to be, which is in my arms, I'm declaring myself her date for the rest of the night."

Kylie didn't have a problem with that. "Are you?"

"Yes. That's one sure way to protect you from the Derek Petersons of the world."

The contempt she heard in his voice proved her earlier assumption had been correct. There was no love lost between Derek, Chance and Morgan. "You and Morgan don't like him," she said, stating what had been so obvious. "Why?"

"Let's just say we don't exactly appreciate the way he's been known to treat women."

Not wanting to talk about Derek Peterson any longer, Chance brought Kylie's body closer to his. He drank in her softness, her nearness, her scent—everything that was woman about her. After seven years of doing without a woman in his life, the one he was holding in his arms made him feel complete.

"Why did you pretend that the two of us hadn't met before?"

Kylie's question invaded Chance's thoughts. He gazed at her, thinking that her question was easy enough to answer. "Something you said a few weeks ago made me want to prove you wrong."

She arched an eyebrow. "And what did I say?"

"You said that we had only met because of our kids and chances were if we'd been at any function together that I would not have given you a second look. It was your opinion that you're not the type of woman I would have shown interest in."

Kylie nodded, remembering she *had* said that. "And?"

"And I've proven you wrong, Kylie," he drawled.

She gave him a bemused look. "How?"

"By being here with you tonight, seeing you walk through that door for the first time. Tonight has nothing to do with our kids. It's a function where we are both in attendance, and I did give you a second look. You are definitely a woman I would be interested in. And to go even further, you *are* a woman I *am* interested in, Kylie. The *only* one I'm interested in."

His words touched her more than he would ever know and Kylie didn't think she could feel more desired and more wanted than at that very moment. The way he was looking at her made her feel hot, feverish. The intensity in his eyes made her pulse flutter and a heat wave consumed her, sending blood thrumming through her veins. She felt her nipples puckering against his chest. What was passing between them was too arousing for a dance floor.

The music ended and she felt him curl his fingers around her upper arm to lead her toward the exit doors. "Where are we going?" she asked breathlessly, trying to keep up with his long strides.

"Outside to get some fresh air."

Kylie swallowed. She had a feeling that fresh air wasn't the only thing Chance intended to get.

* * *

When Chance finally came to a stop beneath a cascade of low-hanging branches, he turned to Kylie and gently pulled her to him. And when his lips creased into that sexy smile that could automatically turn her on, she didn't think twice about tilting her head back for his kiss.

Her breath escaped in a shallow sigh the moment he slanted his mouth across hers, causing her already heated body to become a blazing flame. And when the glide of his tongue across hers caused her stomach to clench, she reached up and wound her arms around his neck, bringing their bodies closer.

She felt his erection pressed so strongly against her, actually wedged between her thighs, and moaned in his mouth at the same time her body instinctively rocked against him. A part of her didn't know what to make of her actions. She had never been this loose, this free with any man. The couple of times she and Sam had made out, she'd been too busy worrying about whether they would get caught to fully enjoy the experience.

Now getting caught was the last thing on her mind. If an entire ballroom discovered her and Chance outside kissing beneath a bunch of willow branches, then so be it. Nothing, and she meant nothing, could make her stop being a participant in this. She'd needed his mouth on hers, his seductive taste mingling with her own tongue more than she had known. She had been hungry and now he was feeding her with a skill that only he possessed. He tasted, stroked and tangled his way around her mouth, pleasuring her as only he could do.

And then she felt him smooth a hand up her silken thigh. As it eased beneath her short dress and inched its way to her waist, she moaned deep within her throat. The sensations his touch invoked overwhelmed her and instinctively she arched closer to him.

Slowly he released her mouth, raised his head and met her gaze, and she knew he saw the longing that was there in the dark depths of her eyes, mirroring what she saw in his. He reached up and skimmed a fingertip across her lips and she moaned against his finger. Heat shot down to the area between her legs.

"I want to leave here and take you somewhere to be alone with you, Kylie."

She knew what he was asking. She knew what he was saying. He might not love her but he wanted her. And at that moment it was all that mattered to her. What he'd tried telling her all along suddenly made perfect sense. They were adults and they could do whatever they wanted to do within reason. Would it be so awful to take what he was offering? A chance for the two of them to be alone? She had lived the past fifteen years without a man in her life, she didn't need promises of forever.

Right now the only thing she needed was him, the man she knew she loved. And for the first time in a very long time, she would be led by her heart and not her mind. Regrets, if there were any, could come later.

"I want to be alone with you, too, Chance."

"I'm glad to hear that," he whispered, smiling. "I think we should go back inside, mingle, dance a couple more times and then leave. What do you think of that?"

She smiled up at him. The thought of being alone with him later made her heart beat in an erratic rhythm, and the pure male desire shimmering in his eyes wasn't helping matters. "I think that's a wonderful idea."

The moment they stepped back into the ballroom a woman called out to Chance, claiming his attention. They turned and watched two beautiful, and gorgeously dressed women head their way. Chance's hand on Kylie's arm tightened and when she glanced up at him she could detect a frown that he was trying to hide behind a forced smile.

"Chance, I've been looking for you."

"Hello, Cassandra. I'd like you to meet a friend of mine, Kylie Hagan."

Cassandra barely spared Kylie a glance, until she noticed Chance's hand possessively on her arm. Then, after a swift appraisal, she extended her hand. "Oh, hello. Have we met before?"

"I don't think so," Kylie said, noticing the woman's immediate dislike of her. The feeling was reciprocal.

Cassandra then turned her attention back to Chance and to the woman at her side. "This is my cousin, Jamie, the one I told you about who's visiting from Washington, D.C."

"Hello, Jamie. Welcome to Charlotte," Chance said politely. He then turned to Kylie. "And, Jamie, I'd like you to meet Kylie Hagan, a good friend."

After introductions were made Cassandra didn't waste time. "Chance, I think you and Jamie should spend time together while she's in town," she said, disregarding Kylie and Chance's hold on her arm.

"Really? And why would you think that?"

"Because her father is Senator Hollis."

Chance's expression became barely tolerant. It appeared he didn't appreciate Cassandra's lack of manners. "Sorry, but is that supposed to mean something to me?"

Cassandra tilted her head back to look at him. The glint in her eyes said she was annoyed. "Well, I thought it would since you're a businessman interested in world trade and he's on the Fair Trade Commission in Washington."

"Well, that's all rather nice," Chance said, irritation evi-

dent in his tone. "But I don't think I need Jamie to arrange
a meeting with her father if I ever need to discuss business
with him. After all, he is a paid politician representing *all*
the people, right?"

Cassandra's hazel eyes narrowed. "Right."

"Okay, then." In an attempt to save face, he changed
the subject. "The committee did a wonderful job with the
ball tonight, Cassandra. Kylie and I were headed over to
the buffet table."

"Well, enjoy," Cassandra said, clearly not happy that she
hadn't gotten Chance to bend her way.

Chance gave Jamie a smile. "It was nice meeting you.
Give your father my regards." Tightening his hold on Kylie's arm, they walked off.

When they reached the buffet table, Chance let out a
long sigh. "That woman had a lot of nerve to suggest that
I date her cousin while you were standing there. She was
willing to use Jamie's father's political connection to set
her up on a date. I've never seen anything so tacky. I'm
sorry about that."

Kylie chuckled as she picked up a plate. "Don't be. I
learned a long time ago that usually it's people with money
who lack real manners."

"I hope you're not grouping everyone with money in
that category."

She smiled up at him. "No, only some of them. The Cas-
sandras and the Dereks of this world."

Chance grinned. "I agree."

They remained at the ball for an additional hour or so,
long enough to mingle and for Kylie to meet Chance's
three female cousins, and his other two brothers, whom she
thought were as handsome and as well-mannered as Chance

and Morgan. After meeting Sebastian Steele, she couldn't picture him married to someone like Cassandra Tisdale.

"We've hung around long enough," Chance whispered in her ear. "Ready to leave?"

She looked up at him, her smoldering eyes telling him she'd been anxiously counting the minutes. "Yes, I'm ready."

They left the ball, then waited as a valet brought Chance's car to them. It was then that he asked, "Did you need to find Lena and let her know you've left with me?"

She shook her head. "I think she'll have an idea what happened when she doesn't see me anymore tonight."

He opened the passenger door on his car when it came. "Will her knowing bother you?"

"No. Will her knowing bother you?"

"No."

"What about your brothers and cousins?" she asked.

"It wouldn't bother me for anyone to know we're to-gether, Kylie," he said, closing the door when she slid onto the smooth leather seat.

When he got inside the vehicle and slid beneath the steer-ing wheel she said, "Nice car."

He grinned. "Thanks. I decided to leave the truck home and bring my toy."

She chuckled. A Mercedes sports car was some toy. "Where are we going?"

He glanced over at her. "Where do you want to go?"

They could go to either her place or his since there weren't any kids at home. That thought made a girlish gig-gle escape her lips. He glanced over at her when he pulled out of the parking lot and headed toward the interstate. "Are you okay?"

She grinned. "Yes. I was just thinking that with the kids away the parents will play. I feel like being naughty tonight, Chance."

He surprised her when he braked and veered off to the shoulder of the road.

"Why are we stopping, Chance?"

"I feel like being naughty tonight, too, starting now," he replied simply, before leaning over and connecting her mouth with his again. Her lips parted without any hesitation and his aggressive tongue mingled diligently with hers. He tasted of the wine he had consumed earlier and it only raised her body's temperature. She returned his intensity with her own, and as their tongues mingled, her insides turned to molten liquid.

When he pulled back, they were both breathless. He captured her gaze, held it. "So, will it be my place or yours?"

She reached out and placed her palm against his cheek. "Mine. I want you in *my* bed, Chance Steele."

Chapter 11

Less than a half hour later, they entered Kylie's home. As she closed the door, a warm, tingly, tantalizing sensation began building up inside of her in anticipation of what was to come.

There in the middle of the room stood Chance. The dark eyes looking at her were smoldering and, as always, he looked the embodiment of extreme male sexuality. And there was no doubt that he was the most tempting sight she'd ever seen.

Neither of them spoke.

He continued to look at her, long and hard, making her already heated body that much hotter, making her fully aroused. When she thought there was no way she could stand the intensity of his gaze any longer, he smiled, that slow, sexy smile that was meant to warm her. Instead it ignited everything woman within her, making her body respond to his physical presence in the most primitive way.

When she thought she couldn't possibly take any more, he slowly closed the distance separating them.

"Are you sure about this, Kylie?" he whispered huskily, taking her hand in his and bringing her closer to him. So close that she felt his huge erection.

Kylie felt off balance and her mind became a mass of desire, of wanting, of need. "I've never been so sure of anything in my life, Chance," she whispered back. "But…"

"But what?"

"But I don't have any real experience at this and I don't want to disappoint you."

He wrapped his arms around her waist and pulled her closer still. "Trust me, sweetheart, you won't. There's no way you can."

He leaned down and took her lips, and seconds later she felt herself being lifted in his strong arms. He carried her up the stairs. "Which room is yours?" he asked when he'd reached the landing.

"The first door to your right."

She had left a low lamp burning in her bedroom and now it cast an intimate glow in the room.

"I love that dress you have on but it's coming off, Kylie," he said as he set her on her feet. Without hesitation he stripped off his tuxedo jacket and bow tie, and unbuttoned his white shirt.

She tilted her head back. "If you want it off, you'll have to take it off," she said with sass.

He accepted the sensuous challenge in her voice. "I have no problem doing that, because it *is* coming off. I have a lot of plans for you tonight."

She smiled. Whether he knew it or not, she had a lot of plans for him as well. "I take it you're going to teach me a few things."

"Yes," he said, undoing the last of his buttons, exposing his muscular chest. She had seen his chest before, when they'd gone camping and he had taken a swim in the lake. And then, like now, she thought it was definitely a chest worth looking at, worth sliding her hands over, worth teasing with her tongue.

Her gaze followed Chance's fingers as he removed his shirt and tossed it aside, but when those same fingers went to the fastener of his pants her breath caught. Still, she couldn't avert her eyes. They watched as he eased his zipper down. A heaviness settled in her stomach and every nerve ending within her came vibrantly alive when he pushed those same pants down his hips.

She had never seen a man undress before. At sixteen she had actually closed her eyes when Sam had done it. As an adult she was now seeing a male in the flesh for the first time. She'd always suspected Chance had a nice body, but now, she saw first hand just how nice it was. And she saw just how aroused he was since the black briefs he wore showed the large ridge of his erection. She couldn't help but stare when he proceeded to remove the last stitch of clothing.

"Now it's time for your clothes to come off."

Her gaze flew up to his face, fighting the panic of not knowing just how her body would be able to accommodate such a well-endowed man. But when her eyes met his, that sexy smile of his aroused her even more and she knew that she wouldn't worry. The two of them would fit perfectly.

With slow and precise steps, he covered the short distance separating them and his hand, as gentle as it could be, reached out and stroked her arm. "Do you know how often I've dreamed about undressing you?" he whispered huskily as he lifted her hand to his mouth and kissed her palm.

She took a deep breath to steady herself. The touch of his moist tongue on her hand only fueled the fire that was steadily burning inside of her. "No, how often?" she managed to get out in a raspy breath.

"Too often," he said, reaching behind her to undo the clasp at the nape of her neck. "And seeing you in this dress tonight didn't help matters any."

He took a step back, loosened the straps away from her neck and the black georgette material slid down her legs. And when he offered her his hand for assistance, she took it and stepped out of the dress. Now she was naked except for her thong, thigh-high hose and shoes.

His gaze, she noticed, was fastened on her breasts and she watched, as if in slow motion, when he reached out and fondled them, caressing them, shaping them to the feel of his hands.

At his touch, her breathing became erratic, and she leaned into him to grip his shoulders, for fear she would melt to the floor. She clutched him when he leaned forward and took a nipple into his mouth, licking and sucking first one then the other. Each and every tug sent sensuous sensations all the way to her womb.

"Chance," she whispered, arching toward him even more. She gasped when he scooped her into his arms and carried her over to the bed, placed her on it. Gently he removed her shoes and then his hand slid up her legs to get rid of her hose. Taking off her thong was easy since there wasn't much to it but Kylie saw how dark his eyes got when the most intimate part of her body became exposed.

His smoldering gaze focused on the mound between her thighs, and Kylie began to feel nervous with all the attention. Chance was definitely enjoying the view, but if he only knew how fast her heart was beating, he wouldn't be looking at her this way.

"I want you, Kylie," he said silkily.

She met his gaze and replied softly, "I want you, too, Chance."

Her words, spoken honestly and seductively, zapped Chance of what little control he had. Placing a knee on the bed, he reached down and drew her naked body to his and kissed her with all the love he had in his heart. The moment he slipped his tongue inside her mouth she latched on to it, returning his kiss with an intensity he knew the both of them felt.

He reluctantly broke the kiss and began caressing her all over, becoming familiar with the soft feel of her body and the sexy scent of her arousal. He kissed her all over, starting with her breasts and moving down to her navel, but as he went lower still, he felt her tense. Knowing he was about to carry her through unchartered waters, he lifted his head and met her gaze. "Kylie?"

The eyes that met his were glazed with desire and shadowed in uncertainty. "Yes?"

"Do you trust me?"

"Yes," she responded in a breathy sound. "I trust you."

"How much?" he asked, giving her one of those sexy smiles again.

Her voice was soft and throaty when she said, "Considering all you know about me, I trust you a lot. I haven't been with anyone in fifteen years, Chance. That in itself should say something."

"It does. And your trust in me is special. I want to make not just tonight, but this entire weekend special for the both of us."

He must have read the question in her eyes, as he chuckled and said. "And no, I don't plan on keeping you in bed all weekend. There's going to be more to our relationship than sex, Kylie. I want to take you on our first official date tomorrow night. Will you let me do that?"

Kylie caught her bottom lip between her teeth. She still wasn't ready for their kids to know they were involved, but with Marcus and Tiffany away for the weekend, she and Chance were finally free to do whatever they wanted to do. "Yes, I'd like that," she said quietly.

He smiled. "Good. And another thing."

She quirked an eyebrow. "What?"

"I want to introduce you to various types of lovemaking but I promise to take things slow and easy. And I also promise not to do anything you're not comfortable with doing. I want to show you that making love is the most intimate act two people can share, as well as the most pleasurable. And I want to share every aspect of it with you." He reached out his hand and slowly traced it up her leg toward the center of her thighs.

The closer he got to a certain part of her, the harder it became for Kylie to concentrate and to breathe. "Every aspect?" she asked breathlessly.

"Yes. I want to take you to a place you've never been before. Pleasureland. I want us to go there together and participate in the kind of pleasure that only the two of us can generate." His voice went lower when he asked, "Will you go there with me?"

She swallowed when his knuckles nudged her thighs apart and his fingers touched her—right there in what had to be her hot spot. And she knew he'd found her not only hot but wet as well. "Yes, I'll go there with you," she said, barely able to get the words out.

"Anyplace? At any time…within reason?"

Chance was stroking her and she could feel pressure building inside of her. Pressure she needed to release. "Yes."

"My touching you this way is just the beginning," he said as he continued to stroke her. "I want to take you on one hell of an adventure. Are you okay with that?"

Biting back a moan, she closed her eyes. "Yes, I'm okay with it." The feathery touch of his fingers was slowly driving her insane. It seemed as if he was touching every sensitive cell that was located between her legs.

"You sure?"

"Yes, I'm sure."

"And what if I replaced my fingers with my tongue?" he leaned over and whispered hotly in her ear.

Her eyes flew open. And she knew the flush that had suddenly appeared on her face told him everything. She took a deep breath as she melted inside with the thought of him doing that. "Why would you want to do that?" she somehow managed to ask.

"Because I want to satisfy my taste for you in a way that kissing won't do, Kylie."

"But no one has ever… I've never…"

"Yes, I know," he said silkily. "But I want to be your first. May I?"

Her heart pounded erratically in her chest. She had to swallow twice before she spoke. "Yes, if you're sure you want to do that."

"Oh, baby, more than anything, I do."

As soon as he had spoken those words, Chance slid off the bed, gently brought her body closer to the edge and knelt in front of her open legs. Then he leaned forward, inhaled her scent and took her into his mouth.

Kylie's body bucked at the first touch of his tongue. A deep groan escaped her throat when he proceeded to taste her with a hunger that appeared unquenched. She clutched the bedspread, needing something to hold on to. His mouth was literally driving her insane and she had to clamp her lips closed to stop herself from screaming.

Chance lifted his mouth only long enough to say, "Just let go, baby, and come for me."

No sooner had he replaced his mouth on her, she did just what he had asked. The force of the climax hit her. And when it did she forgot everything except how all of her senses seemed to be gathered at this one particular spot, making it impossible to hold back. She screamed out his name when her body splintered into a thousand pieces. Waves and waves of pleasure washed over her and through her. She cried out several more times as her body, soul and mind were transported to a place where only pleasure resided.

Pleasureland.

It was a place that only Chance could take her.

Chance reluctantly pulled his mouth away and sat back on his heels, watching the last contractions of Kylie's orgasm move through her. He had dreamed of taking her this way for so long, the only thing he could do for the moment was to sit there and inhale the womanly scent of her, savor her taste.

Hearing the woman he loved scream out his name had filled him with a joy he'd never felt before. But he knew for them, this was just the beginning of one hell of a weekend, one hell of a relationship, and one hell of a future.

Driven by an intense need to become a part of her in yet another way, he reached for the pants he had discarded earlier. He pulled his wallet out of the back pocket to get one of the condoms he'd put there. He quickly slipped it on, wanting to join their bodies while she was still in the throes of lingering passion.

He eased her back to the center of the bed and joined her there. When his face was mere inches from hers she slowly opened her eyes and met his gaze. A satisfied curve touched the corners of her mouth. "Hi."

He smiled back. "Hi."

"I came," she said like it had been a miracle, a pleasure she would remember always.

He smiled. "Yes, you did and I'm going to make you come again."

She blinked at him as if such a thing wasn't possible. "You will," he assured her.

And then he kissed her, taking her mouth in a way that let her know just how intent he was on making it happen for her again. Moments later, his mouth left hers to skim down her jaw, past her neck, as it traced a damp trail toward her breasts, tasting them as he'd done earlier, while reaching down to sink his fingers in the flesh he had just tasted a while ago.

"Chance." She called out his name when she felt her body getting all heated again.

He eased over her. "Open your eyes, Kylie, and look at me." He wanted to be caught in her gaze the exact moment he joined with her. If she wasn't quite ready to hear about his love, he wanted her to at least feel it.

Desire and love pulsed through his veins, made his erection just that much harder, thicker, and when she opened her eyes he knew he needed to be inside of her, feel the length of him stroking her, claiming her as his, totally consuming her.

He raised her hands above her head and with their fingers laced together, their gazes locked, he slowly eased inside of her, finding her wet, ready, yet tight.

"Oh, Chance. I need this. I need you," she whispered.

His response was a hard thrust that shook him to the core, and as he went deeper inside of her, she moaned out her pleasure. "Yes!"

And then her body arched beneath him and he began moving inside of her, in and out, as her moans grew louder, more intense, more demanding and the eyes holding his looked at him with amazement and wonder. She began moving with him, their bodies in perfect rhythm.

Then she came again.

He felt the explosion of pleasure rip through her. Her fingers dug into his back and her legs locked around his waist, and he kept making love to her. Reality was better than any dream he could possibly have. He moved in and out of her, intensifying both their pleasure with every movement, feeling the urgency building up inside of her again.

Her next explosion triggered his and he screamed her name the exact moment she screamed his. He took her mouth in one final deep kiss, putting into it everything that he had, everything that was him. And moments later when the waves finally subsided, he was too weak, too satisfied, too far spent to move. But not wanting to crush her with his weight, he somehow managed to shift while keeping their bodies connected. He wasn't ready to sever the ties yet.

Feeling an aftermath of pleasure that he hadn't ever felt before, he buried his face in her breasts and wrapped his legs around her to lock her body in place with his, as they both closed their eyes in sheer exhaustion. The only word he could think of to describe what they had just shared was incredible.

As Chance's breathing began to slow, he knew that Kylie becoming a part of his life was a gift that he would cherish forever.

Chapter 12

Chance lay there and watched as Kylie awakened. Even before she fully opened her eyes, she covered her yawn, and it was then that he leaned over and gently pulled her hand away before capturing her mouth in his. Seconds later the same desire that was raging through him took over her. She sighed into his mouth and wrapped her arms around his neck, surrendering to the passion he evoked.

The mere memory of all the things they had done last night sent heat escalating through his body and making it harder not to take her again. The intensity of his love for her went well beyond the scope of his understanding, but as far as he was concerned it didn't really matter as long as he was smart enough to accept it. And he did.

He couldn't imagine ever being without her and while he'd watched her sleep, he had felt as if he couldn't breathe unless he had kissed her again. Now he was getting his fill, as he'd done last night while making love to her. They had made love more times than he could count, but he wasn't keeping numbers so it hadn't mattered. The important thing was that each time he'd open his arms she had come into them willingly, without any hesitation or reservation, and that had meant a lot to him.

When he slowly released her mouth he watched as she dragged in a shaky breath. It was pretty obvious that she had never been awakened in such a manner before. "Wow," she said softly. "What was that for?"

He smiled and brought her body closer to him. He wished he could tell her it was for being the woman he loved, but there was no way he could do that. At least not yet. "That was for being the special person you are, and for allowing me to spend so much time with you last night."

A crooked smile claimed her lips as she remembered. "Yes, we did spend a lot of time together, didn't we?" Even now the rock-solid feel of him pressed against her belly was making her hot and achy all over again.

His lips formed into a half grin. "Sweetheart, we did more than that. I spent so much time inside of you that a certain part of my body actually thinks that's where it belongs. It wants another visit and is worse than a junkie in need of a fix."

"Really?" she said, arching her back and automatically pressing her pelvis against his hard erection.

"Yeah, and if you keep that up—"

"What are you going to do?"

She gasped when he quickly took hold of her hips and lifted her leg to cross over his, locking their position. Before she could gather her next breath he shifted his body and entered her.

Once inside her warm depth, he began thrusting back and forth inside of her, while his hands, wrapped tightly around her waist, held her immobile. His mouth feasted on hers with the same intensity as the lower part of his body was taking her. Mating with her.

She reluctantly tore her mouth from his. "Wh-what about protection?" she asked, barely able to get the words out.

He withdrew slowly and then sank back deep inside of her to the hilt. "I got it covered." And then he took her mouth again and her hips automatically bucked against his, reestablishing the rhythm they had created the night before.

After last night he should have been exhausted, but after sleeping with her nestled in his arms, his entire body was primed with more sexual energy than he'd ever had before. He could mate like this with her for hours. She was just that wet and he was just that needy.

She tore her mouth from his and dropped her head into his chest and moaned with each thrust he made into her body.

"Had enough?" he asked, refusing to stop or slow down. The sensations flowing through him were giving him added stamina, making him greedy.

She lifted her head and looked him in the eye. "No."

A single chuckle escaped him. "That's good," he said adjusting his angle. He started making little circles around her lips with his tongue. And then he began thrusting his tongue back and forth inside her mouth, mimicking the action going on below, using the same rhythm.

"Chance!"

He latched his gaze on her face, saw the intensity in her features and knew she was about ready to explode. "Let go, baby," he coaxed, knowing whenever she came he would, too.

She arched toward him, locked her body tighter to his. It was obvious from the way she was digging her fingers into his shoulders that he'd hit gold again and zeroed in on her G-spot, that sexually sensitive area that he had discovered last night had made her have multiple orgasms back-to-back, several times over.

He grabbed hold of her butt and slowed down his strokes, although it tortured him to do so. But he was attuned to her pleasure. He stroked slowly in and out of her, hitting her in that very special spot that made her moans become louder and her breath deeper. When she glanced down and saw the way he was moving in and out of her, she began mumbling. "Oh, yes, that's the spot. Go deeper, Chance. Please. Deeper."

He did what she asked and she surprised him when she began flexing her inner muscles, milking him for all it was worth. He began feeling sensuous contractions inch all through his groin. "Aw, hell."

He began stroking her with an intensity that almost bordered on obsession, intent on pushing her over the edge, the same way she was pushing him. She dropped her head back against his chest again and he was getting turned on even more from the way their bodies were vigorously mating.

"Had enough yet?" he asked, his voice ragged. He hoped she hadn't.

She lifted her face and shook her head. Her eyes, glazed with desire met his and she arched into him, letting him know her answer before she said the words. "Not enough. More."

"Be careful what you ask for, sweetheart," he said. "I'm a Steele, remember. I'm made to last."

And then he withdrew slowly, just long enough to adjust positions, and in a flash Kylie found herself on her back with her legs wrapped around the upper part of Chance's shoulders. And then he thrust inside of her to the hilt, harder and faster.

She screamed out his name, clung to him and succumbed to him as a rush of molten heat speared through her. When he screamed her name and pressed her hips she knew he had gotten caught up in the same exhilarating passion as she had.

She nipped at the corner of his lip and he leaned down and opened his mouth fully over hers, deepening the kiss to taste as much of her as he could. And at that moment, Kylie knew if another fifteen years went by without ever having taken part in something like this, she would survive because in a mere twelve hours Chance had given her enough lovemaking to last a lifetime.

"You have a beautiful home, Chance," she called out to him.

"Thanks," he answered from the bedroom.

Kylie stood leaning against the marble counter in Chance's kitchen. After enjoying their early-morning delight, she had lain in bed, convinced that she couldn't move, and had wondered if she would ever be able to do so again. But he had gathered her into his arms like a newborn baby and had taken her into the bathroom to shower with him. It was a shower she doubted she would ever forget. She managed a smile and shook her head thinking that even now it was hard to believe that the woman who had made love to him beneath the spray of water had actually been her.

She had changed into her favorite capri pants after their shower, then she had fixed them a quick breakfast and he had talked her into going with him to the gym to watch him and his brothers play their regular Saturday morning game of basketball. But first he needed to swing by his place to change clothes. Showing up on the courts wearing his tux would definitely give his brothers something to talk about for a long time.

On the drive over to his place he had told her that he'd had the house built a few years after his wife died, because he felt he could not get on with his life while still living in the home they'd shared together. Now here she was, waiting patiently while he changed into a T-shirt and jogging pants.

"Sure I can't get you anything?" he asked, coming into the kitchen and setting his gym bag on the counter beside her.

A smile touched her lips. "No thanks. You've given me too much already."

"You haven't seen or felt everything yet," he said, as he smoothed his hand over the bare skin of her arm before grabbing her curvy bottom to bring her closer to the fit of him. He dipped his head, kissing her still-swollen lips thoroughly.

"You know we can skip that game with my brothers," he murmured softly against her lips.

"Hmm, and deny them the chance to work off their competitive frustrations? I wouldn't dare," she said, grinning.

He gave her one of his most charming smiles. "Forget my brothers. I promise if we were to stay here I'd make it worth your while."

Her grin broadened. "There's no doubt in my mind that you would, but I'm not sure I can keep up with you, Chance."

He bent his head and nipped gently at her neck. "Hey, you've been doing a pretty good job so far."

Her laughter was low and husky. "Thanks, but I have only so much energy to spare. I may be younger than you but I'm definitely out of practice."

He took her hand, raised it to his lips and kissed her fingers. "If you're sure you're not ready to try the springs in my bed then I guess we'd better go."

While walking her out to the car, he said, "I've made reservations for us tonight at Cedar Keys."

She glanced up at him. "Cedar Keys?" She'd heard the place was rather expensive.

"Yes, Cedar Keys. My special lady deserves special treatment," he said, opening the car door for her.

My special lady. A part of Kylie wished that she was indeed his special lady and then immediately regretted the thought. Just because she was in love with him didn't mean he had to love her back. She had to remind herself that this weekend was about absolute pleasure. Love had nothing to do with it.

"Will your brothers wonder why I'm with you?"

Chance glanced over at her before starting the ignition. "They know we left the ball together last night, Kylie."

The insinuation of his statement gave her a moment's pause. "So chances are they know we spent the night together." It was a statement more so than a question.

"Not necessarily. For all they know I took you home and I went to my place after inviting you to join me this morning. But will it bother you if they've figured things out?"

"I know that it shouldn't," she said quietly. "But I am the mother of the girl their nephew has a crush on."

Chance lifted an eyebrow. "So?"

"So they might figure that I should be setting a better example."

Chance frowned. He reached over and took her hand in his. "Hey, we're spending time in Pleasureland this weekend, remember? We don't have time to take any guilt trips. Besides, there's no need for one," he said gently. "One day you're going to have to accept that what we do is our business, Kylie. And we don't have to answer to anyone."

She drew in a long, unsteady breath. "I wish it was that easy for me to think that way, Chance. But after I got pregnant with Tiffany, my parents made sure that all their friends knew they had nothing to do with the way I turned out. I heard them call me a bad seed once. Since then I've tried so hard to be good and to raise Tiffany the right way."

He reached over and pulled her into his arms, hugging her close. "Oh, baby, you have. You're being too hard on yourself. No one is perfect, not even your parents. And they had no right to lay something that heavy on you. We all make mistakes. I bet if you were to clean out their closets you'll find something they'd rather leave hidden."

She shook her head. "I doubt it. You don't know my parents."

"Yes, I think I do. They aren't one of a kind, you know. There are others out there just like them."

A smile she couldn't contain curved her lips. "Yes, I know."

"Then remember that. Always keep that thought in mind."

He released her and Kylie thought she fell in love with him even more at that moment. "You're good at that, you know."

He glanced over at her as he began backing the car out the driveway. "Good at what?"

"Soothing my ruffled feathers."

He smiled. "Glad I could help."

"Hey, man, did you have to bring your own personal cheerleader?" Bas whispered as he set a screen for Chance to shoot.

Chance laughed as he made yet another shot and Kylie

stood and cheered again. "Jealousy won't get you any points, Bas. You could have brought Cassandra."

Bas frowned. "Are you kidding? Can any of you imagine her sitting over there on the bleachers watching me get hot and sweaty?"

Donovan chuckled. "No, I don't think we can."

"Hey, will the three of you cut the crap and let's get some playtime?" Morgan growled, pushing Bas out of the way and getting the ball from Chance.

"Hey, that's a foul, Morgan," Chance called out, watching Morgan dribble the ball down the court to make a shot. He then turned to Bas. "What's his problem?"

"Seems like some lady he was interested in last night at the ball wasn't all that receptive," Bas said as they ran down the court to retrieve the stolen ball.

"Who?"

"The woman who could be Queen Latifah's twin, Helena Spears. He asked her out and she declined. She's probably the first woman who's ever turned down a dinner date with him. He evidently doesn't handle rejection well."

Chance grinned. "Evidently."

The game ended an hour or so later with Bas and Chance winning. Morgan, who'd made six fouls, would have gotten thrown out of the game had they been playing by real basketball rules.

Kylie sat patiently on the bleachers waiting for the men to come out of the locker room, where they had gone to shower and change. When Bas came out first, he crossed the gym to come over to talk to her.

"So," he asked, dropping in the seat next to her, "what did you think of our game?"

She couldn't help but smile. "Interesting. A lot of rules were broken."

Bas chuckled. "Yeah, better broken rules than broken noses. We need this game every week to work off frustrations. Otherwise, we'd be at each other's throats at some point during the week."

"So I heard."

After a few moments of silence, Bas, who had a habit of shooting straight from the hip, said, "Chance has never brought a woman to watch us play before, so I figure you must be special."

Kylie gave him a wry glance. "Do you?"

"Yes, I do."

"That's good to know because I think he's special, too."

Bas shook his head and chuckled softly. "You don't seem too happy about it."

Kylie let out a sigh. "We should be concentrating on our kids."

"Hey, Marcus is a smart guy and from what I hear your Tiffany is a smart girl."

"Yes, but trouble has a way of finding even smart people."

"You're talking to someone who knows. Trouble used to be my middle name."

Kylie caught her bottom lip between her teeth. "Chance is a nice guy," she said quietly. "Marcus is lucky to have him for a father."

"That's the same thing Chance said about you."

Kylie glanced over at Bas. "What?"

"That you were a nice person and that Tiffany was lucky to have you as a mother." Bas then leaned forward. "Hey, do me a favor, will you?"

"And what favor is that?"

"You've made him happy and—"

"Me?"

"Yes, you. I've never seen him in such a good mood. Sometimes I think that smile is plastered to his face."

Kylie shook her head. "I have nothing to do with it."

"Yes, you do. At first he was all bent out of shape at the thought that Marcus's attention had gotten off his books and shifted to a girl, but once he met you then he saw why."

Kylie's eyebrows pulled together in a frown. "What do you mean?"

Bas smiled. "He was so taken with you that he could see how Marcus could be taken with Tiffany." When Kylie didn't say anything, Bas said, "Now getting back to that favor…"

"Yes?"

"Keep making Chance happy. He's had a lot of sadness in his life and if there's anyone who deserves to be happy, it's him. I think he's a pretty great guy."

Before Kylie could say anything, Bas stood, jumped off the bleachers to the court and called over his shoulder, "I'll go see what's keeping him."

Kylie leaned back and thought about what Bas had said. Before she could give it too much thought, every nerve ending in her body came instantly alive when Chance walked out of the locker room. He had changed into a pair of jeans and another T-shirt. He crossed the gym to her with a heart-stopping smile on his face.

Catching her breath, she decided to go down to meet him. As soon as she got close he leaned down and brushed his lips over hers. "Sorry for the delay. I had to talk to Morgan about something."

She nodded as he took her hand in his and led her out of the gym. "That's okay. I enjoyed chatting with Bas while I waited. Is Morgan okay? He was playing a mean game today. He committed a lot of fouls."

Chance's smile curved into a full grin. "Yes, they were intentional. He had a lot of frustrations to work off."

"Oh."

Snaking his arm around her waist, Chance snuggled her closer to his side as they walked to the car. "What were your plans for today?"

"I was going grocery shopping."

He laughed. "Hey, so was I. Do you want to go together?"

When Chance opened the car door and she slid inside, she glanced up at him and smiled. "Why not? It just might be fun."

Later that evening as Kylie finished getting dressed for dinner she thought that grocery shopping with Chance had not only been fun, it had been educational as well.

He had known what fruits were in season, he made sure she checked the expiration date on everything she purchased and he advised her to stay away from the generic brands, claiming there was a difference in taste.

And she had discovered that they liked the same foods, and the same flavor ice cream. In fact, they had almost argued about who would get the last half gallon of chocolate-chip cookie dough until one of the store clerks assured them there was a case in the back.

After their shopping adventure he had brought her home to unload her groceries and indicated he would return around seven to take her to dinner. It was almost seven now and she was ready.

Kylie smiled as she glanced at herself in the mirror. She was wearing a dress she had purchased earlier that year when she had attended her father's retirement party. Her mother had complimented her on how good she'd looked in it, and now she hoped Chance shared that same opinion. She was just about to add strawberry lip color to her lips when the phone rang. She quickly picked it up. "Hello."

"Hi, Mom."

"Tiffany! I'm glad you called. How's Disney World?"

"Disney World is fine but I think Gramma had too much of Mickey and Minnie for one day. Me and Gramps are going to leave her at the hotel and go to Epcot later. How was the ball last night?"

Kylie was surprised her daughter remembered anything about the ball. "It was nice. Your godmother's committee did an excellent job."

"Was Marcus's father there?"

Kylie raised an eyebrow, wondering why Tiffany wanted to know. "Yes, he was there."

"So you saw him?"

"Yes, I saw him."

"Was he with someone?"

Kylie refused to answer that. "Tiffany, why are you asking me questions about Marcus's father?"

"Oh, just curious. Marcus and I talked before I left and he's concerned that his dad doesn't date much."

"It's not the end of the world for a person not to date, Tiffany."

"I know and that's what I told Marcus since you don't date, either. Okay, Mom, I got to go, Gramps is waiting for me. Talk to you later."

"Okay, sweetheart, have fun and tell Mom and Dad hello."

After she hung up the phone Kylie decided to cover all her bases in case Tiffany hit up her godmother for answers about the ball. She quickly picked up the phone and dialed Lena's number. "Don't be surprised if you receive a call from Tiffany asking questions about last night's ball," she told her friend.

"What kind of questions?"

"Like who Chance was with."

Lena chuckled. "He was with you."

"Yes, but I prefer her not knowing that, Lena."

"Sure, if that's the way you want it."

"It is." Something in Lena's voice made Kylie wonder if her friend was all right and she decided to ask.

"No, not really. I met this gorgeous man last night at the ball. He asked me out and I turned him down."

"Why?"

"Kylie, you know the score. Do you know how many times I've been dropped, sometimes even before the first date, when the guy finds out Mom and I come as a pair."

"Not all guys will make a big deal out of it, Lena."

"Yes, but I'm tired of trying to figure out those who will and those who won't. I don't plan on dating for a while."

Kylie frowned. "I don't know if that's a good idea."

Lena chuckled. "Looks who's talking."

"My situation is different and you know it. I don't date because I prefer not to. You want to date but you're afraid to."

"I am not."

"You are, too."

"Okay, so maybe I am. What's wrong with me protecting myself against heartbreak?"

"You don't know that will happen for sure. And if a man doesn't want you because you care enough to see to your mother's welfare, then screw him."

"Umm, speaking of screw...where did you and Chance disappear to last night?"

Silence pulsed over the line for a brief second and then Kylie said, "He took me home."

"And?"

"And what?"

"And why do I think there's more to this story?"

"There is but I'd rather not discuss it now."

"Okay, just know that I'll be all ears at lunch on Wednesday."

"I doubt if you'll let me forget. Goodbye, and remember what to say if Tiffany calls asking questions."

As soon as Kylie hung up the phone she thought about her conversation with Lena. Lena was her very best friend, but there was no way Kylie would confess to her all she'd done with Chance last night and this morning. Just thinking about it made her feel mortified on one hand and giddy with pleasure on the other. Still, some things had to be kept from even your best friend. She could just imagine the look on Lena's face if she told her what had happened in the shower this morning, and how Chance had taken her against the wall while water sprayed down on them.

She glanced at the overnight bag on her bed. Chance had asked her to spend the night at his place and she'd agreed. Since this weekend was the only one they would share, she planned on making the most of it.

Chapter 13

"I hope you enjoyed tonight, Kylie."

She glanced up from studying the wine in her glass, locked gazes with Chance and smiled. "How could I not? Everything was wonderful. The food, the service, the location...my dinner date. Thanks for bringing me here, Chance."

A smile touched the corners of his lips. "I wanted our first real date to be special, somewhere that didn't serve hamburgers."

Kylie grinned. "And it was special." She was suddenly filled with regret knowing this had been their first real date and also their last. There was no way they could continue seeing each other after Marcus and Tiffany returned, but she didn't want to think about that now. They still had tonight and all day tomorrow.

"Do you want any dessert?" he asked, and she thought his voice had a kind of husky purr to it. The expression in his eyes wasn't helping matters any, either. She'd have dessert later, she thought. Chance wanted the same thing she wanted. A bed with both of them in it.

"None for me tonight, but thanks for asking. What about you? Do you have a sweet tooth?"

He shook his head and grinned. "No, not exactly. I think I'll pass, too."

He leaned over the table to make sure she was the only one who would hear his next words. "What I really want is to take you to my place, strip you naked and make love to you. All night long."

Only the flicker of her eyelids told him she had been shocked by such honesty. But then the heated look in her eyes told him how much she wanted what he wanted.

With self-control, she neatly folder her napkin and placed it on the table. Then she looked up and shot him a sexy grin. "Then I guess we should leave now, don't you?"

Kylie found herself glancing around Chance's home for the second time that day. She had given him her overnight bag and he had taken it to the bedroom.

He had surprised her. With the heated looks he'd been giving her all evening, she'd figured he would have pounced on her the first chance he got. She'd even expected him to pull the car to the side of the road like he'd done last night and kiss her senseless. If nothing else, she had fully expected him to strip her naked the moment she had stepped inside his home.

But he hadn't done any of those things and she thought he was controlling himself admirably. So much so that she was tempted to see just how far that control could go.

"Would you like a cup of coffee or anything?"

She turned when he reentered the room. He had removed

his dinner jacket and tie, and now her gaze lingered on his white shirt as she thought about the chest it covered and remembered how she had smothered her face in that chest while he'd rocked back and forth inside her body, making her moan, groan and scream.

"No, I don't want any coffee. Thanks for asking. But there is something I want."

"What?"

"A kiss. It seems I've gotten addicted to them."

"Kisses?" he asked, slowly crossing the room to her.

"Yes, but only yours."

When he came to a stop in front of her, he reached out and wrapped his arms around her waist. In response, her arms wound around his neck. She raised her chin and looked him dead in the eyes and almost melted at the heat she saw there. When he leaned forward, she lifted her lips up for the kiss she knew she would get.

As soon as his mouth touched hers, she let out a deep, satisfied moan that she felt all the way to the pit of her stomach. And when he began stroking her tongue, with all the mastery that he possessed, she moaned some more. He tasted of the wine they'd had at dinner and of the peppermint he had popped into his mouth while walking her to the car. She enjoyed the flavor of both. When he deepened the kiss she forgot everything except for the way he was making her feel.

His arms were no longer around her waist. At some point in time they had moved and his hands were now cupping her bottom, pressing her closer to him, letting her feel the strength of his growing arousal.

He released her mouth long enough for her to draw in a breath. The same breath that hitched when his lips trailed to her throat and he branded her neck again.

"Chance," she whispered.

"Yes, sweetheart?"

She tilted her head back and met his gaze. "I thought you wanted to strip my clothes off."

"I do."

"What's stopping you?"

"You never said that I could."

Kylie stared at him, remembering that last night he had asked if it was okay to undress her. It seemed that Chance Steele operated with a code of honor and that endeared him to her even more. "All right, then, I'm giving you my permission."

He took a step back and she watched his gaze travel slowly over her body, from head to toe. When he looked up, his eyes lingered on the curves of her breasts visible in the low V-neckline. He realized she wasn't wearing a bra. She could tell by the look in his eyes. That same look made her nipples harden, become sensitive to the point where she could actually feel desire roll around in her stomach.

His gaze then moved to the hemline of her dress. It was longer than the one she'd worn last night, but he seemed mesmerized by the front split, probably wondering what she had or didn't have on underneath.

"Last night I thought you looked simply gorgeous in black. But tonight I think you look sexy as hell in red," he said in a husky voice.

She blinked when she watched him back up a few steps and then walk over to the sofa and sit down. "Come here, Kylie," he said in a voice that sounded strained even to her ears.

She stared at him, confused. How was he going to strip her bare while sitting down?

"Kylie?"

Deciding she would soon find out, she crossed the room to him.

"Lift your leg in my lap so I can take off your shoes."

She did what he asked and he took off her shoes one at a time. When she was about ready to place her foot back on the floor, he kept it in his lap, resting against his hard erection while he slid his hand up her leg a little farther, going underneath her dress to touch the center of her thighs, only to discover her panty hose was a barrier.

Apparently deciding a pair of Hanes wouldn't stop him from doing what he wanted, he placed her foot on the floor then eased to the edge of the sofa and reached both hands under her dress to work the panty hose down her hips. She stepped out of them and then kicked them aside.

"Now put your right leg back in my lap."

Again she did as he requested and this time he was able to slide his hand a little farther up her leg than before. She moaned out loud when his finger touched her center and slowly stroked her.

"Ahh, just as I thought," he leaned in closer to say. "You aren't wearing any panties."

His words hardly registered. All she could think about was the feel of his fingers inside of her, making her even wetter.

"Let me see just what else you aren't wearing tonight, Kylie."

Before she could gather her next breath, he reached up with his free hand and yanked the top part of her dress down. Her breasts spilled free right in his face.

"Place your hands on my shoulders, bend your knee a little more and lean toward me."

The moment she did so, he captured a breast in his mouth

and his tongue stroked it, just like his fingers were stroking her.

She clutched at his shoulders, unable to hold back just how his mouth and fingers were making her feel. Chance definitely knew how to work both ends at the same time. She was melting from the inside out. If he continued doing this for much longer she doubted even his shoulders would be able to support her.

He let go of her breast and leaned forward. "Are you ready for me, Kylie?" he whispered hotly in her ear.

Unable to answer, she nodded.

"That's good because I've been ready for you all day. And tonight at dinner it was hard for me not to spread you out on the table and make you the only entrée I wanted to feast on."

At his words an all-consuming need raced through her body and she cried out his name when she felt the first sign of an explosion on the horizon. "Chance, I need you."

"And where do you need me, baby?"

"Inside of me," she whispered.

He suddenly lifted her in strong arms, and she closed her eyes and pressed her face against his chest.

Her eyes opened when she felt herself being placed on a hard, solid surface. He had sat her on his kitchen counter. "Chance?"

He smiled as he began taking off his shirt and removing his pants. "When I saw you in here today, standing in this very spot, I knew I had to do this. I want to take you right here. Right now," he said, quickly putting on a condom.

"Here? Now? Are you serious?"

"Oh, yes."

He then pulled her dress over her head and tossed it to the floor to join his own discarded clothing. Before she could say another word, or let out another breath, he took hold of her hips, opened her thighs and guided his shaft inside of her.

And then the thrusting began. She wrapped her arms around his neck as delicious sensations began engulfing her. "This is insane," she said, leaning forward and nipping the corner of his mouth.

"No," he said in a husky voice as his body continued to mate with hers. "This is a dream come true. A fantasy in the making. So enjoy."

And she did. He drew her closer and she spread her legs wider to accommodate him. He kissed her deeply. Then he released her mouth to pay homage to her breasts again, flicking his tongue across each nipple, sucking one and then the other, causing a sensuous tension to coil deep within her womb.

"Chance!"

The explosion hit and she cried out, dug her fingers deep in his shoulders as sensation after sensation engulfed her. She thought she would die then and there from consuming so much pleasure.

And then she felt his body jerk and knew he was experiencing one hell of an orgasm as well. She reached out and held him as he shuddered uncontrollably with his release.

It was a while before either could catch their breaths, and when they did, neither seemed inclined to move. So she inched closer, and with as much strength as she could muster, she tightened her legs around him, enjoying the feel of him still buried inside of her. When he was finally able to lift his head to meet her eyes, she gave him a sated smile. "I've heard that things can get pretty hot in a kitchen, but this is a bit much, don't you think?" she whispered with barely enough breath.

He reached out and caressed her cheek. "And this isn't as hot as it will get for us."

That bit of news made her inch even closer to him. "It's not?"

"No, it's not. You haven't seen or experienced anything yet."

Kylie wondered what else there was. They had made love in a bed, in the shower, on the kitchen counter...

"You ever do it in a hot tub?"

His question got her immediate attention. "No."

He smiled. "Good. Then this ought to be fun."

Late Sunday afternoon after returning home, Kylie stood in front of her bedroom mirror and gazed at her reflection. With her messed up hair, kiss-swollen lips and hickeys on both sides of her neck, she definitely looked like a woman who had let go and indulged in her sensuous side. Naughty was too mild a word to describe how she had acted this weekend. Wanton and loose were probably better.

"Hey, what are you doing? Looking for a spot that I missed?" Chance asked, entering the room. He walked up behind her, wrapped his arms around her and settled her body back against his.

Kylie thought him missing a spot was impossible. It had started out very innocent with them enjoying a bowl of ice cream after lunch. Then for no reason at all he had squirted caramel topping all over her, and moments later began licking every inch of her skin to get it off. And she had reciprocated, squirted him and licked every inch of him. She had to admit that for once in her life she had thrown caution to the wind and yielded to temptation.

"What are you thinking about, sweetheart?"

She met his gaze in the mirror and leaned back against

him when he tightened his arms around her. "You. Me. And what a wonderful weekend we had. I wish it didn't have to end."

"It doesn't."

She shook her head and grinned. "Yes, it does. Have you forgotten the kids will be back tomorrow?"

"No, I didn't forget but that shouldn't have any bearing on us."

She turned around to face him. "Of course it does. Surely you don't expect us to still swap beds with the kids around?"

He frowned. "No, but I do expect us to continue to see each other. And if we have to be discreet whenever we do share a bed, then we will."

"And what about the kids?"

"Tomorrow we can tell them that we've decided to start seeing each other."

She took a step back. "No, I don't think that's a good idea."

Chance rubbed his hand down his face. "Don't tell me we're back to that again."

"As far as I'm concerned we never left it."

"Then what was this weekend about, Kylie?"

"It was about us indulging in our fantasies. But now it's time to return to the real world, Chance, and there's no way I can let Tiffany know that I was involved in a weekend affair with you."

Angrily, he reached out and gripped her shoulders. "A weekend affair? That's all this was to you?"

She yanked away from him. "Why? Was it supposed to be something else?"

"I had hoped so," he said quietly, trying to get his anger

and frustrations under control. "The start of a committed relationship was how I saw things."

"But I can't become involved with anyone until Tiffany leaves home."

"Why?"

"Because I can't!"

"Then let me tell you what I think is your reason, which in my opinion is a damn poor excuse. Your parents have convinced you that getting pregnant at sixteen was a bad thing, and every since then you have worked your ass off trying to be a good girl in their eyes. So much so that you won't allow a man in your life. At first I thought it was all about the men in your life letting you down and not being dependable, and that still may be a part of it. But since you claim you trust me, why are you so afraid of letting me into your life?"

"I have to set an example for my daughter. Why can't you understand that?"

He frowned. "And not having a real life, not having a man around to show her how two people can share a loving relationship is setting an example for her?"

"There's more to life than people getting involved, Chance."

"What about people falling in love? Would it mean anything if I were to tell you that I love you? That I fell in love with you probably the first time I saw you that day?"

Kylie's eyes widened and then she shook her head and felt the tears that stung her eyes. "No, it wouldn't matter because I could tell you the same thing, Chance. I love you, too. And I probably fell in love with you that day as well."

"But then—"

"No. You loving me and me loving you won't make it okay. We still have to put our kids first. They think they're in love, too, and we can't downplay their feelings just because we've discovered ours. Just think of how it will look. The father loves the mother and the daughter loves the son. How dysfunctional can that be?"

His frown deepened. "So what are you suggesting? That we wait to see what becomes of our kids' romance before seeking our own? Well, I don't plan to do that. If you love me, and I mean truly love me, you'll know that we'll work things out together. But you have to be willing to step out on love and believe it."

She bowed her head and took a deep breath and then she looked back at him. "No, it won't work, Chance. Please try to understand. There are times in life when sacrifices have to be made."

"Well, if you're willing to let your love for me be the sacrificial lamb then it must not be the real thing, Kylie, because I can't think of anything that will ever stop me from loving you and wanting a committed relationship with you."

Without saying anything else he walked out of the room, and moments later Kylie heard the door slam shut behind him.

Chapter 14

"Mom?"

"Hmm?"

"Are you sure you're okay?"

Kylie pulled two bottles of apple juice out of the refrigerator before turning to her daughter. "I'm okay, sweetheart. What makes you think I'm not?"

Tiffany lifted one shoulder in a dainty shrug. "I don't know. It's just a feeling I have. Every since you picked me up from the airport yesterday you've been quiet."

"Well, I guess I have a lot on my mind, but I'm okay."

"Why are you still wearing that scarf? You usually don't wear scarfs."

Kylie's hand automatically went to the scarf around her neck, the one she was wearing to hide the two hickeys that Chance had placed there. "My throat had gotten sort of scratchy with the changing of the weather, I guess. I thought I'd take all precautions. The last thing I need to catch is a cold."

"But you're wearing it in the house."

Kylie gave Tiffany a pointed look. "I'm aware of where I am, Tiffany. Is wearing a scarf in the house a crime?"

"No, ma'am."

"Okay, then."

The kitchen got silent and Kylie regretted having gotten upset with Tiffany when she was only showing her concern. With a mantle of guilt on her shoulders, Kylie crossed the room and sat down at the table opposite her daughter. "Hey, how about you and I going to a movie this weekend?" she asked, trying to reclaim the easy camaraderie they'd started recently, at least before this past weekend.

Tiffany smiled. "Oh, that'll be neat. Will it be okay to invite Marcus and his dad?"

Kylie's body tensed with her daughter's question. The last person she wanted to be around this weekend was Chance. "I was hoping we could make it a girls' thing. We could even invite Lena to come with us."

"That sounds like fun, Mom, but I was hoping I could get to see Marcus this weekend."

"Didn't you see him at school today?"

"Yes."

"And won't you see him again tomorrow?"

"Yes."

"And the next day and the day after?"

"Yes, Mom, but you and Mr. Steele promised that we could have supervised outings and it's been almost three weeks since we went camping."

Kylie sighed. A part of her regretted having made that promise but at the time both she and Chance had known it was the best thing to keep the budding romance between their offspring under control. "Okay, then I'll take the both of you. There's no need to bother Chance this weekend and—"

"Mom, if you take us, it'll seem as if you're babysitting us. If both you and Mr. Steele go then it will be a foursome and it won't be so obvious that you're there to spy on us."

Kylie rolled her eyes. "I'd be there as a chaperone, Tiffany."

"Same difference."

Not wanting to get into an argument with her daughter, Kylie stood and said, "Have Marcus check to see if his father is free this weekend. Chance is a busy man and might have made other plans."

Later that night Kylie lay in bed and every so often she would glance over at the phone. Chance had made it a habit to call her around this time every night, but she knew after Sunday chances were that he wouldn't be calling anytime soon, if ever. And a part of her thought maybe it was for the best. He thought he had all the answers, but he would never understand the guilt trip her parents had placed on her shoulders after she'd gotten pregnant.

As she cuddled under the covers she thought about the weekend she had spent with Chance. There was no denying that it had been a fantasy come true, and heat flooded through her just thinking about all they had done. In fact today at the florist when she'd been alone her body actually trembled with the memories that were so vivid in her mind.

Their first date had been everything a first date should be, and what he probably hadn't even realized was, although it had been their first date, it had been her *first* date period. She and Sam had been too young to actually date and she hadn't gone out to dinner with any other man. So in reality, Chance had been her first in a lot of ways.

Tears blurring her eyes, she glanced over at the phone. She might as well get used to him not calling her ever again.

Chance threw onto his desk the document he'd been reading and glanced at the clock. Not that he was counting, but it had been three days, sixteen hours and forty-five minutes since he had last seen and talked to Kylie.

After what she had said to him on Sunday evening, she should have been the last person on his mind. She had decided that love or no love, there would not be a future for them.

Chance leaned back in his chair and hooked his hands behind his head. Dammit, he didn't want that. He wanted a life with her, a life that included marriage. Kylie was being more than stubborn. She was being downright difficult.

He couldn't help but remember their weekend together, and the days and nights they had shared. Those memories would sustain him in the coming months. He would need them.

He walked over to the window and stared out at Charlotte's skyline. It was almost two in the afternoon. Kylie would be at her shop. Was she thinking about him the way he was thinking about her? Probably not.

But she had admitted that she loved him.

He should have known that when a woman gave herself as completely to a man as Kylie had done to him this past weekend that love was involved. One thing was for certain: there was still Marcus and Tiffany to deal with, and because of their kids, Kylie couldn't put distance between them regardless of how much she might want to.

Whether she liked it or not, she hadn't seen the last of him.

"I don't know what, but something happened this weekend between our parents, Marcus," Tiffany whispered.

Marcus, who was sitting across from her in the library, glanced around to make sure Mrs. Kennard, the librarian who had a strict no-talking policy, wasn't anywhere close by. "Yes, I know," he whispered back. "This weekend was supposed to get them to together, not pull them apart. What do you think happened?"

Tiffany shook her head. "I don't know but I do know they spent time together this weekend."

Marcus lifted a brow. "And how do you know that?"

"Because Carly Owens said she saw them together at the grocery store."

"The grocery store? What were they doing at the grocery store?"

"Carly said they were actually shopping together. They didn't see her but she saw them. She said my mom had her cart and your dad had his, but they had come together in the same car."

"And she's sure it was *our* parents?"

"Yes, she's sure. She's met the both of them before but at different times."

"Umm, I find that interesting. If they were friendly enough to go grocery shopping together then what happened?"

Tiffany sighed. "I don't know. And there's also something else." She leaned in closer to make sure the students sitting at the other table didn't hear her. "My mom had a hickey on her neck and I think your dad put it there."

Disbelief flickered in Marcus's eyes. "You're kidding."

"No. She's been wearing a scarf to hide it, but I saw it anyway when she took the scarf off thinking I wasn't around."

Marcus nodded. "That means they had to have kissed."

"Right."

"Then what happened to make them start acting funny?"

Tiffany shook her head. "Who knows? Adults can be weird that way. Did your dad say that he would be available to go to the movies with us on Saturday?" Tiffany asked.

"I haven't asked him yet. He hasn't been in the best of moods since I got back."

"Neither has my mom. If after this weekend at the movies they're still not getting along, then we have to do something. I know they really like each other, but now I'm worried because your dad hasn't been calling at night like he used to do. I've been checking the caller ID every morning but your phone number isn't showing up."

"So what do you think we should do?"

Tiffany scrunched her forehead and then moments later a smile touched her features. "I have an idea but we may have to get an adult to help us pull it off."

Marcus glanced around again for Mrs. Kennard, and then turned back to Tiffany. "An adult like who?"

Tiffany thought about her godmother and decided it wouldn't be a good idea to solicit her help. "How about one of your uncles? The one you said who likes to have fun."

Marcus sighed. "That's Uncle Donovan, and this sounds serious."

"It is. We'll see how things go with them this weekend, but if they still aren't on the best of terms, we go to Plan B."

"What's Plan B?" Marcus asked.

Tiffany leaned in closer. "Here it is, so listen up."

Kylie chewed the corner of her lip as she watched Chance and Marcus get out of the SUV and begin walking toward her front door. That deep fluttering in her heart and the sensations that rolled around in her stomach whenever she saw Chance made her release the breath she'd been holding. She could only stand at the window and stare out at him, providing irrefutable proof of just how much she had missed seeing him these past few days, missed talking with him…making love with him.

A part of her questioned the sanity in not giving in to the love she felt for him. Even Lena had raked her over the coals during their lunch meeting that week when she'd told her best friend that Chance had admitted his love and she had admitted hers. Lena staunchly refused to agree with Kylie that this was one of those no-win situations where love wasn't enough.

"Mom, are Marcus and Mr. Steele here?"

Kylie turned away from the window upon hearing the excitement in her daughter's voice. "Yes, they just arrived."

"Good. I'll go open the door for them." And then Tiffany raced off.

A few moments later Kylie could hear the deep sexiness of Chance's voice all the way from the foyer, and the sound sent sizzling heat all through her body. Taking a deep breath, she grabbed her coat off the back of the sofa and left the living room to join everyone in the foyer.

The moment she rounded the corner she felt Chance's gaze on her. And the moment her eyes locked with his dark brown ones, she almost forgot to breathe. For some reason she couldn't look away.

"Hi, Kylie."

"Chance."

"You look nice."

"Thanks." Kylie inwardly sighed. Holding a conversation with him used to be so easy and now she was finding it too hard.

"Hi, Ms. Hagan."

Her gaze moved from Chance to Marcus and for a second she thought she saw a worried glint in his eyes. She smiled affectionately. "Hello, Marcus. How was your trip to Busch Gardens?"

"It was fun. I was telling Tiffany about it. Maybe the four of us could go there this summer."

Kylie nodded, although she doubted it.

"Is everyone ready to go?" Chance asked. "We don't want to be late for the movie."

Marcus and Tiffany rushed out the door leaving their parents alone in the foyer. Chance turned to her. "I meant what I said earlier, Kylie. You look nice in that pantsuit. That color looks good on you. But I think any color looks good on you."

"Thanks." She had decided to wear a lime-green linen pantsuit and instead of pinning her braids up she let them tumble about her shoulders.

She stared at the floor for a second and then glanced back up at him. "You look nice, too." She decided not to tell him that she'd always thought he looked suave in a suit, but sexy as hell in a pair of jeans.

"Thanks. Are you ready to go?"

"Yes."

"And, Kylie, no matter what's going on with us, let's make sure the kids have a good time tonight, all right?"

"All right."

They then walked out the door to join their kids in the SUV.

They saw the new Harry Potter movie.

Kylie was certain it had been a good movie but she hadn't fully concentrated on what was happening on the big screen. Instead her concentration had been on the man who had sat next to her. They had barely exchanged a single word but all during the movie she could feel the weight of his heavy stare. More than once she had glanced his way in the semidarkened theater to find him watching her.

Too often she had been tempted to reach out and slip her hand in his, filled with an intense desire to touch him, to feel his heat. It didn't take much for her to remember that heat, how he had consumed her with it whenever he touched her, kissed her or made love to her.

"Wasn't the movie awesome, Mom?" Tiffany said with enthusiasm in her voice as they left the theater and walked through the parking lot back to Chance's truck.

"Yes, it was nice."

Then Marcus and Tiffany got into conversations about all their favorite scenes and left Kylie and Chance to do nothing but remain silent. He didn't seem inclined to make idle chatter and neither did she. He opened the truck door for her and when their hands brushed she felt him tense the exact moment she did.

"Can we stop for ice cream?" Tiffany asked when everyone was inside the truck and buckled up.

"No," Kylie and Chance called out simultaneously, and then glanced over at each other. Chance cleared his throat and said in a more subdued voice, "I'm going out of town on Monday and there's a lot I need to do to get prepared for the trip."

"And I need to look over my accounting books tonight," Kylie added.

Both Chance and Kylie heard the disappointment in Tiffany's and Marcus's voices but decided that a movie had been enough. There was no way they could sit across from each other and eat ice cream without remembering what had happened the last time they'd done so. It had been the cause of their "lick me all over" party.

All it took was a memory—of Chance stripping her naked in her kitchen, licking sticky caramel sauce off her body—and Kylie's palms started to tingle. Her breasts suddenly felt heavy, her nipples tight, and erotic sensations built up inside of her, settling right smack between her legs. She forced a deep breath of air into her lungs thinking that this was definitely not the time nor the place for arousal.

She glanced over at Chance, and as if he felt her gaze on him, he turned to her. From the heated look in his eyes she could tell he too was remembering what they'd done that Sunday afternoon in her kitchen.

Kylie settled back in her seat. This was going to be one long and extremely hot ride home.

It was time for Plan B.

Marcus and Tiffany wasted no time putting it into action. On Tuesday they had Donovan Steele's full attention as they filled him in on the failure of Plan A. "So as you can see, Uncle Donovan, we need your help."

Donovan leaned back and looked at the both of them. Marcus had contacted him on his cell phone asking that he meet them after school on the football bleachers.

Donovan shook his head. "Let me get this straight. The two of you aren't girlfriend and boyfriend? You aren't madly in love? And you only pretended you were to get your parents together?" he asked incredulously.

Both Tiffany and Marcus nodded. "That's right," Marcus said. "Tiffany and I are best friends and we thought it was a good plan. Things were going along smoothly but something happened that weekend the two of us left town."

Donovan lifted a brow. "And what do you think happened?"

"We don't know but before we left they were beginning to like each other a lot, but now we're not sure how they feel."

Donovan had heard the story from Bas and Morgan but he wasn't about to share the information with these two. "So what do you need for me to do?"

"Help us," Tiffany said.

Donovan was confused. "Help you do what?"

It was Marcus who answered. "Carry out our plan to get our parents together."

Donovan crossed his arms over his chest, not believing what they were asking of him. He loved his nephew but was he willing to incur his oldest brother's wrath? "I think you had better tell me about this plan first."

Marcus nodded. "I'll let Tiffany explain things since it's her idea. But I think it's a good one."

Donovan doubted it was all that good but decided to listen anyway. Twenty minutes later a smile touched his lips. He hated to admit it but he liked their idea, although it could use a little tweaking here and there to make sure neither Chance nor Kylie panicked and got the police involved. There was no doubt that Chance would be mad in the beginning, but in the end odds were he would be a very happy man. "Okay, count me in. I'll help but only on one condition."

"What?" Marcus asked.

"That you modify your plan somewhat."

Marcus and Tiffany quickly agreed.

Donovan then smiled and said, "Now, I think that this is the way we should handle things…"

Chapter 15

Late Friday night Kylie glanced over at the clock on her nightstand the moment the telephone rang. It was almost midnight. She suddenly got a funny feeling in her stomach. Was it Chance? The last time she had seen him was Sunday night when they had all gone to the movies.

Deciding that answering was the only way to determine who her caller was, she reached out and picked up the phone. "Hello?"

"Mom?"

Kylie shot straight up in bed. The voice sounded like Tiffany's, but there was no way her daughter could be calling her when she was down the hall in her bed sleeping.

"Mom? Are you there? It's me."

Kylie jumped out of bed to her feet. "Tiffany! Where are you?"

"Mom, I'm fine."

Kylie angrily began pacing her bedroom. "Fine, nothing!

Where are you, young lady? No one gave you permission to leave this house. How dare you pull something like that!"

"Mom, please calm down. I'm fine. Marcus and I are together."

"What?" Kylie screamed at the top of her lungs, before collapsing in the wingback chair in her room. "What do you mean you and Marcus are together? It's after midnight. No one gave you permission to—"

"Mom, Marcus and I have been thinking."

Kylie gripped the phone tightly in her hand. "Thinking? The two of you have been thinking? Fine, then think at your own houses. I want you home immediately!"

"Not until you and Mr. Steele promise to become friends again."

Kylie frowned. What was Tiffany talking about? "Listen, honey, Chance and I are friends. You need to come home."

"The two of you didn't act like it Sunday night. You barely said two words to each other. If Mr. Steele is going to be our in-law one day, then the two of you are going to have to get along."

Kylie threw her head back and began silently counting to ten, not believing the conversation she and her daughter were having. "Look, Tiffany, I don't know where you are but I want you to end this call right now and come home. Better yet, tell me where you are and I'll come and get you."

"No, Mom, I can't do that. Marcus and I aren't going to do anything we shouldn't, so don't worry about that."

"But I am worried about that! You're only fifteen, it's after midnight and you're out somewhere with a boy when you should be home sleeping in your bed. How dare you tell me not to worry!"

"Then maybe I should ask you to trust me, and to also

trust Marcus. We're in a safe location and we won't do anything that you and Mr. Steele will be ashamed of."

"That's not the point!"

"It is the point, Mom. You and Mr. Steele are going to
have to trust us. Marcus and I figured the reason the two
of you can't get along is because you don't trust each other
and you don't trust us."

Kylie struggled to keep her voice calm. "I do trust
Chance and I've tried to stop being so uptight and to start
trusting you more, but I see doing so was a mistake. You
either come home within the next thirty minutes or I'm
calling the police."

"Mom, please don't. All it will do is cause unnecessary
embarrassment for me and Marcus."

"Tough! The two of you should have thought of that
sooner."

"Mom, I'm serious. If you call the police then we won't
come back. All we need is time to talk."

"And just what do the two of you have to talk about that
you had to sneak out in the middle of the night to do it?"

"We need to talk about you and Mr. Steele and your in-
ability to get along."

"We can get along!"

"Then you sure fooled us. You *were* getting along, then
something happened. We don't know what but the two of
you sure acted like you were avoiding each other on Sunday."

"Tiffany, I—"

"Good night, Mom. We'll call you in the morning and
tell you our decision."

Kylie's stomach dropped to the floor. "Your decision
about what?"

"About whatever we decide. Marcus has to call his father now. Goodbye, Mom. I'll talk to you in the morning, and I promise Marcus and I won't do anything."

Before Kylie could open her mouth to say another word, there was a resounding click in her ear.

Kylie quickly snatched up the phone the moment it rang again five minutes later knowing it was Chance.

"Kylie, you okay?"

His deep, husky voice had a comforting effect on her. "Oh, Chance, what are we going to do?"

"You didn't call the police, did you?"

"No."

"Good. I got a chance to talk to the both of them and—"

"Can you believe what they've done? Just wait until I see them. I'm going to—"

"Calm down, Kylie."

"Calm down? My child is out somewhere after midnight and you want me to calm down?"

"Yes. My child is out there, too. One good thing is that they're together."

"You think that's a good thing?"

"I trust Marcus, Kylie. He won't let anything happen to Tiffany. And he gave me his word that they won't do anything they aren't supposed to do."

Kylie glanced out her bedroom window. A fist tightened around her heart knowing her little girl was out there somewhere. "Yes, that's the same thing Tiffany said," she murmured quietly. "And you're right, we're going to have to trust them."

Kylie was quiet for a long while, then she said, "Did Marcus tell you why they did it?"

"Yes, he told me."

"I thought we acted pretty normal on Sunday night," she said.

"Yeah, but I guess they still picked up on something."

"Well, even if they thought we weren't on the best of terms, it wasn't any of their business!"

"Oh? You finally agree with me about that?"

Kylie frowned. "I'm serious, Chance."

"I've always been serious about that." He then asked, "Where are you now?"

"In my bedroom."

"How about going downstairs and putting some coffee on. I doubt if either of us will get much sleep tonight and if we're going to worry, we might as well do it together. I'm on my way over."

"All right. I'll have the coffee ready when you get here."

Chance made it to Kylie's house in less than ten minutes. She met him at the door with a cup of steaming hot coffee.

As if it was the most natural thing to do, he leaned over and kissed her lips. "You okay?" he asked quietly, after taking the cup from her hand and following her into her living room, where he sat down on the leather sofa beside her.

"Yes, I'm okay. But I'm still worried about them, Chance. I didn't think to ask how they were getting around. I assumed Marcus took his car."

Chance nodded after taking a sip of his coffee. "Yes, he has it. Boy, he's going to be grounded for life."

"So is Tiffany and she hasn't started driving yet. And just to think I had considered surprising her with a car for her sixteenth birthday. She might as well kiss that surprise goodbye."

"And they pulled this just to make a statement that they

didn't like the way we acted on Sunday. If that doesn't beat all," Chance said.

"Yeah, I guess it means a lot to them for us to get along."

"But it's not like we argued or anything, Kylie."

She inhaled deeply. "I know but I guess they were watching us more closely then we thought. You have to admit we were rather distant to each other."

"Yes, we were," he readily admitted it. "And I didn't like it."

She met his gaze and said, "Neither did I."

After a few moments of silence she added, "Do you think we're doing the right thing by not calling the police?"

"Yes. But I did contact my brothers. There was no way I could not let them know. At least I was able to reach Bas and Morgan. Evidently Donovan is still somewhere out on the town and he isn't answering his cell. But I'll talk to him tomorrow. And I notified my cousins, as well, in case Marcus contacts them."

Kylie nodded. "I forgot about your basketball game in the morning."

Chance shook his head. "Yeah, but there's no way I'm going to go anyplace until the kids come home."

"They will come home, won't they, Chance?"

When he heard the trembling in her voice, he set his cup on the table and wrapped his arms around her shoulders. It felt good to hold her again. "Yes, they'll come home. When they get hungry, they'll be back."

His words made Kylie smile. "Yeah, Tiffany definitely likes to eat."

"And so does Marcus."

Kylie cuddled deeper into Chance's warm embrace. It felt good to be held by a man who cared about her. A man who'd told her he loved her. A man she knew she could depend on. "Where do you think they'll sleep tonight?"

Chance shrugged. "Either in the car or at a hotel."

Kylie pulled back and looked at Chance. "Are they old enough to get a hotel room on their own?"

"It depends on where they go. To some hotel owners, money and not age is the determining factor."

Kylie really hadn't wanted to hear that. More than anything she had to remember that Tiffany said she and Marcus wouldn't do anything. She had promised.

"Come here and lay beside me. You must be tired."

She automatically did what he suggested without thinking twice about it. He stretched out his legs on the sofa to accommodate her and gently held her as they lay side by side. Before he had arrived, she had changed out of her nightgown into a pair of silk lounging pants and top. Heat curled through her when he wrapped his arms around her. It felt good knowing she wasn't alone now.

"Try to get some sleep."

"I don't think I can, Chance. I want my baby home." A few moments later, sleepily she said, "Did I ever tell you about the first time I let Tiffany sleep somewhere other than her own bed?"

"No, I don't think that you did."

"She was two and my parents had finally acknowledged that they had a grandchild and wanted some bonding time. At first I wasn't going to let her go but then Lena convinced me that I should. I barely slept that entire night knowing she wasn't in the house. I finally was able to sleep only after going into her room and stretching out on the floor beside her little bed. Now isn't that pathetic?"

"No, it sounds to me like you were a mother who had missed her child and needed the connection." After a few moments he added, "It works like that for adults, too, you know."

She lifted her head and met his gaze. "Does it?"

"Yes." He reached out and stroked her cheek with one finger. "You slept in my bed that one night but that's all it took for me to get used to your presence. All this week I found myself reaching out, as if you were still there, wanting that connection."

Kylie's stomach knotted when her gaze slipped to his mouth and she remembered how that mouth had driven her crazy in so many different ways. She remembered the taste of it, the feel of it. She also remembered something else. The amount of love she had in her heart for this one particular man.

"Oh, Chance." She reached up and tightened her arms around his neck at the same time she leaned up for his kiss.

With agonizing slowness he took her mouth, claimed it, branded it. His tongue made love to her mouth. The more it did, the more she became fully aware of the steady, strong arms holding her. They were protective arms. They were arms that would shield her from any storm, whether raging or mild. They were arms that would always be there to hold her when she needed to be held. It had been late in coming but she realized that now.

Moments later when he lifted his mouth she let out a satisfied sigh. "Thanks. I needed that."

He looked at her and smiled. "So did I."

Determined to maintain control of the situation he then said, "Now let's try to get some rest so we can be well-rested to give our kids hell when they come back home."

"Yes, *our* kids." Kylie said the words as if they suddenly had new meaning to her.

As he pulled her closer she settled against his comforting muscular form and believed that from this time forward somehow everything was going to be all right.

"Mom?"

"Dad?"

Chance slowly opened his eyes. Had he been dreaming or had he actually heard Tiffany's and Marcus's voices? The first thing he noticed was that he was stretched out on the sofa with Kylie lying beside him, her head resting on his chest. That would not have been so bad if his hand wasn't possessively cupping her bottom or one of her legs wasn't entwined with his. Even her hand was resting pretty darn close to the fly on his jeans.

He sucked in a deep breath, letting the scent of her fill his nostrils. She was still asleep, but he could remember a time that weekend when he had patiently waited for her to wake up so that he could—

"Dad?"

"Mom?"

Chance swallowed as he slowly glanced across the room and his gaze lit on two pairs of curious eyes. He blinked. No, make that three.

He quickly sat up and the movement startled Kylie out of a sound sleep. "Chance, what's wrong?" she asked sluggishly, slowly coming awake.

He shifted his gaze from the three sets of eyes to her still-drowsy ones. "Wake up, sweetheart, the kids are back," he whispered.

She blinked. "What?"

"The kids are home."

She was off the sofa in a flash. He had to catch her to keep her from stumbling. "Tiffany! Marcus! We've been so worried about you," she said hugging them so tight Chance wondered how they were able to breathe.

Then as if it finally hit her what they had done, she stepped back, placed her hands on her hips and gave them one hell of a fierce frown. "The two of you have a lot of explaining to do."

"Seems they aren't the only ones," Donovan Steele said in a low voice, after clearing his throat.

Kylie jumped and jerked her head around. She hadn't seen Chance's youngest brother standing at the edge of the foyer. "Where did you find them?" she asked, tossing her mussed-up braids over her shoulders.

Before Donovan could answer, Tiffany said, "He didn't find us. We were with him the entire time. We spent the night over at his house."

"What?" That loud exclamation came from both Kylie and Chance at the same time.

"And we had so much fun," Marcus said, smiling. "The three of us played video games until—"

"What the hell do you mean you were with him the entire time?" Chance shouted, coming to his feet beside Kylie.

"Dad, don't get mad at Uncle Donovan," Marcus said, rushing in. "I can explain."

Donovan smiled as he leaned against the wall. "Yes, Chance, let him explain. And trust me, it's a doozy. And I think you and Kylie might want to be sitting down when you hear it."

Chapter 16

"Let me make sure I have this right," Chance said as he paced back and forth in front of the two teenagers, who were now the ones sitting on Kylie's sofa. To say they were in the hot seat was an understatement. "Are the two of you saying you aren't madly in love and that you never were?"

It had taken the kids twenty minutes to explain to their parents what it had only taken ten to confess to Donovan a few days ago. But Kylie and Chance had stopped them periodically to ask questions.

"Yes, Mr. Steele, that's what we're saying. Marcus and I are good friends and have been since the first day I started at Myers Park High. One day while talking we decided that neither you nor my mom had a life that didn't center around us, so we decided to give you one," Tiffany said, smiling.

Chance frowned. "You decided? Just like that?"

"Yes, sir, we decided just like that. Wasn't that cool?"

Kylie came to stand next to Chance. "No, that wasn't

cool. Did it ever occur to either of you that we liked the life we had?"

"Yes, it did occur to me, but then I wondered what you would do when I left for college in a few years, Mom," Tiffany said quietly. "Just the thought of you being here all alone almost made me give up the idea of leaving home and going off to school. But then I figured it wouldn't be fair for me to give up my life just because you didn't have one. So I decided to help you find one. And when Marcus mentioned how handsome his dad was, and I told him how beautiful you are, we decided the two of you would make the perfect solid soul."

Chance lifted a confused brow. "Solid soul?"

"Yes, it's where two souls combine into one. A very solid one that can withstand anything."

Kylie crossed her arms over her chest and glared at them. "The two of you deceived us. You had us almost pulling our hair out by pretending you were so much in love."

"We kept asking you to trust us, Ms. Hagan," Marcus spoke up and said. "Even if we were in love, Tiffany and I had been raised right. You and Dad have done a good job. We know right from wrong and we know what to do and what not to do. We kept telling you and Dad that, but you wouldn't listen."

"That's beside the point. What the two of you did last night was—"

"Necessary, Mom," Tiffany cut in and said. "I'm not a child. I knew you were beginning to really like Mr. Steele. I could tell. And I could also tell that you wouldn't let yourself like him fully because you probably thought I wouldn't go along with it when all I ever wanted was someone to come into your life and treat you nice, take you places and make you smile. And Mr. Steele made you smile, Mom.

I've never seen you smile so much as when you were around him or talked to him every night on the phone. And I knew our plan was working because Marcus said his dad was smiling, too."

Marcus picked up their defense. "But we also knew something happened, Dad, that weekend Tiffany and I went out of town. When I got back to town the smile was gone and you were acting like you had lost your best friend. Tiffany told me that her mom was acting the same way so we figured the two of you had had an argument. We knew we needed to do something."

Chance sighed deeply. "Is that the reason for the stunt the two of you pulled last night?"

"Yes," Tiffany said softly. "I figured if you cared for my mom that you would come over and make sure she was okay. And you did just what I knew you would do, Mr. Steele."

"In other words, we played right into your hands," Chance said, frowning.

"No, you played right into each other's hearts," Donovan said, coming to stand next to Chance. "I think you've drilled them long enough, and yes, I let them talk me into being a part of their shenanigans because I saw the same thing they did. The two of you cared for each other and you *were* smiling a lot, Chance, when you were together." Donovan grinned. "You were even smiling when you weren't together. You don't know how many times when we were in your office for a meeting that Bas, Morgan and I were tempted to slap that smile off your face. The two of you were meant to be together."

"That's not the point," Kylie snapped.

"Then what is the point?" Donovan asked crossing his arms over his chest. "Your kids cared enough about the two of you to do something. I admit their plan might have needed a little polishing but what the hell. It worked, didn't it?"

The room got quiet. Chance met Kylie's gaze and held it for a long moment. Then he said, "Yes, it worked. Only thing, Marcus and Tiffany, I really don't *like* Kylie. And the reason I don't like her is because I'm deeply in love with her. There's a difference."

Both Tiffany and Marcus smiled and pumped their fists in triumph. "Yes!"

"And how do you feel about my dad, Ms. Hagan?" Marcus asked a few moments later. Kylie knew all eyes were on her, especially Chance's. He knew she loved him. She had admitted as much—but she had also declared that she wouldn't act on that love. Now he was waiting to see if she would reconsider.

What he didn't know was that she had reconsidered the exact moment she had opened the door to him last night. He had come to her when she had needed him most. He had been there with her and had shown her just what a dependable man he was.

And something else. What he'd told her was true. For the past fifteen years she had been trying to be a good girl for her parents. But even her daughter had been able to see something that she hadn't. She needed a life that didn't revolve around Tiffany or her parents. She was a grown woman and if she made mistakes they were hers to make.

She slowly took the couple of steps that brought her in front of Chance. "And I love your dad, too, Marcus. I discovered just how much I cared for him that weekend and it scared me because I didn't think I was ready to take such a big step as that."

"And are you ready now?" Chance asked her quietly, taking her hand in his.

She held his gaze and said softly, "Yes, I'm ready."

Again Marcus and Tiffany grinned.

"Okay, time for me to take the two of you out for breakfast," Donovan said, sensing his brother and Kylie needed to be alone. "And since we won't be playing our basketball game today, I'll go pick up Bas and Morgan and we can work out our competitive frustrations on the video games."

"That's a wonderful idea," Marcus said, rushing for the door. "And now that Dad knows there's nothing going on with me and Tiffany, I can give Rhonda Denton my phone number."

"And I can give Brad Reagan mine," Tiffany added, following right on Marcus's heels.

Donovan turned to his brother and chuckled. "Boy, the two of you will have a lot to deal with after you get married, with two dating-age teens in the house." He then patted Chance on the back. "We're leaving so the two of you can settle things."

Chance gave his brother an appreciative nod. "And give us a courtesy call before you come back."

Understanding completely, Donovan laughed before he walked out the door, closing and locking it behind him.

"You admitted that you love me in front of them," Chance said huskily, still holding Kylie's hand in his. "I didn't think that you would."

She nodded. "I had to because it's the truth and I couldn't pretend otherwise."

"You know what this means, don't you?"

Yes, she knew what this meant. Chance had told her once that if there was something that he wanted, he wouldn't give up until he got it. "Yes, I know and now, since you have me, what are you going to do with me?"

He smiled that sexy smile that could make her heart race

and make her dizzy. "My long term goal is to marry you by next summer, if not before. But my short-term goal is to make love to you, right here and now."

And with that said he captured her mouth in a soul-searing kiss that left her trembling. And then he began removing her clothes as well as his own.

"No visitors and no kids for a while," she whispered when he had gotten her completely naked and stretched out on the sofa.

He smiled. "I would go get the caramel topping but that would be too messy, so I'm just going to have to use my imagination."

He did and enjoyed taking the long, lazy swipes of his tongue over every inch of her body, liking the sound of her moaning and groaning while he did so. By the time he had slid back up her body he knew he was about to take her in a way he had never taken her before. He had already slipped on the condom and the moment he was poised between her thighs, he looked down at her and remembered the term Tiffany had used.

Solid soul.

And as he began sinking deep within her silken heat, he knew that the love the two of them shared was solid soul. It was also something else. It was a love meant to be. A love destined to last a lifetime. A love forged in steel.

He lifted his head and looked into her eyes, then whispered a heartfelt request. "Marry me, baby."

Kylie smiled at him and when he hit her G-spot at an angle that made her moan deep in her throat, he smiled and asked softly, "Was that a yes?"

Her darkened eyes took on a positive gleam when she tightened her arms around his neck and groaned a resounding, "Yes."

Epilogue

Chance couldn't wait until the summer. He and Kylie were married on Christmas Day in the presence of family and friends. Considering how they had met, it seemed very fitting for Marcus to be his best man and Tiffany to be Kylie's maid of honor.

The deafening sounds of cheers, catcalls, whistles and applause shook the room when Chance pulled Kylie into his arms and kissed his bride. It was evident to anyone looking on that the two of them were in love and extremely happy.

At least it was evident to everyone but Cassandra Tisdale. She leaned in and angrily whispered to Bas, "I can't believe he married her when he had a chance with my cousin Jamie. Jamie is a lot prettier and has a lot more class. Kylie works at a florist for heaven sakes! Chance is the CEO of one of the largest corporations in Charlotte. He needs a wife that will complement him."

Bas stared at her, not believing anyone could be that rude

or snobbish. But he was seeing a side of Cassandra that he'd always seen. For some reason he'd convinced himself that he could live with it, but now he knew there was no way in hell he could. He wanted to one day have the same thing his brother had—a marriage built on love and mutual respect.

"So you don't think them loving each other is enough?" he asked after taking a sip of his wine.

She gave a ladylike snort. "Of course not. Love is never enough and no one should foolishly think otherwise. According to my mother, who as you know is an expert on social decorum, a good wife, one with the proper breeding like I have, is to be seen and not heard. Her manners and refinements are so ingrained that her husband knows her job is to keep the household running smoothly and make sure they establish the perfect family tree."

Bas lifted a brow. "The perfect family tree?"

"Yes, when they have children. Everything has to be skillfully planned."

Bas thought he'd heard enough. He really didn't give a damn for manners and refinements. Hell, he would settle for a woman oozing in scandal and sin to one who was nothing but a boring social trophy. And he would definitely prefer to come home every night to a wife who would be wearing sexy lace nighties than to one in a starched, buttoned-up-to-her-neck gown.

He shook his head knowing that later, when he took Cassandra home, he would give her the ultimate blow. There was no way in hell he would marry her. "Come on, they're about ready to cut the cake."

"It's not much of a cake if you ask me."

He had heard enough. "I don't recall anyone asking you, Cassandra. If all you're going to do is find fault and be negative, then I'd rather you keep your damn refined and proper mouth closed."

Bas smiled, certain his statement had pretty much shut her up for a while.

Across the room Chance pulled Kylie into his arms. "I love you, Mrs. Steele."

She smiled up at him. "And I love you, Mr. Steele." She then leaned over and whispered, "So what do you think of my parents?"

He smiled. "I can deal with them. They might have preferred you as their good little girl, but frankly I'd rather have you as my bad one. In fact, I plan for the two of us to get downright naughty tonight."

"You plan on teaching me some more moves?" she asked saucily.

"Yeah, among other things."

Kylie's gaze tangled intimately with his. After this small reception they would catch a plane for Hawaii. Chance's parents had returned for the wedding and volunteered to watch Marcus and their newest grandchild Tiffany, who they were anxious to get to know.

"We are going to make one big happy family," Chance said, leading Kylie over to the cake they would be cutting together.

"Yes," she agreed as she paused to place a kiss on her husband's lips. "One big happy family."

* * * * *

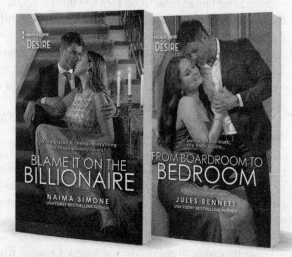

SPECIAL EXCERPT FROM

⊕ **HARLEQUIN**

DESIRE

*Alaskan senator Jessup Outlaw needs an escape...
and he finds just what he needs on his Napa Valley vacation:
actress Paige Novak. What starts as a fling soon gets serious,
but a familiar face from Paige's past may ruin everything...*

Read on for a sneak peek of
What Happens on Vacation...
by New York Times *bestselling author Brenda Jackson.*

"Hey, aren't you going to join me?" Paige asked, pushing wet hair back from her face and treading water in the center of the pool. "Swimming is on my list of fun things. We might as well kick things off with a bang."

Bang? Why had she said that? Lust immediately took over his senses. Desire beyond madness consumed him. He was determined that by the time they parted ways at the end of the month their sexual needs, wants and desires would be fulfilled and under control.

Quickly removing his shirt, Jess's hands went to his zipper, inched it down and slid the pants, along with his briefs, down his legs. He knew Paige was watching him and he was glad that he was the man she wanted.

"Come here, Paige."

She smiled and shook her head. "If you want me, Jess, you have to come and get me." She then swam to the far end of the pool, away from him.

Oh, so now she wanted to play hard to get? He had no problem going after her. Maybe now was a good time to tell her that not only had he been captain of his dog sled team, but he'd also been captain of his college swim team.

He glided through the water like an Olympic swimmer going after the gold, and it didn't take long to reach her. When she saw him getting close, she laughed and swam to the other side. Without missing a stroke or losing speed, he did a freestyle flip turn and reached out and caught her by the ankles. The capture was swift and the minute he touched her, more desire rammed through him to the point where water couldn't cool him down.

"I got you," he said, pulling her toward him and swimming with her in his arms to the edge of the pool.

When they reached the shallow end, he allowed her to stand, and the minute her feet touched the bottom she circled her arms around his neck. "No, Jess, I got you and I'm ready for you." Then she leaned in and took his mouth.

Don't miss what happens next in...
What Happens on Vacation…
by Brenda Jackson, the next book in her
Westmoreland Legacy: The Outlaws series!

Available March 2022 wherever
Harlequin Desire books and ebooks are sold.

Harlequin.com

Love Harlequin romance?

DISCOVER.

Be the first to find out about promotions, news and
exclusive content!

 Facebook.com/HarlequinBooks

 Twitter.com/HarlequinBooks

 Instagram.com/HarlequinBooks

 Pinterest.com/HarlequinBooks

 YouTube.com/HarlequinBooks

ReaderService.com

EXPLORE.

Sign up for the Harlequin e-newsletter and
download a free book from any series at
TryHarlequin.com

CONNECT.

Join our Harlequin community to
share your thoughts and connect
with other romance readers!
Facebook.com/groups/HarlequinConnection

"I remember. I remember it all, Bethany."

Jeez. He hadn't meant for his voice to turn so serious, so
reverent. But there was very little chance of hiding his real feelings
when she was around.

"Me, too," she said.

For a few moments they ate in silence.

"Thanks for helping me here," she said. "You've done a lot of
that since I've been back."

"Anytime. And I mean that."

"Ditto," she said.

He reached over and squeezed her hand but didn't let go.
And suddenly he was looking—with that seriousness, with that
reverence—into those green eyes that had also kept him up those
nights when he couldn't stop thinking about her. They both leaned
in at the same time, the kiss soft, tender, then with all the pent-up
passion they'd clearly both been feeling these last days.

She pulled slightly away. "Uh-oh."

He let out a rough exhale, trying to pull himself together. "Right? You're leaving in a couple weeks. Maybe three tops. And I'm solely focused on being the best father I can be. So that's two really good reasons why we shouldn't kiss again." Except he leaned in again.

And so did she. This time there was nothing soft or tender about the kiss. Instead, it was pure passion. His hand wound in her silky brown hair, her hands on his face.

A puppy started barking, then another, then yet another. The three cockapoos.

"They're saving us from getting into trouble," Bethany said, glancing at the time on her phone. "Time for their potty break. They'll be interrupting us all night, so that should keep us in line."

He smiled. "We can get into a lot of trouble in between, though."

Don't miss
Home is Where the Hound Is *by* Melissa Senate,
available March 2022 wherever
Harlequin Special Edition books and ebooks are sold.

Harlequin.com

HARLEQUIN

Heartfelt or thrilling, passionate or uplifting—Harlequin is more than just happily-ever-after.

With twelve different series to choose from and new books available every month, you are sure to find stories that will move you, uplift you, inspire and delight you.

HNEWS2021MAX